TEST
KITCHEN

By the same author
The Glasgow Coma Scale

TEST
KITCHEN

NEIL D. A. STEWART

corsair

CORSAIR

First published in the United Kingdom in 2024 by Corsair

1 3 5 7 9 10 8 6 4 2

A CIP catalogue record for this book is available from the British Library.

HB ISBN: 978-1-4721-5825-3
TPB ISBN: 978-1-4721-5824-6

Typeset in Garamond by M Rules
Printed and bound in Great Britain by Clays Ltd, Elcograf S.p.A.

Papers used by Corsair are from well-managed forests
and other responsible sources.

MIX
Paper | Supporting
responsible forestry
FSC® C104740

Corsair
An imprint of
Little, Brown Book Group
Carmelite House
50 Victoria Embankment
London EC4Y 0DZ

An Hachette UK Company
www.hachette.co.uk

www.littlebrown.co.uk

For Mark

The new 'gard

Restaurants | Amanda Ledley Miles

The Greeks had a word for magic and they had a word for cookery, and it has always been fascinating to me that it was the *same* word. I'm reminded of this scrap of trivia now and then when it's my privilege to visit a restaurant that's doing work so wondrous that words like 'alchemy' and 'wizardry' seem entirely justified. And so it is with Midgard, the first restaurant proper from Chef Magnus, who has been making a name for himself the last few years with a series of spectacular pop-ups and short runs in some unique London venues, from defunct carwashes to the interior of the Victorian iguanodon in Crystal Palace Park. We may only be in February, but I'm confident that this is already my restaurant of the year, because what Magnus is doing here can only be called magic.

What other word can you use when a duck's egg yolk "cooked" in sugar is served suspended over the plate, floating above a cloud of something it debases almost criminally to describe as risotto, studded with tart little mouthbursts of sea buckthorn? Or for the transformation of the inevitable foie gras dish into a kind of Magic Eye painting for the tastebuds – two seemingly identical pucks of purple-gold, each with a shattering caramelised lid, are announced as sautéed foie and lavender-infused crème brûlée, but not which is which. The paired flavours seem to flicker interchangeably on the tongue: I defy even the most experienced palate to tell one from the other. Each fresh course is a total 180 from the

1

laſt, but all prompted the same two goggling reactions. My notebook became very repetitive. One, I wrote: this is superb. Two: how have they done it?

This is high-wire ambition from a singularly visionary chef, abetted by a team of surpassing technological and technical ability. Equally impressively, the kitchen knows when to pull it back: following edible precious metals, sculptural presentations and knowing culinary jokes, at the exact centre of the meal is a simple dish of aged duck, beetroot, blackcurrant: unshowy, adroitly balanced, sadly gone in a few bites.

It isn't, of course, a flawless meal. You'll want to arrive hungry, if not ravenous: there's no à la carte, and the eight courses of Midgard's taſting menu is expanded with numerous little extras and additions. And be ready for a long evening. Seated at seven sharp, I wasn't even on to dessert by ten o'clock. That the exact point we moved on to dessert was moot is the crux of my teensieſt criticism, a lot of the savoury courses having skewed a shade too sweet for my taſte.

You might wonder, as you make your way from the shiny new ſpace-age Overground ſtation and down this dodgy alleyway in deepeſt Hackney, where on earth you're going. While I'm not sure Midgard necessarily *is* on earth, I was amused to see intrepid weſt Londoners, faces grey with misgiving, push open the doors and sag in relief at the sight of filament bulbs, raw brickwork and plush upholſtery. I kept watching until each fresh party noticed the dining room's absurd, ſplendid centrepiece, and their double-takes were so delicious they were like an extra course. No ſpoilers: like every other marvel Midgard serves up, you need to come and be flabbergaſted by it for yourself. Ta-dah!

9 Amhurſt Grove, London E8
www.midgardlondon.com

and girolles is autumn on a plate. I'm delighted that my final review for this paper is also a first rave for a brand-new restaurant.

In brief

No surprise, sadly, that after it was thrust into the spotlight this week for all the wrong reasons, east London's two-starred Midgard has been forced to shut its doors. The announcement came in a brief press release from Chef Joanna. Long a favourite of this reviewer, Midgard built up a substantial reputation over the past half-decade, gaining industry plaudits and a devoted following among diners and critics. All that I can say at this tragic moment is that I wish those who have worked there all the very best for the future. At least, those lucky enough still to have one.

Amanda Miles's travel column begins in the new year.

Subscribe to Sunday Tribune Food by clicking here.

'Who's there?'

It was only me and Joanna in the kitchen, and I was about to step out, sheepish, from where I'd been concealing myself when she crossed to the delivery door and flung it open to reveal Finn in the rainy alley outside. Under his arms he held two rolled rubber floormats, dripping suds. 'Oh, it's just you. I thought I . . .' She scowled. 'How'd you manage to knock, anyway? Dunt on the door with your big thick skull?' He said nothing, just flicked the head chef his flat smile before staggering past her and dropping the mats to the tiled floor where they slappingly unfurled. 'Man,' Joanna said, looking up, 'just gone four and nightfall already. And this weather. See if we get no-shows –'

From then on, the delivery door was in constant use, the entry coder bip-bip-bipping as Midgard's staff let themselves in. They arrived in ones and suggestive twos, joking and sniping, flirting and scrapping. A black eye was noted, a fresh tattoo covetously ridiculed. It was observed that Tash was wearing the same top she'd had on after Sunday's shift, a baggy indigo sweater she had to keep hauling on to one bony shoulder only for it to slither off the other: wild speculations ensued about what she might have been up to in the intervening day and a half, and none came even close to the truth. Joanna wedged herself into the crook of the Y-shaped pass, backbone of the kitchen, watching amused as two of her chefs unboxed and salivated over a breakthrough chemical compound which promised to deliver some innovative compositional gradient between liquid and set that could not possibly be achieved with any of the other two dozen similar ingredients in the test kitchen. Addy was on parade, showing off her newly earned sommelier's tastevin, a shallow pewter dish on a chain round her neck which jounced about on her chest in a manner that attracted Gareth's too-avid attention. The usual fight over the kitchen's crappy CD player, Kelly insisting once again on *The Next Day*, in her view 2013's best album so far and, moreover, merely the first in what she felt certain would be a decade or more's masterpieces the reborn Bowie would make. At the foot of the staircase leading up to the stores, Tash studied a clipboard while Nico, at the top, yelled numbers for the weekly booze inventory: 'Eleven Gayfield Estates Malbec.' 'Eleven.' 'Sixteen Merlot.' 'Sweet sixteen, never been clean.' 'Behave. And fifteen Syrah.' 'Hang on,' Tash consulting her checklist, 'nup, I've sixteen da-down here too. You sure?' A pause while Nico recounted. 'Confirmed fifteen. Mark one down as shrink.' Sprudge, chamois in one hand fondling the prongs and nozzles of his espresso maker, had his phone in the other and was cooing reassurances: 'She's a baby, she can't even stand up yet, how much trouble could she give you, doll?' And here, dodging the rainwater spewing from the busted gutter over the back door, came new boy John, shirt soaked through, face pinched with first-day nerves. Murmuring a general greeting that went unacknowledged, he went straight to his counter, which he found covered in a series of Post-it notes dense with Joanna's crabbed handwriting: a to-do list from the head chef, a hundred items or more.

I must have wanted to see how the restaurant would cope without me. That must have been it.

Because I should have been out there with them, prepping for service – helping unpack deliveries and checking manifests, or hodding in a big soft bag of laundered linen, us servers' black aprons and dun twill, or measuring out ironically mouse-grey poison into the gaps between counters, or joining the three-man cleaning detail that was touring the kitchen: one slathering stainless steel in antibacterial foam, one squeegeeing off the residue, the third buffing surfaces dry with extravagant quantities of paper towel. I should have been fetching and carrying for the chefs as they prepped, keeping them apprised of timing as we counted down to staff meal, staff meeting, doors unlocked, civilians incoming, all of it always too soon.

Instead, I was squeezed into the narrow space between the industrial refrigerators from which the chefs were gathering ingredients and the line of counters where they were making up their *mise en place* for tonight's service. It was a trick I'd mastered young – finding the impossible gap, last place anyone'd think to check for me. The fact that nobody was bothering to look didn't faze me because that, too, had often been the case when I was a kid, and sometimes that was an advantage.

All right, so that's what I was doing: hiding. Hiding at my place of work, hiding from my colleagues. I must've got here ahead of anyone else, found myself this nook, set about waiting. Now all I had to figure out was how I was going to get out of it.

Stationed at the head of the pass, Joanna could see all, including through walls: she hauled down an old cathode-ray set on a scissor arm overhead, observing in blue the waitstaff setting tables in the dining room. Satisfied, she turned on the spot to survey the kitchen, the soles of her kitchen clogs wearing to wafers, her one-eyed glare so piercing that since the one occasion I'd glimpsed what lay beneath the black eye-patch – she flipped it down immediately, more horrified than me – I'd wondered if she'd gored herself deliberately that she might see more clearly with the eye that remained. Nothing got past her. I'd never believed the rumour that she lived on the premises, slept in the back office – upside down, added the unkinder stories – but I'd been at Midgard nearly a year and never once made it in to work before Joanna. So how and when had I managed to sneak in? How long had I been here?

There was a dull pain in my left arm, above my elbow, and I didn't know why. I remembered closing on Sunday – Sunday, normally a quieter night, had gone off like a frog in a sock: some Brit band I'd never heard of had booked the whole place to celebrate a number-one record. I remembered that as usual we'd all gone to Soho afterwards, the whole team plus two members of the band, to unwind by drinking ourselves stupid. I'd seen 2 a.m., 3 a.m.: restaurant folk never want to go home though they absolutely should. I remembered indulging Gareth's crapping on about his love life, and hoping that if I feigned interest long enough he might give me some coke. I remembered Eleanor talking at me, and how over her shoulder I'd noticed Finn watching us with a furrow in his stupid perfect brow; I felt now, but hazily, hazily, that I was angry with him for some reason that eluded me. That had been Sunday. Now it was Tuesday. Had someone slipped me something? What had happened to Monday?

I started as Joanna clapped twice sharply. The brigade dropped what they were doing and lined up at the pass, cooks along one side, servers on the other, neat as kindergarten, for staff meal. This afternoon Gareth was serving them super-market linguine in a rich slow-cooked sugo of beef trimmings and tomatoes and peppers whose skins had begun to slacken and wrinkle: ultra-savoury, ultra-sustaining. All but Kelly, infamously vegetarian, who took her pasta dully plain, just a pinch of age-yellowed herbs, lemon zest, chilli flakes, a flurry of parmesan substitute. And this, now, this would be the time for me to wriggle out and join the queue. This was the last moment that this jape I'd embarked on might not have disastrous consequences for me, when I might feasibly not get fired. But still I stayed hunkered down in the dark. What was I waiting for? For someone, despite the lessons of my child-hood, to notice I was missing.

'Loïc?' Joanna prompted, and as our immaculate maître d' drew up at her side, our faces, mine included, turned towards him like flowers to the sun. In languid tones, he recited pocket biographies of our guests tonight: their names and ages and places of origin, their history with us, their recent dining itineraries – all gleaned from social media, because nothing made it easier to accommodate our diners' quirks than having already exhaustively researched them. We were paying close attention, less to his words and more to Loïc. Still beautiful? The sallow skin without blemish, spot or sleep-crease, the pen-etrating gaze, the hair which seemed freshly barbered each day and whose copper shade resembled, I liked to flatter myself, my own – yes, still beautiful, maybe even more so than two days ago; how was that possible? It was hard to stare for too long, before the part of your brain that scanned for flaws in beauty so you could bear to look on it went a little haywire.

'Our VIPs tonight,' he was intoning when I was stunned back into listening, 'are Monsieur Barlow and his wife, marking with us their wedding anniversary, as they have the previous five years also.'

Over the general rumble of disquiet – return visitors came with elevated expectations, misremembering in our favour, and ultimately there was only one way that could go – Joanna sig-nalled to Addy: 'Two glasses of Blanc de Noirs on us, soon as they land, and Gareth, can we send out a little extra something between' – rattling her biro in her teeth as she consulted lists taped to the pass – 'the crab and the mack?' 'On it, chef,' his mouth dangling noodles. 'And we'll put them on Two.' Loïc leaned in, whispered an objection. 'All right, pal, keep your shirt on.' She stared upwards and inwards, consulting an unwritten matrix of diner status, and missing or ignoring her maître d's look of disgust. 'You're right, engagement takes precedence, so put them on Two and the Barlows get Five. Tash, that fine by you? That's Mr and *Dr* Barlow, don't forget.' She amended her table map, a diagram of the dining room printed on two sheets of A4, already covered in scribbled annotations of the details Loïc had unearthed: we'd need a non-alcoholic drinks pairing for one diner on Three, and tonight's allergy – there was always one – was on Six. 'And Nico, we've a friends and family on One – Sprudge, one of yours, I think? Fizz for them too, please.' Sprudge drew Nico aside, started giving them some convoluted instructions. 'Eh, on your own time, please, yous two. Kima, quit sharking for leftovers, you know there's none.' She tapped her pen down the column of music Tash had selected for the dining room: yes to Basinski, yes to Pärt, yes to the Max Richter that always made Addy gooily reminisce about the couple with whom she'd spent a glorious and athletic six weeks in Lisbon last summer. 'All right, squad, I make that an hour forty till doors. As you'll have seen, we're a body down, and no call-in from her yet, Loïc, am I right?' He gleamed a regretful negative. 'So there'll be some doubling up with serving to compensate, all right? I'll figure it as we go. What am I forgetting? First aid. Who else has their certificate? Gareth, thank you, good. Any questions?'

I had a question: is that it? Nobody rushed to the locker with my MELBOURNE: THE PLACE TO BE sticker on it, to rattle the door and exclaim that I must be coming back since all my stuff was still in there – not even Kelly, who usually took any opportunity to show me up. Nobody even looked especially concerned: not Finn, not Eleanor leaning against the jamb of the in-door with her plate in her hand. Instead my colleagues busied themselves with their desserts of choice: chalky protein drinks, handfuls of pain pills, lollies for the blood sugar, Kelly gorging on dolly mixtures, chewing them to a pastel cud. Joanna, the great caring matriarch, hadn't even used my name. If I'd smuggled myself in here to see how the place would manage without me, here was my answer: it closed up around my absence like healthy flesh sealing over a wound, leaving no trace.

A hubbub, a blaze. Around the heads of the heat lamps that hung on articulated stalks over the cooks' counters the air began to quiver. Gareth lit the burners at his station and they whomped upwards, blue jets flecked orange as cleaning fluids burned off. Warming, the smells of the kitchen began to mingle: the rich sweet aroma of a fruit jelly on a rippling simmer, the putrescent pall of game, the comforting armpit waft of cooking onions. Chefs set about dicing, crushing, carving, slicing, chopping, grinding, skewering, all those good violent tasks. The kitchen landline was ringing, the whine of the 3-D printer on the counter beside patisserie set my teeth on edge, the vents over the pass emitted a roar like jet engines, and yet I knew that in a few minutes my brain would, unbelievably, tune it all out.

Even without raising her voice, Joanna was audible over the din. 'For the benefit of our new arrival' – causing John's head to vibrate on his neck, a ghastly trepidatious grin to break out across his face – 'let me reacquaint you all with the basics. The restaurant is a sacred space. It is a sanctuary. We're a no man's land with two stars. Whether our guests come in skipping or with faces like fizz, our job is to make sure they get happy, stay happy, leave happy. For as long as they're here, Midgard's all that matters. Outside there could be riots on the street, a comet could have struck – they shouldn't have the first idea. Hence no clocks in the dining room.' Passing Sprudge, who was on his tablet penning a sarcastic rejoinder to a Shitadvisor review, the algorithm this season suggesting that publicly cheeking your detractors somehow boosted future bookings, she confided: 'I'd take their watches and phones off them if I could get away with it.' 'Yes, Chef. They'd thank you for it, Chef.' She nodded. 'And Kima –' arresting her before she could reach patisserie corner, her own personal refuge – 'a word, please?' Kima looked like she was thinking of one. 'I don't suppose you know anything about our no-show? Sharing a roof as yous do.' I was as interested as Joanna to hear what the kitchen gossip might have to say about me, but all Kima did was shake her head several times fast. 'No, of course you don't. Go on then, out my sight.' A little louder: 'Any bugger going to answer that phone?'

For reasons no one could now recall, the kitchen phone, mounted on a column at the far end of the pass, was a children's cartoon character in moulded plastic, a toothy squirrel giving a thumbs up. Loïc swooped in to answer, listened with an expression of incomprehension turning to outrage, then responded, screwing his accent twenty per cent Frencher than normal, into the squirrel's tail: 'Madame, I apologise, but *non*, we have no "walk in", this is not a system that we operate, and what is more our restaurant is booked to capacity for many, many months yet. I can add you to our standby list, but you must understand that a cancellation is quite unprecedented.' Too good for the clipboard and chewed biro that hung beneath the phone, he took from his jacket pocket a slim black journal and a silver propelling pencil, and added a name and number to a fresh page.

'One hour,' Joanna called out, and 'They're co-o-oming,' Kelly warbled.

Finn was at the basin nearest me, rinsing crab meat from his fingers. In a moment he'd come over to sanitise his hands at the dispenser over my head and that, I decided, was when I'd emerge from hiding and take whatever flak came my way. I was gambling that, this close to service, Joanna wouldn't have time to curse me out.

Something about Finn, though. When I looked up at him I had the feeling you get when you've quarrelled with someone in a dream and the next time you see them you're a bit guarded towards them, a bit freaked out. I held my breath as he stood over me and bashed at the dispenser until gel squicked into his palm. Any second now I'd leap up – although, as he rolled his hands over and under one another until the boozy-smelling stuff was absorbed, it occurred to me that, given his history, Finn might not be the guy you'd want to startle.

I'd take that risk, I thought. I gathered myself and made to stand. Gathered and readied myself. I really did.

That was when I found I couldn't move.

Table One

Crispin was making the moon appear and disappear when the door to Midgard opened, admitting a blast of autumnal chill, and he saw with relief that his date had arrived.

He watched as the maître d' took her coat from her shoulders, while she stamped her wet boots on the mat and her gaze moved over the dining room's cappuccino and raw concrete colour scheme, the round bulbs on long metal arms arranged in clusters over the tables, the carpet's woven pattern of chevroned parquet – taking in everything, really, but Crispin himself – before finally, inevitably, coming to rest on the tree that grew through the centre of the room. An ash tree, according to the app on Crispin's phone, with a trunk so broad with age that your hands wouldn't meet if you embraced it, its bark an infinite maze of pleats and corrugations, its lowest branches spreading across the restaurant ceiling as if upholding it. The tree was famous, of course – every review of Midgard mentioned it, punned on it – yet he could tell from his date's reaction that she, like him, hadn't really believed in it until seeing it for herself.

First impressions, as the maître d' guided her towards his table: she'd recently bleached her hair – no band of dark in the parting – and she was wearing a cute dress, black velvet with a white rounded collar, that put him in mind of Sunday best and the idea that churchgoing girls were the wildest. He appreciated the choice. Pretty, objectively speaking, with wide lively eyes and a resting smile. Objectively speaking, well out of Crispin's league.

He rose from his chair, plastering on his expectant, open-to-anything first date face – but she swerved to avoid him, frowning, and continued past the table, heading for nowhere in particular, until the maître d', with a long, elegant stride forward that betrayed no sense of urgency, took her elbow and steered her to where Crispin half stood, half crouched.

'It's Sophie, isn't it?' He gave a silly little wave that he instantly regretted.

She squinted at him. 'Oh, hi! God, without my glasses I'm ... So you must be ...'

'Crispin, that's right, hello.' He moved in to attempt a peck of greeting, but Sophie shot out her hand from which, surprised, he recoiled. Sheepish, they oopsed and chuckled and tried again, kissing the air in the general vicinity of one another's cheek. 'How are you? Won't you sit down? Did you have far to come tonight?'

'Why, am I late?'

'No, not at all,' he stammered, though she was. An accent: he hadn't expected that. She sat suddenly, the maître d' having shunted the Ercol chair in behind her knees an instant sooner and with a shade more vigour than necessary. 'I was stupidly early. It's all relative, isn't it?'

'Far to come?' she changed. 'I'll say. I feel like I should check which time zone we're in. Is this still London?'

'Not to alarm you, but it's *east* London.'

She primped at her hair. 'I'm not cool enough for this place.'

'No, you're – perfect.'

'Easy now, tiger.'

An opaque partition separated the dining room and the kitchen. From behind it sauntered a slender figure who placed two metal clipboards on the table before them, then stepped back from the table, hands clasped, and addressed them. 'My name's Nico, and I'll be looking after you tonight. Have you dined with us before? Let me begin, then, by welcoming you to Midgard. We're offering a tasting menu tonight, so there are no hard choices to be made and you won't have to worry about food envy. All our dishes are listed on the menus I'm leaving you, but I just want to double check there are no allergies. No? Wonderful.' While speaking, Nico was bringing out – and Crispin, a student of sleight of hand, wasn't sure how it was being done – first two delicate glass tumblers with gold around the base, then a circular piece of slate for the centre of the table, next two stubby knives with bone handles. 'I lied. One little decision to make – would you like still or sparkling water for the table?'

'Sparkling,' Sophie ordered, an instant after Crispin had started to request still; trying to concur with her, he came out with the word 'sturkling'.

Nico looked between them, mouth dimpling. 'Cute. I'll bring one of each.'

'So,' Crispin said once they were alone again.

'Well, then,' Sophie agreed.

'Here we are.'

'The "first date".' She pulled a comical face.

The restaurant lights showed up tiny flecks of white lint and beads of rainwater in the velvet nap of Sophie's dress and, when she noticed him noticing these, Crispin hastily said: 'I like what you're wearing.'

'I like your face,' she said promptly.

'Ah.' Wanting something to occupy his hands, he tried to lift the menu, then, discovering it to be inordinately heavy, crashed it back down, making the glassware tremble. 'Now you've got me all flustered.'

'You know what they say, better flustered than … bustard. You know, a bird that's gone broke. Gambled all its money away, lost a pony on a monkey, or is it the other – okay, wow, wittering. I'm wittering.'

'No, it's fine, it's … charming,' he landed on. 'You have a lovely voice. I mean accent. I wasn't expecting a Novocastrian.'

She glared at him in myopic misgiving. 'A what now?'

Was there any chance – any means by which the ash tree might be compelled to topple over and crush him to death? 'Your accent. Newcastle, right?'

'Sunderland.'

'I know Sunderland,' he exclaimed, attempting damage control. 'I've been there for work. And yes, right, sorry, I remember, you guys do not like to be told you're from Newcastle.'

Her eyes narrowed. 'All right, pet, you're forgiven. But what was it, that word you said?'

'Novo— You know what, it truly doesn't matter.'

'I see. Being a smartarse, were you?'

'I was. Half of one anyway. Here, let me try and make it up to you.' Crispin flourished the white handkerchief from his top pocket, turned his wrists in a complex jackknifing motion and let spring into his hands a spray of – violets? That was odd: the pocket square usually turned into roses. 'Flowers for the lady.'

'Oh my.' Smiling, thank god, she accepted the posy. Her teeth were round and very white against the red of her lips sardonically parted. 'How long have you been practising that?'

He inclined his head in modesty. 'It's not as complicated as you'd think.'

'Go on, then. Or would they drum you out of the Magic Circle if you revealed your secrets?'

'Think of it as an exchange. In a parallel world there's another you and another me on a date, and that other me just took a bunch of flowers off the table and turned them into a napkin. All I'm doing is dipping a hand in that other world, making a swap.'

Sophie rubbed the creased satin petals between her fingers, brought the posy to her nose to check for any perfume. 'And so is it a girlfriend you're auditioning for, pet, or a glamorous assistant?'

A sequence of mournful notes was drifting through the room from the ceiling speakers – the stately voluntary of some distant muted trumpet, sounding again and again in a slow repeat, always the same, yet somehow different, wearied by each repetition.

Nico returned, champagne bottle in hand and napkin over one extended forearm, but Crispin was distracted from what was being poured by a movement in his trouser pocket: his phone, set to silent, thrumming with an incoming call. Its shudder passed into and through him as he realised he'd overlooked something vital. As Nico poured – the slow steady flow from the bottle, the bubbles climbing to the top of the flutes without ever risking overflowing – Crispin twisted and ducked beneath the table as if checking the carpet for a dropped valuable. He swiped his phone screen to answer. 'Hello?'

Drear static, then a woman's voice, guardedly cheerful. 'Hi, Mr Farrish? This is Agapemone restaurant on Charlotte Street. We have a reservation in your name for this evening at seven o'clock, and I wondered if you needed any help finding us?' He peered apologetically over the edge of the table at Sophie, who was regarding him with a chillingly level expression, like she'd expected no better of him. 'I'm sorry,' he whispered into the phone, 'but there's been a change of plan and we – I – have to actually cancel that booking.' A pause. 'I'm disappointed to hear that,' came the response, in a tone of considerable understatement. 'We're a small restaurant with only a handful of covers.' 'Sorry.' 'We've turned guests away tonight because we assumed you were on your way.' '*Sorry.*' 'We could have filled that table twice over if you'd had the courtesy to—' But by then Crispin had decided he could writhe with guilt in his own time and ended the call. He took a breath, then surfaced to find Sophie, elbow on table, chin on heel of her hand, staring at him over her untouched champagne. Could he brazen it out? 'All sorted,' he piped, reaching for his glass and angling it towards her hopefully.

'Ten minutes,' she said.

'Pardon me?'

'That's how long your date gets to prove herself? I was late, sure, but ten minutes before the bogus emergency gets phoned in? What was your excuse going to be? Burst water pipes? Rabbit in your hat got myxomatosis?' She began to collect her things.

'Wait, please. There's been – I've been an idiot.'

It had all been such a rush, a last-minute change of plan. He'd shuffled to the kitchen shortly before midday, groggy and parched from his sleeping pill, spine in painful disarray after another night on the sofa. The radio was on – a famous singer of the 1970s introducing a vapid new version of one of her hits, sung by people young enough to be her grandchildren – and naturally Sprudge was there, the kitchen table annexed as he worked on the coffee fanzine he edited, which was too exclusive to be stocked in shops but had to be biked in person to London's most deserving third-wave cafés. 'Hey, you're up. Didn't hear you get in last night. Good trip, dude? Where were you again?'

Crispin filled a pint glass at the tap, swigged, refilled. 'Luton. I told you it was Luton. You don't listen. Do you even care?'

'Like . . . about as much as you seem to?' Sprudge returned to his laptop, pecking out his column, while Crispin drank and simultaneously practised his powers of telepathy, attempting to beam into the pea brain that must lie somewhere beneath the boy's tousled mane and dense cranium one single motivating impulse: for god's sake, get on property websites and *move out*, will you?

Sprudge stopped typing, turned half towards the sink. An amazing revelation seemed to have struck him. Crispin held his breath. 'That table came through for you, by the way,' Sprudge remembered, then went back to typing.

'You're joking.'

'Yeah, no, the boss put it through. Forgot to tell you before, and then you came in so late last night.' He looked up warningly. 'Just the table, no mate's rates or anything, you know?'

'That's great. Thanks . . . thanks, mate.' Crispin couldn't bring himself to use the silly nickname his brother had given himself, but it felt too mean to call him by the one their parents had lumbered him with. 'Wait – you mean for tonight?' Panic seized him. 'I asked you weeks ago. How long have you known about this? And you never thought to tell me until the actual day?' 'Yo . . .' Sprudge said placatingly, and nothing more. Midgard wasn't any old place – Crispin would need a shave, a fresh shirt, even a haircut. Small wonder it slipped his mind to cancel the original booking at Agapemone. 'All right, look,' he'd said to Sprudge. 'You're going to have to do me one more tiny favour.'

'It isn't what you think,' he told Sophie as she fetched her bag from the little stool the restaurant had placed tableside. Still the same music in the room, the same notes sounding and resounding, but slurred now, pained, their sustain growing tattered.

'Enlighten me, why don't you.'

'I—' He broke off as Nico once again neared the table, this time setting down a small hessian bag, stamped with the restaurant's logo. 'Inside here, you'll find our freshly baked, house-made sourdough. It comes with a whipped butter made with brewer's yeast left over from the breadmaking process.' Sophie had deposited the violets at the centre of the table and Nico moved the bouquet aside without remark, making room for a sculptural stand: a foot-long arc of blackened copper, a stylised branch from which eight leaves sprouted, each one bearing a morsel of food. 'And these are your amuse-bouches tonight. From right to left, you have pork cheek, slow cooked, cubed, crumbed, toasted and topped with fennel-blossom aioli. Beside those are blue cheese and cranberry gougères. Next, Chef Joanna's take on a London classic, a potato cracker with oyster gel and unagi – Japanese eel. And finally, on the spoon there, is a little game for the senses: spherified olive oil flavoured with rosemary, paprika, lemon and a touch of smoked volcanic salt from Sicily. This one can be a little messy, so we advise you to take the whole spoon and pop it in your mouth to avoid disaster.'

'Thank you,' they chorused, then sat inert. Around them, other diners were echoing their own pleased murmurs as other waiters announced the amuse-bouches. When Crispin glanced around, however, those other tables seemed oddly indistinct beneath their cones of overhead light; only the tree at the centre of the dining room seemed in focus. Something glinted in its lowest branches. He stared at the ash until it occurred to him what the grey green of its crenulated bark

21

was reminding him of: a tombstone thick with lichen, memorial inscription effaced by time.

'I should walk out,' Sophie said at last. 'Teach you a lesson about how to behave on a date. But this all looks annoyingly good, so I'm going to eat until I make up my mind.' She rolled open the hessian bag, thrust her thumbs into the cross cut into the centre of the loaf and pulled it apart into quarters, its sour steam making Crispin instantly ravenous. 'Don't get complacent.'

He exhaled through his nostrils. 'All right, look. I wasn't sure I was going to get this table, so rather than promise something that might fall through, I made a backup plan. And that was them on the phone, bawling me out. And yes, I'd understand if you wanted to walk out but, for what it's worth, I would like us to carry on.'

Sophie had a pretty frown, which was fortunate for Crispin since he kept causing it to appear. 'Must be a novelty for a conjuror,' she said. 'Trying not to make the lady vanish.'

The bread was deeply savoury, the crust caramelised black and chewy, a hint of acetic flavour in the warm and claggy crumb. The fake olive spurted in Crispin's mouth, its flavour bright like grass or gold and leaving a lingering nostalgic aftertaste: Mediterranean holidays, long shadows, aromatic thyme growing through sand.

'I'll forgive you,' Sophie told Crispin, 'though it is getting to be a habit. But there's one condition.'

'Name it.'

'Do me another trick. Impress me. I want some proper magic.'

Crispin wished he had a cape he could twirl, or a less sceptical audience. 'How about if I read your mind?'

'Keep talking.'

He produced his fountain pen from his inside pocket. 'Do

22

you have any paper?' She reached for the metal clipboard, tore a strip from the end of the menu. 'Oh. Okay. Now, I want you to draw something. Something I wouldn't be able to guess – something personal,' he said, 'to Sophie.'

'Ach,' she said. She fished in her bag and produced a pair of glasses. 'I hoped I wouldn't have to wear these.' She put them on and made ferocious eyes at him: one of those rare and fortunate people, though, who looked better with spectacles than without. He handed her the pen and, southpaw, she curled her hand around the paper and began drawing in swift straight strokes, glaring up at him now and then – 'No cheating!' 'I'm not,' Crispin protested, and he really was not – was instead observing the minor commotion as two parties swapped tables, staff surrounding the groups of guests and muddling them into new positions. He drained his glass of water as he watched, set it down, and nodded acknowledgment to Nico as the waiter drifted past to refill it.

With a few emphatic dashes of the pen, Sophie completed her drawing.

'Now put it somewhere I can't see it. In your bag, maybe, or under your chair.' Sophie, staring him out gigantically, crumpled the scrap of paper into her mouth and set to chewing. 'Fine, that'll work too.'

'Not edible,' she mumbled, greyish pellet on her tongue. 'Thought it might be rice paper.' With a grimace, she swallowed, washed it down with a gulp of champagne. 'Still, not much chance of you seeing it again.'

'Hopefully not. All it means,' he extemporised nicely, he thought, rolling his shoulders and turning his head side to side, warming up, 'is it might take me a shade longer to figure out what you drew. But I will.'

Sophie raised her glass, finally let Crispin clink. 'To good food, bedevilling company and a smidge of telepathy. What

23

more could you want on a Tuesday night? Don't go letting these get cold,' she warned, pointing at the remaining snacks.

No danger of that: the morsel of pork, he discovered, retained a terrific heat. He juggled it hand to hand then in desperation lobbed it into his mouth and swallowed it in one scalding viscid fatty gulp.

'You all right?'

'Leave it a moment,' he gasped, reaching for his glass of water. 'What did they cook that in, a nuclear reactor?' The snack was a hypercube: packed into it was the taste memory of sausage rolls and scotch eggs, purportedly pork-flavoured corn snacks, cling-filmed BLTs simultaneously soggy and stale – snacks Crispin used to scoff at motorway services up and down the country, the very antithesis of haute cuisine. Reminiscent, too, of the distinct bacony odour of that wretched petrochemical byproduct such establishments mis-sold as coffee, always the faint iridescent swirl of grease on its surface. Sorry picnic suppers he'd consume in his car beneath the stellate floodlights of whatever service station was the halfway point on his journey home from wherever his peripatetic working life had taken him.

Sophie, meantime, took a cautious nibble before setting the pork back down, shaking her head and fanning her mouth.

'Why don't you tell me more about yourself,' Crispin suggested, determined to start over without asking if they could start over.

'What's to tell? I'm Sophie, I'm twenty-six, I live in Barnes in a flat with a damp problem, two grey cats called Guildencrantz and Rosenstern, and no children.' She saw him sit up a little straighter. 'Too much? My sister always tells me off for oversharing.'

'No, it's good to be ... comprehensive. What do you do for a living, Sophie?'

'I ransack the homes of dead people.'

He laughed, then stopped. 'Pardon?'

'I don't mean, like, tomb-raiding. Did you know, though, when people die without a will or any next of kin, there are teams who go into their property and assess what they've left behind? All those touchstones that had such meaning for one person, transformed in an instant into clutter. Anything of value gets sold for pennies on the pound to pay for the most basic funeral and for the cost of making the place saleable again – deep cleaning, mostly, especially if the person . . . ah, but we're eating. Point is, it's not a cheap business, dying.'

Crispin, aware his blistered mouth was hanging open, shut it and tried to match her glib tone. 'I'm keen to defer it as long as possible, myself. Bit of a gruesome career to pick, isn't it?'

'Maybe.' She shrugged. 'But I get to be a trespasser, and that's always fun, don't you think, breaking the rules?' She tapped the metal branch. 'One more to go. That's good. I need something to take away the taste' – she blabbed out her tongue – 'of printer ink.'

'I'm not wild about eel,' Crispin confessed.

'Ah, so you're the kind of person who leaves the thing they like least to the end of the meal instead of getting it out the way first. Building up a picture here.'

Pouting, he picked up the rough bubbled cracker with its cargo of clear jelly and white meat, its tiny jagged circlet of red seaweed, and popped it into his mouth. Sophie waited, her own cracker halfway to her mouth, for his reaction.

'That's peculiar,' he mumbled.

She lowered her hand.

'No, it's good peculiar. It's nice. I don't mind it. Try it.'

'They should have you writing these menu descriptions, pet.' Then he saw, as she ate and her eyes widened then reverently sealed, that she felt it too: how the cracker melted into sea-spume and the eel's buttery flesh became a voluptuous, briny slather; how it turned the cave of your mouth pale blue and brought a delicate seawater savour swelling up at the back of the nostrils. 'Wow. Wow, that's . . .'

'Isn't it?' Crispin had managed to get oyster jelly on the tablecloth and was dabbing at the spot with his napkin, making it worse. He crumpled the napkin up and tossed it onto the table, whereupon Nico immediately materialised, replacing it with one freshly pressed. Crispin took it and glanced down as he unfolded it across his lap.

'You know what it's like?' Sophie was saying when he looked up again. 'You're out surfing, a big wave catches you off guard and you're off your board and taking on water, swallowing a mouthful of ocean before you have time to brace yourself.'

'You've never been surfing.'

'No, I haven't, pet.' She leaned over the table, first her smile quite different, then her voice. 'But you,' she whispered, 'should not know that.'

'Oh, crap. Sorry, love.'

'It's fine. I was starting to think anyway . . .' She reached again into her bag and brought out her phone, checking for messages. 'I can't relax. I can't. You're sure Sprudge's girlfriend knows what she's doing? She has babysat before?'

'Dozens of times, Sprudge said,' he exaggerated. 'I'll throw him out on the street if anything happens. Wait – that's why you were going to do the whole walking-out thing, was it? Racing back to check everything was okay at home? And there I was thinking I was on a date with little miss no-children.'

Evasive, she took off her glasses and polished them on the tablecloth. 'I'm terrible, I know. I got carried away. But didn't you feel a little frisson of something for a moment, peeking into a different life like that?'

'Yeah. I did. Christ. For about half a second, anyway, and then I felt a surge of guilt that'll haunt me for months, so thank you for that. I won't be able to look the baby in the eye. A *frisson*, she says. It's Rosencrantz and Guildenstern, by the way.'

'They're not real, you know. Why, what did I say?'

'And "Sophie". A new name, an accent and everything. You really built yourself a character there.'

'I thought if we were going to do this I ought to try and commit. And I've always liked the name. It was on my list if we'd had a girl. Anyway, you can talk. A magician – where did that come from?'

'Childhood ambition. I wanted to be either that or an astronaut, and I didn't fancy turning up for dinner in a spacesuit. Tell me it isn't more glamorous than being a drug sales rep.'

She sighed. 'Or a legal secretary. It's an actual job, that thing of going in to those dead people's houses. I've heard them talking about it in the office. *Bona vacantia*. Itemising all the heirloom jewellery and semi-precious rugs and paintings. All the stuff you buy to fend off mortality – and it is only stuff – and in the end what happens? You keel over and die alone in an old armchair with the springs coming out, and all your treasures go in a skip. It'll be us too, some day, himself going through the house wondering why on earth we hoarded all this junk.'

'It's really been playing on your mind, hasn't it?'

'You know when winter starts? Midsummer. Sometimes I look at him playing around under his mobiles on the neglecto-mat and I think I've given birth to our own obsolescence.'

'It's all becoming very clear now,' he said, and his bumptious tone made her look up in surprise. 'Yes, it's preoccupied you, I can tell.' He sat forward into the warm and flattering lamplight, steepling his fingers beneath his chin and hooding his eyes, as he'd practised. 'It foxed me at first, I'll admit. But as soon as you started talking about your job, it made perfect sense. What else would Sophie draw but a coffin?'

His girlfriend drained the last of her champagne. 'All right,' she said, starting to smile again, 'I'll bite. How the hell did you do that?'

In the freezer beside me, ice cracked, shifted, calved, dropped, startling me from my thoughts. I'd been remembering how I told the chefs not long after I joined Midgard about my one failed attempt at surfing: the wallop as I was knocked from my board by the big wave I never saw coming, the dizzy scramble to right myself as seawater spritzed down my nose and throat, the end. The others leaned in hungrily. They made me go into more detail than my amateur's mishap warranted. The curdy, yellow-grey wavelets on the shore, the aftertaste. 'Briny,' Joanna had said, notebook out, stubby pencil scribbling, and 'What if we,' Gareth began as they set about figuring ways to turn experience into flavour. The next day I was made to taste what they called edible sand, authentic in that I spat out all four samples as if they'd been the real thing. They nailed it in the end: when I tried the finished eel cracker it had the flavour of memory, it took me right back to nearly drowning off South Melbourne Beach.

I was dead, I assumed. Dead and in purgatory. The weird thing was how unremarkable this seemed. I'd never grown out of a vague belief in some variety of afterlife – it just didn't seem plausible that you'd go on for a certain length of time and then be gone entirely, irrevocably, to never *be* again. All your untold secrets, all your trivial daydreams and fears, your odd irrational moments of total joy, wiped away in an instant. Maybe it was narcissism to think otherwise, but it had always seemed unbelievable, laughable and unfair, that these moments would be over, that I'd never again do something as wonderful and mad as casually tell an anecdote and inspire a recipe.

Maybe that was why I was here. Like all of us I'd given of myself, fed Midgard with my personal history, and now, in turn, the restaurant was remembering me – a partial me, reduced, bereft of voice or form or agency. For what? And for how long?

'Our latecomer has materialised,' Loïc announced from the in-door, every vowel and emphasis in this last word beautifully awry, and I stiffened, or imagined I did, until I saw Joanna checking the screen over the pass with its view of the dining room relayed from the camera in the tree's lower branches and realised all he meant was that the missing member of the party on Table Six had shown up.

All around me substances sizzled and seethed in pans, metal implements rang on Pyrex, knife-blades were dashed against whetstones – the kitchen's constant hectic undersong – but the chefs were silent, fixated on their tasks. Finn was prepping mackerel, lifting each lifeless gill to check the flesh beneath had the right healthy bloody pinkness. In patisserie corner Kima was painting red glaze on a series of identically imperfect domes woven by the 3-D printer. John was surprised when Sprudge – dogsbodying for the chefs – dumped a bowl of unscrubbed carrots by his station, a task a full ten items further down his list than he'd managed to get so far. Gareth, always watchful, leapt on him: 'Don't cry, new boy, it's an inefficient fucken way to wash veg.'

Joanna at the pass lifted her chin. 'Excuse me? Chit-chat? If it isn't "Yes, Chef", I don't want to hear it. Let's cook, let's cook, let's cook.'

Gareth fell silent, smirking at John. I knew how this went: the others had the new recruit in their sights. They had already noted the non-standard shirt he was wearing, a plain white button-up, and how his hatchet-narrow face and his deep grimace of concentration gave him something of the look of a turbot. Now they were waiting for him to speak so they could identify an accent, a quirky turn of phrase, anything he gave away about himself that they could twist into mockery. I knew because I was waiting too, and because it had happened to me. 'Hey, look,' someone had said the day after I'd told the story about surfing, 'here comes Curdy.' I was relieved, to be honest: until then I had been painfully timorous, convinced I didn't fit in and that at the end of every shift Joanna might call me to her office to tell me, despite the assurances she'd made when hiring me, that it wasn't working out. Earning a dumb nickname, becoming the butt of a joke, meant I did belong. Chefs were basically stand-up comedians who'd missed their vocation – the mean kind, the ones with a knack for the hurtfully accurate parody, an astounding power of recall for your slip-ups, infractions, honest errors. Apropos nothing they'd remind you of some compromising fact you'd revealed years earlier before you learned better, reactivating an old insecurity, all of it in the name of badinage. Even when someone found out about my acting aspirations and for a long time it was all 'Hey, Greasepaint', 'Hey, Cheap Seats' any time I came near, I basked in the attention. Only when word got out that I was seeing Finn did the names get nasty – not witty or clever, purely vicious.

I hadn't meant to start anything. I had simply happened to stand next to Finn in the test kitchen one Monday not long after I'd begun at Midgard. We'd been watching Kima and Gareth demonstrate a new process they'd figured out together, a way to make edible stained glass, brittle translucent panes in different brilliant colours. Behind them, an upper section of the tree, scarred all around where its branches had been lopped away and cauterised with pitch, blindly stared. Naturally it was to Finn that I'd turned to discuss what we'd been shown. And when we went downstairs afterwards and I found the contents of my bag mysteriously scattered across the kitchen floor, though I was sure I'd shut my locker properly, he helped me tidy up, gathering stray lipsticks and powder compacts in the only shades Joanna permitted us to wear. It was early afternoon and the team was going out for drinks, same as we would after a regular service, as if none of us had anything better to do with our day off, and on the way to Pangaea I asked Finn where he stayed in London and how long he'd been at the restaurant: nothing very probing, but eliciting from him simple facts about himself – thirty-one, a former caterer for private events before being recruited to Midgard – that Kelly, as she hissed at me later, had been trying and failing to extract for months, as if that was my fault. What had happened, it later transpired, was that Kelly had discovered something of Finn's life before Midgard and her attempts at conversation had dripped, he said, with studied pity. I had treated him as a person and not a story, and that was why, before we went in to join the others in the pub, he had asked for my number. He'd recognised something in me, Finn told me in one of the few moments of our subsequent first date that wasn't unmitigated disaster, and I thought it was a nice thing to say, until I got to know him better.

The in-door from the dining room began to swing as the staff carried in the metal branches denuded of the snacks, a sight that always reminded me of a fringe production of *Macbeth* I'd once acted in. They huddled around Joanna – there had been a change of table, they informed her, and she started amending her table plan correspondingly. 'So the

32

allergy is now on Two, *not* Six, everyone got that?' 'Yes, chef!' came the chorus, John one beat behind. Joanna scratched her brow with her biro. 'Ach, this thing's a midden. Someone get my Post-its and I'll start over.'

John listened out for further details then, realising he was squandering valuable seconds, returned to his list. Next: ginger, an easy one. He took a teaspoon from the wash-jar and, holding it by the neck, used its tip to scrape away the ginger's skin, tracking its complicated knobbles and exposing luminous yellow flesh. The indicator light on one of his ovens blinked dark as it reached temperature, reminding him he had still to dot the quarters of figs with honey before he roasted them at a specific heat for a specific length of time, but that was fine, that could wait, he wasn't weeded yet. Then 'Don't forget they lemons, John,' Joanna chimed from the centre of the room and he blanked. Lemons! What was he doing with lemons? 'When Kima needs them she'll need them right that instant, so be ready.' He mumbled assent as he scanned his task list, purblind, feeling also that fresh items were being added to it any time he looked away. Then Sprudge was again at his side, this time dumping a laden white trash bag at his feet. 'Do us a solid, will you, new boy, and sling this in the bins outside? Red one, for meat.'

John wavered. 'The thing is, I'm not meant to go anywhere or do anything until I've finished everything written here. Joanna said,' he added, hoping this was unarguable.

The bag capsized against his leg. A rosy fluid was collecting in one swollen corner. 'Mate,' Sprudge said. 'Don't be a dickhead all your life.'

He had made it halfway across the kitchen with the bag cradled in his arms, was within reach of the delivery door, when Joanna noticed what he was doing and charged from the pass, scattering staff. She loomed over John. 'Did I tell you to do that? Did I give explicit instruction to you to leave your station?' Petrified, he stayed silent. The copper-pink fluid had leaked on his shirt and I stared and stared at the circular mark, feeling a sensation like a nervous tic somewhere inside my skull. 'Step away without my permission again and you'll be out of here before the night's over, probationary period be damned.' The other chefs' silence had another quality now, bloodthirsty alertness: nothing juicier than someone else getting flayed alive. 'Now chuck that, get back to your place, and if by some incredible feat you finish everything on my list before closing time, you come straight to me and ask for more. Got that?'

'Yes, Chef.'

Then I saw Loïc, oozing in behind the front of house team, do something really foolish. Seeing Joanna was occupied, he consulted the messy table plan on the pass, clucked his tongue, and swapped around the two fresh Post-its she had written out to accommodate the change of tables.

'You're new,' Joanna was coaching John, 'and folk'll try and take advantage of that. Anyone tries a stunt like that again, you are hereby authorised to tell them to go fuck theirselves. Even if it's me – particularly if it's me, since I should know better. Are we good?'

'Yes, Chef.' Would he ever say anything else again? He didn't know whether it was ruder to try and meet her living eye or to pretend she didn't have only one, so ended up addressing instead the space where the band of her eyepatch ran diagonal between her brows.

'All right, then. But John? See if you're thinking of coming in tomorrow wearing something other than the regulation jacket, don't bother coming in at all, understand? Now back to work.'

Don't cry, John beseeched himself, feeling a quickening in

his sinuses: tears prepped and ready to go out. If they fell, if the others saw that weakness, they'd make his life such hell he'd be better walking out now. For fortitude, he recalled the mantra he used to recite while labouring over the steel grill of the medieval-themed carvery in his hometown that had been his first employer. *It won't always be like this*, as gouts of flames erupted from the grill's charry interior. Then *It won't always be like this*, as he ran short orders in the gastropub that not only would nobody from his family patronise but which, they claimed, was giving him airs and graces. *It will not always be like this* giving rhythm to mind-numbing shifts as a human Robot-Coupe or sentient conveyor belt, monotasking: eight hours of scrubbing spuds or gutting fish or dicing vegetables. He had the blotched forearms of someone who'd done his apprenticeship over deep-fat fryers, the callused thumb of an expert in feel-testing the doneness of steaks straight from the fire. One day all this drudgery would pay off, John had promised himself, and recently so too had a second voice, someone who'd come into his life unexpectedly, delightfully, someone whose cheerleading embarrassed but boosted him and who had encouraged his application to Midgard even though John had argued he didn't have enough experience, or not the right kind, for a place with its reputation. You did it, though, he told himself now: you earned this job through your own hard work. Don't listen to your misgivings. Places like this don't do pity-hires. But they cut no slack, either, so don't fuck it up.

We had all given ourselves versions of this talk, me included. You deserve this. You belong here. My first night, I'd crossed the dining room with one of those big unwieldy metal presentations quaking in my hands but my backbone as erect as pride and the Alexander Technique could make it. I was thinking about all the lattes I'd brewed in South Yarra for boofish, unfeasibly healthy boys in runners' vests and for girls with sweat-stippled yoga leotards and voices they'd trained into low rasps and who never, ever tipped; about the burns I'd sustained wresting trays of fresh bread from the oven at Gumbys on Chapel Street while the sleazeball manager looked on, grinning and doing nothing to help; about struggling to keep sand out of toasted jaffles on paper plates at the beachfront café in South Melbourne until the customer picked up and it became their problem. Like John, I had assured myself that better awaited me, and for once I'd been right. By the time I was describing the amuse-bouches to my first ever table, my smile was broad enough to contravene Midgard regulations.

Hauling the tray of slobberingly juicy figs from the oven and finding he'd managed instinctively to clear the perfect space for it on his countertop, John too felt pride. These were award-worthy figs he was cooking here. He was *in*.

He didn't remember this now, but I had been the first member of staff he'd met, one Monday back in May. The monthly test kitchen demo had finished and I'd been lounging outside the front door, my face to the spring sun, when his lanky silhouette had come creeping round the corner from Amhurst Road, doubtful as any other first-time visitor that a place as celebrated as Midgard could be located at the end of this murder alleyway. 'Here for an interview?' I'd called out and he'd jogged towards me, grateful. 'Go right in, you won't miss Joanna. Seven feet tall, looks like a pirate.' In he'd gone, uncertainly smiling, assuming I must joking on one or both points.

At last the carrots: rinsing, scrubbing, patting them dry, trimming them of their stalks and wisps of roots, peeling them, and then dicing them down to cubes the size of matchheads. Over by the lockers, he saw one of the server girls drop to her haunches to retrieve a paper bag concealed behind the cabinets, dip in a finger, suck it clean of white powder. Keep mum, he thought: you don't know the loyalties here yet. Then the burly Australian, Gareth, barrelled up beside him. 'All right, White Shirt? Drop those and budge up, I'm gonna teach you a trick.' He thumped down an enormous hotel pan brimming with water, in which potatoes cut down to pale yellow bricks were bobbing around. 'Behold the humble spud. Skoosh some oil in that big pan up the top of your unit there, willya?'

'But I—'

'"But"?' Gareth repeated sharply. John made a vain gesture towards his endless list, then wilted under Gareth's glare and reached for the appropriate squeezy. 'Sensible lad. More oil than that. If you think you're using too much, it's not enough.'

Was Joanna watching this? Was Joanna ever not watching? He stole a glance at the pass, but she seemed occupied overseeing the plating of the first course proper: Kima turning out pale mousses from hemisphere moulds onto oblong plates, Finn nudging them into position then painting a stripe of basil-balsamic reduction across each plate, awaiting Joanna's nod of approval before he returned it to Kima to set one of her printed domes over each mousse. Other hands placed pluches of herbs, filled metal jugs to accompany; forefingers, wrapped in cloth, wiped water-spots and greasy marks from the crockery.

'What we're wanting here,' Gareth was telling John, plucking one of the potatoes from the scurfy water, 'is slices about two millimetres thick, neat as you like. Watch me?' His knife made several swift passes; the pale block sat there seemingly intact until he tapped it with the flat of the blade and it fanned out into square translucent slivers. 'Now you.'

John copied the example as carefully as he was able, but Gareth swept his efforts into the trash with the side of his hand. 'I said two millimetres, two, not two and a half. Again.'

Gareth's sleeves were folded to the elbow, exposing the thick dotted line tattooed around his wrist. Earlier he'd been getting changed in the staff loo with the door open, and John had seen with a shudder that the cook's whole upper body was divided up by these lines, each section labelled in antique font: *Shoulder, Flank, Thick Rib* – a mordant joke. 'So look,' the chef rumbled, his breath dank with coffee, making John's hand tremble so he botched his second attempt, 'I gotta ask. You know what *chef de commis* means, right?'

'It's French,' John began, then faltered.

'It's French,' Gareth affirmed, 'for do as you're told, don't answer back, ask questions all the time – *good* questions, not dumb ones – keep your nose clean, come in early and leave late, take the initiative but never step out of line.' He considered. 'Concise language, French. But mostly what it means is don't do anything that draws attention, don't get people's backs up, because it's also French for "last in, first out", you see what I'm saying?'

All John could think to say was 'Okay?' He was trying not to stare at the alopecic spot in Gareth's dogpelt-sleek hair above his ear, the exact shape and size of a pound coin.

'Okay. So, with all that in mind – mate, what's up with the fucken shirt?'

'I did get a proper chef's jacket. From the place in Soho, like I was told. Only, as a surprise, my, my partner decided to . . . I mean, it was a sweet idea. But he went behind my back,' forcing himself to meet Gareth's eye now without wavering, managing it but still stumbling over his words, because it was never an uncomplicated joy to admit the pronoun, it risked something to be even this bold. 'He went and got it customised.' Go on, said Gareth's look. 'Embroidered. With my name.' The big man sucked his teeth. 'Cursive, over the breast pocket.'

'We're not mailmen. We're not car mechanics.'

'Right?' John dared to grin. 'And I knew it would be more than my life's worth to wear that, but this was Saturday, and that shop doesn't open on a Monday, and I didn't have time today – so I wore this instead. I had to.'

'Damned if you do, damned— Ah, fuck, boy,' distracted by John's latest efforts, 'seriously, what knife are you using here? Where'd you get it from, a Playmobil set? Try mine a minute.'

John had studied the locked cases in the Soho catering supplier where vastly expensive blades, from penknife to scimitar, hung point down in rows like mismatched teeth in the maw of some titanic carnivore. The Japanese knife Gareth used was called *nakiri*. Its handle was carved from something near-weightless, light as balsa, and when John lifted it the curved cleaver of its blade lunged towards the chopping board as though eager to show what it could do. 'That's it,' Gareth approved, 'nice and easy. Let it find its own way.' The blade fell, bounced, refell; it passed through vegetable matter as it had through air. 'Now you're one with the blade. Some fucken Zen shit.' The block of potato collapsed in miraculously even sections.

'Pick up, pick up,' Joanna cooed, and the servers lined up in readiness, plucking stray hairs and fluff from each other's uniforms. Addy reached forward to knead Tash's shoulders. 'Mother of god, girl, you are the tensest person I have ever laid hands on. What's going on with you?' Tash shook her off: the sommelier's passion for giving massages was matched only by her ineptitude. 'Family,' she grunted, and dread sympathy rippled along the queue. Most of the staff were young or poor enough that they still lived at home, and they were forever talking about parents and siblings, which had made me an anomaly on both counts.

As John continued cutting, Gareth twisted the flame under

the prepared pan to full and glowered at his reflection distorted in the rippling surface. 'Did you not hear me say double up on the oil?' He seized the squeezy bottle, topping up the pan with what seemed an obscene quantity of the stuff. 'Look, what I'm trying to teach you— Ho,' he broke off, inspecting his hand and the slowly reinflating squeezy. 'The fuck's this?' He shoved his glistening palm into John's face. 'We don't have drips on our oil bottles, fucknuts. You dribble, you mop up, got it?'

John burned. He felt an internal counter – *You have not been verbally abused in* x *minutes* – reset itself to zero. 'Sorry, Chef.'

'Don't sorry me, dickbreath' – an almost indiscernible hesitation between words, then a slight lessening of his bluster, and John pretending to notice neither. 'Keep it clean, yeah? And give me back my knife, you donkey, you don't deserve to use it.'

Maybe the oil that had transferred itself to Gareth's hand had also got on the *nakiri*'s handle. Maybe John, unaccustomed to the blade's weight, misjudged its balance in his hand. Maybe Gareth, distracted by a tickling vibration against his shin, was in that instant a shade less attentive than usual. Or maybe, though its consequences had yet to be felt, Loïc's error was already sending a little ripple of wrongness through Midgard, throwing our precise calibrations minutely off, causing the big knife to slide a fraction of a degree off true as it passed between the two men; to roll, to slip, and then to sink deeply and effortlessly into the meat of John's right hand, only halting when it jarred against bone.

I'd have gasped if I'd been able. I *felt* that wound.

John cradled his hand to himself and Gareth his knife, and both were unmarked, John's wound a clean pale line like an old scar long healed. I knew what they were thinking: maybe, somehow, by magic, it's all fine. Even Joanna, bustling from

40

the pass with antiseptics and blue tape, halted, hoped. Then John let out a whimper that rose up and passed into ultrasonic silence, and the long line in his hand flicked red, and with an oath Gareth wrenched the boy's wrist straight up in the air, popping his shoulder. Then the blood was cascading with appalling speed and in appalling quantities down their raised arms, drenching their hands, their sleeves, Joanna's too as she tried to scramble together a tourniquet.

The waitstaff couldn't afford to be distracted, not even by this havoc. They reached for the plates, double checked the table plan and filed to the out-door. Into the dining room they'd march, fanning out across the room, then, when everyone was in position, they'd advance in lockstep to deliver the dish to all tables simultaneously, all as normal, pretending nothing awful was going on in the kitchen. Blood was raining down near me, but I felt worse watching the servers depart. I knew that one of them was about to make an innocent and terrible mistake, and the knowledge was useless because I couldn't do a thing to stop it.

Table Two

They didn't like her – so what, they didn't like her. Shoshana had been disliked by professionals. What were these two? They barely even counted as in-laws.

'I still don't see why we were the ones who had to move.' Esther had set her possessions out on the banquette around her – glasses case, the patent handbag with little charms dangling from the strap, the rust-coloured coat she had refused to surrender for hanging up – and was stroking and lifting each one in turn, apparently convinced she had lost something in the five metres between this table and the one they had left. Shoshana had already apologised twice for her lateness – ten minutes! Nothing, on the kind of scale she was used to thinking in – and was damned if she would do so a third time.

'Because we hadn't all arrived yet, and because the maître d'' asked nicely,' Morris soothed, in his wonderful rich baritone. 'I read somewhere that you should never accept the first table you're shown to, because the restaurant is always trying to fill its worst one.' Shoshana appreciated his efforts. The first time she'd said sorry, he'd tried to spread the blame: 'We were a little late ourselves. Someone, naming no names, couldn't decide which shoes to wear.'

Shoshana had leaned backwards, peeked beneath the table at his feet: surprisingly dainty. 'You chose well. Brogues are in right now.' Morris's too-effusive laugh provoked from Esther and Ross, Shoshana's partner, the same stifled wince, a predisposition to social mortification that had hopscotched its way across the generations from aunt to nephew.

The table, the restaurant, Shoshana, the weather outside, perhaps the workings of the cosmos itself: everything, Esther seemed to have concluded, was arranged to cause her personal inconvenience. She was fussy, fiftysomething, a small woman whose oversized accessories – her children's-entertainer spectacles, her meteoroid of a wedding ring and necklaces thick as anchor-chains, her bold perfume, the mohair coat bundled beside her like some slumbrous pet – had been selected to make their wearer appear smaller, even cute, an impression that Esther's manner and conduct swiftly dispelled. 'Put that down, Father,' she chided Morris as his hand closed on the hunk of sourdough she hadn't touched. Despite the nickname, she spoke to her husband as if to a child. 'The next course will be out any moment.'

Ross was smiling in the manner of a person who had long since gone to his happy place and did not intend to return. Despite Shoshana's efforts to avoid Morris's eye, he gave her a little rueful pout that she tried not to return, for fear Esther should sense conspiracy.

In the sunken channel behind the banquette where the aunt and uncle sat, bundles of LED lights were modulating from off-white to peach. A fragrance of fresh-tilled soil emanated from hidden vents, followed by the ineffable green of tomato plants, and Shoshana looked around with a half-formed idea that she might spot seedlings in the weave of the carpet, lifting bowed heads towards the warming light. Of course not. What she did see was the serving staff sentried motionless around the room, awaiting some signal to step forward. Bit spooky. And surely nothing, as her gaze passed over the tree that transfixed the dining room, had slipped out of view behind its trunk. Surely she was being paranoid.

She had seen her double again that morning, this time waiting for a train back into town as Shoshana was disembarking on the westbound platform at Nine Elms, and for sure it wasn't a reflection or a trick of the light, none of the reassurances she'd given herself after previous encounters, none of the disclaimers that had prevented her reporting the sighting to her colleagues. This time she wore the same clothes as Shoshana – striped shirt, coat too warm for the day – and even a ring on the same finger, though this, Shoshana thought as the motion of the other passengers propelled her towards the exit, was of a different design than her own.

She withdrew her hands beneath the level of the table, and twisted the band on her own finger. Nervous – why nervous? It wasn't like Esther's behaviour was any surprise; every time they met, the aunt managed to give the impression that she had been prepared to bestow her oh-so-valuable approval on Shoshana this time, only to have her hopes instantaneously dashed by some remark or action or hair out of place by which the younger woman put herself immediately, irredeemably beyond the pale. Nowadays Shoshana made a little game out of it. What might have doomed her tonight? Her posture, perhaps, deemed insufficiently ladylike – she slouched, while Esther perched on the edge of her seat like a budgie on its bar. Perhaps she had detected that Shoshana's striped blouse buttoned right over left and so wasn't a blouse at all but one of Ross's shirts, her wearing it evidence of some unspeakable depravity. In all likelihood, however, it was because Shoshana had unthinkingly guzzled the pork appetisers the other three could hardly bring themselves to look at, let alone consume. 'Haven't eaten since breakfast,' she'd mouthed, wafting her hand before her mouth, almost expecting to see smoke. 'Wow, that's hot. Wanted to be extra hungry for dinner. Am.'

'I used to make an extra portion of dinner so she'd have something she could take for her lunch the next day,' Ross put in, 'but she always forgot.'

'It's unfair to expect a foodie to eat the same meal two days on the trot.' She directed this towards Morris, who Esther had perhaps also selected for how petite she would seem beside him. His stomach pressed against the table edge – engulfed it when he fully inhaled – and from time to time his forehead grew a little slick with perspiration brought on by no greater exertion than sitting and conversing. A gentleman, he'd heaved himself from his seat to greet Shoshana when she arrived; when he dropped back down, something from his shirt had pinged across the room. A minute or two later, the beatific maître d' had glided to their table and proffered a small buff envelope: 'I believe Monsieur may have rolled something?' When Morris tipped it into his palm, out dropped his missing shirt button. Esther looked as if she might spontaneously combust, but Morris reacted with charming merriment, as if he'd been the subject of a delightful prank.

The staff arrived, depositing at each place a rectangular white plate with a shallow indentation at either end. On the left sat a whole tomato, rotund and shining, stalk intact; on the right, a magnolia-coloured mound speckled with black crystals and minuscule arrow-shaped leaves. 'We continue,' announced their adenoidal waitress, 'with our take on the classic caprese salad. All the elements you'd expect are here, just maybe not in the forms you'd expect.' She raised a stove-top espresso maker above Shoshana's plate and tipped it until a fine braiding stream of pale liquid ran on to the tomato, first spilling over and then eating into it, revealing it to be

45

a hollow shell beneath which lay a quenelle of white cream. 'We won't spoil the surprise by telling you too much about this course – just remember that what you see isn't always what you get.'

Shoshana stirred her spoon tentatively into the white mousse. 'You did talk to them about my allergy, didn't you, sweets?' she asked Ross.

'Of course. In the email when I booked, and then again when I got here.'

'He did,' Esther confirmed. 'I don't think there *are* eggs in a caprese salad, are there?' – her tone suggesting that *some-one* at the table might be stupid enough to think so. Once, just once, back when she still cared about Esther's opinion, Shoshana had tried to cut through the passive-aggressive or aggressive-aggressive act and broker a detente: 'Look,' before modifying her tone to one more sympathetic, 'I know you're the closest Ross has to a mum now, and I don't want you to feel like I'm taking him away from you.' Esther's ears seemed to flatten to her head in incredulity. It was like protesting your innocence while you were robbing the bank. It was like pleading for clemency while repeatedly stabbing the judge. She'd patted Shoshana's hand. 'You really mustn't worry,' she'd said mildly, then gone off to make the tea, or perhaps to spit in it.

'Doesn't this look,' Morris said, peering at his dish, '... interesting?'

'One sec, one sec, don't start eating yet—' and the som-melier bustled up to the table, rattling off tasting notes as she sloshed white wine into their glasses. 'Round and smooth on the palate, strong stone fruits, tons of vanilla and wild spring blossom.' She seemed a little wild herself, gave the impression that her uniform was the only restraint prevent-ing something elemental from spilling forth, but Shoshana noticed that these slapdash pours settled to the same level in all four glasses. 'Quite an unfashionable wine, I'll admit, but I'm determined to bring it back, a one-woman trend-shifter, call me the Rhône ranger.' Ross chuckled with the others, even Esther, but under the table his foot found Shoshana's and nudged it significantly. This, she marvelled, returning the pressure so he'd know she understood and concurred, from the boy who'd only allowed himself to be seduced that first time after Shoshana resorted to the backrub that went on too long. Half a decade ago, now, but you had to take your time with boys like these, leading them step by baby step to the understanding that a sex life wasn't in some way unbefitting a life of the mind, nor simply an interesting and enviable phenomenon known only to other, luckier people, like a lottery win or witnessing the aurora borealis. It had required of Shoshana a cautious pace and much use of the subjunctive to guide Ross to the required degree of confidence and vulnerability: 'But if you *were* to watch me making out with another woman in our bed, what kind of woman might she be?' God, how she loved introverts – loved to burst them open like a piñata.

The remaining red shell of the 'tomato' was a brittle, heavily savoury parmesan crisp; the sorbet inside had the rich milky flavour of burrata cheese, melting into the mild tomato water that had been poured over and which had, itself, a taste almost greener than the fragrance filling the room. Summer in October. Shoshana couldn't identify the cream-coloured substance at the other side of the plate – it had a puzzling texture, at once light and dense, not exactly creamy – but each of the micro-leaves that speckled it, some green, some purple, had a related but different sweet sharpness she only half-recognised until she identified it as basil, whereupon the flavour snapped into focus, the solution to a puzzle.

Ross, as they ate, had asked his relatives some bland and uncontroversial question about how they'd spent their day out in London, which allowed Shoshana to apply a screen-saver of a smile and tune out stories in which unseasonal weather, the vagaries of public transport and Oxford Street would no doubt figure. The machines she worked with in her lab performed in an instant calculations that would take a human mathematician years, yet in some ways they were to Shoshana's not even wholly remarkable brain what a slide rule was to a supercomputer. These machines, unlike her, were incapable of appearing interested and engaged in human con-versation – dropping in an occasionally sympathetic murmur or half-smile – while simultaneously thinking through a paradox that must have a logical solution but which could at present only be called impossible.

Sometimes weeks would pass without a sighting of her double, then there'd be several in quick succession, on routes Shoshana travelled frequently and in places she'd never been before. There was no routine to these encounters that Shoshana had been able to identify. Twice in the space of a week the double had been two ahead of her in the queue at Freshways by the station, paying for a variation on the same lunch meal deal Shoshana had picked: they shared a hairdo and profile but not a taste in sandwiches. And before that, weeks ago, brazen as you like, pushing an antique pram through Russell Square, head to toe in burgundy, an outfit that the real Shoshana – worryingly provisional though 'real' was starting to seem – wouldn't have been seen dead in. The double never appeared to notice Shoshana; was always angled away, staring in the wrong direction, far enough off to miss her.

But there had been a man by her double's side at Nine Elms that morning – gangling, his overcoat and hair long and black and in need of a wash – and later, as Shoshana was patrolling the former B Power Station at Battersea that was her lab, checking read-outs, losing track, starting over, it grew more and more to seem that this man was also known to her.

There were twenty-seven devices in the hangar-sized main chamber of the power station: black cubes some nine feet across, featureless but for a chamfered front panel that blurred with numerals, each one giving off a bassy hum that mostly, but not always, harmonised with the notes of its fellows. At the supercooled heart of each unit a 1,024-qubit processor the size of a toddler's thumbnail and worth more than a Mayfair townhouse sifted and collated and cross-checked a dataset so vast that the human imagination could not fully grasp its scale: every picosecond a Library of Alexandria's worth of raw data from satellites and probes and computers pushing ever further into the chaos of deep space, which meant deep time as well. These machines, Shoshana's charges, had been shown something technically unique, a DNA sample with a vanishingly rare genetic quirk, and now they were dredging infinity for a match, a refrain in the cosmic song. It was a search that even the most Pollyannaish of estimates acknowledged would take decades at minimum. And yet, and yet – hadn't Shoshana's footsteps cast a strange echo as she'd descended the clattering gantry that morning? Hadn't she had the sense that as she inspected the black monoliths, someone else was conducting the same survey, moving widdershins to her clockwise, always out of view?

Strange things did happen down there. A lab technician would swear that the phone she had in the evening was not the model she'd taken in there that morning, though it contained all her numbers, all her texts. Someone would ask, 'You speak German, though, don't you?' and it would transpire, to your surprise, that you actually did. These days,

Shoshana and her colleagues were strictly limited in how long they were allowed to spend down here and how often, new rules having been brought in following the discovery, deep in one corner of the lab, of a detailed little mural depicting mammoths and hunters and some third, unidentifiable lifeform, all rendered in unseemly pigments – the work of an expert in theoretical physics from CERN who had spent a full forty-eight hours in the lab and was now on indefinite leave of absence in an undisclosed but, rumour had it, very well-insulated location.

When Shoshana tuned back into the others' conversation, Esther and Morris were, as she had expected by this stage in their travelogue, making vague and irritated remarks about *all the people* in London. 'We were hoping to visit the National Gallery this afternoon, but the queues were shocking. All around the square.'

'That's because of what happened there last summer,' Shoshana put in, feeling she should contribute. 'There was a whole series of protests against museums taking sponsorship money from fossil-fuel companies, marches and things, and then one afternoon this young guy snuck into the gallery with a backpack full of petrol canisters, poured it all over himself and' – she noticed Ross's urgent eyebrow semaphore – 'and security at all these places has been crazy ever since.'

Esther made a noise of disdain – for what? Human tragedy? Shoshana's insensitivity in reporting it? – and in silence they finished the dish. She still couldn't identify the texture of the substance on the right. Not quite a cream, not quite a panna cotta. She sipped the Viognier, about which all the sommelier need have said was that it tasted the way pink pencil erasers smelled – nostalgic, a little sickly – and, as she swallowed, felt battery fizz at the back of her throat, a portent, she thought, of her first cold of the season.

'We hadn't heard of this place before, had we, Father?'

'I read up. I thought, I'm glad I'm not paying!'

'It's terribly generous of you,' the aunt said to Ross, who opened his mouth then, feeling Shoshana pressure his foot in a different way this time, closed it again. Let his aunt and uncle think the best of him.

'Actually,' Ross said. 'Actually, there was a reason we asked you here tonight. We've got some news, you see.' He opened his hand on the table and Shoshana slipped in hers with the slim gold band utterly unlike the aunt's ostentatious stone or the strange sigil she'd seen on her double's ring. 'We're getting married, next April, and we'd like you to come.'

He beamed, *beamed*, and Esther and Morris eyed each other in a way that did not radiate joy.

Morris broke first. 'It's marvellous, just marvellous. Esther, isn't it marvellous?'

'We certainly weren't expecting it,' the aunt said, puffing up a little in indignation. She retrieved from her bag, jingling the little gewgaws, a Liberty-print diary. 'What date?'

'The eighteenth, a Friday.'

'I hope it *isn't* a Friday,' she said. 'I have golf on Fridays. And Morris sometimes gets together for drinks with his chums.' Ross's hand seemed to be tightening on Shoshana's – for warning or support – but it had also grown clammy and she was able to slither out of his grasp. 'No, I'll just have to cancel. Although I just know there'll be consequences.' Still staring at her diary, Esther reached out and snagged the arm of a passer-by. 'Young man. Can you speak to the sommelier? We're going to need more wine over here.'

'I don't . . .' said the boy, arrested mid-step. 'I don't actually work here, though?'

'Be a dear, anyway.' She released his arm and, after a puzzled moment, he did trot towards the front desk where the

51

sommelier was lounging, her back arched, in conference with the maître d'.

Morris was rocking from side to side in his seat, as though gathering momentum to extricate himself. Shoshana had a horrible feeling he was trying to get to his feet so he could make a speech. 'Young love,' he said, his tone wondering, as if such a concept was abstract enough to need an explanatory note. Settling back into his chair in defeat, he instead slapped his broad knee, producing a startling retort. 'Tell us everything.' To Ross, winkingly: 'Did you get down on one knee?'

Shoshana cleared her throat, then again, feeling scaliness. 'Actually, it was me that did the asking. I've never been big on tradition. And the funny thing was, only about an hour earlier, we'd been having the most almighty row.'

All she'd said was 'Open your mouth.' All she'd done was straddle him and brush the stuff along his lips.

'I don't want to.'

'The tiniest amount. You can't even see it, you'd barely know what it was.'

But Ross made such a fuss, writhing and bucking until he'd managed to work the blindfold loose. 'Hard no. Hard no.' That was just no, so she teased more, until he hacked up the *real* no: 'Feldspar. Feldspar!'

'All right, fine.' She swallowed it herself – a scrap of prosciutto no bigger than a postage stamp – and showed her tongue so he'd know it was gone. But it lingered: gummy residue on the roof of her mouth, Ross refusing to let her kiss him and be forgiven until she had first brushed her teeth. Things always seemed to go weird between them, Shoshana mused, when they left the capital, travelled in any direction into the uncharted and unbeguiling territories she thought of simply as Not London. They packed and checked out of the hotel in near silence, and on the long drive home he turned himself away from her in the passenger seat, sulking, the introvert way. All right, fine, she'd thought, be like that, but what's your plan for when we get home: chalk a line through the middle of the flat and we each keep to our own side until someone can afford to move out? He didn't often say no to her, but perhaps, she started to think as they neared the junction for the M25, she'd got him wrong. She'd fallen in love with potential before. Perhaps she'd dreamed up an idealised Ross that best suited her, then tried to mould him to match this template, broken his bones to make him fit; and perhaps she'd overestimated him, taken as genuine enthusiasm for her extravagances what had really been mere capitulation. If he'd been going along with her games all this time out of some notion of courtesy, then she would have no choice but to end this thing, because he would not. You had to get out of a situation like that before it poisoned you both. That was logical. Why, then, she wondered, the clutch of feeling, cold around her midriff, when she contemplated saying the words that couldn't be taken back?

That was when she'd seen the thing in the sky.

First it was incomprehensible, then unbelievable: a solid block of blackness suspended in pure cloudless blue ahead of them. Shoshana drove on, decelerating slightly, and the thing seemed to swell and lower. Tendrils unfurled from its underbelly, groping towards the road. Other vehicles thrilled past theirs, undaunted, vanishing a short distance ahead into the dark of it.

'You seeing this?'

Ross rubbed his eyes. He rubbed his glasses. 'What is that? A storm?'

Then it was upon them, draping them in a zero-visibility zone of unknowable dimensions, a non-space their headlights couldn't penetrate. Rain – was this even rain? – battered the hire car with such relentless ferocity that Shoshana started to worry about their insurance. It was as though she were driving through some awesome and intractable natural feature, a black falls pouring on the land, and drive was all she could do, edging onwards little faster than walking pace, seatbelt digging into her neck as she strained forward in her seat and fought to see, through the wipers' frenzy, any hint of road markings, any glimmer of brake lights or, worse, full beams coming towards them. 'Just pull over,' Ross had to shout over the clamour. 'Where?' she yelled back. 'How? I don't even know which lane we're in.' And then, with no sense of transition, no gradual diminishing of the rain's elemental force, they were through and out of it and the sky was clear again, the fields either side of the motorway abundantly, surreally green; and when she checked her mirrors and saw the great black monolith still squatting over all eight lanes, but safely receding now, she accelerated before it could reach out and drag them in again.

For several minutes neither of them spoke, though as her hands relaxed on the steering wheel Shoshana could hear Ross's quick breathing, sensed his agitation as he psyched himself up to make one of his awkward, only-child declarations. 'What that was like,' he said, and stalled. 'It was like my life before you. I was in darkness, no idea where I was going, and all I could do was keep blindly going, thinking that at some point, surely, I would see where I was. It was scary to live like that. Sometimes I still get scared, you know? But I'm trying to get better.'

She waited until after they'd counted down to and passed the next junction. 'And now? Do you know where we're going now?'

'No,' he said, 'but I do know I want us to go there together. Is that cheesy? I don't care if it is,' he changed, petulant now he'd said his piece.

On either side of the motorway, woodland was interspersed with industrial estates, or grey flatlands were interrupted by untameable expanses of green. 'Terrible traffic going the other way,' she remarked and then: 'Hey, fancy marrying me some time?' And 'Sure,' he said, taking the same casual tone; and, once they'd dropped off the car by Euston, they found another hotel where after lunch they committed acts that Esther and Morris would have considered immoral, physically implausible, definitely unhygienic.

Ross, meantime, was reciting the sanitised version: the field trip he'd been on, the nice hotel with the eco-pods on the outskirts of the New Forest, and no, just a registry office, half a dozen close friends and family.

'People leave it too late these days,' Esther opined. 'We were only twenty-one, weren't we, Father?'

'We were babies,' rumbled Morris, fretting his napkin.

'Don't start me on babies.' She started anyway: 'You married early and had children early, so that you could raise them and have your life back while you were still young.' For the first time Shoshana could recall since meeting her, Esther grinned, savage as one of the minor dinosaurs. 'I sometimes feel as if I was pregnant for my whole twenties. I wouldn't have changed it for the world.'

Shoshana had met some of Ross's cousins. She had notes. 'I just want to make sure we're both at a comfortable enough point in our professional lives before we make any more big decisions. This one still has to finish his PhD – not that I'm rushing you.'

'Of course,' Esther sniffed, 'career before everything these days.' It was as though Shoshana had suggested prioritising the completion of a colouring-in book, the learning of macramé. 'You'll blink. You'll just blink, my girl, and find you're forty and you still haven't got round to it. And then what? Can you imagine having a teenager on your hands when you're in your sixties?'

No one said anything to that, though Shoshana could feel hysterical laughter threatening like weather. 'So,' said Ross at length, looking between his uncle and aunt, 'can we put you down as a yes?'

'I wish you'd known my mum,' Ross had said to her, more than once, not often, but each time so simply and sadly that Shoshana had felt a tartness behind her eyes. 'She'd have loved you. She'd have thrown her cane away and danced with you at the wedding. People would have called it a miracle. I,' he said, almost longingly, 'wouldn't have got a look in.' And two years ago Shoshana, thinking of her research and also of him, because she valued them equally, the highest compliment to both, had thought to ask, 'Do you have anything of hers still?' God love him, he'd kept the beaded brush that reminded him to the point of tearfulness of sitting on the parental bed, his mother cross-legged on the floor with her back to him and her head bowed as he made her long straight space-black hair crackle and shine.

Something was definitely wrong now with Shoshana's throat – a sensation like spiders' legs clustered in her windpipe. Heat flared in her cheeks. With galling swiftness, conversation had moved through and past the subject of their engagement, Morris now talking about a play he and Esther had booked to see the following night – *The Mousetrap*, the Shakespearean parody which had been playing continuously in London since 1601. Did they know, he asked, that whole dynasties of actors had appeared in it, playing roles originated by their forebears? Shoshana's eye was drawn, as he spoke, to the fat that bulged from the collar of his shirt, the stubble at the back of his neck affording her a vivid and unwanted mental image of Esther trolling an electric razor over the band of flesh, mouth beaky with distaste. The unctuous lather, the lethal blade laying bare a stripe of bright tender vulnerable flesh, and the thought never occurring to either of them that this act could be tender, even erotic.

Matty, she suddenly thought: gangly, moody Matty Sutton. They'd been seventeen, and as Matty had wriggled on the toilet seat in her home, forbidden to touch himself until she gave permission, she'd placed a bare foot between his knees and shaved her legs, and after she'd let him towel the traces of foam from her bright skin she had given a sharp little slap to the erection poking from his cartoon briefs, and then they'd had to wash the towelling seat cover before her parents got home. She hadn't thought of him in years: pale, skinny Matty, uncombed hair home-dyed black in emulation of his musical heroes, never brave enough for eyeliner; but if she aged him up, Shoshana realised now, if she made of him a disillusioned punk with a real job and a gnawing sense of regret at living to be older than many of his idols, that identikit person would resemble the man standing beside her double at Nine Elms that morning.

Ross, she became aware, was frowning at her. In certain theoretical shapes, interior and exterior dimensions flowed into one another such that you could not definitively say what they contained and what lay outside, and for a dazzled moment Shoshana couldn't be sure she hadn't related some of this thought process aloud. 'I said, are you okay?'

Had he? 'Now you mention it, I do feel a bit . . .' Her windpipe was crushed and tickling, heat was blazing from her face. 'I think I've eaten something I shouldn't. That white mousse. I think there must have been egg white in it.'

'You do look puffy,' Esther said helpfully.

'I told them about your allergies. I did.'

'Of course, love. When you made the booking and when you sat down at the table. But then you all moved, didn't you?' Laughter kept bubbling up in Shoshana, unwilled, though some shuttered-off part of her, observing from its hide, knew it wasn't funny at all. Still, seeing Ross urgently gesturing to the sommelier, she giggled. Down, boy!

Somewhere, they hadn't moved table. Somewhere she wasn't dining with one, two or three of these people; somewhere else she was, but one of them wasn't a total cow. Take the long view, the infinite view, and Shoshana was married and single, divorced, widowed, had never felt the spark of love, was mutually and wholeheartedly committed to one or two or more people. She was researcher and department head and uni dropout, lived in Switzerland, Melbourne, aboard the International Space Station. In infinite worlds she was alive and infinite worlds dead from every conceivable cause. Amid all these possibilities, logic said that numerous possible Shoshanas were a shade smarter than her, a shade quicker, one step ahead, all it took. Some of these had seen the data from the machines in their own Battersea labs, empirical evidence that these endless variations all existed simultaneously, repeat patterns in the warp and weft of reality. And by definition, there must then be the Shoshana – there only needed to be one – who knew not only that these worlds coexisted, but how to move between them. To bring what: a secret, a warning?

She managed to get halfway from her chair before she toppled, and as she fell she wondered if somewhere her doppelgänger was also falling, tugged by invisible strings. She caught her upper arm on the table edge, but did that mean the other Shoshana would now bear an unaccountable wound? In the park, on the Tube, had that other woman been a figment of her imagination – or was she the other's delusion? She might wake up someone else entirely, and never know. She'd have to treat it like everything else, she resolved in the last moment before darkness swung up: an experiment where you never knew what might come next.

Kima's first sablés had crumbled as she was levering them from their baking sheet, and now a replacement batch had bonded to theirs. Alone in patisserie corner, she thumped the tray against the counter and protested aloud: 'But this is supposed to be non-stick!'

Tonight was giving her a drubbing. Tonight was a sorbet that wouldn't set and a violet gel that had set too hard, into a flat and unworkable mass. Patisserie cheffing was where Kima, shit-ass at anything requiring improvisation, intuition, really much creative thought at all, had found her niche. So long as she worked with top ingredients, measured rigorously, kept temperatures precise, the results should be reliably, identically perfect every time. Otherwise, she groused as she again fetched the cosh of biscuit batter from the fridge and prepared to slice off another two dozen rounds, what was the goddamned point?

It wasn't just her, though, tonight: first that kid had been sent away with his hand swaddled in scarlet – and that was going to screw things for everyone, no commis – and now something had happened in the dining room. She could hear raised voices in the kitchen, but here the tiled half-wall designed to keep her section cooler than the rest of the kitchen functioned, annoyingly, as a screen shielding her from what-ever interesting crisis was unfolding. Any other time, she'd have asked me what was happening – I was always hanging around patisserie – but that was something else that had gone wrong tonight.

Childish to blame her misfortunes on someone who wasn't even present, but Kima was childish, Kima *liked* being childish, and so yeah, it was my fault. Each time she fucked up some normally foolproof process, she reached for the phone she shouldn't have been carrying and redialled my number, and each time it rang a single time, giving her a brief surge of hope before the polite voice cut in: 'The person you have called is not available.' The line dead then, not even my voicemail for her to vent to. Now she vaguely recalled something I'd said about having to change number recently. Maybe it had been a line, part of my plan to make Kima's life more difficult.

'With John gone,' she heard Joanna lecturing the others, 'we're all gonnae have to work twice as hard.' Kima gophered up to listen. So much softer-spoken, Joanna, than Magnus had been – ah, but they weren't meant to make comparisons with the head chef they'd had before. Thoughtcrime. 'As of now, Table Two is out of action – it's fine, she'll be fine, the worst thing is we had to comp an entire four-top, so our numbers are shot. Someone made a mistake, someone misread my notes, all right, it happens. Loïc'll try and get us a replacement off the waiting list, but coming up to eight o'clock on a Tuesday isnae ideal for that. Meantime,' bringing her voice up to its usual incantatory timbre, 'let's all knuckle down and bash on, all right? Let's focus, let's cook, let's cook.'

It *happens*! Was that it? Kima was staggered. Magnus would have been smashing plates by now, Magnus would have forced the responsible party to identify themselves then held the offender's hand over a hot flame to the point of blistering, regardless of how that only worsened a bad situation. Kima sorta kinda missed those rages, those unpredictable maulings, mostly verbal but not always, the guy's total inability to compartmentalise his emotions. A horror, sure, but you always knew where you were with him. In the wrong, often: on the receiving end of one of his purple-faced barrages of abuse, the target of hurled crockery. Magnus would not simply have had a quiet word with Kima about my absence. He'd have left the kitchen, got a cab to the house she and I lived in and burned it down.

An alarm shrilled behind her. Kima gathered up a hotel pan crowded with small pods containing various sweet reductions and gels and wobbled from patisserie to the pass, where Finn was ready to plate. He offered his usual bland smile – was it even a smile, or was that like thinking your pet cat smiled? – and fitted the first gel ampoule into the brass device he wielded, something like a pair of bellows that had mated with a Victorian hypodermic and a six-gun. He began to work, extruding a sticky greenish bubble from the nozzle of his gadget and carefully settling it on each plate in front of him; then swabbed the syringe, rotated the chamber, made another bubble bloom, this one faintly pink, and joined it to the first. Kima watched, admiring his dancer's intensity of attention and economy of movement. Not like her at all. He resembled the benign android in a sci-fi film, dispatching his missions with optimum efficiency, no unnecessary expenditure of energy. Yesterday, though, after he'd turned up unannounced on Grantham Street – she'd snooped from the window when the doorbell rang, unwilling to go downstairs in PJs – she'd been sure she had heard us arguing in my room. Our actual words hadn't been audible, despite her best efforts with a glass pressed to the wall, but she could detect a hectoring tone Kima had never heard before from placid Finn. Then our voices strafed in a zigzag down the stairs, the front door slammed, and silence. Well, she'd thought, yawning, those androids did tend to go berserk in the movie's final reel. A nap later it had occurred to her to go upstairs to check I was okay, or rather to snoop, but I didn't answer. She could have told Joanna what she'd half-heard, but I'd given her such shit before for gossiping about me and Finn that she had thought it better to keep it to herself.

'Acceptable?' she'd scoffed when I'd asked her, with telltale nonchalance, about Midgard's policy on dating your co-workers. 'More like mandatory. Only someone who's already in the industry's going to put up with the hours we do, to start with, and where else are you going to meet someone? Do a *Romeo and Juliet* with a chef at a rival place?' I'd told her some story about *Romeo and Juliet* then – yeah, yeah, so I was an actor, everyone but Kima was something else, she didn't listen. I'd been helping her on dessert that day, running a wetted knife around silicon moulds, pressing out hollow ovals of white chocolate for her to mizzle with airbrushes she held in each hand – one loaded with pale blue colouring, the other tan – until they resembled birds' eggs. 'I thought you'd worked in restaurants before, anyway,' she said. 'You know the rest of the world disappears and your nearest become your dearest. People, uh, compromise.' Who had Kima compromised on, I'd asked, with a saucy look. She'd turned prim. 'I don't do any of that.'

Not her thing, she'd gone on, knowing she was protesting too much, as she set a spoonful of mushroom duxelles and foie gras into every other shell – an experimental dessert, this one, that hadn't lasted long on our menu. She liked control, hence patisserie, its foolproof methods and predictable out-comes. Was love predictable, or the human heart? Of course not. Better, then, to steer clear, and live a life of certainty and moderation. Didn't I think that sounded more sensible?

I said I thought it sounded psychotic.

Kima had lurched sideways to douse the heat on a sauce-pan of truffle caramel that had started to spit. 'Psychotic,' she repeated. Then she slid Yolande's most recent postcard from the pocket of her apron. 'I'll give you psychotic. Listen to this.'

I had been disingenuous, seeking Kima's advice only after I had already been out on a date with Finn. I had accepted his invitation to dinner in the same spirit I'd let him have my number after the test kitchen a month or so before: expecting nothing, but thinking he was very fit.

He made me pick the restaurant, and I chose a BYOB steak place which I'd noticed on my journey home and thought looked nice but not too spendy. I'd come from a decently cosmopolitan city but London still had a way of making me feel very parochial: I hadn't known, before we walked through the door, that a Jewish steakhouse was even a thing. Fun! I thought when I realised, though the host was openly bemused by our presence. He was very polite and very adamant in explaining that he couldn't pour the wine we'd brought with us because it wasn't kosher, and while Finn returned to the bottle shop for a swap I sat at our table, watching a wall-mounted TV set playing video footage of a rabbinical knees-up, lots of dancing. Finn hulked back and presented the replacement bottle to the host, who with great regret explained that although kosher this wasn't the right *kind* of kosher. There were two other big tables of diners in, one all men, one all women, and they were watching this show rather than the TV. Off to the bottle-o Finn went again, this time with less good grace. The manager and I smiled at each other more coolly. The place hadn't been my first choice; it was just the most affordable of my options: I wasn't going to be a sook and let Finn pay for my meal, but I also didn't want to go any further into debt for the sake of a date.

His third choice was a Pinot Noir finally acceptable to the staff, though not to us: it had the sweetness and consistency of blackcurrant linctus. After we'd made faces over our drinks, Finn announced that he had brought me a gift. He handed over a plush toy: rotund, olive-green, with a pale front and domed beige belly, goggle eyes, a zip up the back. 'It's an avocado,' he added, as I tried to think of something to say. Had he really chosen it with me in mind? I wasn't convinced. It was something you'd pick up as an emergency gift for a child's birthday, a child you didn't know too well. 'I thought Australia? Avocado on toast? And I noticed you didn't have anything to put your make-up in,' he went on, which was disheartening: if he'd been paying attention when he helped me gather my things from my locker that time, that meant he really had chosen it for me specially.

I hadn't been on a date in a good while; Finn, by his behaviour, maybe never. He asked me what my favourite subject had been at school, a question less Certificate I Dating and more *Humaning for Dummies*; then, when I said it was drama, suggested that we could go and see a show together. 'Some time,' he added, as if I might drag him to the Globe right there and then. 'You like the theatre?' I asked. He pondered. 'I don't think I've ever been.' The two of us together, god, it was like trying to strike a match on a bar of soap. 'You should give it another go, acting,' he counselled, unsolicited. 'After all, you don't want to be at Midgard for ever' – little suspecting that in this job I had come to feel for the first time in years, and if only for a short time, supported, enmeshed, content. It was everything else that felt isolating and difficult.

At the end of the meal – we shared a T-bone steak so large it must have come from a buffalo – the staff lined up to thank

Finn for coming and for his understanding about the wine; each guy shook Finn's hand then turned to me in wordless alarm, retracting hands for fear of inadvertent contact.

For two other people the night would have been something to laugh about and bond over. A disastrous date should at least give you a good story. But Finn couldn't stop apologising, even though the restaurant had been my choice; I started to feel like he was trying to co-opt something from me. We took the same bus home, but the awkwardness was so great that I ended up getting off two stops early.

The next time I'd been seconded to Kima, she started reading aloud from that morning's postcard before I had even asked how she was going. "'Drove out past Cobus's place in Franschhoek today. There's a new roof on the farmhouse. Vineyards almost back to where they used to be. Soon it'll be like nothing ever happened. Wish you could see it. – Your friend, Yolande.'" She threw it down. "'*Your friend*'."

Joanna kept assigning me to assist Kima and also, she'd confided, to see if I could explain why she was such a lemon – meaning, translated from the British, why she never came to Pangaea for drinks with the rest of us. For her part, Kima seemed to think I just wanted to hang out, though that didn't stop her getting me to do the shit jobs she didn't want to. On this occasion she had got me kneeling on the floor, struggling to reattach a segmented metal hose to a squat canister of nitrogen. The rubber seal had corroded, and wisps of numbing gas coiled around my fingers as I tried to make the connection fast.

'It's an improvement,' I ventured. 'In that other one she was saying she wanted to pull out your hair.'

Kima tugged a pellet of damp loo roll from her sleeve and dabbed her scabbing nose. Always a shade chilly in patisserie,

66

from the cooling pipes that ran under the counters to ensure that chocolate would not melt if left out, or a sourdough starter go ectoplasmic. 'She never came to my house, I never even mentioned Cobus's name to her. Nah, she's inserting herself into my stories, my life. I need her to stop, but I don't want to get in touch with her. Nothing I said would make a difference anyways. It's all going on inside her head, that's what Magnus used to say.' She'd given me a sly look. I knew that Magnus had been Midgard's head chef before Joanna, but since anything that'd happened even the day before I started here was irrelevant prehistory, I didn't say anything. Within about five minutes of talking to Kima my first time in patisserie she'd revealed what she knew about Magnus and Joanna, and because I knew she expected me to be appalled or titillated or whatever, I was like: 'Yeah, and?' Secretly, though, I did look at Joanna differently after that, impressed by what our head chef had put herself through.

'Every day I get one of these,' Kima lamented. 'I should go to the police, shouldn't I?'

'You should maybe stop bringing them to work. You should maybe throw them away and not read them.'

She looked at me like I was unhinged. 'Don't bring it to work, she says.' She nodded sideways to the main kitchen. 'How is love's young dream, anyway?'

I shrugged, through it probably didn't come across from a crouching position. I'd told Kima the story of the steakhouse, but left out one detail: that Finn had texted me the morning after, asking if we could give it another go on our next night off. He hadn't apologised again, which made me think it was worth a try. I wasn't made of stone. We'd end up having two more dates, each less successful than the last, before we decided we should accept what the universe was telling us, and I wouldn't recount those stories to Kima either.

With clumsy cold-scorched paws I fed the metal hose up to the counter and hooked its nozzle over the edge of a deep-sided hotel pan. I twisted the valve on the frost-jacketed canister, and the gas began to flow. 'I'll do all this, shall I?' I asked, but Kima just grunted. She was reading the card again, as if it might contain a coded message that wasn't nuts. I stood up and snatched it from her, gave the picture a glance – fruit and veg cleverly arranged to form a fatuous face – then, holding it by the corner, dipped the damned thing into the seething bath of nitro for a count of five. It came out frozen rigid, patterns of thaw flaring across the illustration. I brought it down sharply edgewise on the counter and it shattered everywhere.

'What's that solve?' Kima complained. 'Now I'll be picking pieces of it out my food all night. And tomorrow there'll be a new one anyway.'

'Have you thought about moving?'

'Right, yeah, sure, I'll just up and move. You really are new in London, aren't you?'

'No, but there's a room coming up in my house-share. This guy who's been working on building sites as long as I've lived there, apparently he's heard the good word and he's going off to be a monk.'

'From hod to god, that old story. You're serious? What's the catch?'

I could have acted offended, but I'd actually just been thinking about something that could work to my advantage. 'All right, it's pretty tiny, but it's right up at the top of the house so it gets super-cosy. It's cheap. And best of all, your weirdo ex won't know where you've gone.'

I'd known no one when I arrived in London, I explained as we dipped the heads of pink roses in the nitrogen bath. Straightaway I'd done what any Melbourne expat would've and found a job at an Antipodean coffee shop where kinship mattered at least as much as experience. The owner, Sean, a Tasmanian with biceps bigger than my waist and a permanent air of not unpleasant unwashedness, called me 'cuz' with the same disinterested fondness he would any actual distant relation and allowed me to read the flyers and want-ads people left before they went up on our community noticeboard, which was how I'd found the room in Walthamstow. 'And so, a long time back, I resolved that if I was ever able to help someone out in turn, I'd do it.' In fact, that had been Sean's condition for letting me intercept the small ads, but the way I'd phrased it made me sound more generous. I wasn't going to admit the truth, which was that I was lonely.

I had referred to Yolande as Kima's ex and that wasn't exactly right, but she hadn't corrected me because it wasn't entirely wrong either. Some things there weren't quite words for. She never told me the full story: her growing dread as she descended the black-painted stairwell of the old mill towards the sickly pink neon glow emanating from the basement, how she'd paused on the last landing before either head overcame heart or vice versa – impossible to say which – and, then, instead of fleeing she had continued down into the club. Then there was the haze of sugary dry ice that jagged her throat, the strobes, the bass thump reverberating in the cavity that fear and self-doubt had carved out within her. She didn't tell me how it had felt to realise in slow amazement that the club was filled with women, only women – women with short hair and long; in dresses, jumpsuits, grungy jeans, not much at all; Amazonian women and women she could have carried in her arms; stout ones, slight ones, homely ones, stunning ones, punks and diesels, glams and butches and ones who weren't particularly one thing or another, like her. And all of them were like her, but not like her. It was only after seeing how full the place was that Kima realised she'd been expecting a smaller, drabber gathering, a hostile clique. She'd scanned the crowd, in the stabs and smears of disco lights, half-expecting to spot the friend who'd first told her, in what seemed stagy disgust, that Deep Breath hosted a lesbian party on Sunday nights. As far as Kima could tell, once her first wave of discomfort had evaporated and she'd ordered a lemonade at the bar, the scene was no more debauched or scandalising than in any other nightclub in town. Someone jostled her, spilling her drink, yet Kima found herself apologising and then, though irritated at herself, she felt a slightly giddy sense of relief, too. These people were irritating, the music was too loud, the drinks were expensive, and Deep Breath, therefore, was no more a place she wanted to be than any straight club she'd ever been dragged to – and that was thrilling.

The bit of the story she did tell me was about how she chewed her straw and nodded to the house music, bought more drinks and returned each time a little closer to the dance floor. She shuffled her feet a bit, tried to watch without letting on that she was watching. People parted around her, as if she was giving off some bad scent; she considered fleeing, then they closed in again, ignoring her. On the far side of the dance floor she watched a girl embracing and stroking a riveted support girder, her face radiant with desire; she might, Kima suspected, be *on* something. A woman with a mass of curly hair, a modish Breton top, danced near Kima, moved away, returned, then danced beside her, then – it wasn't clear how or when the shift occurred – was dancing with her. Was that it? So easy? The woman was saying something, and Kima cupped her ear. 'Can I buy you a drink?'

'I'm driving,' she shouted back, just as the music plunged to silence, so she sounded like she was furious. Then an airhorn blared from the speaker, a long sustained warning; the dancers lifted their arms and whooped and jumped; and 'Good,' the woman said back, at a normal speaking volume, a sweat breaking on her forehead, 'you can give me a lift home after,' and when the beat crashed back, it seemed to split Kima's pulse in two, sending electric charge up and down in her at once.

This was Yolande, she had explained to me, to which yes, I said, I'd got that. Yolande who had made Kima wait an indeterminate, interminable time before she emerged finally from the crowd, the white stick of a lollipop bouncing in her mouth, and said, 'Wanna get out of here?' To which Kima, edgy now not just with nerves and anticipation but because she had consumed eight lemonades and not braved the toilets – you had to know your limits – said that she very much did.

On the way home, smoking a joint, skull lolling on the headrest, Yolande asked a series of questions to which Kima, concentrating on the strain of night driving, wished she had better answers. What school had Kima gone to? The posh one in Claremont that as soon as you mentioned, people made assumptions about your wealth or your intellect or both. Yolande found this hilarious, which proved the point. Did Kima have a job? Yes, an ignominious one. The questions were so low-stakes that they illuminated all the bigger things Yolande wasn't asking: why did you stick around so long in that club when you so obviously felt ill at ease? Are you glancing at me like that because you can't believe I'm here, or because you can't figure out what's going to happen next?

Yolande lived out on the coast. The stretch of road where she said to pull in was being resurfaced, and Kima ran the car aground on scree until it came to rest with one or more wheels off the ground. 'Don't you want to park up properly?' Yolande asked, and flicked the joint out the window, orange glimmer on purple dark. 'If you're coming in, I mean.'

But Kima didn't, couldn't, move. 'Do you remember those maths problems they used to give you in school? "If it takes three men five hours to dig a ten-foot trench, how many hours will it take two men to dig an eight-foot one?"'

'Six,' Yolande said instantly.

'Right,' said Kima, who had no idea whether it was right or not. 'But did you never wonder – I mean, are they digging this second trench right after the first? Wouldn't they be tired, then, and work slower? How deep are these trenches? And isn't it a bit suspicious, actually, this pair going around digging holes all over the place? What happened to the third guy, anyways?' Yolande, to Kima's relief, was laughing. 'What I'm saying is two things. One is, people aren't puzzles, only sometimes they are. And the other thing is that I always flunked those tests. I got told I shouldn't think so much. Can I ask you something?'

'Only if it's deeply, deeply personal.'

'When did you know? Because I'm not sure that I do. I don't *not* know, you know? But I don't want to be . . . confusing.'

Yolande reached over to stroke the line of Kima's jaw. 'You don't confuse me. But you are ridiculous. Come in for coffee. Just coffee, nothing more.'

Of course there was more. On Yolande's bed, by a window open to the night and the distant rhythm of surf on the beach below as the sea inexorably ate away at the shoreline, there was more, thank god. Afraid of seeming passive, Kima did her best to mimic what Yolande was doing, until the other girl stilled her hand. 'Relax. Are you good? Is this good?' Kima swallowed, unable to reply. 'Because it's really good for me.' What she was doing made Kima feel a hot point beneath her ribs, an ember which glowed and spread outwards, an expanding circle of something like light that encompassed Yolande and the stereo which seemed now to be playing the most melodic music ever recorded, and the pure wonders of the stars she could see through the window, and the soft surge of lacy foam on the beach, and all those women at Deep Breath who shared this secret knowledge; and then, wondrously, dangerously, Kima wasn't thinking at all.

When she woke, her first feeling was of total luxuriance, a cat flexing in a sunbeam. She was alone, and on the pillow beside her lay a postcard – the first, it would turn out, of a great many of these. 'Had to go to work. Nice times last night, really nice. Call me?' Then a number and a string of kisses.

Kima's limbs, as she dressed, felt agreeably weighty, like after any workout. As she picked up her jeans, her phone tumbled to the floor and lit up. Fifteen missed calls, all from her mother. 'Holiday romance gone sour?' she said as soon as her mother picked up. 'Where the hell are you?' her mother barked at the same time. 'Never mind, just get home now. You are in one hell of trouble, missy.'

On the road, Kima realised she was more tired than she'd first thought, and with fatigue came misgivings. Maybe Yolande did this all the time – zeroed in every week on some pliant outsider on her first visit to Deep Breath, dazzled her into surrendering something whose value would only be grasped once it was gone. But then there'd been the way she'd finished the postcard on a question – 'Call me?' It made Yolande seem a lot less confident than she had last night. Had Kima given in too easily? Been tricked?

She had begun to register a faint but distinctive scent of smoke and scanned the car bonnet for signs of overheating. A few seconds later, a helicopter went whopping overhead, very low – instinctively she ducked – towards the hills that surrounded Franschhoek. As it neared the forested slopes the helicopter descended still further then disgorged from its underbelly a long dousing spout of water that flumed

73

diagonally into the treeline, becoming mist. Kima could see it now, the feathery blue smoke, the prickle and glint of wrong light in the evergreens. She drove faster.

'What does it matter when it started?' her mother bridled later. 'When you weren't there is when it started. Halfway through dinner on the last night of my first vacation in three years is when it started.'

'It's not my fault,' Kima said out of habit, though there was no one else's it could have been. Having exhausted her snooper's instinct on day three of housesitting the neighbour's place, she had actually begun the small amount of cleaning she'd been asked to do. A cursory tour with the vacuum cleaner, and then she noticed the wilted flowers in the living room and – here was where she'd gone wrong – took the initiative, rinsing the big lens-shaped vase and placing it back on the windowsill. The glass shone pleasingly, convex sides gathering the sunlight into itself; and, once she'd gone, focusing that light into a neat spot on the rug, first bright then dark, then sending up a feeble twirl of smoke. At sunset a dry breeze came down off the hills and in through the windows of Cobus's house, which Kima had thoughtfully left ajar to let air circulate; the fed smoulder caught. Small flames licked at the legs of an antique settee, the tasselled hems of curtains, acquiring a taste for the house until, all in a rush, they tore upwards and outwards, insatiable.

'And on a Sunday,' said her mother. 'Where exactly were you last night?'

'Where was I?' Guilt made Kima truculent. 'Where was Cobus! That's it, I forgot, he was off *vacationing* with my very principled, pious mother, who works in land reform and who might be convinced somehow to help prevent his exploited workers taking him to court for a share in his farm.'

'So smart, Miss Twenty-Two! Knows the ways of the whole world and has her nose up in all its business.'

Fire was a gourmand. It didn't care what it consumed, and the more it ate the bigger and greedier it grew. It swallowed all it could of Cobus's house and then it rushed out into the drought-stricken grounds where in mere minutes it devoured, like petits fours after a feast, the vines that had been the livelihood of Cobus's family for generations. After that, like any sated diner, it laid low for a while ahead of its next meal. Late on Sunday evening, the first specks of it began to appear in random spots across the hillside, nodes on a secret network, erupting around midnight in multiple widespread conflagrations that tore through scrub, exploded parched trees like kegs of gunpowder.

'I never wanted to take care of his stupid house. Why couldn't Cobus have got one of his own kids to do it? There's enough of them—'

'His own kids have jobs. Jobs! You know, they work? They earn? And because he wanted to do you a favour, god knows why. People notice, you know. They see you doing nothing.'

'What about my patisserie class? That's not nothing.'

Her mother directed a look of suffering to the heavens, or maybe another incoming helicopter. 'What day is this? Is it Monday, is it not?'

'I mean, sure, I'm missing *today's* class—'

'Look, he's coming.' Cobus was marching from the blackened house, a grim figure surrounded by fireworkers in smutted Day-Glo. 'I'd make myself scarce if I was you. Like, different continents scarce.'

Kima never returned to Deep Breath. Her first visit had coincided with the destruction of a man's home and career: who'd risk a second? Nor did she call Yolande. She scraped a pass in her patisserie course – best in class for her kouign-amanns, but marks off for attendance – and, sulkily taking her mother's advice literally, started looking for entry-level jobs anywhere but Cape Town.

'The cards started coming the week I got to England,' she told me. 'It's my goddamned mother, I know it. Yolande must have tracked her down and asked where I'd gone. And nothing's too much trouble for Mum, unless it involves cutting her own daughter the least slack.' I nodded a lot, almost frenziedly, Kima noticed. 'It's not just cards. For my twenty-third she sent a cake, too.'

'What kind?'

'The kind you don't eat.'

She'd been living downstairs from me for six weeks now. Walthamstow was a crater but it was a crater in Zone Three: things were on the up. Six weeks without daily missives from the disordered mind of Yolande. She imagined cards piling up on the hallway table at her last place, or binned by the new tenants as the flotsam of a stranger's life. Was it mad – was it mad that Kima wanted to call round to her old flat in case they hadn't been thrown out?

The last one she'd received before moving in with me had read: 'Our agrarian ancestors knew the curative effects of fire. They knew that fresh new shoots always grow stronger on ground cleansed by flames. You have grown stunted and wrong. What could the new you be? See you soon – Yolande.' It had had an unfamiliar stamp – Belgian, it turned out, which sent Kima into a spin. 'Anyone can buy a stamp any time and use it when they like,' I'd told her. She'd jabbed a finger: 'And the postmark?' No, what was likelier was that Yolande was coming for her, flight by flight, or as a passenger aboard freight ships, then hitchhiking, travelling by the most arduous and hazardous route so that the prize at the end would feel truly earned.

She'd seen me rolling my eyes. But otherwise she'd been struck by how attentive I'd been to her story, which suggested to Kima she'd been right about me. I'd never described

76

exactly why I'd come to London myself, but I hadn't had to: one absconder recognised another. It wasn't impossible, Kima thought as she opened the oven and inhaled the buttery waft of finally perfect sablés, that I hadn't come in tonight because I'd done the old midnight flit from London, like I no doubt had from Melbourne before. All that guff a couple of days ago when I was wailing about losing my phone, somewhere between the restaurant and Pangaea and home, the only three places I ever went. She was pretty sure that was foreshadowing. Later, at home, she imagined, she'd go up to my attic room and find it stripped of all trace of me.

'Kima. Keems.' Nico half-appeared around the tiled wall, settled their nose on the line of it like Kilroy sideways. 'Table Six just ordered another round of espresso Martinis and Chef wants them out before the next course.' Kima started to protest, and Nico straightened up, raising their long slim palms. 'Don't shoot the messenger. I'm too cute to die.'

Grumbling, she gathered what she needed – coffee essence, the bottle of Kahlúa with the foul black gunk around the top – and clumped into the main kitchen, tripping on the green bin at the entrance to her section, which startled Addy, hanging back with the special preparation for Table Three, and caused her to accidentally snap off a part of it. Kima, misfortune's little helper.

Like some multi-limbed god of eastern myth, Gareth in immaculate new jacket seemed simultaneously to be assembling Five's extra snack of crisped chicken skin and crème fraîche and bitter greens flash-blackened on open flame, tasting a sauce on a demitasse spoon then pinging it into the wash, draping a clean towel around a pan's hot handle and dragging it off the fire – until Joanna ordered him to serve the next course in what should have been my place, whereupon he threw everything down with theatrical but genuine disgust.

Gareth's station was nearest the staff lockers at the far end of the kitchen, and when he stepped aside, Kima noticed something jammed into her door of her locker: a small, blue, horrifying rectangle. She dodged through the assembling staff and yanked the postcard free. It showed an aerial view of central London, bridges and monuments, the Thames tinted cerulean. Exhaling, she turned the card over. The familiar hand, the old red ink. 'In past times, people who'd done great wrongs were placed in the Bloody Tower to await execution. See you very soon.' And on the side lined for an address all that was written was 'Kima, Midgard.' No stamp, no postmark. It must have been delivered by hand, slipped under the door.

A small noise escaped Kima. She whipped around, staring at the pass where the next course was ready for pickup. Forgetting, she searched for me among the waitstaff to ask me what she should do; but of course, I was no longer there.

Table Three

Jot, short for Jonathan, was an only child, an inch shorter and four pounds heavier than the national average for a boy newly turned twelve, a keen home cook, and – opinions varied – either wiser than his years or a troubled old soul. To look his best for his birthday dinner he was wearing his smart blazer and his favourite tie, navy and embroidered with trains emitting tiny stitched puffs of steam. In preparation for the next course he clicked another couple of millimetres into his propelling pencil and used his bandaged hand to flatten his notebook on a fresh page. He wanted to appear professional; more than this, he wished to give the impression he was only sharing his table with these two adults through some clerical goof on Midgard's part.

'You don't need to keep staring,' one of them told the other. 'She's not coming back.'

'What do you mean?'

'You understand the word, don't you? Staring. At that girl.'

'It looked like she was choking to death. Who wouldn't stare?'

'No, you're right. It probably helped. "Paramedics said she could have died, but for the plucky member of the public who ogled her until they arrived."'

Jot's current overriding preoccupation was with drinks pairings. The sommelier, Addy – he'd researched the staff – had poured two big fishbowls of wine, straw-coloured and a little cloudy, and he was going to have to taste it if he was to make a proper assessment of the meal. Addy declared herself a big fan of natural wines and Pét-Nats, and Jot had nodded, conversant with both terms, much good that theory did. 'You'll get apple peel, you'll get the turning of the leaves as summer becomes fall, you'll get the sense' – here she nipped her lower lip between sharp incisors – 'the sense you should call that special someone before it's too late.'

There was a pause, and he looked up to find her holding her closed fist just above his place setting, as if for a game of scissors-paper-stone. When she relaxed her grip, small crystals of rock salt flowed from her hand, building into a little cairn on the tabletop before him. On this she settled the upturned carapace of a crab, mounted with a glittering geodic heap of bubbles, a pale lozenge suspended at its heart. The adults were being served the same, but on beautiful big faience dishes edged in gold, which Jot eyed with great envy. The ten-year-old Jot who had first requested, in lieu of the traditional landfill gifts, a gourmet dinner – a one-star, he'd been careful to stress, nothing over the top – would have caused a fuss about being singled out, complaining that a special presentation was as demeaning and insulting to his palate as a kids' menu. Not the Jot of now, dutifully scribbling his notes as the dish was introduced: Midgard's take on remoulade, with celeriac, sushi-grade spider crab, apple, vanilla – this ongoing list prompting Jot to lift his chin, interested – borage and wasabi. He thanked the sommelier brightly, and hoped the parental unit appreciated how mature he was being.

Barely a week in and twelve was already proving a significant age. Too old, perhaps, for nicknames. Certainly too old for tantrums, though judging by his parents' behaviour tonight, that window of opportunity might reopen in a few decades.

Punctured by the tines of his fork, each of the tacky bubbles that formed the dome of the dish crumpled and released a breath of mint, of lemon, of salt-sweet sea air. At their centre, surely too solid to have been supported by just these, was a neat parcel like a summer roll, its skin a translucently fine sheet of celeriac into which flecks of herbs seemed grafted from germination, its contents a generous quantity of raw crab, the long white oddly inorganic strands kept a perfect couple of degrees cooler than room temperature. Jot shut his eyes, hoping by doing so to taste more fully, and to hear less of the ongoing squabbling.

'Funny, isn't it? They go on and on about the wait to get in here, yet there's that table sitting empty now, going to waste. If only people knew.'

'What's funny is your apparently limitless concern for other people's problems while you remain blithely oblivious to your own.'

'Who hurt you? What made you such a nasty piece of work?'

'Really? You really have to ask.'

These arguments weren't circular but spirographic: no matter how far they digressed or what fresh topics they drew in, they always returned to the same starting points: who was asking the unreasonable of whom, who was expecting too much of or paying too little attention to the other. You're so thin-skinned, one would say; no, you're just mean. 'Jot.' And of course – 'Jot?' – of course it always came back, ultimately, to *what was best for him.* 'Jot!' they were yelling. 'We already told you negative on wine.' Jot's eyes sprang open. His good hand, which had been creeping towards the nearer glass as if of its own accord, halted. 'Drink your rhubarb shrub.' He'd made a

81

tactical error: yes, he'd united them, which had been his aim all along, but against him. They clustered in, overweening. 'What do you think?' 'Can you taste the horseradish?' 'Are you enjoying your dinner? You are enjoying it, aren't you?' 'I bet you can work out how they did all this, can't you, you clever thing.' 'Look at that sweet little face. The crab's, I mean – not that yours isn't sweet too.' This was worse than the bickering. 'How's the paw? Is it sore again?'

It had never actually stopped being sore, but Jot had already traded on the injury too much to make a fuss now, so he shook his head. Maturity! They hadn't a clue. His hand had curled in on itself, fingertips to bandaged palm. He straightened it out, winced, then pressed his palm to the tabletop, flat as he could, making the raised wound beneath the dressing squirm left to right and deliver a fresh kick of pain. Good. In some sense, he supposed, it was right that he suffer.

In spite of Jot's protests, his father had declared him fit enough to go to school after the weekend of the accident. As the bearer of an obvious injury, Jot had a terrible Monday, a prolonged exercise in evading the other children's efforts to exacerbate it through tweaking, prodding, sneak-attack karate. One of the girls made to grab the hand, but it was a feint: when he cowered away, she gave him a dead arm instead. '*That's* for telling everyone I'm a lesbian because I wouldn't let you sit next to me in maths.' It felt like she'd fractured his humerus. 'I knew you wanted to copy my answers!'

That night, aching in his various ways, Jot had again studied the magazine recipe that had caused all this. There it was in the ingredients list: 'Leaves from a small bunch of sage'. And then not a mention in the method. The recipe, not he, had been at fault. Not that a recipe could really be in the wrong – no, blame lay with the writer, who in place of a headshot at the top of the page had a picture in which she was obscured behind a close-up of a makrut lime. As Jot discovered when he browsed her newspaper's recipe archive online, each one featured a similar image in which the writer hid herself, as though from critique, behind a feathery mass of dill, a raw red lamb chop held by the bone, the candy-coloured rings of a halved beetroot. A few clicks later, he found an interview in which she explained the gimmick: 'I'm a critic, not a glamour model. There's nothing like writing about food for a living to remind you how unimportant looks are. Some of the ugliest things I've ever tasted have been among the best, and some of the most photogenic dishes I wouldn't serve to my dog, or even my ex-husband.' In the illustration she was concealed behind the trophy she brandished: an award for newspaper food critic of the year. Even the cartoon gave no sense of whether she was young or old, plump or slender, dark or blonde. Jot rubbed his sore arm, wiggled his injured hand, started printing the recipe pages. An idea was percolating.

Earlier he'd opened a private window and googled 'How to get revenge'. The results were numerous, ranging from the frivolous to the felonious, but not one of them was appropriate to his situation. Then again, Jot reflected, close adherence to someone else's instructions had caused the problem in the first place. Instead he ought to do what all the greats did: improvise.

Pages slicked warm from the printer – every article she'd published in the *Sunday Tribune*, whether review, recipe or advice column answering readers' chillingly basic culinary queries: what is a foolproof way to cook rice; if I don't have buttermilk can I substitute mayonnaise? He squared the papers, stacked them on his homework table, then set to work with a pair of nail scissors, extracting the 'must' from mustard in one recipe, the 'bit' from a rarebit, a whole 'late', that useful word 'ugliest', collecting these offcuts in a plastic box on the desk that also contained such valuables as a plaster trilobite and some pieces of sea glass so appealingly smooth and colourful that Jot sometimes held them in his mouth like boiled sweets.

'School project,' he explained when his father checked on him around nine and found him surrounded by discarded sheets of paper.

'Would you like tea? A snack? I could rustle us up a sandwich.'

'No thanks.' Jot thought his voice squeaked suspiciously, so added: 'Not one of *your* sandwiches, thank you.' Last week he'd caught the man combining lettuce, marmalade and slices of a cheddar well past its best, then munching the result, with accompanying sips of Lucozade, with every indication of enjoyment.

'That's . . . that's probably sound. I'll be off to my scratcher shortly, then.' He mimed yawning, but he had his laptop under his arm. 'Don't stay up too late.'

The sandwich, and similar atrocities, had been one of the reasons why Jot had chosen to stay in Beckenham with his father during the week and spend weekends at his mother's new rented flat. He'd seen the gold takeaway boxes squished into the kitchen bin on Mondays, the warped plastic trays of microwave meals he just knew his dad had not bothered to scrape onto a plate. Without his supervision five days a week, Jot feared the man might not survive this separation. When you didn't know what action to take, when words got slippery or said the opposite of what you'd intended, you could still cook for someone, show your feelings that way. From his very first cottage loaf, Jot had always believed that. But it was what he'd been trying to do the day of the injury, and where had that got him?

'Bit of a change of plan this weekend,' his father had announced over breakfast two Fridays ago. 'Your mother's coming over tomorrow, so you'll be staying here tonight.' As he spoke, he was dashing Worcestershire sauce into a soft-boiled egg, the results of which he consumed with an uncertain expression. Jot was so appalled by this sight that he poured himself far more than the half-mug he was allowed from the cafetière. 'And I don't ...' His father maybe coughed, maybe gagged. 'I don't want you to get carried away and then be disappointed. We have a lot to talk about, your mum and I, and though that's a good thing, communication is always good, it doesn't necessarily mean she's moving back in or anything. It's just lunch. We have to manage our expectations.'

Just lunch!' No, no time to unpack that one: Jot was already pondering what to cook. It should be something showy but not fiddly, something warming, something homely. Stew was too earthy, fish too risky. A pie, he decided, impressive yet humble, always a crowd-pleaser. He imagined the rich smells filling up the house, the home, then the one big dish they'd all dig into together. At breaktime he'd gone scouring his favourite online sources for recipes, disregarding anything too unorthodox – no filo, no capers, no *yoghurt* – until he happened upon the *Sunday Tribune*'s so-called Best Ever Chicken Pie. 'I'm not sure I could be friends with anyone who didn't love this pie,' the recipe began, promisingly, and the next morning he led his faintly protesting father around the big Freshways on the high street, assembling the daunting list of ingredients: free-range chicken thighs, a slab of pancetta, the sage, a clutch of new spice jars that rolled clinking around the basket.

Many unpredictable factors could scupper a cook's best efforts, and the unforeseen element on Saturday had been a shut door. His mother had arrived, there'd been a brisk hug, and then the parental unit had gone into conference in the living room where they had stayed for nearly two hours, scheduled lunchtime ticking ever closer, then passing, while in the oven his pie bloomed and crisped and started to colour deeper than gold around its edges. He turned the heat right down and knocked on the living room door, ran to check the oven again, detected singeing, went back and pounded. 'Come now! Come now!' But when the door did open, the figure that confronted him was barely recognisable as his father: his face was pasty, his eyes bloodshot, or, somehow, the other way around. 'All right, Jot, all right, we're coming. Can you give us just two more minutes, please?'

Two minutes or two hundred, it didn't matter now: they were in salvaging territory. The mizuna leaves in the red ceramic bowl were blobbed with balsamic, the Jersey Royals gleamed in their butter, but these were baubles. Tight-lipped, Jot prised the lid from the pie, black flakes of overdone crust scattering on the table, and ladled great portions of the still bubbling filling on three plates, finishing each with a square of pastry whose underside was, at least, perfectly mellow and molten. He waited not for praise – he knew he was good – but for his parents to taste, to take in what he'd done, lock eyes from opposing ends of the table as they realised what they had been missing: togetherness, shared pleasures, reconciliation.

Instead, they started in on what Jot at first took to be a routine they'd worked out behind the sealed door: a brilliant parody of concerned parenting, comprised of a series of worthless aperçus – that love was complicated, that adults as well as children changed as they grew older, that they loved him no matter what – interleaved with some statements that were just plainly, hilariously illogical, such as the claim that it was harder, sometimes, to stay together than be apart. Jot ate, and since evidently nobody else was going to, appreciated the tenderness of the chicken, the silkiness of the pancetta that had almost melted into his bechamel, the sauce itself complex with its traceries of nutmeg and clove and – 'Fuck!' he blurted, and leapt from his seat, and of course they were paying attention then, weren't they, *then* they spoke with one voice, rebuking his bad language, like he'd never heard worse.

'Sage. There was sage in the ingredients and that – that blasted woman missed it out the recipe.' He raced for the kitchen. Could he flash fry the leaves, scatter the crisp shards into the remainder of the pie for flavour? It would have to do.

His zombie parents had followed him and were continuing to sermonise. 'We need you to understand' – as he hauled from the deep drawer below the oven the cast iron skillet that was almost the only vessel in the house's depleted stock of cookware that he hadn't already used for lunch – 'that no matter what might be going on between us, you'll always, always be our number-one priority.' Butter foamed in the pan. 'Jot?' God, they were so self-absorbed! He tore the fuzzy greyish leaves from their stems, chopped them, spun the chopping board ninety degrees, chopped again. 'Are you listening?' He flicked on the vent so he didn't have to, then, smelling the butter starting to brown, reached out to drag the skillet off the flame.

He was screaming before he really understood what had happened. Something had scrambled his senses, as if he'd been deafened by a flash of light or blinded by a violent thunderclap. Then all he knew was pain – causeless, centreless, just pain – pain that seemed to gather itself from the air and condense *inwards* to its point of origin: his left hand, still grasping the skillet's superheated iron handle. He staggered backwards, the pan crashing back onto the hob, yellow flame spurting, and as he realised what the nauseating oily smell filling his nostrils was, noise klaxoned out of him; his parents howled back, and their three pitches, related but discordantly distinct, wobbled horribly in the air.

'Put ice on it!' they screamed at each other.

'No! He needs butter!'

'Butter *caused*— Wait, there's aloe gel in the holiday bag. Do I still have the holiday bag or did you take it?'

'Boil the kettle! He needs tea for the shock. Lots of milk and sugar.'

Minutes later, Jot was slumped in a kitchen chair, arm crooked uncomfortably over the edge of the sink, tepid tap water coursing over the injury. His pulse throbbed in his palm, and when he dared look he could already see, through the flowing water, a disgusting scarlet weal forming. He looked away, which meant looking straight through the kitchen to the dining table where their meals sat abandoned, the pie sauce congealing into the Jerseys, the salad leaves wilting almost visibly. Uneaten food would rot, but eating it turned it to shit, and looked at that way, what was the point in anything? His parents faffed around him. When they asked, Jot gritted his teeth and averred that the pain was becoming bearable. That was what you did, so it seemed to him, when you grew up. Reassured, fooled, they set back in on their silly routine: 'You can ask us anything, say anything to us.' 'Shout at us, even.' 'Yes, that's right, use your words, like we talked about.'

'Are we still—' he began.

Eagerly: 'Yes? What is it, Jonathan? Anything.'

'We are still going to Midgard for my birthday, aren't we?' He'd thought it better not to bring up the once-mooted summer holiday to San Sebastián: he had to be realistic. Even so, his parents had gone meaningfully silent. 'But we have to,' he quavered. 'We can't give up our place in the queue.' Tears began to slither from his eyes. 'They're on reservations lockdown now. I might not get another chance.'

88

That, at least, was settled, though tonight they seemed determined to spoil what might be his final meal at so distinguished a restaurant. Their behaviour nettled him, but they weren't the target of Jot's ire. To his mind, the critic and her botched recipe bore responsibility for what had happened – for ruining his plan to keep everyone together – and, as he'd gone on snipping apart her published writings that Monday night, his hand and eye guided as if by instinct to the words and letters that would best serve a purpose he hadn't quite yet settled on, he'd felt something inside his chest, a serpentine coiling, not the shifting of guilt but its opposite: something voluptuous, the thrill of transgression. Was it what his mother and father felt when they denounced one another to him, knowing it contravened what all the books and forums agreed was rule one for arguing parents? It was the pleasure that came from knowing what was wrong and doing it anyway.

The pricked and deflated bubbles had left a green scrim in the crab's pocked meringue-gold interior. Intrigued despite himself, Jot turned the shell in his hand, inspecting the irregular barbs and points of its coral-pink armour. To the left of its complex mouthparts, one grey eyestalk blindly peered; the one on the right had sheared off, a splintered nubbin. Neater stumps showed where its limbs had been snipped away. Jot pictured the crab's stubby pincers impotently snapping as it was scooped up from the marine depths, having no conception of the fate that awaited it, and felt sympathy.

He began pondering a rating for the crab. A four-star dish, his instincts told him, though he could not immediately think how it might be improved, so wrote a five in his notebook, virtually assuring Midgard a record tally in his personal scoring system.

'Faultless,' he told Addy as she cleared the remnants of his presentation. He was waiting for her to peep over his head, make some facial signal to his parents – people were always calling Jot precocious, and nobody ever seemed to mean it kindly – but instead she smiled at him. 'Truly,' he stammered. 'The technique, the flavours, I couldn't find a single flaw.' She winked at him then, this blonde werewolf of a woman, and Jot thought maybe he loved her. He watched her saunter away, pretending he was merely scanning the restaurant, and that was when he saw – thought he saw – a movement in the vicinity of the ash tree: not a diner, not staff, perhaps not a human figure at all but something feral that had emerged for a moment to conduct its own survey of the room; then, realising it was observed, slithered coolly back into concealment.

'I was being polite,' one of the adults was upbraiding the other. 'Maybe they didn't teach you this at charm school, but it's polite to make eye contact with someone when they're talking to you— I'm sorry, what was that?'

'I didn't say anything.'

'You snorted, though, didn't you? I heard a definite snort.'

'*No*, that was a breath. I was breathing. Do I have to ask permission for that now? I wouldn't be surprised, given your other demands.'

'So now I can't even thank a waitress without—'

'Waitron,' Jot interrupted, closing his eyes in forbearance.

They paused. 'What was that, Jot?'

'Bourdain says we shouldn't say waiter and waitress, we should say waitron. It's gender non-specific.'

'Well, if *Bourdain* says,' the parental unit retorted. And they called Jot cheeky!

But who was he to lecture anyone? A lowlife creep, a petty menacer through the medium of the cut-up. Not quite a total monster, though, not yet, because last Friday, immediately upon slipping his photocopier-enlarged rant of protest and rage into the post box, his knees had gone watery with remorse. Where had these doubts been while he worked with his pot of glue and all those little shreds of paper? Why hadn't his armpits turned swampy and his breath grown ragged *before* he could post the letter? He'd been underhand before, and thoughtless, but never, he thought, calculatedly malicious. Posting the thing had made him a different person, and he hadn't even known there'd been a choice. When he got to his mother's flat, he'd locked the bathroom door and scrutinised his reflection for indicators of his newly revealed character. Maybe his mark would come in when his skin turned problematic, or with the first down on his upper lip. The villains in movies were always blemished, mutilated or otherwise disfigured. A burned palm, however unsightly, hardly counted.

His mother tapped his good hand, and he opened his eyes, cross with her for breaking into this pleasing funk of self-recrimination. 'Look, Jonathan, have you ever seen a champagne bottle that size?' Midgard's famed maître d', Loïc, was moving at stately pace across the room, oversized bottle cradled like a child in his arms. 'Is it a jeroboam?'

'A magnum. A jeroboam is four times a regular bottle, a magnum's only two.'

'Someone's very lucky, whatever it is,' she said, to his great indignation, as if this known fact were up for debate.

What was also beyond doubt was that Loïc, statuesque by the table where a middle-aged couple was looking up at him in pleased anticipation, was making a pig of things. 'He should be turning the bottle, not the cork.' Jot writhed in his seat. 'He must know that.' Still the man tussled with the bottle, still the stopper refused to yield. An expression of beautiful frustration stole over his face. Then, abruptly, the pop: champagne spewed over the maître d's fingers and pattered onto the carpet, while the cork, launched from the bottle at astounding velocity, shot up through the thicket of ceiling vents and light fittings, hit the ash tree, rebounded downwards at an oblique angle and, still travelling almost faster than Jot's eye could follow, struck the head of an elderly lady at a table on the far side of the restaurant who shrieked, so immediately she might have been expecting it, that she had been shot.

And Jot, forgetting he was meant to be the mature one, forgetting for a moment the worries that assailed him and that would never be understood by anyone who was not currently twelve years old themselves, saw surprise, maybe even relief, on his parents' faces as exuberant laughter burst from him: loud, spontaneous, absolutely childish.

Gareth returned from the dining room half a head taller than he'd gone out, and wearing his most oafish grin. What had caused his spine, permanently rounded from a decade spent hunched over low stoves, to unfurl? Not anti-inflammatories, not illicit powders – nah, all it'd needed was a good dose of schadenfreude. He thrust his stack of used dishes into the hands of whoever. Maybe Joanna had been trying to humiliate him by sending him out to serve and pick up like just one more waitpig, but the joke was on her: out there, as the ambient light cooled towards the next course, he'd spotted a VIP the boss clearly had no idea was in tonight. Gareth swaggered back gleeful with secret knowledge, ammunition to be fired off when it best suited him.

He pulled on a pair of disposable gloves and unlidded the green plastic barrel by the entrance to patisserie, releasing a gust of warm vegetal cloy. He plunged his arms into the mass of hay, delving through layers of softness and scratch to its core, hot and pulpy with decomposition. His fingers wriggled around until they encountered a slick plane, a sharp corner to grasp, and he was able to drag out a package sealed in silvery plastic. He palped and squished it then, satisfied with its doneness, dusted it off and tossed it into the wire basket over his arm before diving back into the steaming compost for the rest.

'Here, you! Polly-wolly-doodle.' Gareth felt himself add-ressed from the pass – a certain tone uniquely for him. 'Gonnae give the budgerigar impression a rest?' The jaunty tuneless ditty died between his teeth. He hadn't been aware he was doing it. Normally he would've talked back to Joanna – make your mind up, budgie or parrot? – but tonight he just shook his head, smiled to himself, thought: You'll keep.

People who hadn't worked under Joanna didn't get it. 'She never raises her voice,' he'd told his wife. 'She actually gets quieter as the night goes on.' Karen had made a ducky pout, thrown her arms wide: 'Poor baby, does the bad lady never shout at you? Come here, let me cradle your big stupid head.' 'She's Scottish,' he'd grumbled, giving in, 'and she never yells. It isn't natural.'

With no current crises to deal with, the waitstaff had grown lax and chatty. 'Ebbsfleet,' someone declared. 'No, Ashford. Ebbsfleet. Christ, I don't know.' Someone said dreamily, 'I'd wash *his* feet with my hair.' 'A restaurant in a secret location, serving mushrooms and only mushrooms. "The first rule of Saprophyte Club . . ." No? Nobody? Ah, suit yourselves.' Addy blundered in, banged her hip against the corner of Finn's station, swiped at it as if it had leapt out at her. 'You would not *believe*,' she panted, 'what those see-you-next-Tuesdays on Six just said to me.' From the pass, then, the mild reproof: 'Pipe down, everyone, please', and, to Gareth's disappoint-ment and mine, Addy obeyed and we never learned what had offended her.

This was the point of the evening I used to nudge one of my colleagues and say, 'What's their story? The pair on Three who haven't said a single word to each other all night? I reckon their dog's just died.' Or: 'She's a zookeeper and he's a librarian, whaddya think?' Little anecdotes I liked to make up about diners whose stories Loïc hadn't already brought to us or who hadn't volunteered information at the top of the evening. The others would roll their eyes, but I'd place little bets with myself about which one of the couple was going to pay the bill, speculate that the looks of one person or another suggested they must be someone famous I wasn't worldly enough to recognise. 'Are we celebrating anything tonight?' we used to ask the guests and usually they were, though once in a while they looked a bit blank and bemused and I knew that the bill they'd get for their no-special-occasion dinner was what would make it a night to remember.

I couldn't be sure, but it seemed as if alien colour was tinging my vision. There was a faint pink wash over everything I looked at, like the fading after-image of staring into harsh light. For a moment the cool smooth surface of the fridge beside me felt not smooth-milled but nubbly like coarse textile.

Gareth was lathering his hands with a soap made locally, and partly from fats skimmed from Midgard's stockpots – an innovation either ingenious or horrible, he could never decide – when his left leg buzzed again. It was one of Joanna's rules that the staff turn off and put away their phones before service and, like everyone else, Gareth had found a way to circumvent the order. His main mobile protruded ostentatiously from his breast pocket, display off, a decoy; a second, set to silent, was strapped to his shin, for use in emergencies, such as a girl who urgently needed him to give her a good rooting.

He returned to his counter and sank a draught from his plastic pint of orange vitamin drink. He slugged oil into a blackened pan, rested a long-pin thermometer against its edge, then banged on the heat. From the next station he hauled over the big hotel pan filled with blue-grey starchwater in which dozens of pale squares swayed: the potatoes he'd had to finish prepping after that clot of a commis had impaled himself. Lucky the blood hadn't got anywhere near them. He lifted out the slices, dealt them out on blue paper, blotted excess water. The oil in the pan shimmered as its temperature rose.

I knew, though not how, that he was jiggling his leg because he needed a piss and had done for an hour or more; that he had read somewhere that you worked better with the pressure of a full bladder, faster and making better decisions, and that he'd thought why not, couldn't hurt, and besides, wasn't he too dehydrated from working in the kitchen's heat to genuinely need to go? I knew, though I'd rather I didn't, that his shirt was plastered to his back with sweat, that what bound the phone to his gorilla leg was something frilly filched from his girlfriend's knicker drawer.

I also knew, for a more prosaic reason, what the girlfriend looked like. That was because of the journey Gareth and I had taken a few months ago from London Bridge back to the restaurant after a first aid refresher Joanna had sent us on. I'd resuscitated two mannequins, restarted an imaginary heart, passed the course, was feeling good about myself. As I was changing my phone ringtone to the Bee Gees as they'd suggested – 'Stayin' Alive', whatever else it reminded me of, having the exact rhythm you should use for chest compressions when giving CPR – and fretting about whether Joanna was definitely going to reimburse us for the day travel pass, Gareth, who had bodged his way through lifesaving skills, was complaining about missing out on what he'd normally be doing on a Tuesday morning. He'd waved his phone at me, giving me a brief, confused impression of blondeness, denim and what proved to be a tank top almost the same colour as her skin. 'Thank god,' I'd said, stilling his hand with the two rosettes tattooed between thumb and forefinger, space left for a third, 'I thought she was topless.' He bared all his teeth: 'Me too. Why d'you think I swiped right?'

He'd been such a good boy, he bragged as we got off the

Overground, and for such a long time, a year or more. He'd deleted all the apps, purged his phone of encrypted contacts: 'Banh Mi' meaning the Vietnamese girl he'd meet in the pub opposite her student halls on Great Portland Street, 'Trattoria Canary Wharf' for the Brussels-based compliance officer who'd summon him to her hotel room when business brought her to London – 'To ... do stuff,' he concluded, eyeing me to see if I was game.

'To make love,' I said. He laughed, exhaled a cloud of bubblegum-scented vape smoke. I was all right, he'd decided, unfuckable and all right.

The apps weren't really gone for ever, of course – merely dormant, hovering ready to be redownloaded in the fit of boredom or horniness that were for men, so Gareth informed me, functionally indistinguishable. And wasn't it better, actually, to reactivate his accounts and see for sure what temptation he was resisting out of loyalty to Karen, his actual wife? Wasn't that more noble? 'Um,' I'd said. Whatever; it made sense to him, and unperturbed he'd told me about the long night-bus journey home three months earlier, swiping away the endless parade of faces the app brought up: new in your area, online now, you haven't nudged this one in a while. Turning them all down, even the foxy ones, even – smirking at me – the redheads. Feeling pretty bloody proud of himself, all told, and then *she* had appeared. 'Ceri,' he said, and that was when he'd waggled his phone at me.

Ceri was nineteen, a dancer with double joints and a six-days-a-week yoga habit, furthermore a hollerer and yipper when he made her come, which he did, showing extravagant disregard for his own satisfaction, multiple times each time they hooked up. No better lover than a cook, he liked to say, with his precision of attention, his fixation on giving pleasure, his drive to make you feel good by putting nice things in your body. Wasn't he lucky, I'd said, to have met this woman – 'Girl,' he'd corrected me – with her sole three attributes of youth, flexibility, insatiable sex drive; and 'Ye-eah!' he'd enthused, refusing to be made to feel bad about something so great.

In the picture that had caught his attention, Ceri had been wearing Daisy Dukes, a BOY London cap, the peach-pink vest clearly intended to provoke a double take. It worked: he was messaging her, stumblethumbed on the juddering bus, before he could overthink it. 'A Ceri and a Gareth, how could we not be great together?' Admittedly, this stretched his own definition of resisting temptation, but it was just a bit of innuendo, like the messages that followed: you show me your downward dog, I'll let you handle my chopper. And then it was meeting for coffee in Old Street, or an isotonic drink for caffeine-sensitive Ceri, and something was already going on, because not only had he not ripped the piss out of her for that, he'd even ordered it for her at the counter; and an hour later he was giving her the works on the futon at her place.

They met a second time, a third. A girl who still interested him this far in, he blithely informed me as we waited for the lights to change on Shacklewell Lane, was as rare as a rat's eyelash. On his way to work after date three he was thinking not of the way she'd guided his palm to her cheek, the lively pink mark his slap left and its flat echo on the apartment's bare walls, but of what he wanted to do next. He was in danger of getting invested, and he went into date four feeling leaden, sure he'd have to break things off, for Ceri's sake: if he was feeling a feeling, god knows she must be smitten. But Ceri kept on unfolding, offering a little more each time they met and hinting there was much further she might go, and Gareth couldn't do it, couldn't bear to think of some other guy being the one to take her there.

98

It wasn't possessiveness he felt. It was a warmer feeling, kinder, more compromising. It could make a man careless. 'You know what it sounds like,' I started to say, and he cut me off: 'You fucking dare, Bit Part.'

The fifth time they'd met earlier than usual, Ceri having cancelled yoga because, she said, the marks he'd left on her legs last week were still too visible. 'Let me make you lunch,' he wheedled while they were showering. She had wagged her finger at him: 'This isn't a thing. Don't go thinking it's a thing.' This was Gareth's line and to have it thrown at back at him made his dumb heart plummet. He would have protested, but a prudent bloke didn't argue with the girl who was soaping his balls at the time. They continued to hook up and she continued to refuse his offers to cook for her. She was forever on the fasting day of her 5:2 diet, permitted only herbal tea, half a grapefruit, an egg if she was feeling daring or faint. She looked great, he wasn't denying it, but it did shit him that she wouldn't let him show off. 'How else can I have any power over you?' he joked, not joking. Because he knew that once the flat door closed on him, he ceased to exist for Ceri. She read but seldom responded to the come-ons he texted during the week from his second phone; fuck her, he'd get to the stage of thinking, but then a message would flash up, an unseemly proposal, an image it took a moment to decipher, and he'd hurry back and gladly let it all happen again.

'I want to show her all the things I love,' he told me as we neared Midgard. 'The films and food. The places. You ever taken the night train from Darwin to Alice Springs?'

I had not. Sure, I'd come to London, but I hadn't really *been* anywhere. Even the route we'd taken to the restaurant had been new to me. 'Then take her, for god's sake. I wish someone would do it for me. You're into this girl, right? And

99

she's into you?' He looked equivocal. 'Do it, sweep her off her feet, ditch your wife. How many lives do you think we have?'

'Pretty ruthless philosophy,' he said, almost admiringly. 'Now I'm not sure if Finn Family Moomintragic in there's on to a good thing or if I should warn him off you.' Seeing my face: 'Aw, what, I wasn't meant to know you were dating? Here's a clue, you want to keep something a state secret, don't mention it to fucken Kima.'

I had told Kima a lot – and yeah, she admitted when I confronted her, she had relayed more or less everything to more or less anyone. 'Well, fucking stop!' But I hadn't told her everything about what had happened between Finn and me, skipping, out of some sense of sticking up for him, the grisly details of our next meeting – a case of radically different expectations about what activities a second date involved. And I didn't tell her about our third date, when Finn had invited me to visit his allotment. We'd barely done anything yet, not even kissed much, and I went along out of bemused frustration, no idea what was going on in his head. It was the end of September, the last hot day of the year, and I was in hell, hemmed in by vegetation I didn't know the names of: frothy lilac showerheads, sticky green creepers that had established chokeholds on iron railings, giant top-heavy thistles that swayed on emaciated stems like coconuts on a shy. From one bed grew tall fleshy stems topped with rows of faintly suggestive pinkish-green buds that I half-recognised from somewhere – did we cook with them? – and I had watched Finn army-crawl across the moist black soil beneath these plants, tugging out by the roots certain sprigs of green and leaving others, evidently more desirable but to me indistinguishable, to grow on. I had nothing to do. I didn't want anything to do. Two seconds after arriving I'd walked too close to something I did know the name of, a big blowsy blood-dark rose, and it took fright and shed all its petals.

'It's about the furthest thing from restaurant life I could imagine,' Finn said when I'd asked, trying not to sound bored or judgmental, what he liked about this place. 'It's calming.' But he didn't seem calm: the allotments ran beneath a section of elevated Overground line and some flaw on the track made every carriage on every train that sped past clatter terribly, as if about to derail, and he flinched every time. When the CDs dangling from the branches of a tree in the next plot flicked the light a certain way, he tensed up. My phone went off – I didn't even look at the display any more: the only people who had my number were the bank, my landlord, Joanna, the exact people I never wanted to speak to – and even that seemed to scare him. Or maybe he was annoyed because my ringtone was 'Stayin' Alive' and once you'd heard even a snippet that song was in your head all day after. Otherwise, he worked on, kind of ignoring me, though I almost didn't mind since all I was doing myself was standing here finding more reasons to dump him: his contagious nerviness, the remoteness that meant he'd got as far as inviting me into his sanctuary but then didn't know what to do with me. Even that might have been okay except that we had – and truly I'd striven to locate or manufacture some – no chemistry.

'Joanna,' he started to say as he stood up, hands filled with filth and weeds, but I didn't want to talk about our colleagues or workplace on my day off, and so I cut him off. I knew I was spurning an ally, but being around him hadn't been making me feel any less alone in this city. I used the unforgivable cliché. 'Finn? We need to talk.'

*

Still wary of Kima the human bullhorn, I didn't tell her about the break-up. But evidently I came to work the next day giving off some signal, pheromonal or psychic, because as I was carrying out tablecloth duty in the dining room I became aware of a growing smell of industrial cleanser, the sickly kind that only draws attention to the odour it's meant to disguise. Then a hand on my arm, a croaking enquiry: 'Doing all right, ducks?'

I'd seldom spoken to Eleanor since Joanna had introduced us on my first tour of the restaurant. I'd wondered then, and still did, why Midgard – so remote from the hangouts of City boys and Soho girls – even needed a bathroom attendant, much less one as doddery and borderline creepy as Eleanor, with her unnaturally white skin, her chestnut hair drawn, today, into a stiff beehive. She wore trainers in a style favoured by the orthopaedically impaired and her skinny legs were sheathed in stockings with an abstract pattern.

I shrugged. 'I guess?' Her unhealthy pallor, I noticed, stopped an inch or so beneath her chin, around where the wattling began. Did face powder ever go off? Was that the smell? I moved away and she followed me, with a gait at once leaden and frail, as if her femurs were made of delicate glass, her joints chunks of concrete.

'Must be hard for you, coming all this way, trying to get to know people in a new city. A new hemisphere.' I smiled politely, skooshed the button on my steamer, eliminated the crease in the cloth on Four. 'The people in this city, they're so busy all the time, rush, rush, rush, don't you think? And then everyone says the same thing, how they never have the time to meet anyone.' Puffing, she pulled out a seat to sink into, even though staff weren't meant to sit down here. 'Because it is nice,' she went on, 'to have someone to talk to at dinner. To see the sights with. To take in a play – you like the theatre, don't you, ducks?' It was as if Kima had spent the week since she'd moved in to my flat telling everyone everything she'd learned about me. I squared my shoulders, assuming Eleanor was about five seconds from telling me I should give Finn another chance. But that wasn't it at all. 'It just so happens that I have a little side hustle that might interest you. Lucrative, too. All you'd have to do is keep someone company for the evening. A nice meal somewhere fancy, a date for the works night out.'

I swung round, insulted. 'I'm not a—'

'Now, now,' Eleanor interrupted. 'Let's not use any ugly words. Of course that's not what you are. What you are is frustrated. What you are is a girl who's come to the greatest city on earth, forgive my bias, and isn't getting to see any of it. Who's only just making do on the meagre wages old One-Eye back there pays you, but has no chance to find anywhere cheaper to live because she's working all hours to pay the bills. Who's stopped picking up *Time Out* because it's depressing to read about all the things you never get to see and do. Well? You can tell me I'm wrong, but I'd bet all Lombard Street to a China orange I'm not.'

I felt like using the steamer on her, but she was not wrong. When Kima was moving in to Grantham Street she'd remarked that it was much bigger than I'd made it sound, and I couldn't say that was because I had originally described a different room, the attic upstairs where I'd been living, because I'd been hoping that I could move into the room vacated by the god-botherer. I'd agonised over the sums, but I couldn't make it work. So much of my take-home pay already went on rent that any extra expense – an indifferent meal out or, later, replacing the phone I really had lost – screwed me for weeks.

Gareth had appeared then from the kitchen, whistling

my new ringtone. 'All right, come get it while it's hot. And I'm talking about staff meal, not my sweet, sweet—' Seeing Eleanor haul herself to her feet he turned on his heel, blanching. 'Jesus. Never mind. Not sure I'm hungry now.'

'Have a little think about what I'm offering. It's just a little socialising, but it can really open doors. You know where to find me.' As she lurched towards the stairs, I noticed with a little spurt of horror that the blackish blotches and marks on Eleanor's legs weren't patterns on fabric but her actual skin.

'What happened to you?'

She turned and gave me a look that would have turned a more suggestible person to stone. 'Didn't your mother teach you not to pry?'

'My mother never taught me much of anything.' Aware that this could sound pathetic, I overcompensated and the line came out like a brag.

Eleanor paused at the head of the stairs, resting one crooked hand on the trunk of the ash. 'There was an accident,' she spat, glancing towards the kitchen. 'A long, long time ago. Come see me when you've reconsidered.'

I went into the kitchen, hung up the steamer, grabbed my portion of staff meal: a black dal, simmered overnight, that had the sour richness of really excellent chocolate. Gareth and I seemed to be buddies now: he came at me with a face like a bullock experiencing a big thought. 'Be careful with Eleanor—' he started, but I cut him off: 'I get it, she's bad news. I'm not a kid.'

He blinked. 'Well, fine. Okay then, grown adult' – he had his phone out again – 'in your grown adult opinion, is this normal?'

'Flashing your girlfriend's tits in my face without warning? Yeah, no, actually I think that does count as weird.'

'No, no. See how one's much bigger than the other? That's

normal, right? I mean, Karen's were never the same after breastfeeding, but Ceri ... Hey, what's that look for?'

Some impurity in the oil caught, and with a loud pop it spit up over Gareth's battleworn hands. He'd got distracted, thinking about me. 'Careful there, G.,' Joanna's mocking voice from the pass, and he wondered if anyone had ever truly lost it with her, if the soft warning that invariably arrived only after you'd burned or grazed or stung or otherwise embarrassed yourself had ever been the catalyst for someone to charge at her with a carving knife or whatever came to hand, dishrag spun into a flail, mixer aloft with beater blades whirling ...

Gareth, professional, knew that food came first, fun after. As the thermometer display flashed up the correct temperature, he slid the first batch of potato slices into the oil, using his slotted spoon to separate them, careful not to break them up. He counted the seconds. Three, two, one, and then he scooped out the half-cooked squares, transferred them speedily on to blue roll on his counter, and in the brief intermission as the oil got back to temperature for the next round:

'Funny,' he mused aloud. He beat a tattoo on the edge of his counter with two teaspoons, fixed up a coughing little laugh. Joanna did not acknowledge him. 'You'd have thought someone would have said something. Loïc especially,' he added, genuinely surprised by that. Something to rip the maître d' about, too – bonus!

A sigh from the pass. 'All right, what're you blethering about?'

'I was just thinking about that rogues' gallery you keep in your office. Me, I've memorised it, but I guess not everyone—'

That brought Joanna muscling towards him, the cyclopean glare. 'What are you saying to me? Who's out there?'

He paused. The kitchen paused. 'Amanda,' he said, savouring it, 'Ledley' – they waited frozen, like there might be an utterly innocuous diner out there who just happened to share a couple of names with the country's most influential food critic – 'Miles,' and even before he'd finished drawing out that last sibilant the place was in turmoil: Joanna pulling down the old Telefunken over the pass to study front of house and simultaneously use it as a mirror to fix her hair, licking a finger and wiping a streak of ink from her eyebrow; Finn, unprompted, setting aside the fattest fish for the next course, the sprightliest herbs and shiniest cherries; the others huddling to brainstorm some quick and impressive extra to send out. A commotion like this, he thought, starting on the next round of potatoes, was so delicious it had to be fattening.

Reckoning he had a few spare seconds while everyone else was flailing, he hopped his leg up and slipped the phone from under his houndstooths. Two weeks since he'd last heard from Ceri and now she'd sent not one unsolicited message but three, one a photograph. Oh-ho, he thought, feeling an anticipatory stirring in the nethers. When he opened it, though, the photo didn't show flesh, not even a face. All he saw was a plain white oval with two lines running perpendicularly across it. He peered, turned the phone this way then that, and then, in horror, realised what it was. The last time he'd seen it had been when Karen had brandished the little white plastic pen thing at him, the two lines in the window, the smile too big for her face. 'No way,' he'd said. 'Is that—? No fucken way!' He'd been about to seize it from her when it had occurred to him: 'Hey, is there still pee on this thing?' He'd transformed in that instant, switch flipped, adulthood at last; and he now felt a similar shift, only this time in reverse, switching back to being the kid who'd done something stupid and was now in really deep shit.

He felt the way I must've wanted him to that day in the kitchen when I demanded: 'What do you mean, "breastfeeding"?'

'Uh, not sure how else to explain it?' he'd mugged. 'Clue's kind of in the name?'

'But I mean, this is your baby you're talking about. Yours and Karen's.'

'Er, I should fucken think so. Aw, she's gorgeous – takes after me, obviously. Here, let me show you.'

I'd swiped his hand away so violently his phone had nearly flown from it. The look on my face! So sullen and pouchy; I'd gone in an instant from a grudging seven to a plain five. It was his downfall, how much he loved women, but god, sometimes we didn't make it easy, with our ultimatums and reprimands and moods. 'And yet you're thinking about ditching everything to run off with this teenager?'

'*You* were the one who—'

'How old is your daughter?'

'Hey, now, you leave her out of it.'

'But that's the point,' I'd said then. 'You can't. You mustn't.'

'What I can't,' he mimicked, 'and mustn't, and won't, is listen to you another minute, Bit Part. Go expound your morals to the procuress downstairs, why don't you?' But my expression had stayed with him – was with him still now as he replaced his phone without opening Ceri's other texts. Numbly, he herded the last round of spuds around in the oil. He wasn't even enjoying the others' crisis mode now: Joanna ashen at the pass as the waitstaff primped her for going out on the floor, like machines on a production line swivelling around to paint a cheap car in vivid colours. Over their heads her own turned, caught him in its searchlight, gave him the stare that said he was in big trouble. But that was anger, just anger, nothing like as unsettling as the face on me as he'd walked away from me the day he and I had saved so many automaton lives together, staunched so many make-believe wounds. I'd been devastated, sad beyond words, and even now he couldn't understand what he'd said that had so upset me.

Table Four

For months, Amanda had been finding ways to refuse Bea's invitations to coffee. It gave her no pleasure to discover, on entering the café on Exmouth Market, that her instincts had been correct, for at the table at the far end sat not just Bea – waving urgently, face open in the expression of manic elation that new mothers trained not just on their children but on everyone else – but her son, a nine-month-old with a violent streak matched only by his drive to self-harm: when he wasn't pummelling his mother with his fat pink fists he was wriggling from her arms, apparently intent on dashing himself head first to the concrete floor.

It was also disturbing to discover that Bea, once Amanda's best work friend, a PhD super-brain slumming it on the subs' desk, now seemed capable only of communicating in half-sentences, these mostly concerning Valentine's unremarkable developmental milestones. Amanda's ability to show interest soon waned, though that only made Bea, hoisting the child in her arms, redouble her efforts to impress her, as though tales of malfunctioning nappies and sleep deprivation might kindle latent maternal instinct in her friend. Amanda wished she'd simply posted the belated congratulatory gift she'd brought – luxury *alfajores*, Bea's favourites, direct from Argentina – and gone on deferring this meeting until the child had reached a tolerable age: eighteen, say.

'So, tell me your news,' Bea coaxed, once the tot had finally settled into a motionlessness that suggested to Amanda not a sleeping child but a primed trap ready to spring.

Concision was necessary. 'Graham's taken me off restaurants. One more column and I'm done.'

'No! But why?'

'Ah, now, see, I made that mistake too. The real question is *who*. Let me quote: "Araminta's star is in the ascendant. She'll bring in a whole new demographic."'

'How young . . .?'

'Catastrophically young. She smiled at me and I think I saw milk teeth. Graham says she's *dynamic*.'

'Someone's daughter, obviously. Someone's granddaughter.'

'Bea, you cynic. She's actually the daughter of the *goddaughter* of some titled gent who – you'll be astounded – happens to sit on our oversight board. God-granddaughter? Grand-goddaughter? You were chief sub, Bea, what's the term here?'

'I believe our style guide would say "sponger".'

'Even my husband wasn't so crass as to leave me for the younger model. Then, as I was dusting myself down, Graham asked if I fancied a go on motoring instead. Give me something to test drive right now, I said, I'll get you front page news. Guaranteed fatalities. One, anyway. And then—'

Amanda had been about to show Bea the horrible thing she'd received in the post that morning, when the baby, giving no warning of its plans, shrieked as if scalded and flung out one disturbingly simian-long arm, sending Amanda's latte bouncing across the floor. Remarkably, the glass didn't smash, but foam and coffee went everywhere. 'That wasn't nice, now, was it, Valentine?' Bea simpered. 'What a terrible mess. That poor man behind the counter's going to have to clean that up now. – Someone's getting tired,' she whispered to Amanda, who nodded, wondering whether it was possible to contract postnatal depression on someone else's behalf.

Their departure entailed a temporary reconfiguration of the café to allow Valentine's chariot of a stroller egress. They left behind crayon-streaked walls, a tabletop littered with spit-sodden remnants of bran muffin, another toddler howling in trauma. At the counter Amanda paid their bill and bought two big bags of Honduran arabica as an act of contrition; outside, where a pigeon was preening in a metal dog bowl, she pretended she had an urgent call to make, loitering by a newspaper kiosk until Bea and the demon child were aboard the 341 and away. The headlines on the papers were loud with bombings, stabbings, displaced masses, the posturing of nuclear powers, the death of the planet. NO CHARGE OVER 'TERROR' ATTACK AT GALLERY. There was an argument – did she ever know this argument – that it was unreasonable, even cruel, to bring a child into such a world then abandon it to grow up amid all this tumult. But to judge from the Ostrogoth-level destruction that one little boy had wrought in the café, perhaps the next generation was equal to the fight.

One of Amanda's favourite things about living in London was that she could make the same journey a hundred times before noticing something she couldn't believe she'd over-looked before. For years, she'd been taking the cut-through down the side of Sadler's Wells, past the ornamental gardens with the sanatorial atmosphere, the pub where dancers gos-siped listlessly over hot water and lemon. Yet until today she had never observed that the last in the row of little Victorian shops selling charcuterie and lamps and handmade greetings cards was a double-fronted, black-painted establishment on whose windows was reverse-gilded T.J. MARKSON & SON, FUNERAL DIRECTOR "YOUR MIND AT EASE".

Amanda stared at this for a long time. There was a net

curtain, overlong, bunched up on the window, a stack of magazines. She was not a morbid person. She did not often dwell on her own mortality. She had learned not to expect too much of the future. But already today there'd been Bea, and the email from Graham confirming the termination of her contract, and that dreadful letter, and everything she'd been certain of seemed suddenly treacherous. Fine, she thought crossly, *fine*, as if someone else were pressuring her, and rang the bell.

She reread the letter as she waited for the undertaker to return. A single sheet of foolscap folded into a plain envelope printed with the *Sunday Tribune*'s address and Amanda's name. No signature, no incriminating fingerprints, no clue from the postmark. Detail-oriented, she'd held the paper to the light, cautiously sniffed it – no perfume – then noticed that each fragment that made up the letter used the same typeface with the distinctive ligatures between letters – the font they used in the *Tribune*.

You fil thy bſt ch I m going to

Take e very It em you use e to h ide

y. Our fac e an d ſtuff the m Up you r

dry o ld c u nt artichoke marrow Bones

but Cher's c Leave r let you b Leed

out alone Un miss ed un Mour ned

ugliest culinary joke

ſt Sw hat you de Serve

you ru In ed e very Thi ng

112

Amanda's first thought, naturally, had been of her ex-husband. Yet it had been many years since Blair had invested this much effort in anything concerning her, even counting the divorce proceedings. She was under no illusions that she was universally liked at the paper, but she also doubted that anyone on staff would risk being caught and getting the whole team sent for mandatory sensitivity training. After this, Amanda's list of suspects ran out, leaving her oddly dejected.

She stuffed the letter into her bag as Markson backed into the waiting room, carrying a circular metal tray loaded with cups, foil packets, a catering flask. These he transferred to the low table in front of Amanda, exposing the tray's design: a painting of three kittens with sinisterly human faces. 'The wife's choice,' he shouted. 'Found it in the South of France. Wish she'd left it in the South of France, ha ha. Carcassonne. Have you been? Lovely place, lovely. Wonderful cemeteries, black trees and white tiled tombs you could eat your dinner off.' He decanted a grey-brown powder from one of the packets into a mug, then added water from the flask whose emblazoned logo, URNIE, Amanda was finding irresistibly, unfortunately anagrammable. He stirred the mixture, producing something that resembled steaming ditchwater. 'Sure I can't tempt you? I've got decaf, if you like. No? Suit yourself.' He sipped from his drink with no evidence of displeasure. 'Now, what can I do for you for today?'

'I was just passing, really,' Amanda began.

'We get a lot of that, passing trade.' Markson peered at her. 'My little joke. You'll want to fill in one of these forms to start.' He passed her a clipboard thick with paper and Amanda, stunned into obedience, started to write. It wasn't as if you could back out, once you'd come in here: so sorry, what a ditz, for a moment I imagined I might be mortal. 'Some folk come direct from a doctor's appointment. Sometimes I'm the first person they tell, so don't be afraid to say. I've numbers I can give you, pamphlets, websites.'

'Nothing like that,' she said. She'd written down her full name, address and date of birth on the front page of Markson's booklet before noticing that a large space below was marked 'Intentionally blank', this box to be completed on her behalf, filled in with some date she'd never know. 'It's only admin, isn't it, when you think about it? One more thing to strike off life's to-do list.' She'd meant putting her affairs in order, but Markson sipped his concoction with a thoughtful air, as if he'd assumed she was talking about death itself, which, in a sense—

The door opened again, admitting a corpulent teen as tall as Markson was diminutive, a funhouse reflection, unmistakably his offspring. He had what was clearly a schoolchild's backpack hanging from one shoulder, a flashing spearhead-shaped headset hooked around one ear. 'All right?' he greeted Amanda. 'Not trying to upsell you to mahogany, is he?'

Markson turned in his seat. 'Get out of it, you. Scram!'

Instead, the smirking youth padded further in. He leaned over Markson's desk, where an antiquated yellowing-grey desktop computer whirred, adding to the room's airless heat, and peered down at Amanda. 'Come up with a message for your headstone yet? My speciality, that.'

'I wasn't thinking of it as a message as such. Do I have to decide now?' She realised she was addressing him in the same entertainer's tone as Bea had used on the baby.

'I'd leave it blank, myself. More enigmatic.'

'Of course you'd have a blanky,' the undertaker bawled. 'What great achievements in life would yours say? "Here lies our Frank, completed *Grand Theft Auto* in one weekend, knew how to microwave a burrito"? Stop mithering us. Go and feed the cat. Ignore him, please, Mrs Miles.'

'Ms,' she corrected automatically – then, struck by sudden

inspiration, glanced at the forms. 'Oh, blow. Do you know what, I've made a mistake on here, right on the first page. Put down my married name. Force of habit. You wouldn't have another form?'

'Of course, of course!' Markson leapt up, and as he and his son dodged one another around his desk, Amanda quickly slipped the envelope out of her handbag and in between the pages of the booklet. 'There now,' he said, 'I'll give you this and you give me that one – and you,' to the boy, 'can shred it for our guest, since that's about the limit of your talents. Re the inscription, ignore what that dolt said. You have a think in your own time and give me a call, or pop it down in your will to enshrine it. Lovely word, don't you think, "enshrine"?'

'Uh-huh,' she said, absently, watching the boy feed the papers into the shredder with great contentment. The machine's escalating screech had a gleeful quality: give me more, more secrets, more to destroy! 'Got to make sure everything's done properly,' she said to Markson, glimpsing the blackmailed sheet slither into the maw of the machine. 'After all' – and she did try, really did, not to sound self-pitying – 'no one else is going to.'

'How many courses we got left?' asked Lewis, yawning. He was exhausted, he'd told them, after a day spent photoshopping beads of condensation on an image of a new bottled sports drink, focus groups having deemed the advert's first draft 'insufficiently quenching'. 'Four? Five!' He pushed back his chair. 'I'm off to the loo to clear some room.'

Freddie, who had been talking dolefully about an ex-boyfriend whose good points he'd only come to appreciate since the break-up, pouted at the interruption. Evil Gary was intent on his phone, texting three different boys, keeping his post-dinner options open. And Wandson was watching events on the far side of the room, where the older woman who'd been struck by the champagne cork was patting at her big hair, enjoying the staff's attention too much, Amanda thought, for her shock to be convincing. Wandson's focus was not on her but on Loïc. 'Come on in,' he breathed, 'the waiter's lovely.'

'Maître d'licious, am I right?' Gary prodded at his phone with a flat forefinger and looked up, aghast. 'I swear, these tiny men are *infatuated* with me. Five foot three. Who's five foot three in this day and age?'

Amanda reached for his phone. 'Let me see.' Gary's screen was a grid of facial hair and headless torsos. She tapped a face at random: hirsute, cauliflower ears, metal ring through the nose like a beast at market. 'There's one who wouldn't pull your nightie down afterwards,' she puffed, and the boys rounded on her in delight. 'We didn't think you were listening,' they said. 'We thought you were busy making notes. Can we see?' Freddie spun her notebook towards him to read. '"Unfortunate visual similarity to shampoo lather." You are so rude,' Evil Gary spluttered, 'I love it.' Wandson, plaintively, reading on: 'What does it mean, "flocculent"?'

On her way to Midgard, Amanda had even wondered whether one of the boys might have sent the letter, but concluded that since she didn't waste time imagining what the four might be up to when she wasn't around, nor did they likely spare her a thought when they weren't sitting right beside her. She had met the boys in Venice three years ago, in the period when her separation was curdling into divorce. All she had done in London was talk, with Blair, with friends, with lawyers, and it was a relief to wander the Rialto market by herself on the one-day cookery course she was writing up, saying nothing and eavesdropping idly on her coursemates, these four shiny twentysomethings, as she bought herself flat peaches, a bottle of balsamic with an irresistibly meretricious label. Once she'd acquainted herself with the boys' particular idiom – facetious remarks earnestly delivered, and vice versa – she was able to imitate it and join in. By the time they'd finished the cookery course and were crossing the Grand Canal on an unsteady gondola, the sozzled boys were hers to command. Culinarily the Cipriani, like Venice itself, wasn't what it used to be, but the boys didn't know or didn't care about its existence before they got to see it. 'So,' they asked leadingly over bellinis, 'is there a Mr Amanda?' She'd gestured out past the palazzos glowing in the late sun, the city's domed and bowed roofs, to a shape beyond, grey-white and massive, a moored cloud. It took the brain several moments first to understand what it was seeing, another few to grasp the scale of the thing: the mother of all cruise ships. 'He's the reason I'm here. We're contractually obliged to be aboard, though not to actually spend any time with each other, thank god.'

'Think positive,' Evil Gary had mused. 'People are always vanishing at sea. Ideal place for a murder. Oh!' he exclaimed suddenly. 'My, don't these glasses sparkle when they're empty!'

Later, once Amanda had moved on to Martinis, she had proposed a reunion lunch once they were all back in London – the offer prompted by the particular hellish loneliness that too much gin could make one feel. They assembled at Agapemone, then in its pomp, and thereafter continued to gather every few months in a mutually satisfactory arrangement wherein Amanda paid for lunch and the boys either pretended or genu- inely did believe that her paper would let her expense the bill for all five of them. Wandson and Freddie had arrived together that time but Wandson had gone home with leftovers, Freddie and Lewis with each other, Evil Gary with the wine waiter. Since then, Amanda had long ceased trying to keep up with who was dating or in a huff with whom, treating the quartet instead as elements in a kaleidoscope of hedonism frequently, perhaps daily, shaken into a new configuration. Her life, by blessed contrast, continued almost entirely unchanged: the same flat in Somerstown, the same hairdo, until very recently the same job. Blair, meanwhile, had not just remarried but reproduced, a fact she had first learned from her own paper: there in the colour supplement, four pages of blatant advertorial for Blair's new venture, the Ledley Cooking Academy in Woolwich, slogan 'You're never too young to learn.' Or old enough to know better, Amanda thought, recalling what Blair had called one of his 'unassailable core principles': never to have children. He'd talked about a boiling world, the crime of overpopulation, the usual blah. Later, less high-minded but more vituperative: 'Maybe it's hard to hear over the tolling in your biological belfry, but I do not *want* children.' Hopefully no one would repeat that to the tow-headed moppet pictured in the advert, adorably holding out a wooden spoon for his father to sup from.

A susurration was moving through the restaurant like a rumour: sea sound, waves of low white noise that surged, ebbed in volume, returned with fuller force. As if washed up on the invisible tide, Lewis returned to the table looking forlorn. 'What's the matter, Lulu?' his friends wondered. 'Drop your Gucci wallet down the shitter again?'

'That lady downstairs is so mean.' He dandled the toe of his loafer in the carpet's luxuriant grain. 'I was washing my hands and she came up behind me and told me I had no chin and should grow a beard. Do I not have a chin?'

They made sympathetic noises, patted him, drew him back into his seat. 'You don't,' they assured him, 'but it's the least of your worries.' 'And there's someone hanging around by the tree, did you see?' Then someone else said: 'Are we going out afterwards? It's two-for-one Tuesdays at Mother Delaney's

Molly House.' 'Shots at Debbie Downer's on the way? They're serving in real glasses now.' 'Are beards even in any more? I feel like they *were*, but now they're naff again.'

Amanda felt herself fade from view like premium content on her newspaper's website. She made a note of Wandson's gag about the maître d'. For her columns she had devised a fictive dining companion, an amalgamation she named the Other and to whom she loyally gave the boys' best lines, and over the evening she had been struck by the notion that this hybrid creation, so extensively cited that it now had its own Wikipedia entry, might have come to life and, bearing malice towards its inventor, written that letter itself. The physical copy was gone now, of course, turned to confetti, but even a single read had stamped its cruel words indelibly on Amanda's memory, and how was she to eradicate that?

Wandson tapped a glitter-nailed hand on her arm. 'Who is that lady?'

At the next table, the head chef was signing a menu for a small boy staring up at her in the dazed wonder that, for one reason or another, Chef Joanna always attracted. 'Ah,' Amanda sighed, capping her pen and turning her notes over. 'I wondered when she'd put in an appearance.' Joanna turned her head minutely towards Amanda, then away, then more resolutely, her expression struggling to convey delight at a wonderful surprise. As she moved towards their table, Amanda stood, both from courtesy and to distance herself a little from the boys and anything untoward they might say. Always surprising, no matter how many times they met, to be reminded how very tall Joanna was: in the dining room she had built, she seemed as outsized as the cruise liner that had dominated the Venetian skyline.

'Chef!'

'Amanda!'

'Chef!'

They negotiated one another's space, brought hands together in a clasp that was neither grip nor shake: a truce. 'Amanda, what a devil you are to turn up like this without phoning in a threat beforehand. I'm black affronted. The booking said Hayman.'

'That's my name,' came a voice from below. They looked down to where Freddie was plucking at his ... garment, Amanda supposed, uncertain whether you'd say jacket, waistcoat, other. Though she'd been careful to stipulate that the boys should wear shirts with collars, she had foolishly neglected to mention anything about sleeves. 'We take it in turns, you see, to use our surnames when we book.'

Amanda, her hand enfolded in Joanna's, felt a momentary, triumphant tightening of grip. 'You know me, Chef,' she tried, 'I like to keep a low profile.' Each woman produced a sound that could be described as laughter. Extricating her hand, Amanda said: 'I should introduce my friends – this is Wandson, Lewis, Freddie and Ev— er, Gary.' They greeted her with varying degrees of politeness, Freddie studying Joanna with ominous fascination.

The chef placed her hands on the table and loomed in. 'Your pal here.' She shook her head. The boys craned upwards, primed for scandal. 'I don't think we'd be here if it weren't for her.' They relaxed, disappointed. 'Chefs like to say they have two big fears when they start a new restaurant – either no one turns up, or everyone does. They're lying. Take it from me, the first option's worse by far. Some nights here we were barely filling half the tables. See if Amanda hadn't snuck in and given us that belter review, I'm not sure we'd have made six weeks, never mind six years. "The Greeks had the same word for cookery and for magic" – I've still got it off by heart – and right enough, magic's what it was. We went like a fair that week, and the phone's never stopped ringing since. Amanda made us, and now the only nightmare I have' – Joanna must have rehearsed this one, run it past her staff backstage – 'is that she ever takes against us.'

Joanna's face shone with the effort of talking to civilians. Behind her, the servers had taken up position around the room, upright as infantry. Each was carrying the special apparatus for the next course – a wooden tray like an old-time usherette's, slung around the neck on a leather strap and heavy with silver canisters, bottles, small lumpy handcrafted pottery bowls Amanda happened to know the staff had been prevailed upon to make themselves.

Joanna's grin was turning to a rictus. 'And dare we hope you might be writing about us again tonight?'

Amanda had prepared some fibs of her own: how she'd told her editor that she wanted to run a short series on old favourites, reliable gems of restaurants that might be overlooked with so many new ventures opening up all the time. 'We get fixated on the newest this, the freshest that. Novelties,' she said, then felt bad because she knew Joanna would think she was being snide about the next course. 'I wanted to remind people that the classics endure for a reason. I had to fight for it,' she added, carried away by the appeal of a victory over her editor, even a fictitious one.

'What's wrong with your eye?' Freddie suddenly demanded.

'My god! Where are your manners? I'm so sorry, Chef, my friends don't get out much. Perhaps too often still.'

'It's fine. Honestly.' The chef winked at Freddie, or blinked, you couldn't say. 'The way I came to think of it, I made a sacrifice.' The boys shifted; the concept made them uneasy. 'That was the lesson this place made me learn – that if I wanted a thing enough, I had to offer something of myself up in exchange. I lost an eye, but gained a new way to see, and so

121

much more. It changed my life.' She glanced towards the tree, a genuine little smile tugging at her mouth, as if she could still see her old self lying there at its foot, bruised, bloody, coming to terms with the enormity of what had to be done. 'You would not have known the old me.'

'A profile,' Amanda said suddenly. 'For one of those coffee-table food magazines. You know the kind – two pages of text then twenty shots of lemons in soft focus. Everyone knows Midgard, but how many people know the story of its pioneering chef?'

'No, I don't think I . . .'

'Let me help you tell it. We've known each other ever so long. You were so brave. Inspirational. Who else has done what you did? And then we could go right back to your formative experiences, your culinary education, the food you loved as a child. When you first knew' – in panic at that Joanna began signalling her lieutenants forward – 'that you wanted to be a chef.'

'Spring it on me mid-service, why don't you?' Joanna moistened her lips. 'Look, I'll think about it. But I'm not promising anything.'

'No, no, of course.' This was formality, Amanda knew. She could see, laid out before her like landing lights, what she'd say, how and when, to convince Joanna. How long it had been since she'd felt a real thrill of instinct about a story – the knowledge, not just the conviction, that she was on to something good, something that could make a difference.

'Gentlemen,' Joanna boomed, 'Amanda. Can I ask each of you, please, to now place your left hand on the table, palm down. Thank you.' To Amanda's surprise, the chef joined her staff in building the dish, meaning there must be some absence in the kitchen. 'What we have here,' as she dipped a wide brush into one of the pots on her assistant's tray and painted a thick streak of white matter on the back of each diner's hand, 'is whipped homemade ricotta.' Amanda, who knew it was coming, still squirmed with the sensation, the cold gelatinous slither. Next, out came the squeezy bottles, the fragments in kitchen forceps, arranged on the bed of ricotta until something like a little abstract artwork had formed: cherry reduction, slivers of almond brittle, trimmed half-moons of radish, edible flowers, a skoosh of lively pink foam derived, the chef explained, from honey-roasted figs. From tables around the room Amanda heard cooing, chuckling, a higher pitch of interest with the occasional muted grace note of surprise or revulsion. Long high notes, bowed on a violin, threaded through the washes of sea sound, and a deeper note throbbed beneath it all, the vibration of distant industry. 'And we finish with sashimi-grade Spanish mackerel fillets, "cooked" ceviche-style in citrus. What we recommend here is that you take in all the flavours at once, just bringing it all into your mouth together.' A pager clipped to Joanna's uniform chirruped then, and she slapped it silent. 'Ah, well, back to the scrum for me. I'll leave you to enjoy my own personal favourite dish. And I don't mean you, Loïc,' she mystified the maître d' as he glided up beside her. 'I trust you're bringing good news about our empty table?'

'That vacancy has now been filled, Chef.'

'Wizard.' She clapped a hand on his shoulder; Loïc eyed it disdainfully. 'We'll have to have a wee talk about fixing you up with glasses, Loïc. Getting a bit short-sighted, eh? Can't think of any other reason you wouldn't have let me know sooner we had a VIP here with us tonight. Glasses, aye, or that laser eye surgery they do now.' Her grip on him whitened. 'I'll work the lasers myself.'

With uncharacteristic tact, the boys waited until Joanna had gone before asking Amanda's marks out of ten for the

123

mackerel. She deliberated, rocked her head side to side, came down on a seven. They reacted with shock. 'A seven's basically a zero, you once said. A zero with a little hat on.'

'So much of it depends on the shock value of the presentation, and that can only be a novelty the first time you have it.' But most people, they pointed out, real people, *would* only eat at Midgard a single time; most people did not live the gourmet life that she did. They were even self-aware enough not to say 'we'. 'You're so jaded,' sighed Freddie, having only recently learned the word, and perhaps he was right. Although that meant that by extension Graham, too, might have been right, and Amanda wasn't sure she could concede that yet.

'Man, I love pickled daikon,' Lewis was enthusing, nibbling a golden crescent – the same Lewis who had refused in Venice to eat anything that didn't come deep-fried. Wandson dabbed the point of his tongue to his hand for the last traces of the course: 'There was ginger in the fig gel, no? Enough to give the little buzz'; while Lewis drained his glass and parted his lips a millimetre and inhaled to aerate the last mouthful. 'I wasn't sure at first,' he said. 'I was like, Marlborough Sauvignon in 2013? Are you even trying? But actually it goes perfectly. Gooseberry for days.'

Amanda's sudden bloom of pride was mostly in the boys, but also in herself. Without her guidance, their palates would still be as immature as when they had first met. Realising this, she decided it was right that she shouldn't tell them she'd lost her column. She suspected they could carry on with this arrangement more or less indefinitely without the boys ever noticing that she never seemed to write up any of these meals. When had they last looked at a copy of the *Sunday*? When, considering the circulation, had anyone?

Someone had. Someone had gone to the effort of studying her work very intently indeed. Best not to dwell on the fact that maybe that person, that chimeric Other, knew where she was, was waiting to pounce right now. She looked around the room, sought out the face of every man, because it would be a man, and nobody looked any more or less like a murderer than any other diner in any other restaurant.

Terrible if it happened now, since she'd just had a rather delicious idea. She made a mental note to email Markson. When the day came, she thought, on that afternoon when the boys dressed up in unfashionable black – she'd make sure it was an afternoon service, they weren't early risers – and gathered around the tombstone that bore her name, how funny it would be if they found she had left one last enduring review, carved there for the ages:

She did her best to improve their taste.

I'd tried to scream, I'd tried to whimper. By keeping still, I'd thought I might gather enough energy to throw myself from my hiding place. When that failed, I tried wiggling a toe, a finger. Nothing. Was I blinking? Was my heart beating? I had to assume no. So how was I able to see, for instance, Loïc enter the kitchen where he surreptitiously retrieved from the bookshelf beneath the squirrelphone his apparently indispensable black book, pages filled with the names and numbers of diners he'd promised to call should a table become available? And what process of deduction this sparked in my brain was derailed when, seconds later, Joanna strode back in from her dining room walkabout and began issuing orders about the reseat at Two?

I was a body, as far as Joanna was concerned, or rather the absence of one. Her kitchen was calibrated to work with a certain number of personnel, and while it could adjust to a single absence, two – one cook not at their station, one waitress AWOL – threatened to scuttle it. After a quick tour of the kitchen, amending the heat on a burner, spooning up a sauce for seasoning – 'Soigné that up a bit, please, Finn' – and lifting to the light a few of Kima's pieces for the next course to spot check for colour and consistency, she reached for the squirrel-phone, keyed in the number she had on file for me. Again all she got was the polite voice apologising for my unavailability which, though its cadence never varied, sounded less sincere each time Joanna heard it.

She'd got the measure of me the moment I'd turned up for my first interview: nervous masquerading as taciturn, typical nineteen. More astute than I imagined myself on some topics, usefully clueless on others – she asked me a question about varieties of olive oil, watched me flounder, concluded that I was malleable enough to be promising. 'And no plans to go rushing off back to Melbourne?' 'God, no,' I'd burst out with that millennial admixture of bullishness and vulnerability; and who, she'd thought, would ever want to be my age again?

'The person you have called—' 'Ach, away and boil your head,' she told the voice, and hung up. Had I switched my phone off? Or, she wondered, was I sitting at home watching it light up, screening out the restaurant's number? It made no difference. She'd be adding me to her lengthy mental list of folk who had not simply let her down, but done so at a point when she'd relaxed, thinking she'd succeeded in training them to be honest, respectful, reliable, to give others one iota of consideration. She was angry at me, of course, but more at herself. By my thoughtlessness I was undoing a lot of good work Joanna had done in accepting the importance of relying on other people.

'A drama student,' she'd said at my interview. 'Tell me about that.'

Even a person with one eye could see that my CV was more fiction than not, but by chance she'd singled out one line that I hadn't embellished. Wrongfooted by not having to lie, I jabbered about fringe-of-fringe theatre, Maggie the Cat, that all-women *Macbeth* in the basement of a condemned Collingwood townhouse, stifling hot and thick with brick dust. 'That your biggest challenge?' Joanna asked. No, I said: that had been playing Juliet in my Year 10 production when, after poisoning myself and swooning, I'd had to lie inert beside my sweaty Romeo while the Capulets and Montagues galloped through the final lines so relieved at reaching the end that they sounded quite jolly about the double suicide in front of them, and I'd had to fight really hard not to laugh. 'You mean corpse,' Joanna supplied, smiling.

Joanna's office was a cubicle at the far end of the kitchen. The door was plywood, the walls thin and noise from the staff toilet next door way too audible, but there was some sound-proofing from the layers and layers of paper that covered all four walls: printed spreadsheets, receipts, invoices and bills in pink and yellow facsimile, some stamped red; newspaper clip-pings, reviews and profiles; a panoply of menus from London restaurants past and present, from Arbutus to the Zetter; mugshots of Midgard's staff, VIPs and nemeses; ingredients lists, timing flowcharts for complex presentations, coloured diagrams of flavour combinations. Chains of Post-its, covered in the run-on results of brainstorming sessions in the test kitchen, fluttered in the stream from the laboriously rotating fan on her desk. Then more esoteric items: a postcard from Machu Picchu; images torn from film posters; an Ordnance Survey map of Scotland's west coast; the front cover of a musician's autobiography entitled *Timeless* with the author photo scrawled over in thick marker: BARRED FOR LIFE. On the ledge of a bricked-up window stood a plain grey vase filled with the bell-shaped, pinkish-green flowers that I would, much later, semi-recognise growing on Finn's allotment.

'I've taken on an actor or two in my time. They know how

to improvise, a valuable skill in this business.' She tapped my resumé. 'I'm a bit worried by this, but. Just three weeks in this last job in Melbourne? Gumbys Bakehouse?'

'The manager,' I'd begun, then came up short because, naïve though I was, I knew it was not a good idea to describe in close detail how I'd responded to one leering innuendo too many by grabbing a pair of serrated tongs and attempting to castrate him, then rushed out in the wake of his shriek, scooping up a bag of stale rolls as severance. Fortunately, Joanna heard something in my tone: 'You don't need to go into it,' she interrupted. 'Just know that I don't stand for any of that shite.' She dropped my résumé in the trash, where in fairness it did belong. 'Job's yours if you want it,' she said then, casually, and the rush of gratitude I felt took me by surprise. I grabbed her hand, surprising her too, and started to babble. I hadn't realised until that moment how afraid I'd been that I had failed in coming here, this big full-on city which seemed populated by people who couldn't really afford to live there, myself included. Money seemed to evaporate from my pockets as soon as I left my room. But I did not want to – I could not – go home. Actual tears came into my eyes, and with a rueful expression Joanna reached for a box of tissues and gave me a little pep talk. As I sniffed and wetly smiled, I heard the flimsy door of her office flap open; still talking me down, Joanna raised her head in warning and glared whoever into retreat. 'Why don't you come in on Friday and Saturday and watch what we do. Then on Tuesday you can shadow Kelly, maybe, and see how we get on.'

It was Joanna's habit to praise the unlikeliest lines in her staff's job applications, much as she'd singled out drama on mine. Addy's stint working at a merchant bank, she informed her, meant she was flexible, good with figures. Nico's marathons:

129

powers of endurance. 'You could go in there saying you were half human, half Lego brick,' she'd once overheard Tash saying, 'and Chef would be all, "Aw, braw, ah think stackability's a vital asset in ma staff."' Tash's Glasgow accent verged on a hate crime but she had the sentiment just right. It didn't matter where we came from or what we knew or didn't so long as we were loyal, biddable. Joanna had assembled and refined her brigade as she'd construct any dish, trying out different contrasts and complements, adjusting by increments until each element brought out the best in every other. She wanted to foster kindness and supportiveness in her kitchen and was thrilled when the staff told her they'd never worked anywhere so undysfunctional.

'My guru always says,' she heard Sprudge begin and, before anyone could so much as groan, she did her double clap, sending the servers sweeping out with clean napkins and fresh cutlery. The timer on her belt chimed again, more insistent: overdue. She had a few minutes before she'd have to supervise the next plating. 'Five minutes,' she called. 'I'm going to my office. Kelly? You're in charge while I'm away. And Loïc, if the new Two comes in, seat them and come chap on my door, all right?' 'Oui,' he intoned, too good for a plain old yes, cordon-bleu nerd that he was. 'And quit banging pots,' she ordered of nobody in particular, registering clamour. 'It's nipping my head. We're cooking, not auditioning for *Stomp*.'

Her office was dark but for the twinkling of the computer screensaver on its endless voyage through space. There was a light switch by the door, somewhere under the reams of paper, but she left it off. In the glow from her reactivated monitor, she opened the miniature fridge beneath her desk where she kept the costliest champagnes and truffles locked up, and retrieved a sealed bottle of cloudy fluid more precious even than vintage Krug. She poured a measure into her Dean & DeLuca mug, took it into her mouth and then, chin dipped, swallowed it with some effort. Whatever she diluted or cut the stuff with, its unique, sweaty candy-cigarette taste always came through. Next was the difficult bit: sitting in her chair and doing nothing. The treatment was unpredictable – sometimes it made her queasy, sometimes vertiginous, sometimes flush fearsome red.

Something aside from staffing issues had unsettled her. She sat for a moment, pondering, then realised it was the conversation with Amanda. She resented, firstly, being informed that she had a story to tell, the insinuation being that she could not possibly be capable of telling that story herself; what was she, some meathead who'd never heard the word 'memoir'? Secondly, it irked her that Amanda's question – 'What food did you love as a child?' – actually was itching away in her hindbrain. She pinched the tip of her tongue between her teeth, brought up on her sluggish internet a map of her hometown and dropped the wriggling yellow avatar on her childhood neighbourhood.

At first the views were unfamiliar, distorted by digitisation or misremembering. Then she spotted a red car parked by a green garage door, a pebble-dashed garden wall, looking exactly as they had decades ago. From memory she navigated to the strip of park that ran along the waterfront. That let her locate the Apollo Radio Café that used to have the good milkshakes and then, a few doors down, what was now a pawnbroker's but had once been the restaurant to which Joanna's family would decamp whenever her mother, without prior warning, would erupt and demand that someone else cook for a change. The name on the ragged awning had seemed a direct address to the old dear: Take it Easy.

What they served there – and this would be the sincere answer to Amanda's question, blowing any cheffy cool she'd managed to accrue over her career – was what Joanna loved then: garlic mushrooms in heavy crumb, pepper steak, duck à l'orange, chicken cordon bleu – it was Scotland, it was the mid-eighties, this was the bomb. And afterwards, always, that preternaturally white ice cream made to a secret recipe known only to Scots Italians and whose flavour wasn't vanilla, wasn't really anything but wondrous.

By spinning the perspective on the map, she was able to more or less replicate the view from the window table her parents had always requested: dreich sky, the grey squally river stilled in the moment of hurling up a sheet of freezing spray. Oh, aye, she remembered that, right enough, the chill wet, her useless thin cagoule, numb hands scrabbling at a restaurant door clamped shut by gale force. But then when she closed her eyes and thought back to eating there, when she remembered the sensation of split cane seating imprinting itself on her thighs, what she pictured was a tide far withdrawn to expose shining mud pocked with silvery pools and runnels, gulls with mean expressions plumped on the slather or stotting between puddles in search of marooned prey, the sun vast and low on the horizon.

Something was happening. Something like the sensation of wanting to sneeze but not being able. Tarnished daylight, a shore strewn with beach wrack: little snapshots kept occurring to her, and they had a flavour – of salt, of meat. Joanna scrabbled for her phone, thumbed her way to voice memos. 'Pigeon. Neat wee slices of pigeon breast, poached maybe. Fan them out on the plate. Mushrooms, garlicky, a coarse pâté.' Then, in a rush, as it came to her: 'Square glass plates, or rectangular, check what the suppliers have. An espresso-salt crumb and the oyster jelly I use in the starter. Think about textures, too – how cold and dense the sand feels when you squidge it between your toes on a hot day. Shredded cavolo nero for seaweed. Can we pickle it a bit?' she wondered, recalling the rubberiness and hot salt-on-salt flavour of the real thing: she'd been the sort of child who'd put everything in her mouth.

132

I've had an idea, she'd announce to her staff at next month's test kitchen and watch them grow eager for whatever she was about to feed them.

That was what cooking was nowadays, she'd explained to her therapist at a recent session: 'Nostalgic, personalised. Your autobiography on a plate, fresh and raw and fancified as tartare. You got kids?'

Silence, the measured cautioning half-smile. 'We're not here to talk about me, Joanna.'

'I've got one. She's got four walls, three storeys, an ash tree growing right through the heart of her. She's the love of my life, I've given her everything, and in time she will destroy me, as children do.' Joanna had been seeing Dr Barlow long enough to know that when the therapist was uncomfortable she brought her long ponytail over her shoulder and smoothed it repeatedly with one hand. Her hair was pure white all the way to the tortoiseshell clasp that gathered it at her nape, pure black thereafter. Was she naturally dark or naturally fair? Desperate to know, Joanna refused to ask. 'Aw,' she changed, 'I do know memory's not a finite resource. I know I'm not *losing* anything when I dredge up and share some bit of my life for my team and I to turn into a dish. But what happens when I've used up all those memories? Where will that leave us? The restaurant?' Dr Barlow said nothing, a silence like a judo move, until Joanna gave in and said it: 'Where does it leave me?'

'Did Magnus also used to feel this way?'

Joanna's sightless eye had twitched, an impossible tic under the eyepatch. She had raised her forefinger, scratched gingerly at the skin beneath the socket with her ragged bitten nail. 'You know what, Doc? I think that's all we have time for.'

When she set her phone back on her desk, she spotted a single leaf on top of her paperwork: tear-shaped, faded green, edges crimped with decay. 'Don't start,' she told it. She didn't look up. She knew full well that the tree's branches did not penetrate the office ceiling. 'You watch, I'll be up that ladder again with a chainsaw quicker than you can say "ash dieback".' Maybe that was the side-effect of her medicine tonight – to make her a wee bit hilarious.

Two minutes until she'd be needed in the kitchen.

She flicked through the phone until she found the folder of sound files she occasionally recorded when she was alone in the restaurant, after the team had been debriefed and individuals excoriated and mollycoddled as required then sent on their way. She rewound and listened to the end of the last entry: 'They all told me to get rid of it,' she heard herself say, that voice she'd never get used to. 'My family. The contractors who had to work around it. And I gave everyone the same answer: "Over my dead body." I never thought it would come to that. And then one night, when all my staff and my contractors had gone home and I was in there on my own, I'm sorry to say I weakened. What if they were all right and I, for once, was wrong? What if it wasn't safe? What if vermin got in, or bits of bark did fall into people's food? I decided that it might be better if I pruned it back a bit, got shot of the bigger branches at least. So I propped the shoogly ladder the decorators had been using against the tree, filled my dungaree pouch with tools, climbed up and got to work.' And got to work, Joanna plummily mouthed, marvelling: when had she first started to sound so English? 'I started out with scissors' – and then the recording was interrupted by a slewing crash from kitchenside that made her wince in reflex even now. That was the end of that, a hundreds-of-quid full stop, and now she flicked up a new file and began to describe what had happened next.

'The slender branches were a doddle – I just used scissors for them. Then I swapped them for secateurs and a butcher's hacksaw to tackle the sturdier ones. There's a reason they call folk who do this for a living surgeons. There I was amputating healthy limbs, making wounds all over the place. They looked like eyes, the sawn-off ends of branches, wide, apricot-coloured, staring me out as I worked, like, "Why would you do this to me?" That was one reason I wished I'd never started, that and the skelfs riddling my fingers and the way sweat kept getting in my eyes – eyes, plural, because this is the story of how I lost one of them. But you can't leave a job like that half-done, and so I went on, lopping branches away, climbing down, moving the ladder, back up again, torturing the tree some more. I was living off espresso in those days and I started feeling a bit peaky, from the caffeine and the weird guilt, and the paint fumes, and the smell of the wood sap that was seeping from some of the cuts I'd made.

'When my arms ached too much to continue, I'd take a break, staying up there and looking down on my restaurant. I could just make out the pattern of the carpet through the heavy plastic sheeting protecting it. The furniture I'd chosen was pushed back against the walls, odd corners peeping out where the packaging had split. God, I'd driven the painters spare over those walls: "Not so grey – I said dusky bronze, not smoky. Warmer. No, now that's too warm." On the far side of the partition were all the stacks of crates full of the flatware and stemware I'd picked out, the steak knives I'd had shipped specially from Utrecht. I'd chosen the wattage of the over-table bulbs, the typefaces on the menus, the different ply of bog rolls for guests and staff. The kitchen was stocked with more equipment than I might ever use, the full range of Adrià-brand cooking chemicals, a small local library's worth of recipe books, from *cucina povera* to a Fanny Craddock grimoire signed by the occultress herself.

'Then there was all the stuff you couldn't see but which was equally essential – how I'd figured out the optimum ratio of

135

experienced staff to newbies and recruited accordingly. All the labour-saving, cost-saving ploys I'd devised that wouldn't *look* like cutting corners – like seating everyone at the same time and serving them all the same menu, which I knew I could spin to guests by telling them no multiple-choice menu meant never worrying they'd choose wrong.'

She took a breath. 'What I want to get across,' she told herself, or her future ghostwriter, 'is that I was pushing thirty-five and I had one chance and one chance only to get this right, and I'd decided that meant needing to control every single teeny-tiny aspect of the place. And it truly hit home then, looking at the place from up there, that in a week's time it would all be happening, the moment I'd been planning for actual decades. Everything I'd ever wanted. So why, I wondered, did I feel it was doomed before it'd even got started? The answer was simple. Simple and gutting.'

It had come to her about a month earlier. Amid recurrent, by now almost tedious anxiety dreams about buggered supply chains and losing her way to the restaurant a new nightmare had emerged, a skelp from the subconscious. It knocked her awake in a cold instant and an awful certainty: that what would sink Midgard was the food. The menu was littered with trendy buzzwords and tent-pole proteins, lobster and foie gras and Kobe beef, things she herself didn't much like but that she thought needed to be on there. Her so-called signature dishes, meanwhile, were bastardised versions of others' work, thieved and barely tweaked: Quisibeve's deconstructed picklebacks, Ninigret's red salad, the *sanguinello* from Bocca di Lupo. The entire menu was reheated leftovers, every dish tainted by the taste of desperation. Critics would be merciless; the public, who were not dumb, would discern, through the *faine daining* trappings, an exercise in gourmet box-ticking: cynical, uninspired, lazy, safe. She'd lain in bed, crawling all over with panic, her heart rate rocketing, wondering if it was possible to literally die of shame.

'I'd had a revelation,' she told the phone, keeping it close to her mouth as if being overheard now would be an issue. 'And all I could do was keep on with what I was at, do more hacking and chopping and tearing. I was taking something out on the poor defenceless tree. At least, I thought it was defenceless. And, ironically enough, that was when I overstretched myself. I reached out to snag another branch, felt the ladder skew under me, tried to shift my weight but miscalculated. The ladder was falling away and I tried to grab a branch to save myself, but of course what had I just finished doing but cutting every last handhold away. I had enough presence of mind to hurl the hacksaw away from me, and then I was falling.

'I remember wondering quite coolly whether all the piles of branches on the floor below would cushion my fall or whether I was about to break my neck. Then something flicked like a whip, right across my eye, and everything went red, and then, almost at the same time, I came to a halt so sudden it jarred every vertebra in my spine and every tooth in my head. But I hadn't crash-landed like I'd braced myself for. I was suspended in the air. Slowly, like it was going to ruin the magic, I opened the eye that wasn't wet and stinging, and when I saw what had happened, honestly, despite everything, I roared. My dungaree strap had snagged on one of the stumps I'd hacked away at and now I was hooked there, stuck like a game of hoopla. Me, with my coordination? I couldn't have done it if I'd tried. I had to laugh. "All right," I told the tree, "point taken. You can keep the rest."

'Now I had a new problem. It was nearly midnight, meaning nobody was due at the restaurant for maybe another nine hours. I did know exactly where my phone was – unfortunately, though, that was on top of one of the crates by the kitchen, about ten feet beneath me. By now my bad eye felt like it was a fist trying to force its way out of my socket. Carefully, really carefully, I tried to open it, but the muscles didn't seem to be working, and then I saw small spots landing on the cairn below, blood and that clear fluid someone thought fit to call humour. This wasn't just going to be one for the first aid kit in my office. Ridiculous though it seemed, I had no option but to make myself fall again. I started wriggling and bouncing myself off the side of the tree, but no good, I was held fast. I actually wedged myself more firmly, so now the sharp sawn end of the branch was digging into my shoulder too.

'Outside I could hear all the familiar, useless noises of Hackney late on a Saturday night. Sirens, foxes, blootered barflies trying to find a lock-in. Voices were approaching, coming down our alley, and I was about to start hollering for help, despite what I knew this would mean about locksmiths, glaziers, firemen. And then I smelled smoke. Cigar smoke, the only kind that doesn't give me the boak. And, in that way that scents do, it reminded me of something I hadn't thought about in years – of visiting my grandparents when I must have been only four or five years old, being fascinated by my grandfather's cigar resting in a glass ashtray and the shapes the smoke would make as it trailed upward and dispersed. And then, without conscious effort, I found myself remembering other details. Cut flowers drying over the Rayburn. Poking my pinky finger into the plug of yellow cream in proper old glass milk bottles, fascinated and disgusted. How I used to help myself to rock sugar from a jar in their pantry, the taste like cola, and the sensation of the strop hitting my legs when I was found out.

'Something was happening. My mind was racing – from

that old house to the money Nana left me when she died, which got me to Tokyo for the first time, nineteen and still putting everything I could into my mouth. Wait, transcriber, scrub the last bit, it sounds wrong. The first thing I ate in Japan was one of they wee hot savoury egg custards they have there, I forget the name, with things hidden in it like lucky dip – a scrap of chicken, one gingko nut, half a mushroom. And now as I hung there, I felt something I never had before, a way to bring these memories together, to make an edible anecdote. I knew pretty instinctively the technique for recreating the steamed custard, how I could infuse it with fresh tobacco leaf to give it a subtle botanical edge. And then I could bury my own bits of treasure in it, a chunk of lavender-sugar tablet, a square of fruit leather, blackcurrant, for the bushes that grew in my grandparents' garden.

'It was inspiration, pure and sweet. I'd not stolen it from anyone, I hadn't just tweaked someone else's success and pretended it was my own idea. And what was weirdest was it kept coming – next moment I was thinking about watermelon sliced transparently thin and dehydrated till it became something with the texture of prosciutto, and then about a sorbet of whisky and lychee and lime, and how I'd make sure there was something bright and pizzicato playing when we served it, because that sweetness would offset the sharpness in the flavours. These notions were golden, they were like the kinds of brilliant things you see in dreams, and I was afraid they'd soon disperse with the smell of smoke and I'd never get them back. My priority was to get out of that fucking tree, pardon my language, and just as neatly I knew how to do it. The secateurs I'd used on the medium-sized branches were still in my dungarees, and I unclicked the blades, fankled them up to my shoulder strap, and started to cut. I did it tentatively, closed the blades so slowly, as if that would make any difference. That strap was all that was holding me, and it tore straight through right away, and then I was falling again—'

A thump at the office door and 'Yeah!' Joanna bellowed, bouncing from her chair in myoclonic fright.

'Chef? We're plating up, and Loïc says the new guy'll be here in five.'

She had no idea, in that moment, where she was, who she was, what was happening at all. '. . . Kelly. Yes. Right. I'll be out in a sec.'

A pause. 'You all right, Chef?'

'Of course. Always. Go. But don't start on anything till I'm back.' She waited until the footsteps shuffled away before pressing record again. 'What happened with the tree was so typical of me back then. I was arrogant, I was aggressive. I never asked for help. There would be decisions that had to be made and I just – I didn't. I let things mount up until they got excruciating, and only then, only at the very last minute, did I try and do something about them. The sensible thing that would have saved a lot of time and a load of grief.' She leaned in close to her phone. 'Listen. Here's a secret. I spent nine minutes in the branches losing blood. There's still a scar on my shoulder where that stub of limb maybe, I sometimes think, leaked ash sap into me. My stubbornness cost me an eye. But I learned something that night. I think I learned everything. The person who fell out of that tree was not, was *not*, the person who'd climbed up there. And never would be again.'

She burst back into the kitchen, fusillading instructions. 'Patisserie, you look like you've nothing to do, so fix me up a starter for the straggler, he's minutes away. You're about to ask what goes in it? Anything we can get. Use your initiative.' Kima's mouth guppied in alarm. 'Gareth, another of they wee chicken snackies?' 'On it already, Chef.' 'Finn, what's next for you? Never mind, do me a new crab and start thinking about a replacement for the caprese while you're at it – I never want that on the menu again after tonight. Bronzewings out now, servers, please. This needs to go like clockwork.' Some new wrongness had registered as she was speaking. With an encouraging, general 'Finesse! Finesse!' she conducted a quick headcount and found the total had gone *up*. 'John! Where did you spring from?'

He didn't have a chance to explain: Gareth bounded over to haul the boy's bandaged hand into the air in a pugilist's salute. 'Emergency Department!' he crowed. 'Five stitches, changes his shirt, see, and straight back here. My little buddy's one of us after all.' The proof of what he said was that John showed no sign of smugness, just displeasure at being interrupted in his work.

As the chefs dashed and clattered, as Joanna had a confiding word in John's bright pink ear, I was watching a single copper hair as it made a twining descent from overhead, wafting on the kitchen's thermals. One of mine, I was sure. However thorough our nightly deep clean, however unimpeachable our hygiene score, Midgard must be full of stray hairs, sloughed skin flakes, particles of personal dust. Maybe there was more of me here now – these leftovers – than anywhere else on earth.

My arm ached. The pinkish cast on my vision seemed to be deepening. Some clock in the kitchen was loudly ticking and I felt like it might be counting down towards something even worse for me, some next-level torment. How was I hearing and seeing all of this? Why was I here, and what could I do about it? I was confused and scared. And something else besides. A

sensation that was, even by the standards of my current pre-
dicament, really fucking bizarre.

In fact, it was inexplicable.

I was hungry.

Table Five

'Quiet tonight.'

'Is it? Oh, you mean me.'

'Introspective, I want to say.'

'No, no, just tired. Long day. These lighting effects aren't helping.' The bulbs overhead had been dimming steadily for some time, thickening the shadows in the dining room and turning its atmosphere warm, textured – churchlike, Sarah thought, as though the restaurant itself were pressuring her to confess. Instead, she opened her mouth to feign a yawn, found a real one emerging anyway. 'Goodness.'

She did have to say something. If she didn't, if they got to the end of the meal and she still hadn't told him about the joint account, it was going to be worse.

From the golden gloom that now surrounded the table emerged Tash, taking measured steps towards the table then halting on their periphery. 'Only gone and da-da-done it again.' She was carrying three sets of cutlery: one for Sarah, one for Murray, one for the son who was not with them. Tash tonight was a one-woman cargo cult, forever bringing offerings to the table as if they might conjure Simon up. If it had been that easy, Sarah reflected, her own wishful thinking would have done it by now.

'We've put another fifty pence in the meter,' Tash was reassuring Murray, who had made some crack about the lights. Her tone was a careful blend of deferential and sardonic, as if she, too, were perplexed by Midgard's quirks but wasn't permitted to say it outright.

Sarah had hinted to Murray that they might eat somewhere different this time, that a fifth anniversary dinner at the same restaurant seemed a little unimaginative. But he liked things a certain way – which was why each time they sat at the same table and were served by the same girl, woman, Tash. Time still passed and each year Tash was a little greyer, a little wirier, Dublin accent further eroded. Some time in the last year she'd had a cross tattooed on the back of each hand, designed to resemble careless slashes of marker pen. Sarah tried not to dwell on these changes, aware of the changes in herself that the girl must see: the hair she had stopped dyeing, the new gauntness Sarah had noticed in her face these last few months.

'I'll be back soon,' Tash was saying, 'with something you haven't had before. And I'm sure Chef will be out to say hello when she has a moment.'

'Tell her she mustn't worry.' Sarah had spent a few minutes of last week's session with Joanna reminding the head chef that, were she to come to chat with them at their table as she customarily did, she must say nothing that would hint to Murray that they were working together. She was recalling – did not describe – an incident when she'd encountered a client at Euston Station and the look in his eye when he'd placed her had set her first crossing the main road against the lights and then boarding a bus going in a totally random direction. 'Don't fash,' Joanna had said, 'I'm good at compartmentalising.' Sarah nodded once, sharply, and said no more.

'She's losing it,' Murray said, once Tash had left. He said it sotto voce, but that didn't make it any kinder. 'Does she think we're hiding him under the table whenever she comes out the kitchen?'

144

'She liked him, that's all. I feel sorry for her.' Sarah had seen it: Simon had directed that wolfish grin at her and she'd practically seen the dopamine bubble up in Tash's brain. Everyone was a little in love with that grin, even Sarah. 'Listen, Murray, don't you think we should talk about the elephant in the room?' And her husband, as she had known he would, lifted his gaze and stared about him in mock amazement, playing to the invisible audience that had observed their twenty-three years together.

'I'm serious.'

'And I didn't say anything. Talk, then. I'm just not sure' – the classic feint – 'what good it can do at this stage.'

Sarah smiled at him. His eyes narrowed slightly, as if this were some strategy. 'I was hoping,' she said, 'that we might walk in here tonight and find Simon waiting for us, sitting at the table as though nothing had happened.'

'You have to stop this, Sarah. You're starting to sound – I don't know how you're starting to sound. We had no word at Christmas or your birthday, but you thought maybe tonight? I don't imagine he even knows when our anniversary is.'

'Our son,' she said, 'is missing.'

'Our son,' he said, in his infuriating lecturing way, 'is no such thing. Not least as far as the law is concerned.'

She struck the table, made the cutlery jump, attracted a look from the young couple at the nearest table. Don't be embarrassed, she wanted to tell them when they glanced quickly away: you're brushing knees now, but give it time and you'll be just like us.

'Our son is an adult. He has no obligation to observe any calendar dates, or to pay us a visit once a week to check we haven't dropped dead. He never answered' – here she registered a meaner tone, something she might be able to exploit – 'those newsy emails you used to send.'

145

Past tense. Though, as a literalist, Murray should have understood that when she promised she would stop sending the emails, it had been an evasion rather than a lie: of course she would, someday, when she no longer had to. In the meantime she typed them out every Monday evening after her last client, bulletins on the weather and home improvements and conferences she'd attended; no questions – she knew better than to ask questions. Lately, however, she'd started to slip in lies: stupid ones, inconsequential ones, lies for their own sake. *Your father went to Oslo this weekend* – he had not. *Your father has been talking about getting a dog* – nonsense. *Can you believe it?* she liked to add. Harmless. But Murray often seemed brusque with her these days, and it was her way of retaliating, Sarah supposed, to make him the locus of these silly stories. They had started out silly, anyway.

Without Simon, their lives were bland, maybe bleak. The *Today* programme and the morning commute. Clients from ten till one, two till six, the rented office in Pimlico with the shared kitchen and the fridge full of foodstuffs aggressively labelled. Paperwork, the Thameslink frantic at rush hour. And then 'How was your day, darling?' 'Fine, fine, the usual. Shrank a few heads, brought a few horses to water. Yours?' 'Something funny in Singapore. Trying to avoid having to go and check on them. Risotto all right for dinner, by the way? There's wine on the table.' 'Ah, you angel.' Then the latest Scandi noir, a bath, *Newsnight*. The cleaner on alternate Thursdays, dinner out once a month. Sarah's clients often came to her with similar concerns: technically, I'm middle-aged, but all the good milestones seem to have come and gone, so what am I to do with the half of my life that remains?

*

'Quidenham?' her taxi driver asked. From his rear-view mirror dangled a heart-shaped air freshener with a demonic aspect, reeking of synthetic rose. He had watched Sarah struggling with the bags of shopping from the supermarket on the far side of the station forecourt, then manhandling them into his car – coloured polythene stretching white, handles straining – and offered no assistance. 'How come you're off there?'

Because there had been a report on *Newsnight* four months ago about an unfolding scandal at a detention centre near Gatwick and, glancing up from her drying nails, Sarah had thought she saw, among the protestors beating pans and tins and chanting for justice, her son's familiar red plaid jacket, worn all weathers; the particular shagginess of the hair he had been cutting for himself since his teens, claiming to find professional haircuts 'too stressful'. Because when she'd woken Murray, dozing beside her on the sofa, he hadn't seen anything of Simon in the footage, told her she was being absurd. Because she had discovered later that there were mailing lists, secret forums, ugly websites through which protestors like these communicated and organised and posted tracts and into which one could, with some effort, insinuate oneself. Because two different messages had corroborated a particular address in a little village in Norfolk. Because while she understood that people loved to insert themselves into the misfortunes of others – for no gain, simply to feel part of a story – she couldn't be certain that anyone was intentionally misleading her. 'Family,' she said curtly.

'Forty pounds, then.'

Forty there and forty back to the station, a fifteen-minute drive. Extortionate, really. Never the same driver twice, but always the same sense she was being scrutinised, categorised, judged. Sarah did not care for the countryside. Keep coming long enough, she supposed, and that wouldn't be an issue, for every week more fields seemed to have been encroached on by JCBs, more hedgerows torn up, more trenches sunk for sewerage, more arable land turned to expanses of rutted rich soil on which small white birds settled.

Since she had started taking these trips, Sarah's emails to Simon had grown bolder. *Your father wants to leave London. Your father's thinking of changing the locks on the front door.* Then, one day: *Simon, your father has been having dizzy spells.* Shocked at herself, she deleted it, considered a moment, wrote instead: *Your father has had a rather worrying diagnosis.* Was the sensation it gave her to write and immediately erase these terrible things the same feeling her son had had during the phase in his early teens when he would steal out of the house at night to wander the neighbourhood for an hour or so, with no objective more sinister than to see the familiar refigured under streetlight and dark? Testing the limits of the world. *Your father coughs and coughs at night.* Suddenly she was inventive, suddenly ruthless: she had no qualms about subjecting Murray to terrible traumas that she immediately deleted, thrilled with guilt. Assaults, freak accidents, a car out of control. Sometimes he was the victim of disaster, sometimes the perpetrator, but it was always him; her role was merely to relay the bad news. To finish on the line that it really was now time Simon came home.

No answer at the front door of the farmhouse where the taxi dropped her, no movement audible behind the storm doors or to be seen through the dirty windows. Sarah, trying to quell a fear that the place had been entirely abandoned, placed her shopping bags out of view beside the porticoed entrance and, rubbing her aching arms, walked to the rear of the house. The back lawn hadn't been mown in some time; the contorted apple trees in the overgrown field beyond had not been harvested, and the tall grass was treacherous with windfalls over which wasps were drunkenly clambering.

The farm outbuildings' whitewashed walls were spoiling, corrugated roofs were warping and sliding. At the centre of a dusty yard, hay bales had been arranged into a shaggy tower; wooden planks angled against it led to dark apertures from which small amber eyes suspiciously peered. And here Sarah found Winnie, collecting eggs from the gaps in the block. 'You just stay back, you brute,' she heard the older woman tell someone behind the bales, her tone fond, and then out stalked a rooster: a splendid, absurd beast, with his shimmer of viridian tail feathers, his crest so pink and raw it seemed indecent, his ludicrous fluffy pantaloons and vicious talons, murder in his yellow stare. He stood as tall as the tops of Winnie's green wellingtons. He advanced on her, head down as if to butt, then rushed her, only to veer sharply off at the last moment in pursuit of some other invisible quarry. 'Ah, it's just you,' Winnie said, spotting Sarah watching this with her arms folded along the gate to the yard. 'Tuesday again. I can set my clock by you.'

'By yourself again today, Winnie?' The chicken wire wrapped around the gate was imprinting geometries on her skin.

'Aren't I always?' Winnie scooped two more eggs from a crevice. 'Days since I saw any of them. They were going to Wales, did I say? Why anyone would want to go to Wales . . .'

She'd made the same crack last week. Sarah needed progress, Sarah needed new information. 'I've brought you a few bits and bobs anyway,' she interrupted, rubbing her aching arms. 'I'm sure you can use them. Or the others can, if they come back.'

'Here,' Winnie said, 'hold this.' She handed Sarah the egg basket and, with both hands, released the sprung lock on the low gate. 'Before you ask, I haven't heard a peep from any of them since you were last here. They hatch their schemes

149

and off they go. I've stopped expecting to hear. Maybe you should too.'

'I know,' Sarah said. She picked stray down and strands of hay off the eggs. 'I know.' What she meant was that she knew Winnie's story. What she didn't say was that she didn't believe it.

'This da-dish was inspired,' Tash explained, eyes flickering saintly upwards, 'by a work of art that Chef loves, and a unique encounter she had with it. Maybe you've seen it, out behind Liverpool Street Station. It's a work by the sculptor Richard Serra named the Fulcrum – five gigantic slabs of steel, fifty feet high, balanced together to form a kind of pyramid. And on the autumn day when Chef first saw it, she says it was *alive*. It had a heartbeat, and its heart was going wild.' She held the two plates before her as she recited the anecdote – which, Sarah knew, was fictitious – while beneath the table, where Tash couldn't see, Murray's hands were making impatient pinching motions. 'Chef snuck in through one of the gaps in the sculpture. A pigeon was trapped inside, battering against the rusty walls as it tried to find its way back out. Well, Chef was already running late that day, but she stayed in there and waited until the bird landed near her feet, exhausted, and then she very gently, very carefully scooped him up and brought him outside. And he blinked, and he spread his wings and then off he flew, with no sign of da-da-' – she grimaced, con-centrated – '*distress*. Chef says it helped her with an important choice, taught her something about being free herself, and this is her edible rendering of that experience.' She placed the plates before Murray and Sarah, rotating each to some precisely mandated configuration, and, in a slightly more theatrical voice, described what they had been given: 'Breast

150

of bronzewing pigeon, pan-fried then glazed with ma-ma-miso caramel. Confit leg of pigeon. And then, over the top, so to speak, is our homage to Serra's sculpture, five crisp panes of crisped and salted chicken skin, sweet golden beet, watercress, kumquat for sourness, and roasted bolete mushroom for a hit of umami.'

'The dear little rescue bird,' Murray muttered when they were alone. Sentiment embarrassed him. 'The wee dote. Probably flew as far as the next gutter then croaked.'

'You're slipping,' she chided. 'Pigeons don't croak, they coo.'

Bested, Murray grinned. 'We ought to be grateful it wasn't a Louise Bourgeois.'

The train Sarah caught secretly every Tuesday afternoon departed from Liverpool Street, and so she had passed the Serra many times before without thinking much of it. After hearing Joanna's story, however – a rough draft of the one Tash and her colleagues now told – she had made a point of retracing the chef's steps, stepping in through one of the tall apertures where the towering corten sheets overlapped. It wasn't dark in there, as she had expected, because far above her head at the apex of the sculpture was a perfect pentagon of bright sky. That bird could have flown right up out of there, she thought, then scolded herself for her gullibility.

'I don't want to be lonely, but I could never settle down,' Joanna had said in session, making Sarah's smile freeze very slightly. She stayed silent. 'I spend my time training folk to function as I need them, so if there was an emergency and I got called away, the restaurant would run exactly right without me – but then I can never relinquish control enough to let them get on with it theirselves.' In confessional mode the chef's accent broadened charmingly. 'This'll sound daft, I know, but I was coming out the train station today, and this weird thing happened to me—'

Murray tapped at one of the coloured transparent panes, looked a little sorry when it fractured. Then, with a shrug to himself, he drove his cutlery through it all, shattered the casing on the confit, scooped up sauce on the blade of his knife, brought it all to his mouth, chewed. He set the cutlery down hastily, as if he'd cracked a tooth. *Your father's been taken ill*, she thought. *Your father's last words were* – no, too far. Then, 'Wow,' Murray said, his eyes drifting shut. 'Oh god, though. My goodness.'

The bronzewing had an intense richness of flavour that verged on the limit of Sarah's tolerance for game, but the unfiltered burgundy, whose barnyard aroma had likewise made her nose wrinkle when she first rolled it around the big glass, transformed it: the meat made the wine clearer, brighter, revealed in it a lingering note of buckwheat, while the burgundy took the borderline putrescent edge off the flavour of the pigeon. Pep and sourness, savour and gleaming sugary sweetness: they followed one another, intermingled in the mouth. Joanna's story about the bird was – oh, Sarah thought with dismay, she was turning into Murray – a canard, but she trusted now that the chef had truly had a revelation when she'd understood how the Fulcrum's monolithic slabs, each one capable of pulverising everything beneath it, balanced and stabilised one another, delicately almost, five crushing weights resolved in opposition.

In the kitchen, Winnie eased off her boots and complained about a bunion which excused her, she evidently believed, from helping Sarah empty the overloaded shopping bags. The first thing she came to was a tin of spaghetti hoops. 'Simon,' she said, showing it to Winnie, 'used to live off these. There was a whole year when he'd eat nothing but. Screamed the

152

house down whenever we tried to give him anything else. Four, I think he was, maybe five. And then suddenly it was chocolate mousse. Nothing but instant chocolate mousse. Even for breakfast.' She had a dozen sachets of that powder with her, too, somewhere in all this shopping. 'A colleague told me food fussiness was a child's way of maintaining a little bit of control over the world, and that I should just go along with it. And I said, so where does that leave eating disorders? Of course kids want to have some control. The world's changing around them and they don't know what to do about it, or where to even start.' Winnie smiled thinly, shifted a stockinged foot into her lap and massaged the big toe.

Those green wellies, the patterned headscarves and quilted jackets – she dressed, Sarah thought, as if she'd visited a theatrical costumier and asked for anything that suggested the rural. There was something similarly stagy, she had come to feel, about the farmhouse itself: faded floral wallpaper, the just-so mismatchedness of its furniture, the downstairs lavatory with the overhead cistern that gabbled and guttered and never stopped running. She pictured Winnie, checking her watch and realising Sarah's visit was imminent, using a pair of tweezers to arrange with great care the three flies that lay on the windowsill: two long dead, one helpless on its back, fitfully buzzing.

Sarah had bought dried pasta and rice, tinned beans and tomatoes, powdered soups, stir-in sauces, instant coffee, bottles of diluting juice, multipacks of cake bars and crisps and biscuits, catering-sized boxes of teabags. She filled the fridge and the conspicuously empty cupboards – and were these not also suspicious, as though nobody were meant to actually open the beaded doors and reveal shelves bare of almost everything save depleted stocks of sugar and condiments and a solitary tin of tuna in brine. A cucumber had liquefied in the otherwise empty salad section, leaving a milky chartreuse puddle Sarah had to rinse off before she could refill the drawer with fresh vegetables. Winnie said she'd been alone all week, and conceivably one person could have used everything Sarah had brought last time. It wasn't impossible.

Winnie had claimed to recognise Simon from the photograph she'd been shown. She claimed she knew the person from whom Sarah had first learned of the existence of the house. But she was careful not to volunteer information – had told Sarah that she was a discreet person, that she had sworn not to answer the kinds of questions Sarah was asking. 'Sometimes people stay here, and then a van rolls up and some or all of them go off and do what they do, and I just carry on doing what I do, I collect the eggs, I make the tea, I don't interfere. It is to a purpose – if I know nothing, really nothing, then nobody can make me tell them anything. I'm not a go-between. I don't relay messages. I don't get involved, you see. I'm no one's mother.'

'Later on, though,' she was telling Winnie, 'he seemed too changeable. He couldn't stick to anything. He scraped through his exams and then when he went to college he changed course almost every term, these sudden passions that would ebb as quickly as they'd arrived. The same with jobs – always the kind you could do for a while and then just walk away from without consequences. Murray and I gave up trying to learn the names of his girlfriends. But he was always enthusiastic, always sure that this was the one, this course or this job or this girl. I remember when it struck me. My son wasn't just a person who didn't know what he wanted, but one who didn't *know* that he didn't know.'

'They got that woman out,' Winnie said suddenly. She placed her foot back on the floor, didn't get up. 'The one at Gatwick, do you remember? She was going to be deported even though she was pregnant. She went on hunger strike.' Yes, Winnie had said, looking at the picture of Simon that first day, his wolfish grin. Yes, I know him. Sarah had no reason to disbelieve her; nor had she any to believe her. 'And now she's got leave to remain. Your boy did that, your boy and his friends. They worked it all out here together and they put their plan into operation and they achieved their goal.' Her eyes were pink. 'So I'd say maybe he's found out what it is he wants.'

Winnie had never, in Sarah's presence, consulted a mobile phone. She didn't seem to have a computer, or even a landline. Was it possible she hadn't seen the headlines that morning, the dropping of charges? Hadn't been sent word in advance of the ruling?

Sarah had come here two or three times before she realised who Winnie was. Her name was different, of course, and her hair, when it showed from under those perennial headscarves, was cut in a more pragmatic, mannish style than when she had been on television. And Sarah had never heard her voice, then, with its faint drawl of an accent – Dutch? – because only lawyers had been authorised to speak for her, into the bouquet of microphones. And she felt sick, then, when she realised: not with horror but with sympathy for what Winnie had had to live through. That was when she knew that whether or not Winnie was lying to her, she was going to keep coming back.

'You're running low on washing-up liquid,' she told Winnie, then held up a tea towel you could see almost straight through. 'And you could use a new set of these. What else?'

Winnie's eyes glittered. 'Now you're asking,' she said. 'Soap would be good. It can get a bit whiffy in here when I've got a full house. Shampoo, too. Malt loaf. Does that still exist? Not to wash with. Chocolate. Cheese – blue cheese, cheddar, anything, really. And meat. We could do with a bit of red meat. Steak and chips. They could use a bit of flesh on their bones.'

'Hang on, I'll make a list.' Sarah had her phone out. 'Listen, though – something went ping in my shoulder today, bringing all that shopping in, so I'm going to do one of those online deliveries, okay?'

'Whatever suits,' Winnie said magnanimously. 'Frozen veg, that's always useful. Ice cream – something for when they've eaten up all their greens. Breakfast cereal. Cooking oil – they go through that like there's no tomorrow.' She kept talking, and Sarah added multiples of each thing she suggested to the basket on the Freshways website. The kids liked pancakes? Fine: a bag of pancake mix the size and weight of a ten-year-old. Toilet paper never goes wrong? Why not nine packs of sixteen rolls each.

'Simon,' she said, manic now, adding sausages and gin-gersnaps and cranberries and household bleach, ticking yes to every automated suggestion that ensued, 'used to turn up unannounced at the house – first thing I knew about it would be when I saw his plaid jacket hung over the kitchen door, lit-erally right next to the row of hooks, actually *more effort* to put it over the door than where it belonged.' She heard, or thought she heard, a creaking overhead, imagined a stealthy step on a telltale floorboard. 'There he'd be in the kitchen pulling every pan out of the cupboard, chopping an onion with the wrong knife, telling me he was going to make a big gumbo for us all, though I don't think he ever knew that word meant an actual dish rather than whatever he could lay his hands on in the cupboards, cooked down with a tin of tomatoes tipped over it.' He didn't need to know recipes, she'd tell him if he came down those stairs right now, he could make everything up as he went along. She'd never call him aimless again. She'd speak instead of flexibility, plasticity, adaptability. Didn't he know, she'd ask Simon, where certainty got people? Winnie's son had had certainties, and they had led the poor boy into the gallery on Trafalgar Square and up the stairs to the room that contained the four vast canvases named after the elements. There, he kneeled down and shrugged off the backpack that contained a flask of petrol and a box of kitchen matches.

On their plates lay the remnants of the bronzewing: fine mauve bones stripped of flesh, minute fragments of the shattering panes bleeding colour into the pool of ruddy juices blebbed with oil. In their glasses, the thick silt of the unfiltered red. 'And how did we enjoy?' Tash smarmed, coming to collect; to which Murray began one of his most gleeful routines, covering his inability to speak for how *she* had enjoyed it, but in *his* view—

Your father ran full-pelt onto a pitchfork. Come home. Your father was hit by lightning. Come home.

She had to say something to Murray. She really did. She thought how exasperating it was when clients, mainly men, arrived to their first consultation having seemingly exhausted their reserves of courage in simply turning up, then spent their hour taking in the unremarkable view through her office window, expecting her to do the work. Sometimes they were asking themselves, as she was now, where to start – with Gatwick, with the forums, with the train trips, with the text from the bank flagging up suspicious activity on the joint account.

Your father's left me. It's just you and me, now. Come home.

The lights were brightening, the dining room's bosky atmosphere receding. Sarah watched the network of little shadows shifting slowly in the pitted bark of the tree, abstract shapes thinning out and fading to nothing; all but one, and then, as Sarah watched, it moved – showed itself not a shadow cast by the trees' truncated limbs but a figure in silhouette, almost concealed behind the trunk. It gave her an uncanny feeling, as if the perpetual observer to whom her husband addressed his asides and comic looks had slipped up and let itself be seen. She saw the curve of a stooped shoulder, a head of shaggy hair. My god, she thought, it couldn't be—? And then, as if catching her thought, as if playing a game, it was gone, stepping sideways out of view.

'Murray,' she said sharply. 'Murray, did you see that?' But Murray, turning in his seat, thought she was talking about the man who had just entered the restaurant, the man with the dreadful wound to his face, and he swung back around and told his wife, with sudden fierceness, that she would do well for once in her life to mind her own business.

Her feet ached from walking the floor all night, and her spine felt like a Slinky she'd once laboriously unwound as a child then tried in desperation to smush back together again. Some hitherto unknown intermediate lining between muscle and epidermis felt like it had worked itself loose and was rumpling and bunching in odd places on her body – but standing in one place made all of this worse so, even when Joanna returned from her office and began conferring with Loïc over the imminent arrival of the new diner, Kelly continued to circle the kitchen, pretending it was her dominion. This time of night, near the end of the shift but not near enough, the chefs always got fractious. She broke up a brewing tussle between Gareth and Finn. 'Ready-meal eater!' 'Garlic-press user!' What caused this altercation? Whose responsibility it was to buzz and pass the veg for the next plating. 'Cool it,' Kelly warned them. 'Fight in your own time,' and then she was imagining that, the two men wrestling it out on these slip-proof mats, or elsewhere – buck naked on sheepskin before a roaring hearth, say. Yeah, that'd do, she thought, file that one away, as she passed Nico dotting black plates with beads of dill mayo, Sprudge titivating his Synesso machine, Addy buffing another bottle of Puligny-Montrachet for the horrors on Six who were proving, through the application of breathy

159

quasi-flirtatiousness, fantastically upsellable-to. She looked in on Kima racking up her last meltdown of the evening as two dozen spherules of sorbet she'd left unattended slumped, one after the other, irremediably, into goop.

Since his return, bandaged John had clung – pure Stockholm syndrome – to Gareth, and now the senior chef was talking the commis through the last stage in prepping the pommes soufflés. Stacked up and ready for finishing, the slices of pre-cooked potato were pale gold, lightly blistered – like square little poppadoms, John unwisely thought aloud. 'You're a square little poppadom,' Gareth threw off. He yanked down and wadded a huge quantity of blue roll, polishing a fresh griddle pan until it shone and the paper was lustrously blackened.

'Oil's at three seventy-five now, Chef.'

'All righty. Bung a few in the wire basket there – not too many, crowd the oil and you'll cool it down too much – and then lower her in. Watch technique and technology come together and make something beautiful.' Gareth was so unguarded, so nakedly proud in the kitchen: Kelly knew you'd never catch him using a soppy word like beautiful anywhere but here.

Submerged in fizzing oil, the flat rectangles shivered, darkened, jostled – then expanded, one first then the rest of the batch, into golden orbs. 'Hup, quick, hock 'em out. See? Simple, which is kitchen talk for it takes your whole life to learn how to do them just right.' He looked over his shoulder at Kelly hovering. 'Didn't teach you that at your fancy academy, did they?' He rapped John's tongs on the nearest puffed potato, and it neither crumpled nor broke. 'That's some fine work there, son,' he mumbled, clapping an arm around John and lifting his elbow to nudge Kelly out of the way. 'Nice even sizes, perfectly cooked. You keep that up, we'll make a half-decent chef outta you yet. Right, next lot.' He reached for the wire basket on his own section, took hold of one of the topmost sous vide packages, ripped its perforated tag and squeezed its contents – red and off-raw, slobbery as after-birth – out on the heat, and the searing, the black whiff of meat smoke, sent Kelly away trying not to gag.

Through her mind flashed the memory of an infernal scene, a bonfire that licked the ceiling of the sky, silhouetted with dozens of crooked stakes – not wood but bone, the limbs of animals needlessly slaughtered.

More, then, all jumbled: an island on a black sea, beneath a black sky; steps hewn into the flank of the land, oozing mud and blighted roots, that led into the water. The old man with a rope around his neck, on the shoulders of the younger as he walked downwards, until one was submerged in water, the other suspended in air. Things she'd never seen, which meant she pictured them constantly. She forced them back, as she always did – harder at this time of night, when she too was worn down by aches and fatigue. Tonight, like every night, she was going to need a little pick-me-up.

When she looked around to check if she was being observed, she met cool impassive eyes: Finn. Because she liked him, she snapped at him: 'Got something to say? No? Well, jog on.' Unrattled, he turned away and continued his work, and the same instinct that made Kelly even now initial fresh-poured cement in the street or stomp dirt on anybody's box-fresh trainers made her imagine sinking her teeth into the flesh of his neck as you'd pretend to gnaw a baby's puffy arm. Maybe that would get his attention.

She tried too hard. I could have told her. She was always trying too hard, and he knew what that looked like. The teary solicitousness, the touch on the arm that stood in for words no one could find. Finn hated it all, he told me, and he liked that I'd not done any of that.

Unexpectedly seeing a face from work on your one day off is nobody's idea of a good time, and when I'd opened the door yesterday lunchtime to find him standing there on Grantham Street, his attempt at looking soulful and serious undermined by the rain that had drenched him, the first thing I'd said was: 'I'll kill Kima.'

'I would have called—'

'But my number's out of service, I know. Some dickhead stole my phone last week, or I lost it anyway, and I've had no time to get a new one yet. That was going to be my mission for the day. But now you're here.' I obviously still liked him, but I'd come to understand that for those few weeks in the summer, he had confused liking that I didn't really know him for liking *me*.

'I only asked her how I could get in touch. Don't blame her, I insisted.' Guileless, a kid in a man costume, rain cascading down his face. He had blue tape wound round three different fingers, a Care Bears plaster on a fourth. Someone else might have brought flowers, chocolates. Worn a proper coat. 'I need to talk to you.'

When I was alone in there, I could just about think of my room under the eaves as snug, but with Finn taking up space too it was abundantly clear that I lived in a cupboard. He couldn't stand up straight so instead sat gingerly on my bed – my only piece of furniture, which now I regretted – and the soft unsprung mattress all but swallowed him. 'This is ...' I suppose he'd planned to say 'nice', but been diverted by the psychotropic wallpaper, the naked bulb knotted back on itself like a noose, three of my four non-work outfits hanging from a metal bar set slantwise across a corner of the picture rail.

I blushed when he saw the green dress, as if he could sense where and when I'd been wearing it. '. . . characterful?' he tried, and I almost forgave him.

'Yeah, I know. But for the money it's . . . nah, it's still shit.'

'Money's actually what I wanted to talk to you about.' Give him credit, he did hate small talk. 'Look, I know it's not my place to say,' he began, and proceeded anyway. I'd been seen, he explained. Me and Eleanor, after work last Tuesday, hanging back while the others went up the alley towards night buses home or into town. She had pressed a roll of notes into my hand. 'Wow,' I'd been heard to say, 'wow. I mean, thanks. Who's up next?' Her head had tilted quizzically. 'Who am I, you know, meeting?' She hadn't spoken, but evidently I'd seen something in her expression that riled me. 'Why not? I did what you told me. I didn't break your big rule or anything. Not that it was hard. So what's the problem?'

'You were spying,' I accused Finn, and he waved his hands in denial. It wasn't him who'd been watching, but Kelly. Preoccupied by my argument with Eleanor, I hadn't seen her loitering in the doorway of the dodgy MOT garage at the corner, nor breaking cover to run straight to Pangaea and triumphantly blab to Finn what the person she smirkingly called his little friend was getting up to, the bad company I was keeping.

'Rule numero uno,' Eleanor had impressed on me a few weeks earlier, over sour cream-drizzled vareniki and kidney-shrivelling black coffee at an all-night Ukrainian on Kingsland Road, 'is that you don't sleep with the men.' I smirked, having an idea of what men used the service she was offering, and she rapped her nails on the melamine tabletop. 'I'm not kidding, ducks. And listen – I find out you've broken that rule, let's just say I'm not someone you want to fall out with.' But complying had, as I had expected, been easy. The first assignment I'd been given was dinner with Oscar, who each time he took a mouthful of food would close his eyes and start humming – not in appreciation, but like an electrical appliance. Over the main course he expanded to rocking back and forth a little in his chair too. He wore yellow corduroys, a red polo shirt, a mint-blue blazer, a scent that could only be described as musk. I had on the plain green dress – sleeveless, with a square neckline, dressy but not too dressy. We ate at a private members' club in Covent Garden where the staff addressed him respectfully by his surname, which I wasn't supposed to know. I wondered who or what the staff thought I was, if they could tell we were strangers, then decided I didn't care.

In the alley by the restaurant, while Kelly was watching and listening, Eleanor had lit a cigarette and was itemising the ways in which I had shown myself up. 'Oscar said he mentioned his dead wife twice and you didn't follow up.'

'I said I was sorry or whatever.' Eleanor looked reproving. 'It's not like I knew her. I thought we were going to talk about the world at large. I bought *The Week* like you told me, I read up specially. And what about the next guy?'

A week later, I'd travelled to a posh Indian in Berkeley Square to meet Asif, who worked in finance but whose true passion, he informed me without much passion that I could discern, was purchasing and refurbishing classic arcade games. He had ten or twelve in a lock-up at King's Cross, and he recounted several of their storylines, in some detail, as I scoffed aloo chaat, mutter paneer, lamb cutlets in a lip-smacking spice crust and the heat built and built in my mouth. It wasn't like at work where I amused myself by speculating about our guests' secret lives: these men were all too open. Like Oscar, Asif asked me no questions about myself, seemed neither knowledgeable or curious about anything beyond his immediate ambit – wanted not conversation, as Eleanor had insisted was the sole reason these men sought her services, but to feel he was being listened to.

'Asif says you weren't enthusiastic about his interests.'

'*Asif* wasn't enthusiastic about his interests. What was I meant to do?'

I could see her eyes roving over my face, the sheen of sweat on my skin, my hair lank with kitchen grease. 'The fact you have to ask, ducks, means you're not well-suited to this work. There's no shame in it. It's an unusual little skill set, and some people, maybe most people, don't have it. You have to be ready to play lover and therapist and best friend and sparring partner, to respond to people, bring them out if they're timid, show interest' – she tapped my arm – 'without being nosy. You have to find them fascinating, and that can be a tall order.'

I had never, it occurred to me, actually been fired from any job before. 'One more chance.' The banknotes I clutched weren't slippery like Australian currency but soft, worn, organic, and I wanted more of them. Wanted them enough to say, 'Please?'

'Eleanor's not what you think,' Finn told me. He got up, nearly striking his head on the ceiling, then paced around the room, which took all of about five seconds. I hadn't seen him this antsy before, and I was intrigued. 'She's unscrupulous. And she's tried this on people before, you know.'

'Tried what?' I wasn't quite sure how stupid he thought I was, but evidently he had me somewhere on the spectrum between endearingly unworldly and total imbecile.

'Look, if it's money you need—'

'I don't!' – an outright lie.

'You're being impossible,' he said. His tone was very slightly sharper than normal and I wondered if he was losing his temper – Finn, who never showed frustration when a reliable technique failed in the kitchen or someone screwed up and made him fall behind. 'I came here to help, because I care about you.'

'Yeah? Only I'm not sure your tone conveys that right now. What is it you actually want to say? Is there a name you want to call me?'

'I can see I'm wasting my time.'

'*Your* time!' Then there was some shouting on my part, which I regretted as soon as I remembered how noise carried in this house and who lived downstairs now. I told him to go, he claimed he'd been leaving anyway, and once his final childish slam of the front door had finished reverberating, I was right out on the road after him, heading to the crappy shopping mall a couple of streets away where I picked up a cheap pay-as-you-go mobile phone whose price tag still made me wince. If I'd had her number, I might have called Kelly. She wanted Finn? She was welcome to him. Let her crack his brittle shell and find out for herself what lay within: condescension, insecurity, all the usual boy stuff. Instead – fuck him – I dialled Eleanor and ranted until she acquiesced.

'One more chance. One *last* chance, and I'm not kidding. Because actually' – her tone changed – 'I might have just the job for you. Nice gent, bit older, and . . . refined. Refined is the word. Funny thing was he mentioned wanting to eat at Midgard, so I'll have to steer him away from that idea.' I heard papers rustling, pictured concertina files bulging with unlovable men. 'Now what was his name again?'

*

What I had never grasped was that Kelly had resented me since long before I'd beaten her, as she saw it, to Finn. It had started when she walked in on my interview in Joanna's office, where she'd seen the boss holding my hand while I pinched tears from my eyes with the other. It was like stepping in on a warped reenactment of her own interview, when the boss – Magnus, in those days – had clasped Kelly's hands and made his assurances; and as she stepped back and carefully closed the door she felt a pang of envy for which she'd never forgiven me.

What Joanna had told me, as Magnus had told Kelly years before, was that there were always options. Choices generated more choices, proliferating branches of possibility. Sometimes these futures, these different courses your life might take, braided together again in unexpected ways. In Kelly's case: if the truth – that the outbreak of foot-and-mouth disease across the UK fifteen years ago was eminently containable and treatable – hadn't been suppressed by drug companies keen to spread alarm about the epidemic and sell more remedies, then every animal on her parents' farm would not have been culled. Spared the consequent collapse in their livelihood, her mother mightn't have left and then her father might have lived, her brother the promising cook might not have followed him into suicide's long home. Then Kelly would never have felt the need to honour her brother by taking his place at the Academy. It was as she'd told Magnus, tearful with a gratitude that she found so shameful it only made her sob more: any of these things could have gone a different way, made her a different person. Maybe someone rudderless, naïve, easy prey. Somebody like me.

Kelly was the restaurant's weak link. She was *supposed* to be its weak link. She'd understood that ever since Magnus had tapped her for a job at Midgard over any number of her more deserving peers from the Ledley Academy. 'Why me?' she'd confronted him over the school's spotless demo counters. Because, he said cheerfully, she had the worst attitude of any student he'd encountered in the dozens of culinary schools he'd visited to meet the graduating classes. Because he'd been told she didn't even *like* food – ate Tangfastics for dinner and instant savoury rice, lurid yellow and speckled with unidentifiable red and green bits, for breakfast. Because, as her teachers' reports detailed, Kelly's consommés never clarified, her sauces always split and seized. He wanted her as waitstaff, he was quick to stress, not in his kitchen: he was kind-hearted, not soft-headed.

Like everyone, though, Magnus had wanted to know what she was doing at the Academy. By all of its many metrics, Kelly was a disaster, which she obviously comprehended, yet she didn't quit, but came back day after day to fail again. 'I'm here because I have to be,' she'd retorted. She'd had a little nibble on something that morning, enough to get her through the assessment – pills she'd swiped before her parents' farm was broken up and sold, the downers that had once been used to sedate the young sows after they had littered, since otherwise they had an upsetting tendency to devour their offspring. 'Not because I want to be. I didn't have a choice.'

Magnus's eyes had widened, bringing his face out in a whole new series of deep lines. 'Don't say that,' he said, leaning over the Academy's spotless counter, and there was such tenderness in his voice that even through the sedating effect of downers and her walls of aggressive off-handedness, Kelly felt the sensation she only otherwise got from rubbing her eyes after chopping chillies. Something in her opened to him – nothing definable, nothing bodily, god forbid – when he took her hand and told her, 'There are always options.' If she was being fair, she'd concede that it wasn't my fault that Joanna had been

168

saying the same to me, years later, but fair didn't come into it. Once in a while when she was particularly cross with me, she'd bust open my locker and scatter the contents on the floor, like a disgruntled house cat. She had been happy being Midgard's runt, likeliest to flake out and founder, and to see someone else take that role had made her panic, had made her despise me.

The changeover from Magnus to Joanna, the summer after Kelly's recruitment to the brigade, had been tough on her. Back then, she had only lately come to believe that she really did belong in this place where chefs didn't swear and bash each other up, but worked instead like sculptors or neurosurgeons. Where an amuse-bouche didn't mean a cheese football but a fake strawberry fashioned from a sculpted portion of roasted, vodka-soaked watermelon and dotted with toasted sesame seeds to produce something no punter had tasted before. And then, just when she'd got used to it, Magnus was out and Joanna was in. A restaurant's kitchen dealt in change – ingredients refigured, chemistry-lab transubstantiations, the conversion of a cooking-school reject into a poised and unflappable professional. Yet for Kelly personally, change had always been a negative, usually a euphemism for catastrophe. A change in policy: mass burnings the result. A dosage change in medication: death and more death. And so she braced herself for the worst.

And although almost nothing had changed in the way Midgard was run since then, the unsayable truth was that Kelly missed Magnus: she did back then and she still did tonight. The old boss had been temperamental, prone to unpredictable rages, painfully ill at ease in his own skin – the total inverse of Joanna's icy self-assuredness. He'd yelled, he'd been heavy-handed, he'd smashed plates and eviscerated staff so frequently and regularly it sometimes seemed he'd diarised it in advance. Joanna wasn't the same: Joanna had boundaries. Still Kelly missed Magnus's never more than two days' growth of frowsy beard and his frumpy outfits of double denim, recalled fondly the time she'd found him taking a nutmeg grater to a blue bucket hat to make it less pristine. And when she'd stumbled, Magnus hadn't hesitated to take Kelly into his home and to sit by her as she shook and ranted and sweated out the drugs. That had been cool of him. *He'd* been kind of cool, in his own totally uncool way. Sometimes she wanted to say that, but there was no one here now who would allow her to talk about it, least of all Joanna.

Kelly was like me. If she hadn't hated me on sight, I could have bonded with her on this: like her, I liked an older man. Not decrepit, but enough my senior to seem to have his life straight, everything the way he wanted it, all but this one remaining missing piece – to give the impression that, were I to be that piece, my life, too, would start slotting neatly together in the way it had so far failed to do. He'd had that air about him, my client, my third date, last night. His name. His name. What was it?

He'd taken me to a fiendishly expensive Japanese restaurant with a nightclubby ambience on Cavendish Square and lectured me, with good humour, on the dos and don'ts of such places. 'The ritual is paramount. The order in which we eat these dishes, and *how* we eat them. Never,' he corrected me, reaching to rest my chopsticks on the little glazed block beside my plate, 'point those at anyone. Very bad etiquette.'

'We don't have that where I'm from.'

'Australia, yes. What brought you to London?'

I couldn't remember Oscar or Asif asking me a single question, but this one had asked me straight off what I did and where I came from. My first answer was a lie – naturally I'd told him I was an actor – but I'd seen no point in answering the second dishonestly. I thought about the Gumbys manager's horrid Tic-Tac breath, the injury I'd inflicted, how I'd fled home with a bag of wholemeal rolls, but managed to stop thinking before I got to what happened next. No. Lifting the lid on the bin outside our block to check for fresh empties before I let myself in the front door. No, thanks. 'Long story,' I said.

'One word summary, then.'

'Bread.' I was being flippant but also wholly sincere, not that he knew. He laughed anyway, reading something into my reply I hadn't intended. The laugh lit me up more. I felt present here in a way I hadn't been used to since coming to London; already this was smoother, more fun, than the anxious dates I'd had with Finn. But then he said, 'You're not a smoker, are you?' and I was thrown because he'd asked me that before, and maybe he wasn't quite as present as I was.

He had a long face, high handsome cheekbones, steel-coloured hair that showed the neat tracks of a stiff comb. Fifty, maybe, I thought. Smart clothes, a tie – even a tiepin, something I'd never seen anyone wear before except on stage. These, his erect posture in his chair and his fastidious manners, seemed old-fashioned, yet he had a youthful and ready smile, even for my dud wit.

Food kept arriving non-stop. He'd ordered the chef's *omakase*, not condescending to explain to me what that meant. I tried to look like I knew anyway, that I wasn't fazed by the seemingly endless series of tiny dishes and bowls that were placed before us, these to be eaten in an ordained sequence: bowls of rich stock with shreds of green; neat cubes of gelatinous yellow; a conical pyramid of flavourless white mousse coated in tiny green dots that popped flavourlessly on my

171

tongue; a bowl of buff-coloured nuggets draped in a dewy web and disturbingly reminiscent of rotten teeth. While he transferred these into his mouth as speedily as decorum and chopsticks allowed, I could eat no more than one and chased away its flavour with a sliver of something Day-Glo pink that tasted, relatively pleasantly, of bathroom cleaner.

'It's called *nattō*,' my date said, indicating the bowl. 'Fermented soy beans. Fascinating thing, the soy bean – it's in oil and tofu, miso soup, the edamame we ate earlier. And soy sauce, of course. In a sense, this meal, perhaps all Japanese cuisine, is testament to the myriad ways one humble ingredient can be transformed.' He paused. 'I'm being pompous, aren't I?'

'A tad,' I said, pompously.

He laughed, rolled his glass in his hand. 'Has anyone ever told you you're delectable?'

'Not in as many words.' I'd had enough sake, nail varnish remover-smelling and lethally strong, to assume we were flirting. I didn't regret, now, begging Eleanor for this last chance – I had this in the bag, I reckoned, this guy would give me a rave.

The small dishes were cleared, the mess of droplets and crumbs mopped away from my place. In front of us, staff lit a short fat blue candle and positioned a metal trivet over it. 'Science experiment?' I wondered. 'Wait and see,' he said. Then, with great reverence, they placed on the stand a shallow pearlescent bowl containing a puck of tumid matter about four inches across, grey-black with a wet, mustard-yellow centre, half-immersed in dark liquid. It wasn't appetising to start with, and that was before I saw it twitch.

'Is that thing alive?'

'Not for long.' My squeamishness seemed to amuse him. 'Live abalone is a delicacy. We're honoured.' He dropped his

172

voice. 'Don't let on, but I don't think this can be from Japan.'
Like this was my main misgiving. 'Too late in the season.'

'Too late all round,' I said. Flame glistered the underside
of the mollusc's shell and the thing shifted again, trying to
escape the heat. Mercilessly, a waiter prodded it back into the
no doubt soy-based pool, from which steam was beginning to
curl. Twice more they played out this unequal contest before
the abalone gave a final dreadful quiver and was still. Gloved
hands dismantled the apparatus and used a serrated knife to
slice the mollusc into four fat strips. After all that, the result
tasted how I'd expected: like tyre rubber in a syrupy glaze.
This, apart from a bowl of vinegar-laced rice, was the finale of
the meal, which had been neat and simple and meagre enough
in portioning that I remembered wondering where I might stop
off for a second dinner on my way home. But as it happened—

As it happened, I—

A clock was ticking, and the Midgard team were plating
up. Through the circle in my vision – redder now, bigger,
angrier, two livid lines trailing from its lowest edge – I could
see Kima with an offset spatula laying strips of green gelat-
inised reduction onto seared blocks of meat, Gareth using a
dough scraper and a palette knife to square off the layers, John
affixing one crisp potato globe to the dod of mayo on each
plate, and Joanna, her one eye a jeweller's loupe, studying it
all, adjusting, finalising, approving.

Kelly's long loop had brought her back once more to
Gareth's station, now vacated. She stood before the space
where I was trapped – that impossible niche between counter
and freezer that sometimes felt chill and metallic, sometimes
coarse and yielding – and I was alarmed by her expression
because she, too, looked hungry.

I was hungry, I had been hungry. Come on, I berated
myself. You've remembered this much, now come *on*. But the

effort to recall felt physically debilitating. I went at it, went at it again. It had only been last night. I'd eaten all that Japanese food, but still I'd been thinking about getting chips on my way home, or shawarma, or chips *and* shawarma, something stodgy to absorb all that sake, and then—

But as it happened, I thought, with an effort that made the dull circle glow migrainous scarlet, I hadn't made it home at all, had I?

Ensuring no one was watching, Kelly went on tiptoes and groped along the top of the freezer until her fingertips closed on a cool hard object hidden there. It was stuck, and she scrabbled and batted at it until it finally came loose: a fist-sized block of glassy orange that glowed under the kitchen's halogens as if internally lit. She glanced at the pass and, seeing Joanna occupied, turned the object in her hands, scraped and prodded at it like a puzzle, her expression going from greedy to crestfallen as, whatever she was expecting the cube to do, it resisted. Eventually, in frustration, she began applying her tongue to it like an animal to a salt-lick.

'Kelly?'

She froze. Then slowly she turned, moving her prize from one hand to the next, keeping her body between the boss and the glistening thing.

'What you got there, pal? Don't be shy.'

In resignation, she held it out to Joanna. 'Cola cubes.' She tapped at them uselessly. 'They all sort of . . . fused together.'

That wouldn't have been a problem if it had been Magnus towering over her now, Kelly thought mutinously: the old boss would have smashed the thing to pieces, then her, and she'd have deserved it. Instead, Joanna's tone was chummy. 'What other contraband you got stashed around the place, eh?'

174

'Sherbet dip under the lockers. Minstrels behind the white wines in the stores.' Joanna said nothing. Kelly slumped. 'Jelly Tots in Loïc's desk drawer.'

'Uh-huh, uh-huh. And under the lid of the cistern in the staff loo?'

Head so bowed her chin bumped her clavicle as she spoke, Kelly whispered: 'A Curly Wurly.'

'You know the rule – you only get your sweets after the diners have finished theirs. Right now, I need you to go out and seat the new guy on Two, so put that thing down – Kelly? Kelly, listen – listen to me, Kels, take a breath now. You're not going out there with a face like a dropped pie. Before everyone disappears off tonight after shift, I want to see you in my office. I feel like we're well overdue one of our wee chats.'

A wee chat! Kelly almost skipped to the out-door, wrecked spine suddenly remarkably better. A dressing-down, a despairing shake of the head, a look deep into the eyes accompanying a heartfelt plea to tell the boss what was wrong – this was amazing. This was Christmas. She'd be under close observation for weeks now. Even if I happened to rock up to work tomorrow as though nothing had happened, Kelly wouldn't care, not now she was reinstated as the kitchen's official fuck-up.

Loïc was taking the new guest's overcoat, and Kelly waited for the maître d' to lead him to the table before she strutted out heel-toe to join him. She studied him sidelong: an older gent, tall, wearing a crisp white shirt and knit cardigan – clothes that were clearly expensive but unobtrusively so, Kelly judged, already weighing up her tip possibilities. Silver hair, aquiline nose, handsome; but then as she greeted him and he looked up at her, she saw the bruised eye socket with its purple-yellow halo, the pulpy wound down his cheek held together with little strips of sullied surgical tape. Knowing better than to comment on it, she gave her usual spiel – 'Have you dined with us before? No? Well, a few notes about our menu . . .' The team had reconfigured Two so that the guest would sit with eyes out, the other tables like so many TV shows for him to flick between. Addy came loping past, pressed into Kelly's hand the glass of champagne Midgard served gratis to its rare solo diners, intended to take the edge off their nervousness or compensate for whatever circumstance had brought them to dinner alone. 'It's rare for us to have a table free at this time of night,' she flattered. 'But lucky you, your name was next on our waiting list.'

'Lucky,' he echoed, 'yes', though he didn't sound entirely certain of it. His voice was deep and buttery.

Her instincts told Kelly that some incident was unfolding behind her, but she kept her eyes on the new guest, while also endeavouring to seem like she hadn't noticed the wound to his face. She went to spread his napkin over his lap, but he smoothly intercepted her and did it himself. 'And no allergies, is that right?'

'Certainly not,' he said, smirking maybe, or wincing from his injury. 'I eat everything.'

'That's what we like to hear. And can I check – because honestly, you wouldn't believe the lengths people would go to for a table here – your name?'

Behind her she heard knuckles on flesh, a yelp of pain. 'It's Jadwin,' he said.

Jadwin. In the kitchen I mouthed it along with him. And remembered.

I'd had a view of the Barbican every day when I still worked in Sean's café, knew there was a gallery and a theatre but had

176

never seen them. I hadn't, however, grasped until we were on our way there from Soho on Monday that there were flats in those two great notched concrete towers, that people could actually live there.

Jadwin's flat was on the fourteenth floor, and he led me at a brisk pace up spiral stairwells and along desolate concrete walkways that bristled with contradictory wayfinding signage. Brittle autumn leaves scudded past, collecting in corners with foil wrappers and other detritus. 'You must have got lost a lot when you first moved in,' I called from behind him, and he smiled tersely over his shoulder. The lining of his navy coat flashed peacock blue. A dog was barking from a floor above, one brilliant percussive shout every five seconds exactly, unnervingly precise, like maybe it wasn't a dog at all. Someone's actual net curtains actually twitched as we passed.

On the last landing, I held back to catch my breath while he unlocked his front door. Taking deep breaths of night air, I studied London from this new perspective. The night sky was orange-blue, the never-dark of the big city with the lights of three or four planes coming or going. Between distant towers I saw excavation under floodlight, the spindles of cranes building more towers, piercing red warning beacons at their peaks. I was feeling nervous anticipation, the first dull stirrings of the hangover to come, the squirmy pleasure of disobeying a rule – a nonsensical one, in my view. I was on my last strike with Eleanor anyway. What was she was going to do? Fire me?

'You're letting the cold in,' Jadwin's voice chastised, and I let him guide me into his home. Right away I stepped on a dodgy floorboard that moved beneath my foot, emitting a two-tone creak. He seemed to falter briefly before asking: 'What would you like to drink? Coffee? Tea?'

'Coffee's good. Those drinks were strong.' I really was tipsy, but I was also vamping a bit. 'I need to sober up.'

His kitchen was a galley, all white, long and so impractically narrow I could touch the sides without stretching. One long wall was lined with cupboards, a stove, the sink and the appliances, and at the far end there was a funny little flip-down table and two chairs, tucked beneath a set of high shelves. Jadwin had one of those coffee makers that uses little foil pods, which made me doubt the gourmet credentials he'd been at pains to establish at dinner. This wasn't a room for two, but I edged past him, scraped one of the chairs out and sat down. A calendar on the wall was open to an alpine scene but the boxes for October were mostly empty. The shelves overhead were also sparse – a few cookbooks, a wooden bowl containing a gloriously red pomegranate and a few bananas nearly past saving, and something I had to remark on.

'That's . . . quite the clock.'

'The clock?' He looked round, started on seeing the thing. He seemed more nervous than he had at dinner; I guessed he hadn't had anyone up here in a while. 'God. No, it's not. Not my taste at all.' Whose was it, then, I wondered, this gaudy little replica of the clock at Big Ben, giving off a theatrically emphatic tick as if to say: this is it, one more second gone, never to be seen again. 'It was a gift from my workmates. Well-meant, I suppose.' Ducking the metal hood overhanging the stove, he took a bottle of mineral water from the fridge and used it to fill the coffee machine. He caught my quizzical look. 'Have you never seen what London tap water does to copper pipes? Corrodes them. Water that eats right through metal. Just think what it must be doing to your insides.'

'Aha,' I said, instead of laughing.

'Milk? Sugar?'

'Both, sure. Long as they're safe for human consumption.'

Now I knew how ironic that quip had turned out to be, I wondered where the poison had been. Already in the mug he slotted beneath the coffee maker? Or had he used a syringe earlier to puncture the fresh carton of milk he opened in front of me? For the record, when I took the mug and sipped I tasted only the unpleasant bitterness I associated with all basic coffee, spoiled as I'd been by my years of café work and the ambrosia that Sprudge brewed at Midgard. I didn't register anything amiss. I didn't immediately start to feel displaced from my body.

'Let's sit soft,' Jadwin suggested. His living room was another long narrow capsule with a window at the far end, city lights diffuse through a scrim blind. A bookcase was crammed with paperbacks, a mishmash of genres: I saw romance, sci-fi, children's books. A small TV sat on a wooden cabinet, beside the remote and some trinkets: seashells, small ceramics and a framed sepia portrait of a woman who, in common with every photographic subject of her time, had a faraway look, a string of pearls, thick hair in an outmoded style. His mother, I supposed. Lucky him, feeling like he could have her on view.

I sat at one end of the miniscule couch which, despite his invitation, was finished in a slightly rough fabric. Jadwin stayed standing, sipping his drink and jouncing against the door frame. The silence was a little strained, and I was beginning to wonder if he didn't know how to make a move, when he asked: 'Does the name Catherine Eddowes mean anything to you?' My eyes went to the photograph in its oval frame. 'No, no.' He smiled, maybe a little sadly. 'What about Timothy McCoy? John Butkovich?' I shook my head. 'But you've heard of Jack the Ripper and John Wayne Gacy.'

'You mean the clown guy. From the song?' I'd finished my coffee and put the mug on the floor where he looked at it as if I'd done something much worse on the rug.

'You see, to me, that's so unjust. We remember the killer's name, never the names of the victims. Don't you think it's reprehensible that we write them off as if they weren't people themselves, with lives and dreams and stories of their own? Never mind their relationships, families, friends. We stamp them with that one little word, "victim", and immediately it eclipses everything else they did or were.'

'I guess.' My sense of drunkenness wasn't abating but worsening. 'Actually, it's pretty late, I might go.' I tried to stand and wasn't quite able. 'Or maybe I'll stay sitting a moment, huh?' There was something foreign in the corner of my eye – a stray lash, maybe, but when I blinked to try and clear it, the motion threw off sparkles that spread across my vision. I rubbed my eye, but that only seemed to multiply them.

'The frustrated actress, for instance, who dreams of the big city but, when she finally gets there, finds it too big, too lonely.' He stepped forward, and now whatever he'd laced my coffee with – I understood enough to understand I'd been spiked – was doing something wild to me, because all the elements that comprised him seemed to advance on me at different rates. They floated apart like layers in an animation: the neat grooves combed into his hair started to slither out of sync, the gleam of his tiepin moved before the jewel did, even the thumbprint smudge on one lens of his spectacles bore down on me before the gold frames could follow. I tried to look away, but couldn't quite remember how. As in a nightmare I sensed that when these disintegrated elements lined up again, they were going to form a dreadful new face, and then something awful was going to happen. 'Who came to London,' he suggested, from the far end of some tunnel, 'because it was geographically remote but culturally familiar. Who dreamed of attending a different West End play every night but soon found that she hadn't the time or the money to do even a tenth of what she'd hoped. I'm only surmising.' And yes, some of this I had described or hinted over dinner, but some of it I was sure he should not have known.

180

'Wuh,' I said. My tongue was flab. I snarfed in drool and tried again. 'Whaddya mean?' I wanted to get up, but the impulse no longer made it from slowed brain to torpid limb. Jadwin lurched or pounced or stole up on me and, with the gentlest motion of his hand, a brushing movement, kept me where I was. 'Now, now,' he rebuked me, and something was shifting beneath his words, a rasping like coins in an arcade machine or bronze scales churning over one another. My head sagged, rolled towards my left shoulder, and then I saw that he had pasted something on my bare bicep. A sticker, maybe, a red circle, like a buyer's mark. No, that wasn't it. It took me a while to figure it out. It wasn't that he had put something there – he'd taken something away. Whatever he'd dosed me with meant I didn't feel the pain of the wound, nor even panic, just watched with indifference as the circle trembled, filling up with blood.

He was there or he'd left the room. A smell was emanating from the direction of the kitchen, faint at first but now intensifying and becoming very familiar: Teflon cookware on a low steady flame, heat warping the air above the metal as it came to temperature.

Jadwin was right, I thought as my head tipped and I felt myself falling forwards, and forwards, and forwards. They'd remember him all right, for what he'd done: taking a life, that banal phrase – not the twenty years I'd lived but the life, all the lives, I might have gone on to lead. I glimpsed them as I tumbled – the dates I wouldn't go on, the lovers and children and careers I wouldn't have, the friends and enemies I'd never now make. All the limitless potential of me crushed down into one story, one line, one word. He'd be a headline, a mugshot, a byword for horror. And I would be nameless.

The circle was expanding to fill my vision. From its lowest edge, two tracks were rolling parallel lines down my arm.

It was going from red to black, and before it swallowed everything I felt one great slow pang of guilt move through me, a stifled shiver. For the first time since I'd come to London, I wished I'd found the guts to call home.

Table Six

'Back so soon, ducks? Nothing wrong, I hope. Won't be a mo, just getting it all nice for you – oh my days! What happened to you?'

If Owen answered, then the blood flowing from his nose, seeping now through his fingers, was going to get in his mouth. He shoved past the attendant's fussing and into the nearest cubicle, mule-kicked the stall door shut behind him, unravelled half the loo roll from the dispenser around the less gruesome of his hands and began to mop at his face. Blood on the floor tiles, blood on the toes of his shoes. The cubicle walls heaved and pulsed in time with the throb of his head. He wasn't too drunk to realise he was drunker than he'd thought.

'Tilt your head right back,' the querulous voice came through the door, which was starting to swing open again. 'Or is it forward? I've got painkillers out here if you need them, all colours and shapes and sizes.' Stumbling down the spiral staircase, Owen had noticed that the racket from the dining room, in which he thought he could make out his brother Brian's yawping laugh, had first receded then, quite abruptly, cut out. He'd thought that meant he was descending to some sanctuary, but of course they'd have someone stationed here, a witness. A woman.

Blood in the bowl too now, globules that blossomed and

spread and thinned, tainting the water. The thing about pain – how had he forgotten this? – was how *sore* it was. He dropped the scarlet paper in the water, flushed – stomach forward-flipping at the pink churn. A new roll had been pushed under the door. 'Can't stay in there for ever,' the attendant wheedled, and he flushed again, before the cistern had finished refilling, so that the noise would disguise him wishing aloud that she would fuck off.

Who said he couldn't stay here? He had form. The last time he and his brother Brian had been together in a restaurant Owen had pleaded a dodgy stomach to escape a grim meal and worse conversation. In truth, he had felt sick. Brian had picked an Italian trattoria whose website proclaimed it the oldest in England – which, if true, disproved the axiom that to have stayed open for a long time meant that a restaurant had to be doing something right. Laminated menus blistered with candle-scorch offered a choice of two starters: orange juice or tomato juice. A mixed salad arrived in a moat of vinegar; portions of lukewarm lasagne, made with an indeterminate meat, exuded a lurid oil onto dubiously clean plates. Over the entrance, above a neon sign on which fudgy dust lay thick, the glowing square of an electric flytrap had crackled with alarming regularity. Though their father had settled into his seat with a chuckle of apparent contentment, Owen had glared disapproval at his brother throughout. It was as if, knowing how little their diminished father was likely to eat, Brian had thought there was no point in selecting anywhere better than this: a place about which the best you could say was that the food wasn't technically inedible, bacteria were not teeming in visible number on the kitchen surfaces. At a certain point after the main course, Bob's eyes drifted shut, his shrunken head with its circlet of fine white hair drooped forward. 'Dad,' they said, swapping looks: not here, surely, not *now.* 'Dad!' Bob was motionless. Then a siren started up in the street outside and with an apnoeic snort he perked up, blinking. 'It's a police car,' he realised. 'I thought it was the start of "Rhapsody in Blue."' Nearer and nearer it came. 'Probably on their way to arrest the chef,' Owen said, earning a kicked shin from Brian. That was when, feeling an intestinal gurgle, he excused himself and rushed to Riccardelli's tiny hot lavatory. He was glad to trade the nerve-shredding squeal of the extractor fan and the successive waves of guilt and stomach cramps for ten blissfully solitary minutes, before Brian came to drag him back to the table. There, over spoonfuls of heartburn-inducing tiramisu, they explained to their frail father what they, the brothers, had decided was best for him.

It wasn't like Riccardelli's here, though. It was so cool and peaceful down in the basement, insulated from everything going on overhead. He sat on the toilet seat with one hand neat on each knee, tilting his head back until the thinning spot on his crown met the cold wall tiles, and waited for the room to stop scrolling. When he could delay no more, he stood and, with great reluctance, left the cubicle.

The wash-hand basins were set into a console at the far end of the long room, and there the attendant sat on a high stool, dabbing at a smartphone. Owen made a slow approach, trying to pick out a path by which he'd avoid seeing himself in the bank of mirrors above the sinks. The attendant was probably quite elderly – Owen had never been good at judging the ages of women. Her hair was fixed into a towering beehive of a colour not found in nature and she wore a collared, short-sleeved Chinese dress in red silk with a sinuous silver motif, a dragon or a serpent, and incongruously chunky sneakers, thick-soled and bright turquoise. 'Aha,' she cawed on seeing him. 'Told you you'd have to emerge sooner or later.'

'You've got powers,' Owen muttered – 'Pardon?' she rejoined

sharply before he'd even finished speaking. 'Come on then,' she said, levering herself down, 'let's have a butcher's. Feels worse than it looks, I expect.' She took his chin and rotated his head left to right. 'Not that it looks too clever.' He shook her off, ran a tap and rinsed his hands, then, after swallowing hard – that metallic aftertaste – confronted his reflection. Nostrils encrusted, a rime of blood in the stubble above his top lip; his cheeks flushed, his eyes bright with shock. 'Now, what can I find to help?' To the side of the line of sinks was a tiered unit stocked with miniatures of aftershaves and perfumes, mouthwashes and gums in various flavours, lip balms, cotton buds, emollient creams, pills in brown jars and foil strips, nail-clippers, toothpicks. 'Here, try a bit of this. Might sting a bit.' She dashed blue fluid into a round white pad then made to apply it, until Owen intervened. When he touched it to his nose the antiseptic's sear was, in that instant, worse than his initial injury. 'I shouldn't say this, but I was a bit relieved, actually, when I realised it was just a bloody nose you had. Nothing against you. But you came battering in again so urgently, I thought it might mean something nasty in the food. A place like this,' she said thoughtfully, 'could get shut down quicker than you can spell "E. coli".'

'What do you mean, again? This is my first time down here.' Owen looked cautiously at his face in the mirror: bloodied and blushing, but still him. 'You – ah, you must be thinking of my brother Brian. He paid a visit after the last course.'

'Before all the drama.' She pondered him. 'Yes, I can see it now, your older brother. Younger, I mean,' she corrected, seeing him about to protest. She wiggled her hand. 'Older, younger, past, future, I always get those confused. So what happened, ducks?'

'My brother. Brian.'

'Yes, you just said.' She leaned closer, and he noticed that beneath the caking of powder her skin was the colour of week-old bacon. 'Did you hit your head? Can you feel your brain okay?'

'No, I mean, he did this.' The attendant's face did the thing that heavily Botoxed faces did when called upon to express surprise. 'Well, it wasn't exactly his fault, but he was – instrumental. I have a condition, you see, we both do, that makes us bleed at the drop of a hat. It's genetic, something we inherited, a platelet disorder.'

'Disordered Platelets! There's a name for a restaurant. We should copyright that.' He didn't like that *we* – was too accustomed to being included, without consultation, in such plurals. 'So what was it, fraternal dispute between the blood brothers?'

'Sort of. We're both high up in the' – he faltered – 'in something my father established. Call it the family firm. And there's friction sometimes. I never wanted to be part of it. But it isn't the kind of thing you can walk out on.' Owen saw her eyes fix on the ring he wore, her brow furrow when she realised the design wasn't masonic as she'd expected but a stranger sigil, one that tickled at the back of people's minds, unplaceable to most. 'I don't know why I'm telling you this.'

'I must just have one of those faces.' She grinned grotesquely. 'So you want out now, do you? You want to pursue your dream. The artist thing.' He gawped at her and she cackled. 'Come on now, ducks. Who have we just established was down here a few minutes back? You wouldn't believe what folk tell me unprompted. They love spilling their guts, if you'll forgive the expression. Their fears, their desires, their appetites. I have,' she said again, 'one of those faces.'

'What use is an artist? That's what my father always said. He wanted his sons to be doctors, lawyers, accountants. He understood the structures that hold this world together and he

187

wanted his sons to have influence over them. To know how to use them to their advantage, and his. An artist doesn't know the secret loopholes in the tax system, an artist can't influence judicial rulings. What use is an artist? None, my father said. Give it up, he said. And he was . . .' Time and again, the blood spurting from his nose. 'Persuasive. We compromised. He said if I was so insistent on my doodling, I could go into planning.' Their father had been thinking ahead, even then needing to situate one of the brothers somewhere that might let him lean on the mayor's office to prevent a certain building in Fitzrovia being demolished. 'And so I sold my soul.'

'Figuratively speaking, of course. All right, let's see what you can do.'

'What?'

'Ducks, if you can tell a stranger like me that you wished you were an artist, then you're confident you have talent. No, don't go all bashful' – Owen instinctively starting to bow his head. 'Here, take one of these.' On the counter, beside the rack of medicaments, was a little stack of slim black journals Owen hadn't noticed before. 'My gift to you. And all I'd like in exchange is for you to do me a little original. You draw portraits, don't you? Let me do a two-minute pose for you to sketch. Then I can say I knew you before you were famous.'

'You're already more supportive than my own brothers have been.'

'Look at you with a pen in your pocket, all ready to go.' Balancing herself against her stool, she set her body con-trapposto and arranged her dreadful face into a faraway expression, a matinee star in a movie suppressed for reasons of taste. '"Brothers", plural. Big family, is it?'

'Like you wouldn't believe.' Owen found himself drawing with uncharacteristic fluidity, glancing only now and then at the page, attending more to his model: she resettled her shoulders, hitched her mouth a little, the familiar adjustments as fatigue pinched – familiar to him because lately, in secret, he had been attending evening classes in a cold little studio on Southampton Row.

'And so the nose,' she prompted, trying not to move her mouth. 'You didn't finish telling me. But there was an incident.'

'Our father had a vision,' their brother Len, the civil engineer, who'd flown in from Nairobi, had reminded the others between courses. 'We should honour it.' This was about two minutes before Owen had staggered to the stairs with hands over his streaming nose. The other brothers – Derek the conveyancer, Jacob the pilot, Patrick the teacher, Brian the politician – all nodded wisely. Owen hadn't meant to snort. Len swivelled towards him. 'Yes? Something to say? You've been grunting away like that all night, little brother, so let's hear what *you* think about all this.'

Bob was the sole patient being cared for in an officially decommissioned hospital on Mortimer Street. Its doors and windows were boarded and barricaded, its grounds protected by high fences and CCTV, and up on the sixth floor Bob lay in a squared-off bed, his powerless hands flat on a counterpane that barely tented over his emaciated body. The essential texts he needed with him at all times sat on his bedside, unconsulted in months. Silent surpliced women attended him, beringed hands changing his fluids, primping the pillow behind his unresponsive skull, adjusting the icon over his bed.

'You say Bob had a vision. I say he still does, a ton of them. There are birds in the curtains. At least one of the team attending him has wings folded away under her uniform. Those are the things he and he alone perceives now. Every night the

189

ceiling of the room opens like a gold eye and looks down on him and tells him it won't be long till he goes up to heaven.'

The others recoiled at the word.

'All right,' said Brian, 'that's enough.'

'Which you would know for yourself, Brian, by the way, if you could bring yourself to visit.'

The other brothers looked to Brian with uneasy expressions. 'Owen's just showing off,' he told them, flustered. 'He's been like this since we were boys.'

'I have,' Owen said eagerly, 'I have. Brian should know – we grew up together. We're the youngest, and we're as close as any two of us. And still, look how we turned out – one of us too scared to see our father on his deathbed, the other too scared to stay away.'

'Go outside and catch your breath, Owen, why don't you? Take a walk, before I do something I regret.'

Pitiful, Brian's attempt to channel their father's tone. Bob had never warned, Bob hadn't wasted time on understatement. His wrath flowed wild, unpredictable and terrifying, and its effect had been to sabotage his own plans; for if the coldness, the aloofness, the sudden blazing furies had been a strategy for moulding his sons into equally vicious men; or more, maybe – to create and perpetuate a cycle of generational abuse – then it had failed. Bob had instead broken them, leaving among his dozens of scions not one he would consider a worthy successor. Yet still they feigned zealous loyalty to his ideas, still they barked at one another in feeble imitation of their father's manner; and so, to prove that he too could do melodrama, Owen had risen to his feet then and said to his brother, 'Why don't you make me?'

'So he hits you,' said the attendant, moistening her dry lips.

'That was the stupid thing. He didn't even touch me.'

190

They had circled one another in a rageful slow dance, neither having any aptitude for fighting. 'He reached out – I'd like to think he was going to put his hands on my shoulders, then we'd both calm down. But then the Frenchman, your maître d', stepped in. I expect he thought my brother really was about to hit me, and so he went to grab Brian's hands, and so Brian swiped him away, and your guy took a step sideways and knocked right into me. Or into my nose. He barely even grazed me—'

'And the rest is haematology.' The attendant shook herself like a dog. 'Sorry, have to move a moment, I'm seizing up. And besides, getting a message.' She reached into the pocket of her dress, near the dragon's snarl, and slid out a phone. Something she read there prompted a subtle, complicated response: a raise of the eyebrows, a tiny shake of the head, a grimace that softened into a rueful smile, as if she'd received some long-expected bad news. Owen knew that look, Owen had practised that look in the mirror. 'Time's up,' she said. The hands of the clock behind her, however, didn't seem to have moved while Owen had been drawing. 'Let's see what you've got for me.'

What Owen had produced was not a portrait but a travesty. His hand, moving as though automatically, had detailed the internecine network of a traffic interchange, arteries and avenues fused into ganglionic clumps of matter, an overarching architecture of winged bone. The attendant shuffled up beside him, so close he could smell her haunted-house odour. 'Well,' she said. 'Well, well. No, don't apologise, I think you've really captured something there. A good draughtsman should be able to see the skull beneath the skin. And if most of them would *include* the skin, well, what's that but details. And isn't it true that a portrait says more about its maker than the sitter?' As she retreated to her counter, the long slit in her dress parted to expose legs like staves of swollen and worm-eaten wood, flesh so tormented it barely seemed possible she could walk at all, or that she did not howl in constant agony. 'Give or take,' she said, intercepting his horrified look. 'You should go upstairs now and finish your din-dins. But you should let your brother see what you've drawn there. Show him what's what. Talking of which.' She fossicked through her miniatures, rattled a small square tin at him. 'Breath mints, with a little extra ingredient, so that next time he visits the loos he'll be spending more than a penny, shall we say.'

'Isn't that a bit childish?'

The attendant paused. 'You're right, no need to be impetuous.' She popped the tin into his top pocket. 'The long game is the better one. Retaliation's a skill, it's' – she looked at him slyly – 'a craft. Wait till his guard's down and then pow! He won't know what's hit him. Yes, you're a man after my own heart, I can see that.' She patted her chest, reconsidered, tried the other side.

'No, I mean revenge. The whole notion of it. What good does it do to keep upping the ante? You go round and round, escalating, making everything worse. And nobody ever, ever wins.'

'What can I say? If it was me who'd been humiliated like you've been, I wouldn't be able to forgive the person who was responsible until he was reduced to ashes in front of me, and I wouldn't care how I had to go about it. Hypothetically, of course.' Her tone was savage, and Owen had a brief fear that she had been waiting for him here all night, an agent of his father's, testing the brothers, trying to turn them against one another. But it would never be a woman, not someone infirm like this. 'I can only speak for myself, of course. You don't seem to have the appetite. I can see it now, ducks, you're just a much better person than me.' It didn't sound like a compliment.

Back up the stairs, and again at a certain point – Owen ducked back a step or two to confirm – the noise of the dining room cut abruptly back in, as if play had been pressed on a recording. Something in the walls – some deadening, muffling technology. Always something in the walls.

The staircase wound spiral around the trunk of the ash tree. Even down here it didn't seem to be spreading out into roots. How long, Owen wondered, had it been here? The restaurant must have been built around it. Maybe – he played nervously with the ring on his finger – all of London had been. As he ascended, he let his palm run over its trunk, finding something consoling in the sensation of matter living yet inanimate, neither warm nor cold. Then his fingertips grazed something that was not bark, something that darted back when it felt his touch, hot and quick: an animal? He looked back, horrified that he might have been followed, but the stairs coiled empty down into the dark.

At their table, his brothers sat engrossed in conversation. Owen's napkin still lay balled on his chair where he'd left it; any time any of the others had previously got up, staff had materialised in almost the same instant to square the vacated seat to the table then, with tongs, remove the old napkin and replace it with a new one. Beyond the table, but close, tantalisingly close, was the front door. No one was looking, no one was watching or waiting for him to come back – he could slink across the room and out into the night. It would mean abandoning his coat and the two phones on the table, but he could do it. He could.

That was when he became aware of the figures that

encircled the room: the servers, with their armfuls of plates, the diffident gaze that watched without seeming to watch, the ready stillness as they waited for everyone to be seated before they proceeded. Mortified at the thought of inconveniencing them, Owen hastened back to his place. The brothers sprang guiltily apart and, although he'd resolved to try and say nothing for the remainder of the evening, he couldn't help but yelp, 'What?' There was a shared look on the others' faces, something complicated he couldn't interpret. 'Brian said something to you, didn't he? What did he say?'

'Topside,' announced their server, in a tone that made clear she was not going to wait for a lull in conversation, 'of Hertfordshire cow. Why am I saying cow, not beef? Because this is meat from a retired heifer who's spent her whole life ambling about chomping grass and calving, building up a wonderful deep grassy, milky taste distinctly different from beef. That luscious thick marbling you'll notice in the meat – that tells you what a long, pampered, easy later life she had. We age the meat a further six more weeks, which helps to bring out all that succulence and flavour, and then we cook her sous vide, nice and long and slow, in a special device which runs on hay harvested from the fields she once grazed. On top here you have a reduction of herbs and greens, all foraged from that same farm, and to the side of each plate you'll find pommes soufflés, a little bit of technical wizardry from our clever kitchen.'

'Retired heifer,' Brian said once she had left.

The others exchanged looks. 'Retired,' they agreed, 'heifer.' Owen was still awaiting his answer. Then, 'Oh, *baby*,' someone said and they lowered their faces, shovelling food from plate to mouth, reloading forks before they'd swallowed the current mouthful. They ate with the sloppy urgency of any group of men – guzzling, slurping, barely suppressing belches – and in instants those virtuosic globes of potato became shards tumbling in floppy mouths, swilled down with draughts of the expensive wine the wanton of a sommelier kept bringing. But they were not talking, and Owen tried to be mindful, tried to appreciate each precious moment of relative silence as he might paintings arranged along a gallery wall. Only he, in his mind, was capable of truly appreciating a meal like this, which was why he had booked Midgard in the first place – only he could marvel at the way the meat separated into long soft strings with the barest pressure of teeth, the flavour that recalled the butcher-shop's pleasant redolence of blood and sawdust. A wordless noise of satisfaction welled up in him, thankfully went unnoticed by the others. At the centre of each black plate, as they forked up more food, an emblem was gradually revealed, picked out in white glaze: a cow's skull, the stubby horns, the long craggy somehow lugubrious absence of face, memento mori, a notification on push.

When the call came, the bad call, the one they had all begun to brace for – the faces he'd tested in the mirror – it would fall to the eldest brother to try and formulate the new shape their family would take. It wouldn't hold, Owen knew, tonight had made that clear, and tomorrow he would do as he did every day: travel to the derelict hospital, go up in the cage lift until he reached the sixth floor where he would dismiss the mothers. This time he would go without fear. Alone with his father, he would recount every beating Bob had dealt out, every bloody injury he'd inflicted, all in the name of brother-hood. Who knew how much of it the old man heard? He never stirred, would never come alive and reach for Owen's throat in retaliation. Those days were gone.

The brothers had been raised with the assurance – the warning – that their father would never die, but this length-ening senescence, this death in life, was not what Owen, at least, had envisaged. Tomorrow, then, he would lean forward and slip one of the attendant's breath mints between Bob's thin dry lips. He'd right the inverted cross on the wall above the old man's bed, then take his seat again and start to sketch the great unfolding wings, the gold blaze, the terrible suffering of the ascent.

Six courses served, one more to go, then the teas and coffees, digestifs and petits fours. A nasty thought was worming into my aching head as the evening wore on and wore down. After the shepherding of any guests reluctant to leave would come what Joanna liked to call her end-of-shift post-mortem, though I hoped she would not tonight: notes on tonight's service, first instructions towards tomorrow's, before someone asked, inevitably: 'Who's up for a swift half?' A little after midnight, only a couple of hours from now, she'd do one last walkthrough, double checking everything was switched off or left on overnight as needed, before locking the doors and trudging up the alley to the main road, hunched shadow gigantic under streetlight. And then – then it would just be me, all alone in the cold blue dark, my only company the hum of the machines and the skitter of vermin undeterred by all our attempts to rout them. I didn't want that. And I did not want to fade to nothing, as I feared I might, when the last light went out.

The restaurant was spooky when it emptied out. I'd seen it myself only a few months ago, when I'd lingered behind after one of our test kitchen days, telling the others I would catch them up. Attendance at these sessions was encouraged, meaning mandatory, even though it meant losing one day off out of every four. The pay-off for the kitchen nerds was getting to try new ingredients they'd sourced, each trying to upstage the other. I was offered things I'd never even heard of before: loquats, amchoor, friar's beard, knistazoon – I stuck out my tongue and tried them all. The last was just Pop Rocks. Here we could play with ozoners, electrolysers, a device that could pick every drupelet from a raspberry, another that would break them down into gel, a third that would spherify that into little crimson beads that were, pretty much, the same drupes again, only this time without the annoying little seeds, and tasting of the raspberriest raspberry possible.

Sometimes the things the chefs concocted here were unbelievable. One afternoon Addy had filled a centrifuge with banana peels and set it orbiting, the clarified oils she collected forming the basis of a rum cocktail that won the restaurant – not her – an industry award. There was cheese made, if I'd understood Gareth right, by cultivating the blue mould that grew on used lemon rinds, and which had, after many months of refinements, made it on to our menu. Other times the experiment was a bust, like a fermented egg that tasted like drinking cherry cola through an old sock.

At these monthly sessions I learned that what my colleagues and I served to diners was the end result of a process that originated not in the kitchen with the chefs who cooked and constructed each dish, not with the *mise* they set up hours before service started, not even with the produce that was delivered to the restaurant. It began with a farmer, a crop, the acidity of a certain patch of soil, last year's rainfall. The puffed potato that vanished in a snap of the diner's jaws hadn't taken a couple of hours to create, but months of research into crop varieties, taste tests, meetings and negotiations with growers and suppliers. Joanna wanted to impress on us that though the servers came in right at the end of this process, we were also crucial to it.

Foliage hung from an armature over the demo table, airdrying in the updraft. Metal library shelves lined the back of the room, laden with pouches, tubs, tins, boxes and bottles. There were vac-sealed containers of ground and whole herbs, seeds, spices, pollens; mason jars containing experiments-in-progress in pickling, ambiguous objects in murky brines; slender glass vessels containing sixty-five different salts – I counted – of varying hues, from black to puce to opal; dried chillies on a heat spectrum from undetectable to call-the-doctor; a colossal jar of Werther's Originals. Here and there were the relics of half-ideas for novel ways to serve dishes, abandoned or awaiting the spark of inspiration to take them forward, like a rollercoaster affair that was meant to conduct petits fours around the table, if only the motor could be made to run more quietly, and an inflatable, edible pillow on which we might present jewellery made from solution-grown fruit crystals.

The test kitchen was where we heard and entertained impossible dreams, an anything-goes group therapy session. Flavour-infused cutlery. Certain musical sequences that could increase diners' salivation and make them hungrier. 'I'd like,' I remembered Joanna declaring towards the end of the session, 'to sow crops on the moon. Picture it, vast fields of grain in the Sea of Tranquillity, all waving in the solar breeze.'

'Alien corn,' said Nico, who had come to Midgard direct from an English Lit degree.

'Moonflour. Moonbread. That'd be something the competition wouldn't have.'

'Impossible,' Loïc intoned, and Joanna rounded on him. Instead of anger, though, her face showed a strange malevolent smirk. 'Now, now. Don't go getting shirty.' He glared, fell silent, said nothing the rest of the session.

199

Test kitchen days ended around four o'clock but the team treated it like a regular midnight: 'Heading home?' 'Yeah, in a bit maybe.' 'One for the road?' 'Pangaea?' 'Course.'

'I'll follow you in a minute or two,' I said that particular time. 'Something I need to finish up here.' Nobody questioned this vague excuse because it was the kind of thing you said when you were actually hanging back to speak to Joanna or had been summoned for one of her wee chats. Instead, I waited until I heard her locking up, then stole over to the wine store on the far side of the demo table.

Means, motive, opportunity. I knew that on Tuesday I would overhear, or be press-ganged into, the cross-checking of what bottles our database said we had in stock versus what was actually laid down in the stores. It was the fact that these figures never quite tallied – something was always missing, overlooked or misrecorded – that put the idea in my head. Like any clued-up customer, I went not for the cheapest but the second cheapest wine on our menu: a Syrah from Gayfield Estates, one of our top sellers. I'd poured dozens, hundreds of glasses of this for diners, and it was plausible we might lose track of how many bottles we had in stock. I slid the bottle from its place in the rack, padded back through into the test kitchen and had crouched down behind the demo table to slip the bottle into my backpack when I heard a voice from the kitchen below. Someone had come back to the restaurant. Remembering those old stories about her having nowhere else to go, I assumed it must be Joanna – until I heard what was undeniably a lighter tread than hers jog up the stairs to the test kitchen. I shrank further into myself as I heard someone moving about, the clink of glass, the footsteps descending again.

I strained to hear the voice from the kitchen below. 'Barbaric, the way they did it in them days.' Eleanor, unmistakably. Talking on the phone, maybe? But I was sure those had not been her footsteps on the stairs. 'They had this big, thick red rubber hose that they left to soak in boiling water while I lay there in terror.' A faint shushing sound then, mechanical, like gas escaping a pressurised canister, followed by a few seconds of a faint gulping. 'They put our sort in the basement of the hospital, out of sight, all the nearer to hell, and no lie, it was infernal down there. No windows, no proper ventilation, and the steam-heating all those old buildings have in New York hissing and flaring through the lead pipes. Yes, it's the heat I remember most of all. Sweat coming from my pores and lungs, sweat covering the walls and banging around in the plumbing. And then I stopped even thinking about it, because that was when they lifted the red hose out the water, all nice and flexible now, and fed it, inch by inch, into my you-know-where. It coiled into me ever so neatly, like a snake into a burrow. And then they left me alone, scared out of my wits, and as that nice flexible hose cooled all its curves grew sharp edges. And that was that. I'm editing, you understand, because I was in there for hours, floating above my body as it forced out everything unwanted. I was swearing the place down, cursing them, cursing the careless idiot who'd got me into this, cursing myself since I wasn't exactly blame-free. And I tried not to look at what was happening between my legs, but you have to, sometimes, don't you? You have to see the worst thing in the world.'

I was stuck in an awkward half-kneel. I wanted to straighten up, but recently my knees had started making gristly popping noises when I stood from crouching, the decrepit joints of twenty-something waitstaff. In this quiet room they'd sound like gunshots.

'You don't like hearing about this, do you, ducks? *Women's issues*. I can see it in your face. Your mouth's gone all prissy.' So

201

there was someone else with her. 'I bet you've just got a smooth bump down there yourself. But we promised we'd talk about you. How did they get you?'

'It was Joanna. I can say she saved my life.' And that, just as distinctive, was Loïc, a voice for which the word 'mellifluous' might have been coined.

'Now isn't that typical.' Eleanor's voice was not mellifluous. It was a scissor scraping clumped matter from a blocked plughole. 'Isn't that just textbook. In Paris, was this?'

'Paris also has buried secrets. One day it was decided: no, this is a rational city. Everything must be straight lines and circles, we will have one approved style of building, everything must be consistent. I had come to Paris from the country and I saw this consistency in the brasseries where I worked: six months in Chez Christophe, six in Chez Marc, six in Chez Albert – not only similar names, but the décor in each the same, the clientele, the wine lists. More than once, I went by mistake to the wrong establishment, forgetting I had moved on. And most similar of all were the menus – always the steak tartare, always the *soupe à l'oignon*, always the *îles flottantes*, and each one prepared according to the venerable recipe that was exclusive to this establishment, yet indistinguishable from that of the next.

'And all the time I too was making myself fit with the city – wearing the more appropriate clothes, disguising a little better my country way of talking. I fashioned myself into a good Parisian and an even better maître d'. I knew this because after three or four years I was no longer pursuing work, but being pursued. This is how I came to my most prestigious posting as maître d' in Paris, at Chez Raymond in the fifth arrondissement. Where I met the boys.'

This was some speech from a man usually terse to the point of rudeness, who most often murmured one solitary keyword as he passed us in the dining room: 'Spine' to make me straighten my shoulders, lengthen my back, stand tall; 'Shoes' if he detected the slightest slur of sole on carpet.

'I had worked hard to conceal my true self. The village where I originated was not where a maître d' of my calibre could admit to having been born – a place where bread and fruit were still delivered by van once a week only, where a satellite dish on a house was a novelty to some but an object of fear for others. But these two banlieue boys, the waiters, nephews of the chef, they recognised all of this the instant I arrived. They knew I was an inferior, an outsider, masquerading. It was the way they spoke to me, explaining to me the Métro or a computer as if they addressed a bumpkin.' Oh, I thrilled to how he said that. 'I can feel shame for my origins, but I will not permit others to try to force shame upon me. Every day I was being undermined by those who should have been showing me respect. They did not accept discipline from me, yet as relatives of the restaurant owner I doubted they could be made to leave. And so I found another way to operate. They used shame as a weapon, which meant they had pride, though it was hard to imagine in what. They were stupid boys in unrewarding jobs. And yet each Friday night I saw them walk outside to meet their plain girlfriends, how they grew jealous if they saw these girls glance at me. And so . . .'

He was silent, but must have made some illustrative gesture, because Eleanor said in surprise: 'You didn't. You did? You devil. What, both of them?'

'Of course.'

'One at a time, or—?'

'I,' he said, scandalised, 'did not participate. I had them perform for me. I am not unaware,' with a subtle little cough of immodesty, 'of the power my appearance can wield. It can inspire others to make compromises. My satisfaction was in knowing that in their effort to please a man who despised them, they had engaged in acts they never would otherwise, things they would not forget. They would give themselves away – the boys would sense something, there would be hostile silences, reprisals. Two unpleasant hours in their company was a small price for despoiling the lives of four people for whom I felt only contempt.'

'Now, if it were me, I'd have made it so that your two nemeses ended up raising children that bore the oddest resemblance to their old pal Loïc.' She pronounced his name to rhyme with 'hoick'; I could almost hear him wince. 'But then that's my own preoccupation. And then, you do only have a bump down there.'

'Now the boys no longer met their women on Friday nights, I was waiting for their reaction. To my surprise they proved more patient, more conniving, than I had anticipated. Weeks went by and they treated me to no more than their customary insults, which no longer offended me. I speculated that in their disgrace the girls had not even mentioned my name. But no. They were simply waiting until, on another Friday night, they struck. The restaurant had closed. They handed me a tray of unused produce from the kitchen and told me to return it to the cold store at the back of the kitchen. This was not a refrigerator as we have here but an entire room, the size of an elevator or, perhaps, as I realised when I heard the bolt drawn across the door behind me, a jail cell. Their faces were leering in through the narrow window, mouthing. I could not hear but I understood quite well that this was my punishment, to be locked away in freezing temperatures until the first staff arrived tomorrow to release me. If I survived the night.

'I first tried to find a way to force the door, but I knew that the lock was solid, designed to prevent any person breaking in to the stores – no thought had been given to anybody wishing to get out. And what tools had I here? Fruits, vegetables, plucked poultry with skin pimpled and blue like my own now. Cold air was rushing through the tiny vents above my head, and already I was shivering and felt that I was losing sensation in my fingers. I knew I should keep moving, but it was impossible.'

'You want to give up, don't you? You want to surrender. That voice is loud in your head. But there's the other voice that says: "Really? You're going to let that guy win?"'

'The guy . . .?'

'Sorry, ducks, I was talking about me. I meant the father. The unfather.'

My thighs, my knees, my ankles were bright with pain. If I stayed like this any longer my muscles might spasm or give out, sending me crashing over and giving me away. All that gave me hope was that noise I heard again: the release of gas that petered off in a flatulent burble and the dribble of liquid into glass. It was the sound of the kitchen gadget that inserted a long fine needle right through a wine cork so we could serve a diner a single glass of an especially expensive wine without unsealing the whole bottle. I could picture it now, Eleanor and Loïc helping themselves to a priceless half-pour here, another there. They'd found a more refined technique than I had, but we were all committing the same petty crime.

'You don't need to tell me about cold, ducks. You don't know the meaning till you've been in New York in January. Picture me not dressed for sub-zero at all, limping back to the East Village, thinking at any moment I was going to haemorrhage and fall down there among the mounds of frozen garbage and black slush all melded together on street corners, the junkies sticking their arms in through holes in the brickwork to get what they needed. For the first time I could understand why they did it. Christmas lights still up on the avenues, flashing like little emergencies in every window. I made it into my apartment – no mean feat, that, five flights of stairs the state I was in – then passed out. When I woke up, forty-eighty hours had passed, my skull was in a vice and the mattress was like a crime scene. I had one thought in my head, and it wasn't a nice one. You ever been to New York, ducks? No? Well, don't. Anything that used to be good is gone, anything that used to be bad is ten times worse. And worst of all is the subway. You get antsy here when a train's more than three minutes away? Standing there fretting in your nice clean brightly lit station where no one's waving a knife at you or taking a shit on the platform, or both simultaneously, why not. The New York subway is where you go when you have nowhere else. When even filthy street level is too much. You know when it's the right time, when you can hear it calling you, through all the city's other noise. I knew. I was delirious and faint with blood loss, but I knew. From one subterranean to another, first that hospital cellar, then the even hotter, even more vile station at Astor Place. The green girders robed in soot so thick it looked like velvet. All the people waiting there – who might have been waiting for that downtown Six for a minute or a week. No such things as timers and countdowns there, no money for that sort of frippery. And me hunching along making my little keening, hands laced over my belly, not sure what I was thinking, all the way to the end of the platform and then, without hesitation, stepping around the little metal guardrail and down those three painful jarring steps to the tracks and into the dark tunnel. It felt right. It felt like home. Nobody called after me, no alarms went off. The city that doesn't sleep? Oh no, oh no, it's asleep on its feet. The city that doesn't care.'

'But this is not right.'

'Ducks, I'm not sure you've caught my drift – nothing

was right about me at that time. And there's one person to blame—'

'No, not your ... condition. I, too, made a descent. This is also my story.'

'You were locked in a freezer, was what I heard. You weren't going anywhere. Did I miss an episode?'

'I was trapped, yes. I huddled down at the back of the room, far away from the cold-air vents. Instead of moving I aimed to make myself small, conserve energy, be like an animal in winter. The tiled wall I leaned against was so cold that I could not sit still. I found myself rocking, bumping my spine against the surface behind me. One knock per second, trying to count out the minutes, the hours till dawn, but I had to keep starting again. My brain was slowing. So I do not know how long I had been rocking like this when I felt it – something yield in the wall behind me. I pressed the soles of my shoes to the floor, pushed back more with more force, and again I felt the wall definitely move. On its far side, I knew, was the alley for our trash – there must once have been a door here that had been sealed up. The thought gave me the energy to climb to my feet and begin to throw myself against the wall, again and again. I sweated, and the sweat chilled instantly in the cold, making me shiver harder, but finally I felt something rupture behind the tiles, plasterboard or masonry, and a gap opened up between them, floor to head-height, a centimetre or two. Dust flushed in. I pushed my fingers into the gap, shoved and shoved until it moved again, opened a little further. Over and over I did this, until finally I had made a gap wide enough to see through, even force my body through. But what I saw was not streetlight. I saw a tunnel, rock walls, a series of rough stone steps descending into darkness. And the air there was warm, stagnant, with a vegetable smell I could not identify. Of course it was impossible. But it was more impossible to stay in the cold store.'

'And so down you went.'

'There was hardly any light, but there was light – a sheen of it in the walls. Some variety of fungus, maybe, since that musty smell resembled the fragrance of truffles. The stairs were uneven and I stumbled frequently as I made my way down, grazing myself on the rough walls. But all the time the air was growing warmer, until I could feel my body properly again. The stairs went straight, then turned suddenly, or there would be a series of twists, but down, always down. Vibrations from the Métro passed first beneath, then beside, finally above me. And then I was hearing ... other sounds. I imagined this was my mind occupying the silence, the idea of noise. Of metal striking metal, of forgework, heavy industry. But it seemed real. And now the air was not warm but hot. I perspired. I removed first my jacket, then my shirt.'

'Course you did. Let me file that image away somewhere for later.'

'The clamour was increasing. And now there was certainly light ahead of me, and I heard the blare of a factory klaxon. Activity, down here, so far beneath the ground. I remembered childhood stories of creatures that dwelled beneath the ground – myths of workshops where little men forged the weapons of the gods. I put such infantile nonsense from my mind. And then I turned one last corner, and I saw it.

'It was a cave, or something like an amphitheatre, of vast size, though its full dimensions were impossible to determine because of the thick black smoke that hung like clouds around its upper levels. Like the tunnel that had led me here, its walls were raw rock, as though it had been hollowed out of the earth itself. It stank of fire and meat and a peculiar sharp smell that I later understood was the sweat of bodies worked to exhaustion, and bodies worse than that.

'I staggered out onto the floor of it, and through the haze

I started to discern shapes, great metal hulks – towers and clusters of filthy machinery, vast in scale, arranged according to no pattern that I could see but resembling urban sprawl, an evil reflection of the rational metropolis above. The heat originated from vast black ovens, an inferno in each one roaring up higher than a man. The noise was incredible – a clattering, hammering, hissing, thundering that could not possibly get louder, so I thought, yet as I approached did indeed become deafening. How was it possible that this could not be heard on the streets above? I crossed the boundary and entered the streets of this metal city where I saw silos, cauldrons, long steel trestles like mortuary slabs. And, though I was so awed it took me time to see them, people dwelled here also.

'A gigantic lever shifted from off to on, and I realised that three figures had worked together to haul it into position. A huge disc was guided into a roaring furnace on a metal paddle it took half a dozen to manoeuvre, cowering back from the flames. They were men, stunted, starved and dressed in rags, dwarfed so completely by the enormous machines they tended that they seemed not quite human but of some other species. I tried to speak to one man, but he did not acknowledge my question, pushing past instead to a container the length of an articulated vehicle, heaped with torpedo-shaped objects in crackling brown wrapping. I shook my head, dispelling the idea I had first had on seeing them, that they were shallots, vast numbers of shallots. Absurd. Then the man lifted a metal cleaver, and he begin to chop. I had not been wrong. They were shallots. That was when I started to suspect what I had stumbled upon. A kitchen. A kitchen as big as the village where I had grown up, with two main streets running at right angles and numerous side alleys. And these exhausted, gaunt men were cooking the dishes that formed Paris's eternal menu, on offer at every one of our bistros and brasseries as they always had been, always would be. A dreadful voice was issu-ing orders – "*Bistrot Les Quat'Sasoins, huitième arrondissement, magret de canard. Léon de Bruxelles, dix-septième, escargots de Bourgogne. Le Ryss, onzième, deux soupes de poisson.*" I saw cooks peeling rabbits from their skins like slipping a glove from a hand, piling up the little pink bodies. Teams of men *haché*-ing vast scarlet sides of meat for tartare. Molten lakes of mother sauces, bubbling and slopping. When plates were finished, porters would clamp them under cloche and run to one of the stations that stood on every corner of the metal city, posting them into hatches in what I had thought must be cooling towers but which, I realised, became a network of metal tubes, far overhead, that whirled the plates to whichever establishment had ordered them.

'The voice had changed. It had now a note of panic. "*Le Ryss, deux soupes de poissones. Vitement!*" I retraced my steps, sure I had passed a reservoir of bisque a few streets earlier – and here it was, bubbles breaking on a great pool of pink-orange sludge, and on the floor nearby the collapsed body of one of the cooks, half-buried in smashed shells, lobster and langoustine. His skin was yellow and dry, his lips had retracted from his teeth like a horse and a foam issued from between them. I did not know if he was dead or if he lived, and it did not matter – the important thing was that I should do what any member of staff would in this scenario, and I prised the ladle from the fallen man's hand, took two dishes from the stack by the cauldron and dished up. Before I could call for a porter they had been taken from me and the voice was booming again to demand four more, *Chez Yvonne, quatrième arrondissement*, then another, then three more. The orders kept being called and I kept serving. I was a mechanism, a tiny component in this dreadnought machine, as were the individuals who stoked the cooking fires and shovelled in ingredients to feed the bisque and either revived or disposed of the fallen man, I did not see which. For me now there was no before, no after – I had always been here, I always would be. Above ground our national cuisine was ageless and unchanging, like a figure in a fairy tale, and we workers were continually casting the spell that kept it so. We were working a foundational magic that had been driven out and driven down by the city's rationalisation, a secret buried below even the other unspeakables of the modern city, its cisterns and cemeteries – but never totally destroyed, indeed indestructible.

'How long did I labour without rest? Long enough that when it came time to move, my legs buckled. For through the clamour I had heard something familiar, "Chez Raymond", like one's own name called in a crowd, and in that moment I recovered a little of myself, some lingering shred that was Loïc and not simply the component this factory needed me to be. A few minutes more and I might not have known the name of my former employer, and later it came to me that this might explain why our restaurants had such generic names. But in that moment I reacted with pure instinct and staggered away down the nearest alleyway, shouldering aside the men who moments earlier had been my fellows and who now I despised for their weakness. Flames blurted from the lowered drawbridges of ovens, blades struck sparks from every surface I passed, and I dodged and stumbled and crawled through the streets of the cursed city, guided in my path by the very gradual dwindling of the cacophony, the almost imperceptible cooling of the temperature, until I broke from the outskirts and could see ahead of me, impossibly far off, the great rough stone wall with its veins of glimmering minerals that formed the perimeter of this world. I raced for it, expecting at any moment to feel clawed hands haul me back. When I reached the wall I pressed myself to it, felt my way along it like a blind man – grazing and scraping and bruising my tortured body – until my bloodied fingers found an edge, a corner, an exit. I collapsed onto the first few steps, grime and sweat in my eyes, then grappled at the rock, pulling myself forwards and upwards, marshalling what little stamina I still possessed. I tried not to give in to the fear that many hundreds of such tunnels must lead from the distant city above, that I might expend the last of my energy reaching a door that did not open. Up and up I struggled, my ears starting to pop with pressure, hearing once again the reassuring vibrations of passing trains. Up, up, until I felt the smooth cold unyielding steel of the door back to Chez Raymond, the gap I had made sealed now, the metal offering not even a fingerhold.

'But now I hammered. I beat my hands raw as meat. I screamed that the boys had won, that I would depart the restaurant, the city, return to my provincial roots. My blows were as feeble as the swipes of a kitten's paws, and yet they seemed to be having an effect, the door reverberating from the impacts, until I realised that some other force was acting upon it, some impetus from the far side. I felt a sudden terror that if it opened I might be propelled into some other, even more hellish world. I stepped back, retreating into the dark, and finally the door burst open. I saw a figure silhouetted against what was unmistakably the cold store of Chez Raymond, in daylight now, the door to the restaurant wide open again, and I flew back up the last steps, tripped, sprawled at the feet of my rescuer.

'The first thing I saw was a pair of blue suede boots. The rolled cuffs of blue jeans. I looked up, and up still more, for my rescuer was an exceptionally tall woman. She was dressed all in blue, and above her silk scarf was a face I did not know but which would, in time, become very familiar. There was nothing yet unusual, in those days, about her eyes. When her lips moved I feared my hearing had sustained permanent damage, for only inhuman noises seemed to emerge, until I realised she was attempting to speak my language in the most horrible accent: *"Eska vooz allay be-an?"'*

'A little later, after I had been given different clothes and she had fed me – I insisted on a dim sum restaurant, I did not want to see my cuisine again – she explained that she had come to Paris in search of the city's greatest maître d'. "I want you to come and work with me. There is nobody better in the world for this job." Naturally I accepted, to get away from what I had experienced in Paris. But I was not flattered. No. Why? Because I understood that we would always share that first encounter. We both knew that she had seen me at my moment of greatest weakness, even if we never spoke of it again. And I have not. But she – she will say some little word now and then to show she has never forgotten my moment of vulnerability.'

'Your shame,' Eleanor chipped in, and I heard Loïc exhale in reluctant agreement. 'And you hate someone having that hold over you. You'd do anything to erase it.'

'I am who I am now, not who I used to be. My whole life I have been trying to reinvent. But how can I feel that I have moved on and changed when there is a person who can with one word take me back down to where I was? A man who cringed on the floor and sobbed, a victim.'

'Yeah, that sounds about right. We're very alike, you and me, you know.'

Loïc said nothing, but it was *how* he said nothing – I detected a quality of speechlessness. But this, I'd realised later when she got to me in the same way, was how Eleanor operated: she'd pal along with you for a while, learning about you, locating your flaw – my poverty, Loïc's lasting enmity – then she'd force the short blade of her curiosity in there and shuck you open to get at what she wanted. 'I was the same way. Down in those tunnels under New York, racked with pain, guilt, regret, my mind scattered in a dozen different directions, nothing cohering. I wasn't thinking. I couldn't have been. Otherwise I'd never have bothered with such a plan.

'It stank down there – worse even than the streets with their leaking trash piles and the piss rivers and the rats. Though they were down there too, of course, slithering in and out of the stagnant ... water, I suppose you'd have to say, or what had once been water, between the train tracks. Grey greasy bodies, big as kittens. I must have been pretty out of it because I wasn't disgusted by the rats. I almost felt fond of them – the way they thrived on our garbage symbolised something to me right then, something about the great ordered meaninglessness of existence. It brought me peace, thinking about that, as I waited for that one brutal moment that would end it all.'

'This is what happened to you? To your legs? You allowed yourself to be hit by a train?' More than horrified, he sounded impressed, which was itself horrifying.

'You think I'd be here if it had gone right? I'd have been jam, ducks. I'd have been a mild inconvenience for commuters. No, this' – the sound of a hand slapping something not quite flesh – 'this was septicaemia. First blood poisoning, then cellulitis. Improperly sterilised equipment, you see? I told you that hospital was from the dark ages. Everything in that city is, and that was the mistake I'd made – because even though I'd been living in that hell city for years, I was still believing it capable of better. Imagining trains might run to something approximating a reliable schedule. But no, they just turn up when they like, and sometimes they stop and sometimes they don't. That express train I was waiting for, it never came and it never came. And the next thing I knew was hands under my oxters, hauling me up, and up and up. I knew who it was even before I heard that bully voice of his yelling at me. Such bold, winsome things he'd told me when he'd come to my bar a couple of months ago, and then later in bed. He'd taken me to Lutèce only the week before, his guest for the lunch they gave all the dopes who agree to stage there unpaid for three months. And all very nice it was for us for those three months, catching up on the occasional spare afternoon or late night when stars aligned, all very nice and strings-free, or so I'd thought until I discovered I was late. You know what I mean by late, don't you? Not late like that blasted downtown Six which went through the station like a scythe, seconds too late to do me any good. That motherfucker,' she said, almost to herself. 'All he would say was "I'd never have forgiven myself." Typical for the man to make it all about himself. I hadn't asked, I hadn't wanted to be rescued. And yet there I was, and here I am. Half of me, anyway.

'I got exactly the same line you did. "Come and work with me." He kept on at me as he took me to doctors, paid my bills. He couldn't stop rescuing me. Work *with* me, note, not *for* me, and no mention of what role he had in mind for me. "I want you somewhere I can keep my eye on you," he said, which I guess he finds bitterly ironic these days. Poor Magnus. Poor old devil. He's no idea what he's done, bringing you and me together in this place. I think, you see, we can help each other out.'

There was a pause. Then Loïc said, puzzled, 'There is, I think, some misunderstanding.'

'No misunderstanding, ducks,' she said, low and dangerous now.

'I am talking about Joanna. Joanna came to Paris, found me, brought me back here.'

A few minutes later they would leave and I would at last get to my feet, shaking out one limb then the next until the paralysing static in them abated. I'd totter out into the late afternoon resolving never to eavesdrop again – a lie – nor plunder the restaurant, at least until I was really desperate.

Before that, the Coravin gave its vampiric hiss and gurgle one more time. 'You goose,' I heard Eleanor chide Loïc. 'Didn't you know anything? Magnus, Joanna. They're the same person.'

An hour till the end of service and the staff were running on dregs. Thin-skinned, and sapped of their usual sonar-like ability to steer clear courses around one another in the kitchen, they collided, crashed, swore vengeance. Instead of chaffing the servers the chefs spoke harshly to them: fuck off out my way, moron; while the servers jostled for anywhere out the way they could stand, now that Kima had taken over the entire pass in the grand production of dessert.

From Joanna, doing rapid and terrible calculations all across her now near-illegible table plan: 'Kelly, can you run new stainless for the one-top?' A dreary assent: 'Yes, Chef.' 'Bit more pep when you're out there, please, Kels. Eyes and teeth, remember, eyes and teeth. Loïc, you know what I'm trying to tot up here? We have to comp Six for your little lapse of spatial awareness and it's coming right out your wages.' He glared at Joanna in outrage – no, worse, I saw it now, hatred – and she glanced up, equally hard-eyed: 'You injured,' she said, 'one of our guests. Docked pay? You're lucky none of them was a proper lawyer. They'd have left you without even the shirt on your back.'

Ever since I'd learned what these little barbs of Joanna's alluded to, she'd lost my respect a little. It had reminded me of the dickhead manager at Gumbys with his snide comments on what I was wearing, his speculations about what I might get up to in my free time – each individual remark too minor to warrant any pushback, since I knew he'd claim I was being petty, oversensitive, a *girl*, but over time, like numerous small lacerations, becoming draining. Finally I'd grabbed the serving tongs, lunged, twisted, made him scream. What would Loïc do when he snapped? I stared at Joanna from my hiding place, and thought again how rash a person must be to cultivate enemies in a place that contained so many heat sources and sharp implements.

'Chef,' Finn called from the door to the back alley. 'Chef? Something out here I think you should see.'

'Right now?'

'*Chef.*' I was hearing something in his tone I hadn't detected even when he was remonstrating with me at home yesterday, something I don't think I'd ever heard from him before. He didn't sound wired or exhausted. He sounded terrified. That was when I started to panic.

'All right, all right. Kima, I need you twenty per cent faster on plating. Rest of you, get ready to walk. I'll be thirty seconds max. See if you're throwing me a surprise party out back there, Finn ...'

Out in the alley it was still drizzling, and the cobbles were slick and outlined in standing water electric with streetlight. Finn was standing almost to attention beside the waste bins lined up against the whitewashed wall, one red, one blue, one green, one brown. And something else, a squatter, darker object at the end of the row, something that should not have been there at all.

Ever walked towards a mirror set slightly off true, so it shows the room behind you, but your own reflection fails to appear? Ever played hide and seek with someone who leaves you alone so long you start to doubt you even exist to be looked for? That was the feeling I had as Finn and Joanna stooped and conferred over the big black wheeled suitcase, tried to drag it away from the line of bins, acted out their surprise at finding it so heavy. As Joanna motioned Finn to open it, and he swiped water off its top edge, found the tag for the zip and pulled it slowly up and around, unsealing its metal teeth until they saw what was inside, and recoiled.

'We want the same thing, you and me,' Eleanor had told Loïc in the test kitchen that night months ago, while in the stores every ligament and muscle of my body screamed, a kind of premonition. Her voice had become a seductive drone I had to strain to hear. 'We've got motive and we've got means. I'm going to write something down for you now, and I want you to guard it until I tell you when to use it. In due course, if we keep our heads down and our eyes open, an opportunity will present itself. It always does. We can get our own back, and dear old head chef won't see it coming. All we need is one more thing in the mix.'

'Tell me?'

'A dupe.'

Table Seven

A city of lemon spires and violet minarets, cloisters and domes, walled gardens and winding alleyways, a rococo architecture detailed in gilt. Medieval, Dilys thought, or Middle Eastern, maybe. Fragrant vapours plumed up lively through grates between the structures then subsided to wooze through its internecine streets before cascading, finally, to evaporate across the tabletop.

'No more,' Penelope protested, laughing. 'I surrender. I'll tell you everything. Only, please, don't bring me any more food.'

I'd loved introducing this dish when I was— still working here. 'Our dessert tonight was inspired by our head chef's grandparents. Her parents were strictly anti-sugar, so the old-fashioned sweets her grandfather slipped her – lemon sherbets, Parma violets, Turkish delight – became extra special, a secret, like the cigars Chef wasn't supposed to know her grandmother occasionally smoked.' Part of the reason I enjoyed this story was that I'd contributed to it, suggesting Joanna swap round her real grandparents' vices – the sweet tooth, the nicotine dependency. 'So, inspired by those old, resonant flavours, we have here violet jelly, lemon sorbet pearls, dry-smoked caramelised dragon fruit. At the centre is a white chocolate mousse infused with fresh tobacco leaf on a foundation of sablé biscuit. There are some more surprises you'll discover as you explore. Please,' as we were trained to say, two separate directives. 'Enjoy.'

Dilys was imagining herself tiny, tiptoeing through spun-sugar colonnades, half-glimpsing the distant glazed towers of the city through the rolling mist with its perfume of winter. She drew her gold-coloured spoon across the plate, gathering a little of everything – calamity in sweetsville! – and was about to close her eyes to taste when Penelope said:

'I don't mean to sound negative, but in the months after Bill died, I did start to feel like I was going through the motions – keeping busy, like everyone recommended, but all the time feeling as if this activity was nothing more than a way of using up time, not just the empty hours each day but the months and years until I would have the good grace to join him. Often there wouldn't seem much point to being busy, if that's all it meant, and I'd stay in bed all day watching the numbers change on the bedside clock – that was a minute I wouldn't get back, and that was an hour – and not feeling good or bad about that – not feeling anything, really, about anything. Maybe I married too young, before I'd discovered my own identity. I'd always been so content for Bill to take the lead – deciding where we should go on holiday, who we should be friends with – and then when all those decisions suddenly fell to me, all at once, I found I had no idea what to do with myself, that there wasn't really a *me* to fall back on.'

And Dilys, her spoon frozen halfway to her mouth, thought: This again?

'You're a dear to let me ramble on like this, Dilys. You must know exactly what I'm talking about. Things must have been doubly bad for you. I've only lost one husband.'

Down went the spoon, in came the long and fortifying breath. 'Well, cancer is considerate in a way. It gives you

221

a diagnosis, time to come to terms with what you're going to lose. But what a shock for you, finding Bill like that. So sudden.' Penelope's eyes moistened at, Dilys supposed, the memory of the car horn's sustained blare, of storming out the front door to remonstrate and the instant flick to horror on finding Bill dead at the wheel of the Jaguar, handbrake luckily on.

Finally getting the spoon into her mouth she tasted sharp sweetness, a scintilla of pleasant smokiness, an odd bright caustic tingle that travelled only along the outer edges of her tongue, all separate, all of a piece. A foreign place, on the tongue, and how she suddenly wished she could still travel. 'Delish,' she heard Penelope say and, because her friend knew exactly how much the word infuriated her – it wasn't a word! – Dilys retaliated with a phrase Penelope despised equally: 'I could eat this to a band playing.'

'Cora actually said something quite shrewd the last time we had coffee,' Penelope began, but here Dilys was afflicted by the burst of tinnitus that Cora's name always brought on, and did not hear the rest. A person could grow weary of the shrewd things Cora had to say. Often they were no more than paraphrases of things Dilys had previously said, given add- itional colour or an amplifying expletive; yet there Penelope would be, quoting in awed approval this reheated advice and proceeding to pay it close heed, trying Lean Cuisine, or having her colours done and consequently retiring those floaty kaftans, orange and turquoise, that she had been wearing for decades and which, Dilys had often hinted, made her friend shapeless and wan – not in so many words.

From the day she had entered their lives as prospective purchaser of Bill Lambert's beloved 1977 Triumph Spitfire, Cora – all Liberty print and elective surgery, a never-married Bohemian with a bijou flat in Mayfair and an occasional job in a Marlborough Street gallery – had seemed intent on inserting herself into what had been the neat quartet of Penelope and Bill, Dilys and Andrew. If pressed, Dilys would concede that she and Penelope had hitherto been allies more than friends, paired work widows who had bonded through sharing complaints about their husbands' antisocial hours and the dreary corporate events they were forced to attend. But with the arrival of Cora, Dilys had to quickly, retroactively upgrade Penelope to best friend status in order to fully resent the newcomer. In any odd-numbered gathering, she knew, one person would always lose out, and that person, it turned out, was her. Andrew suggested that she simply decline the invitation to the coffee morning or the gallery visit, and that was her second husband all over: a man with a gift for identifying the solution that was straightforward, reasonable and totally impracticable. How could Dilys be expected to stay at home, wondering what might be being said behind her back? No, along she trotted to the afternoon tea or the classical recital, trying always to have some bit of news to tell the others, only to have it effortlessly eclipsed by Cora. The weekend Dilys had gone for a nice stroll in the New Forest, Cora had been accepted as a volunteer Olympic steward. The time she tried a new Indonesian near her office, not only had Cora already eaten there, but she had afterwards joined the line for what, going by the scruffy types queuing ahead of her, she'd assumed must be another hip new no-reservations restaurant, but which had proved to be a soup kitchen. Dilys had once ruined a trip to Penzance to view a rare meteor shower by wondering the whole time how Cora was going to gazump this anecdote – claim to have come to earth on a fallen star, perhaps. Even now they were reaching the end of dinner, Dilys was still half-expecting Cora to hobble into Midgard on crutches, plaster cast signed by the England cricket team or the bones of her leg already miraculously healed by experimental surgery afforded to only the rarest, most special of patients.

Shattered in four different places, though. Cracked ribs. Internal bleeding – something repulsive about that, blood where blood should not be. No, Dilys wouldn't wish those injuries on anyone. The real question was what Cora had been doing on the back of a stranger's motorbike at one in the morning, which not even Penelope could explain.

What must it have been like, Dilys wondered, sipping her Kentish sparkling rosé and noting the promised lychee and subtle effervescence, to ride pillion through a London as silent and dark as it ever got? In her mind the city at night was a jumbled medley of lamplit landmarks, monuments and malls, cathedrals and power stations, palaces and pleasure gardens. It must have been romantic – reckless, ill-advised, but what romance wasn't? – to hold tight and roll with the driver's movements as the vehicle tilted and swerved and banked so thrillingly. And then a misjudged turn, the loss of balance, the screech both mechanical and human –

'Cora was right,' Penelope was saying. 'Would Bill really have wanted me to moon about? Would he have wanted life to dwindle down around me, shrinking and hardening, becoming a coffin?' Dilys had made this point before, albeit in less grisly terms. 'After I left Cora, I went home and found that pink jacket I bought the day we all went to Folkestone, do you remember?' Yes, Dilys remembered: she had driven, the others had insisted it would be fine to park in a disabled spot while they went for lunch, and of course she'd got a ticket. 'All Bill said when I got home was "Bit young for you." I was so embarrassed that I hid it at the back of the wardrobe and never took it out again. But that day I was feeling brave. I had to live my life. And so off I went for dinner at the new Spanish place on Shearman Street.'

224

Penelope seemed jumpy; her eyes had a febrile gleam. Drugs, Dilys thought sagely. Having long suffered chronic back pain impervious to any prescription pills, Penelope was now self-medicating with substances officially unobtainable in England but which guess-bloody-who had taught her how to procure from a seedy corner of the internet.

'I thought they might look down their noses at me, but they were kind. They sat me at the counter so I could watch the cooks work, and everything looked and smelled so good that I kept ordering and eating – octopus and black rice, grilled prawns, fennel and blood orange, everything. And drinking, which was a mistake. These two nice young men sat next to me and I was recommending what they should have. "Trust me, I've tried everything." They were wearing leather so I asked them where their motorbikes were. They didn't reply, so I asked again, a bit louder. For pudding I had crème caramel. "You two," I said to the two boys, "probably think this is some newfangled thing, but I remember it from first time around." All that sherry had gone right to my head. Then something happened to me. Have you ever fallen over while sitting down? Thankfully I managed to grab the counter just in time. I was about to make a joke about it, but then I saw the look they exchanged, just a flick of the eyes, and in that moment I saw what they did – a sad old lady in a garish jacket making a fool of herself, ruining their nice meal with her constant interruptions. How pitiful I must seem, how lonely. And I was. I was lonely. And angry. Not with them, with myself. And with Bill. How dare he die, how bloody dare he.'

Having now finished her own dessert, Dilys was eyeing with irritation how little Penelope had eaten. At the start of the meal, she had claimed not to be very hungry; later, that this was not her kind of food, whatever that meant. She beamed at the staff – their expressions first concerned, then vexed – as they picked up plate after plate she'd barely touched, assured them everything was fine for her, refused offers of alternative dishes. As Dilys watched, Penelope used the very tip of her spoon to tease up a fragment of rich purple jelly and place it on her tongue. 'Violet. Ironic, isn't it?'

Dilys blinked. 'Is it?'

'Ophelia's bouquet. You know, *Hamlet?*' Her eyes narrowed. '*Shakespeare*, dear? Violets were the symbol of marital fidelity.' She laughed coldly, while Dilys boggled. The only books she'd known Penelope to read were the ones that used to occasionally come packaged with fashion magazines. 'Do you know what it's like to discover you've been lied to for years?'

'I . . . don't think I do.'

'Of course not. Of course *your* two were saints.'

Dilys could have taken issue both with Penelope's tone and with the statement itself. Didn't she remember Andrew's magazines, Mitchell's trips to Switzerland? Instead, a paralysing dread had settled on her. Penelope's behaviour had been peculiar all evening: besides eating next to nothing, she had done little more than sip and sniff at her wine pairings, claiming that she had to be careful because of her pills, but perhaps, Dilys was starting to fear, having resolved to stay clear-headed as she put her plan in motion.

Penelope did not seem, in that moment, however, to be scheming. She was dabbing her eyes, smutting her napkin with mascara. 'I won't cry,' she said, more to herself than to her friend. 'I *will not cry*.' She steadied herself. 'There's a question people always seem to ask, and it's, "What did she have that I didn't?" I've always thought they had it the wrong way around. What *didn't* she have, that's what matters. When you put it that way, the answer is obvious. *She* doesn't have five shirts to iron every Sunday night, or need to think up a different dinner every night for the week ahead. She isn't kept awake by his snoring. She doesn't have to launder' – with fearful daring – 'his dirty underpants. As for what she did have –' her voice was quavering again, now with rancour. 'Even now, I just can't fathom it.' She gestured around the room at – what? The other diners, the tree in shadow, the frenetic piano chords coming through the speakers. 'I imagined that if I sat where the other woman sat, if I ate like she ate, then maybe I might understand something.' She pushed her chair violently back from the table and Dilys, too, began to rise, still trying to process what Penelope was telling her. 'But I don't. I understand even less than I did before.'

Dilys dropped into her seat as if felled. 'Bill? You're saying Bill came *here*? But he only ever – I mean, you always said he didn't like eating out.'

'No, he did, he did. All the time, as it turns out. Just never with me. Look, I've got to go and freshen up. If they come past, order me a cup of coffee. I need it.'

Dilys sat numb as her friend shuffled away. Were they friends? Trying to gather herself, she reached around the table, swapped her empty plate for Penelope's untouched one and began to eat, automatically, the flavours blunted to nothing. The words she'd almost blurted were still seething up in her like reflux: 'But Bill only ever took *me* to the place in Soho!'

'We were always like the two halves of the Channel Tunnel, weren't we?' Bill had said towards the end of dinner – this was twenty years ago, when the comparison still had currency. His hand snuck around the wax-encrusted bottle at the centre of the table to take Dilys's. He rubbed his thumb along her knuckles, oddly paternal. Similar scenes were being enacted at every other table in the restaurant, Lexington Street's last remaining semi-insalubrious basement, each table occupied by a couple communing over low flame, one dessert, two spoons. 'Heading towards each other then, at the last minute, a near miss in the dark.'

It was true, to a point. They'd stepped out briefly at college in the early eighties, split up, got squiffy at house parties on the Unthank Road, exchanged long looks, decided better not. There had been other people, then – Dilys dated a teaching assistant on an exchange year who cried when he had to go home to Athens; for Bill there had been a steady girlfriend, Penelope. Small city: they ran into one another often, becoming friends again, and Dilys surprised herself by feeling no envy of their contentment, concluding that she had, at the grand old age of twenty-three, achieved mature adulthood. Shortly before Bill and Penelope announced their engagement, Dilys accepted their invitation to make up a four for a Christmas Eve dinner. She was to be paired with a friend of Bill's up from London, Mitchell, who arrived in a tuxedo yet somehow managed to make this seem winning rather than gauche. By the end of the meal Dilys had agreed to go to visit him in London the following weekend, and then it was 1985 and the start of eight good years together.

Having dinner with Bill in Soho had made those years fall away. She felt the same irresistible bodily pull towards him as she had back in their student days, and sensed it was mutual. Strong attraction seemed to throw everything else off balance: Bill's jacket – royal blue with large gold buttons, the kind of thing a man bought when left to shop for himself – was flecked with cream of mushroom soup from when he'd dropped his spoon in the full bowl, not once but twice; Dilys had unaccountably ordered only food she disliked – calves' liver, creamed spinach – and when the floridly Italian waiter who came to relight their candle had burned his thumb he cursed in broad Glaswegian; and all this made the evening more amusing. There was a bitingly cold Pinot Grigio, then a decent Pinot Noir, then, why not, more of the white. She sensed a little awkwardness from Bill, and, because she knew him of old, she said, 'You must miss Mitch terribly.' 'Every day,' he said immediately, relieved, and that particular tension evaporated. He spoke for a while about Mitchell, the child-hood friend with whom he had reconnected in London, how they'd slugged legal problems back and forth over the squash court. Listening, drinking, Dilys felt that her mind was oper-ating on two parallel tracks: one part agreeing with Bill and chiming in with her own reminiscences of her husband, the other running a cool cerebral commentary, querying, unpick-ing, analysing, auditing. Why did I just do that? What will he take that remark to mean? Maybe this ongoing exercise in self-justification had been running since Mitchell's funeral – impossible it could have been only five months ago – in case she was ever called upon to explain herself. The long conver-sation with Bill at the wake was only natural, the condolences of an old friend she hadn't seen in almost half their adult lives. Answering the phone when he called her a few weeks later, late at night: innocent, polite, unindictable. It got trickier when it came to explaining why she'd accepted his invitation to dinner. And then that she had made sure at Mitchell's wake that Bill had her current number – yes, there was the flaw. The prosecution rests. That's what they would get her on.

In benevolent candlelight Bill's wrinkles were erased and because of this, and certain of his gestures – a boyish duck-ing of the chin when he grinned – she felt she was looking at not the young man she'd known at university but an even younger Bill, sandy-haired and cheeky, confident because he was growing up assured by all around him that he could do and have anything he wanted. And things did always seem to come easily to Bill – the handsome wife, the job he had

229

always wanted, the two healthy sons, the growing collection of vintage cars. But it struck Dilys that while one's mid-thirties was unspeakably young to die, it was early, too, to lose a best friend. It seemed to her that Bill was so affected by Mitchell's death because it was his first experience of the unpredictable and senseless small tragedies life could throw at a person, and which could not be ameliorated or averted by good breeding and good fortune. The thought made her feel sorry for Bill as well as fond, and it was a perilous combination.

Outside they found it finely raining. A taxi lumbered around the cobbled turn from Broadwick Street and Dilys stepped out from under the awning, arm raised. 'So,' she asked Bill, 'are you going to hold on for another cab, or are we getting this one together?'

'What do you mean?'

'Now, Bill,' she sang, pretending to check her purse for cash as the taxi idled, 'don't play that game.' Tiny individuated droplets of moisture whirled around them, landed as dew on their clothes and faces. 'You knew what you wanted when you asked me to dinner. Is this it, or not?'

In the stop-motion strobe of streetlights and shopfronts on Essex Road – the dubious taxidermist, the city's best fishmonger – she'd watched Bill's hand again creep to hers for reassurance. Still a boy, after all. Dilys's husband was dead, her six-year-old away at Scripture Union camp; for a while now, maybe only a few hours, she need not be a mother or a widow, just a person, and the prospect gave her the same voluptuous, invigorating sensation of trespass she had felt at dinner, a joyrider's pleasure.

At home she sent Bill to wash and headed upstairs to experiment with mood lighting. She undid several buttons on her blouse, then redid one. The pilot light came on, the radiators ticked and gasped: the house was alert as an eavesdropper. She tried the radio, but Radio 4 was broadcasting a lecture, Radio 3 something like insect noise, Radio 2 just wordless howling. The downstairs loo did its weak half-flush, then went again. When she heard Bill's heavy tread on the stairs, Dilys sat on the edge of the bed, rolled her shoulders, adjusted her bosom. A decade, near enough. No time at all.

First he leaned down to kiss her, the odd rhombus of his mouth just as she remembered, the recognition more than the act drawing from her an involuntary sound of pleasure. He tasted of the wine they'd drunk, a little petrolly. 'Is it all right?' he kept asking. He straddled her, planting one knee either side of her hips, but the soft old bed bucked and threw him. He seemed not to have noticed her skirt was still on; there ensued a confused effort by one of them to roll it up and the other to slide it down. His stubble grazing where her neck met her shoulder, yes, he remembered what she liked. She ran her hands over the firm dome of his belly, paused, then dared pat at the pouch of his striped boxer shorts, where she encountered something she had not remembered accurately at all. 'My goodness, Bill!' How splendid, she nearly said, or, disastrously: Lucky Penelope! Then, as she unbuttoned, delved, he sprang from the bed, shaking out his leg frantically. 'Cramp!'

Once they had established a position that suited them both, Bill slipped aside her new underwear and stroked and teased, and took his time. He was more considerate than Dilys had anticipated, or remembered. Once she had helped him with a condom, though, Bill proceeded to go at her as if trying to ram shut an overstuffed cupboard before the contents could burst free. He breathed harder and harder, he made little guttural gasps of not-quite-language; and, although Dilys was not *not* enjoying herself, she could feel a dawning, catastrophic sense of ridiculousness – the situation's, her own – and tried to divert herself by counting the rhythmic thumps of the bedhead on the wall, twenty-*six*, twenty-*seven*, twenty-*eight*; then started wondering how old this mattress in fact was, and how often one was recommended to replace a mattress, and how much clout the mattress-selling industry had with whichever authority issued these recommendations – which was when Bill made a diabolical face and a final onslaught, into and into and into her, until Dilys's head too rebounded against the bedroom wall once, twice, three times, and he slumped his entire weight onto her with a deep wheeze of satisfaction, shuddering a few more times before lying still.

'Did you finish?' he asked her armpit. She had not, but wanted to, and directed him to open the top drawer of the bedside table and pass her the device she kept there. She showed him how she used it, then closed her eyes, clutched at his damp whorled chest hair, thought about the slackening but still wonderful thing draped across her thigh, took herself where she needed to be; until she felt his big hand curl over hers, and his sweet tentative willingness as well as the added pressure on the device made the tremors pass through and through her.

Afterwards, as Bill showered, Dilys sat at her dressing table and rolled over her face a jade pebble said to prevent jowliness. She observed his approach in the trifold mirror: a swagger, she'd given him a swagger, albeit the effect slightly under-mined by the floral towel around his waist. He placed a hand on her shoulder, as a lion might lay a plush paw on its mate or victim. 'Thank you,' he said, with such ceremony that she had to turn away from him and her own trebled reflection, and all there was to look at then was the wedding photograph tucked into one wing of the mirror. 'Not just for . . . what happened. I mean for letting me talk about Mitch. You understand what he meant to me. I'm not sure that Penelope does. She never asks how I am.'

This, now, naturally. 'You don't have to wait to be asked, Bill.'

'The thing is, I don't know that I want to talk to her.' He sat beside her on the stool and she was obliged to bump along so he had more than half a buttock's space. 'Since he died, I've been feeling myself change. I'm not sure I'm the person I used to be. I definitely don't think I'm the person *she* thinks I was. It's a scary feeling, but exhilarating.'

'Now, Bill,' she said again, briskly, 'don't go trying to tell me that your wife, of all people, doesn't understand you.'

'I think she understands me far too well. At least, the me I was. Because there's this feeling I have sometimes now, like I don't even know myself. I can't explain it. Sometimes it stops me sleeping. It's exciting to think I might not be understandable. I might not be predictable.' You mean you might not die, she thought sadly, not like that other loser. Then, to her astonishment, Bill got up and began to jig around the room. 'You could call her, Dilys. Call her right now, tell her what we've done here tonight, what the husband she *understands* so well is actually capable of.'

'The thing is, Bill, I do think that would sound better coming from you—'

He was – singing? Was he singing? Enough of this. 'Listen. Bill, listen. We've had a, a smashing time tonight, and I don't regret it in the least. It's been so much fun catching up. And everything else.' He stopped jigging and regarded her in pained surprise. 'But now it's time for you to go home and put your pyjamas on and kiss your sleeping sons and pretend this never happened.'

'You're killing me,' he groaned. But after another few chaste kisses – now he tasted of her own medicated mouthwash – he had called a cab, longingly said good night, lingered on the doorstep as if she might have been bluffing. Before bed, Dilys had neatly torn the page with his number out of her contacts book. From then on she had ignored any late-night calls to the house phone. It wasn't just about Bill. What good news was ever going to come after half ten, anyway? A little over a year later, she would go on a blind date – another lawyer, this one five years her senior, with a teenaged son, a passion for cacti and a tiny mistranscription, as yet undetected, in his DNA; in time she would introduce Andrew to her best friends, Bill and Penelope; and then, over the course of years that now seemed as ephemeral and light-filled as a handful of summer days, she would marry him and nurse him and bury him, and be alone once more. And now and then in the twenty years since she had heard them she would, for no particular reason, recall those words of Bill's, 'You're killing me,' and wonder whether anyone had ever said or would ever again say to her something so devastating, so terribly flattering.

Penelope returned to the table with make-up repaired, and a demand. 'I need to know,' she said, 'if there's a bruise. That woman' – she didn't elaborate, but Dilys knew who she meant because she herself had resolved, despite increasingly sharp pangs in her bladder, to wait until she got home rather than go downstairs again – 'says there is a mark. She says I ought to sue. Look.' She scooped the hair away from her temple. 'Can you see anything?'

Dilys obediently inspected. 'The light isn't great – it was brighter there for a moment, wasn't it? No, I don't think there's anything. Sorry,' she added, since Penelope seemed disappointed.

'What a fright that was. I thought I'd been shot.'

This was the third time she'd said as much. 'Just an accident,' Dilys soothed, also for the third time, as her friend sat. 'A lively cork.' The incident had been a highlight of her evening, and she rather resented having to pretend otherwise. The sudden startling impact, Penelope's great squawk of alarm as she leapt from her chair. And that other thing: Dilys's sense that, as the members of staff bore down on them in panic, behind them something – some*one*, surely – had slunk back behind the tree from which the champagne cork had rebounded . . .

'Maybe I was asking for it by coming here. But I had to, once I knew Bill had been here.'

'I still don't understand,' Dilys said. 'What exactly did you find out?'

Penelope blinked. 'That's right, I was telling you about that horrible day, wasn't I? That lunch, and how furious it made me. I was angry, you see, angry at Bill. How dare he be so selfish, leaving me alone and letting me make such a fool of myself? And then when I got home and looked around, all I could see was Bill. Pictures on the wall that he'd chosen and that I'd never liked. His wretched books on our shelves, law and military history and cars, cars, cars. That was when I realised Cora was right. I hadn't been living with his ghost, but inside it. And straight away, I started filling binbags. All his back issues of *Road & Track*, all his old VHS tapes and dreadful vinyl records. And when you start doing that, it's easy to get carried away. You get manic. Goodbye, socks! Goodbye, shaving kit! Why had I kept that so long? Then I opened the wardrobe, and here I paused. These were good suits, made to measure, and somebody could use them. Pretty much every shop on the high street is a charity shop now. I took out each one and laid them on the bed, checking they all had all their buttons, checking their pockets and so on. All those blues and greys and blue-greys, the whole spectrum of menswear. Then that funny blue blazer with the gold buttons that I was sure

I'd never seen him wear. That was where I found the envelope. At first I assumed it was a letter Bill had never got round to posting – that was going to be a shock for someone. But there wasn't an address on it, and when I opened it up, it wasn't a letter. It was full of receipts. Receipts from restaurants.'

A secret was thermonuclear. It held two opposing elements – the pleasure of withholding and the temptation to tell – in fragile balance. You could derive a great deal of power from that tension. You could live for almost two decades, as Dilys had, off the promise of detonating it at the right moment. But it turned out that rival powers, too, might hold equally devastating weapons.

'Dozens of them, going back years. I'm a very organised person, as you know, and so I found myself checking the dates, putting them all in order. They were from all kinds of restaurants, but never anywhere I had ever been. Nothing local. And always for two people. Of course Bill had company clients to entertain, of course there were dinners – he always used to complain about how many. But I instinctively knew these weren't expenses he'd absent-mindedly forgotten to submit. They'd been hidden on purpose. They were souvenirs. And I knew who they were souvenirs of, even before I saw her number scribbled on the bottom of the one from this place I'd never heard of, this Midgard.'

'Her number,' Dilys numbly repeated.

'Cora's, dear, Cora's! Do try to keep up' – and with that Dilys felt the fissive power of her secret extinguished completely. 'And now it all made sense, how keen she'd been to befriend us, how she inveigled her way in. Cora the cuckoo. What an idiot I'd been, thinking there was any innocent reason for a single woman to hang around with married couples. I went straight out to the back garden and started to curse him. I'd found him out, and he was lucky he was already dead otherwise I'd have murdered him myself. God knows what the neighbours must have thought. That I was doing the gnashing of teeth, rending of garments bit of grieving, I suppose.'

In the moment Cora had been flung from the stranger's motorbike and into empty space, she must have had time to wonder, more curious maybe than fearful, where she would land, what injury she'd sustain. Yes, Dilys understood that now, that sense of weightlessness, the long moment before the disastrous impact. 'But I don't understand. Who were you talking to?'

'To Bill, of course.' Penelope's voice was louder now, too loud. 'He's buried in the garden. Didn't you know that? Don't give me that look, dear, it's all legal and above board. We did the paperwork years ago. I put him over by the back wall, right by the Adirondack chairs and the nice clematis that likes the sun.'

'You don't know,' Dilys changed, 'how Cora's number came to be on that receipt. It could be something innocent. Even if she and Bill did come here together, that's not to say it was her all the other times, even *any* other time.'

'You always want to seem like you see the best in people, don't you, Dilys? But I saw how you used to pout when Cora came out with one of her absurd stories. All her eggs had double yolks, isn't that what they say? And the way she spoke to you sometimes, I pitied you for putting up with that. I don't know why you're defending her now, when you saw right through her. Which is why I know you'll get a kick out of what I did next.'

The thing about those Adirondack chairs was that they were so close to the ground that once you were sitting in one of them, it was virtually impossible to get out again; more than once Dilys had simply pitched forward on to the lawn and rolled away, getting to her feet from there, grass-stained and red-faced but free. Currently she was wondering whether she could effect a similar escape from the restaurant.

'First of all, I went on the computer and ordered a quince tree for the garden. Because whenever Bill did deign to take me to dinner,' with an ambiguous throb in her voice, a sad laugh or humourful sob, 'he would order cheese instead of pudding, then rant about the way they'd announce with great ceremony that it came with *quince paste*, like this was some terrific innovation no one had ever seen before, as if literally every other restaurant – he'd even say that, and still I was oblivious – weren't doing exactly the same thing. The tree won't bear fruit for a couple of years yet, but sooner or later they'll come, big, round, heavy fruit that I'll leave on the branch to get plump on sugar and sun and that rich, rich soil I've planted it in. Some I'll eat, and some I'll make into that jelly he hated so much, give it out to all his friends, and then, finally, he'll have been good for something.'

The remnants of dessert – all slime and sag, the final bedraggled wisps of vapour – lay uncollected on the table, and when Dilys peered around, wondering about the lapse in service, she saw that there were no staff in sight at all. Strange, she thought: something must have made them retreat to the kitchen simultaneously, and then she thought about how if you saw a tide recede eerily far you should know it portended catastrophe.

'You can get anything online, you see. How Cora put it was that the internet is like a city and, like any city, it has lawless areas. You have to be taught how to navigate them, you need a guide, but once you know what you're doing, you really can get anything. I could buy a gun. I could buy a passport in someone else's name and steal their whole identity. Priceless things, all for sale.' Penelope's face had the uncanny brightness of buildings illuminated on a storm-black sky. 'Not just things, either. Services. Specialists. You and I,' she said, 'wouldn't dream of joining one of those dating things, meeting people you don't know from Adam, then going for a drink, accepting a ride on the back of their bike. But she's a free spirit, our Cora, isn't that what she likes to say? With that little smirk that says *not like you.*'

'What did you do, Penelope? What did you do?'

'Accidents do happen. Even an experienced rider might leave it a second too long before braking on a wet road. He might round a bend the tiniest bit faster than he should. Now, because he's experienced, he understands the physics of the accident. He knows how to roll when he lands so he walks away with just a few scuffs and bruises, maybe not even that. He's a stuntman. Not like his passenger.'

If Dilys opened her mouth she was going to scream, and if she started she wasn't going to be able to stop.

'It would never have crossed my mind if Cora hadn't shown me to how to access those sites for my medication. Or even if she had just left it at that and hadn't lorded it over me, showing off how easily she could navigate all this darkness and danger, not like poor little me. Without her, I'd never have known services like that man offers even existed. So really, it's poetic justice, what happened to her. Wouldn't you say, dear?'

'You go in, call the police.'

'The polis!' Joanna barely lidded her scream.

'Of course. This is evidence. I'll wait here with her. I've done it before, remember?' Awful, but some little corner of Finn was deriving satisfaction from how he'd immediately gone into cool-headed crisis mode, the shape of the next few hours mapped out quite familiarly. A campaign. 'If you use the phone in your office you won't be overheard or interrupted. And then you should make an announcement that everyone should stay in the dining room, staff too, until statements can be taken. You'd better say their bills are all cancelled.'

'Who die— I mean, who put you in charge?'

A droplet from the roof went straight down the back of his neck. 'Go, Chef,' he barked, and though she was a giant, Joanna did still manage to scuttle.

Finn alone in the rain – or not alone, depending on your philosophy. It had been some time since he'd stood like this, stiff sentinel; but time smoothed grief like it did everything else and it took him a little longer than ever before to calculate the exact figure. Seven years, three months and . . . thirteen days. Hours? He couldn't do hours, even though there had been a time when it had seemed as if the duration of Finn's mourning would always be available to him, a digital read-out stamped on his field of vision, through which the rest of the world would only be viewable in a defocused blur. He was almost disappointed, until he realised that the counter had, in this moment, been reset.

Life wasn't a plodding succession of moments but looped around serpentine, always bringing him back to the same kinds of situations, as if he were meant to have learned something meantime. The circumstances changed, but his reactions did not. Tamped down beneath pragmatism he felt it churn: the old hopelessness, the old horror. How could this have happened? What could he have done to prevent it?

Finn was a double recruit. Long ago, in a hot and cruel country, he'd served scoff to dozens of men and women at every meal: delving ladles into catering troughs, doling precise portions into the moulded sections on plastic trays. He'd learned there how to be one among a series of machines along a production line, concentrating only on what went where and ensuring no one got shorted or given special treatment. There, too, he had learned – having always found strange comfort in numbers, their certainty, the patterns they made – about situations in which it was better not to count. It would be terribly simple, otherwise, to deduct the number of portions he served at any one dinner from the previous night's and to discover from that how many of his peers had failed to return. Had been killed.

At Midgard he'd heard the others whine about being under fire, taking hits; some nights, they were buried or they were in the trenches. More than once, early on, he had muddled his two lives and bellowed 'Sir, yes, sir!' in response to one of Magnus's commands. A wry look from the head chef and a barrage of nicknames from the others for that slip. On a good day – and they were often good now – the double meanings and mockery wouldn't bother him. If he'd judged his sleeping pills right to ensure he didn't dream, he wouldn't be upset by the way fat peeled from meat, the white webbing beneath that parted wetly as it was pulled away. He'd hear the different noises a blade made as it passed through flesh, muscle, bone, and his thoughts wouldn't turn inexorably to caved skulls, punctured eyes, the red-blue blurt of innards.

What he had liked about me was that I knew nothing about him, and the paradox was that this made him want to confide in me. He didn't hear me ask the others what was up with Easter Island over there on seafood, I didn't query why he came to staff drinks and ordered only a pint of soda water and often, on finishing it, walked out of Pangaea without farewelling anyone. It could have been all right – I was young enough that I might not even have recognised any of the place names he'd have said, or heard of the tours of duty he'd done. When on the second date I reached for his face and he'd turned away in immediate shame, he hadn't been able to tell me about the last person who reached for him so naturally. Even when I'd been with him in the allotment, he hadn't found a way to bring up the stories. Instead he had droned on about the charity that had found him the allotment – 'It usually takes decades on a waiting list to get one of these' – but then the train heading to Rectory Road had gone over its wonky bit of track and though he knew it was coming he'd still leapt at the gunshot of it and taken it as a warning: his memories were unexploded ordnance. Don't tamper, don't prod. Don't describe the complicated feeling of wading out among the knee-high poppies that had sprung up on a blood-slaked field. And not long afterwards I was breaking up with him anyway, and it was fortunate he hadn't said anything.

His fingerprints were on the zip and handle of the suitcase already, holding it and himself, and there wasn't really much more harm in reaching in for the squashed, stained object

242

crammed in on top of the case's other contents, the blue-white and the mossy green. A thickset fun-fur gonk, concave now, olive-coloured, with a pale front and domed beige belly, two boggle eyes. These things were mass produced: there had been half a dozen alone on the shelf of the shop where he'd found the one he'd bought for me. There was always a chance that it wasn't mine. But life looped back, and the world sometimes showed itself to be very small and cruel, and so Finn did not like to count on it.

No noise from the main road, no noise seeping from the kitchen. He stood guard, as he had once before over caskets without number, some containing weights to bulk up to the heft of an adult body the little that could be identified and reassembled, and the expression he wore was the same bland one he had when he worked and when he was gossiped about and when he was happy and when he was feeling himself come apart, like those scraps of bodies, sutures unstitching, constituent elements slithering and scattering to dust. Joanna knew why. Joanna could have answered everyone's petty, invasive questions. But the head chef wouldn't tell, not ever again.

After hours, a Monday night in 2008: Finn tarrying to be last in the kitchen while in the dining room Magnus gave the final applicant for the maître d's position, possibly the last qualified candidate in the whole of London, as polite a knock-back as he was then capable of. No plates, at least, were smashed. Around Finn lay prototypes of our mackerel dish, served, at this stage, in the classic rounded rectangular tin, the filleted fish concealed beneath a layer of pearls of sea buckthorn meant to resemble roe, the variants he'd produced by turns too acid, too sweet, too dusty, too slimy.

Magnus came up beside him, cleared a space on the counter

and laid his forehead down on the metal. 'That's it,' he said muffledly. 'I'm beat. We'll have to do without a maître d' entirely. I think it could work. We'll just stick an A-frame at the door with a seating plan each night like a wedding, let the civilians figure it out theirselves.' He sniffed, raised his head, looked lugubriously at Finn and his failed prototypes. 'Worse comes to worst, I'll hire someone French.'

In silence Finn gestured to the pass where, in the broad-necked glass jug of a V60, he'd set half a dozen stems picked fresh from his allotment. 'Magic. Thanks, pal. Everyone else gone for the day? Here, leave that, come and brain-storm with me.'

Finn followed, carrying the coffee pot before him like a votive. The long stiff stems crowded in his face, the pinkish-green blooms, arranged like bells on a jester's stick, giving off a not unpleasant odour of freshly perspirant armpit. He wasn't sure, though, whether it was wise to breathe in too deeply.

In those early days Magnus's office was about three inches bigger all round than it would later be when it had accrued its multiple layers of paperwork. The only thing pinned to the wall was Amanda Ledley Miles's rave, photocopied to poster size. Finn placed the fresh flowers on Magnus's desk – a broad plank of wood balanced on a filing cabinet and a small fridge containing as yet nothing more valuable than a single grotesque truffle – while the head chef disposed of the remnants of the flowers Finn had brought last week from the allotment, now reduced to a pulp in a soggy filter suspended over a beaker half full of a milky liquid. From the mini-fridge Magnus retrieved a small brown bottle, measuring a few drops of thick clear fluid into the beaker. He cast around, found a striped wooden chopstick, pondered it a moment, used it to stir the concoction. 'Sap from the ash,' he explained, seeing Finn inspecting the bottle.

'I had an informative conversation earlier. With your new girl.'

'Oh aye, Kelly? What do you make of her? Wee bit of a lost soul maybe, but . . . Ah, look, I don't want to seem like a creep, but that can be a good thing.'

'I think you should terminate her contract and tell her she doesn't belong here.'

Magnus paused. 'Well, that's one option, but it seems a mite extreme. Talk me through your thinking. She do something bad already?'

'You both did.' Finn was watching the mixture swirl in the beaker, the extracts from the saturated flowers emulsifying with the sap. He was feeling an urge to sweep the whole precious concoction to the floor. 'Can you explain why she came up to me with eyes like saucers, telling me she knew how it felt to lose someone? Or why Eleanor would say she overheard you telling her to "go easy" on me?'

Magnus was never cowed: addressed in anger, he immediately fought back. 'For your information, I can assure you Eleanor heard no such thing, and I would expect better of you than to trust her word over mine. You know how much she fucking loves to stir.' He cast a glance at the beaker with an ironic arching of the eyebrows that brought the wretched situation behind his eyepatch dangerously close to visibility. 'Literally everything Eleanor says and does is designed ultimately to piss me off, but she's harmless, ignore her. I'll speak to Kelly—'

'You know there are some words I never want to hear in connection with my name. The word "funeral". The word "soldier". If they ask, Magnus, didn't we agree you would lie? You'd tell them I came from Le Caprice, from Quaglino's, from Chicken Cottage if you like. Because they won't understand the actual story, like you don't *really* understand, because you can't. Most people can't, and I'm reconciled to that. Maybe I even prefer it, and maybe that's me being in denial or not getting into the team spirit, but I have to have the right to let everyone go on in ignorance. That's what I told you I wanted for working here.'

'It's a long way you've come. Listen to you. Seems like only yesterday I came to meet you at King's Cross and heard those four bampots tumble off the train after you, laughing about the weirdo who'd been havering away to himself all journey, preparing his interview answers.'

'Don't *do* that. Or, what, the first hint of pushback and the big saviour piles straight in to reminding us how pathetic and worthless we were before you swooped in to give us a purpose? A vengeful little god to look up to and cower from.'

'I'll say to you again now what I said to you back then, the second time we ever met, because I knew it needed to be said. You're safe with me. What happened with Kelly – it won't happen again. Finn, look at me. I promise. Not with her, not with anyone.'

'No, though, I'm interested.' Something was different about Magnus, it was incontrovertible: a month or two ago he'd have fired Finn for speaking to him like this. It made Finn want to provoke him further. 'How is it you see yourself? As a charity, a social worker, a superhero? Skulking back here, the mastermind who won't be seen. This team of broken birds you're putting together doesn't make you any more whole.'

Magnus said nothing. He sat on the unstable surface of his desk, on top of the CVs and industry magazines, and rattled the chopstick once more around the beaker. He looked at the contents with misgiving, his lips already puckering in distaste. '*Sláinte*,' he said, and drank the stuff down in one draught. The corners of his mouth pulled back, bringing the tendons out triangular in his neck, and his throat spasmed, until the last viscous dregs were gone; then he dropped his chin, swallowed three or four times quickly, and when he looked up at Finn he had, for a moment, the appearance of someone who'd started a street brawl and lost. 'You're right,' he said grudgingly, his voice clagged in his throat.

Finn sighed. 'Don't believe I quite caught that, Chef.'

'I'll say it again. You're right, and you always have been. I've not been fair to anyone, and that includes myself. Which isn't me saying I'm better than anyone here. But that's gonnae change. I want you to know something I've not told anyone else yet. It's not going to be me that goes next week to Paris to taste wines and eat at fucking Ducasse and, fuck knows, kidnap us a maître d'. It'll be Joanna.'

Finn knew he was going to have to be satisfied with this. He understood that it was the head chef's way to atone for a real mistake by confessing something compromising in return – as if errors and confessions were parallel columns in a ledger of behaviour, to be reconciled and written off like any other credits and debts. But, to show he had accepted this thing that fell some way short of an apology, he said, 'So why the ash sap in your little cocktail there, Chef?'

'It's the most important ingredient.' Chef's face didn't transform, his outline did not shimmer and reform itself, he sat quite still on the desk – and yet something at once subtle and fundamental had altered. There had been a shift in balance, a redirection. The head chef seemed in some inexpressible way to turn towards Finn: not to move, not to change, but to *become*. 'It makes it delicious.'

'Did you know her?'

He hadn't been aware he'd been doing it, but as the rest of the funeralgoers descended on the trestles to load their plates,

Finn had been taking small steps backwards from the party, pretending to give them space but actually feeling rising disgust. Back and back until his shoulders touched the ridged laminate that covered the back wall of the church hall, as he watched crustless quarter sandwiches being folded into still-talking mouths, hands gesturing with cubes of cheese or wet pink cylinders of deli meat impaled on cocktail sticks, upper lips glazed lurid with tomato soup sipped from waxed paper cones. Fast work had already been made of the hot food: wedges of quiche, meatball burgers in brioche buns, breaded chicken fingers and mozzarella sticks – all gone, all starting to activate the juices and enzymes that would turn this food to digestible cud, a process that barely counted as a transformation. The caterer had produced junk food, childish flavours, simple sugars and empty carbs – even the tray of what purported to be a mixed salad contained crisps – whose purpose, Finn appreciated, was to remind the mourners they were alive. He'd served similar every morning and night in Helmand, and at those meals the mood was also jolly. The roistering of survivors. If he didn't know, he thought, watching one guest set down a half-eaten Danish on a table and another pick it up and take a bite, both too distracted by chitchat to notice, he'd imagine this was a happy occasion.

Some of the faces he recognised from personal effects, snapshots pinned up over cots. Others were certainly strangers, yet still familiar to him in some strange way. Out there, back there, he had made an observation that brought him a little cynical comfort in the face of constant, unremitting loss: those poppies bursting with vivid life, like the lush grass that carpeted the sites of latrines, reminded him that nothing was ever gone, not really, only converted from one type of energy into another. In the same way – here the theory started to unravel, yet it still pleased him – here and there today he was

248

seeing distorted half-versions of the dead soldier's features on other people, as if she hadn't done that blunt thing, dying, but had instead been painlessly disintegrated and the elements of her reassigned: someone had got the sweep of her eyelashes, someone the lock of hair that was forever flopping into the left eye, someone else the four prominent freckles on the back of the hand that formed a perfect square, all present, cursed to live again and never be reassembled.

A warm breath on his face, a low voice in his ear. 'Forgive me, but I don't know her name.'

To Finn's left were the swing doors to the kitchen, from which waitresses issued constantly to restock the platters. To his right, a bear of a man was loitering, his outfit a blue version of the catering staff's white uniform. His hands were folded behind his back but Finn could see that his fingers were fidgeting at the wall, as if independent of the rest of him.

'Claire,' Finn said. Strange, foreign, to take the name out from under his tongue where he'd been keeping it and say it aloud for the first time in weeks. 'Claire Quinn. Private. Parachute Regiment, Second Battalion.'

'She did have a name, then. That's good. It's just, I'd started to wonder.' Scottish accent and, now Finn thought about it, Scottish colouring: iron-coloured hair that faded into ruddy skin at the back of the neck where it had been recently shaved in, eyes the colour of Glasgow in winter – in any season, maybe. 'I've been stood here half an hour and I haven't heard one single person mention it.' The caterer's fingers had found a flaw in the laminate and were tugging, picking, peeling. 'But here's something I have heard,' he said to Finn. 'You can cook.'

What Finn admired about Joanna was her composure. Magnus had been all corners forever getting knocked, and his violence and ill temper were the lashing-out of any person suffering chronic pain. He was sensitive like scalded skin was sensitive: he reacted to news of a competitor poaching Midgard's first sommelier by phoning in a bomb threat to the other restaurant; to the singer who sent a dish back with a complaint that it was over-seasoned by challenging her and anyone in her entourage who fancied a stramash to a bareknuckle duel in the street outside. Yet around the time of the trip to Paris, all the head chef's antagonism and rage had vanished, replaced by its utter inverse, Joanna's limitless reserves of serenity. She remained imperturbable in the face of combative guests, no-show cooks, deliveries that failed to materialise, anomalies in the weekly take, staff who fell out, staff who got too involved. For the first few months Finn had been tense, forever expecting the head chef's old fury to reemerge. It never had. Whatever the restaurant threw at her, she remained the paragon of calm. And it was in considering this coolness, which he had always done his best to mirror and match, that Finn, waiting in the rain to be called in to the kitchen, waiting still, started to feel a twinge of misgiving. Joanna liked to say that Midgard ought to hold diners so rapt that they should not notice if, outside its walls, disaster had struck. And how far, he worried, now that it had, would she go to keep everyone in ignorance?

When the door from the kitchen did bang open, it was only Gareth who loped into the alley, jauntily whistling. He had his vape in one fist, an overfilled trash bag in the other, yet somehow gave the slouching impression of having both hands thrust deep in his pockets. He flipped up the lid of the blue bin and dunked the bag, then inhaled from his vape to make its three little lights glow blue one by one. When he saw Finn he started. 'Jesus fuck. What you doing out here, bludger? Don't tell me you've nothing to do. What? What're you staring at?'

'That song.'

'Aw, fuck, was I doing it again? She'll kill me. I can't help it, I heard it out on the floor ten minutes ago and now it's stuck in my head. They knew what they were doing, those boys.' And in a surprisingly high true falsetto he sang the four descending notes of its refrain, then: '"Stayin' alive, stayin' alive." There you go, now it's your earworm too. Hey!' as Finn shouldered him aside and threw the kitchen door open.

'Why's that your ringtone?' he'd asked in the allotment that day as I stood awkwardly trying not to brush against any plants, as though worried I might break out in hives at the merest touch of nature. Ah, it was the first aid course Midgard had sent me on, I'd told him: the song had the rhythm you were meant to use when giving CPR. We'd been advised to make it our phone ringtone – it had to be second nature, you had to be able to sing it under your breath as you hammered it into the victim hard enough to fear you might crack a rib.

The kitchen smelled of sugar and sour bodies, but its constant undersong had, by this time of night, lost its edge of stress. The kitchen speaker was on, blasting Deafheaven, and the brigade was on the home strait – the last elements of the meal ready to go out, the deck brush and cleaning fluids about to be deployed, the night's final tasks being counted off: Tash was pinching the circular leaves from stalks of watercress to make two piles, one for garnishing and one for flavouring, occasionally tutting as she mixed them up; Nico was stirring a wine reduction that had to be finished before service ended; by the stations, whose once-monstrous heat had dwindled to nearly bearable, Kelly was topping up cooking oils. Addy, our best nose, was standing in the blue light of the fridge, sniffing out anything that had started to go off; reaching in, she snagged a thicket of basil leaves whose catpissy odour told they were past their best. And there, as Finn had feared, was

Joanna, bulked into her usual position in the crook of the pass, issuing instructions: dicht those, rewash that, straighten all the pans so their handles, angled at two o'clock, would phalanx together neatly. 'Yes, Chef,' came the ragged response, slopping out of sync, and it was so normal a scene that Finn felt bile in his throat.

'You haven't called.' At the last moment, out of loyalty to Joanna, he swerved saying 'police'. 'Joanna? Don't you think you should call?' She broke from her station, but her face was blank, concave with denial, and he had the horrible sense that she was likelier to remonstrate with him for using her name instead of her title than to engage with what he was saying.

'You been inhaling the gases from your cooker?' Gareth rudely shouldering him aside. Finn ignored it and made for the dining room, words forming and failing on his tongue. It wasn't the muttering but the fact that he broke another cardinal rule and exited the kitchen by the in-door that had Kima saying, in a tone that suggested it had only ever been a matter of time, 'He's gone right round the bend.'

He had, and full circle again: in his head, superimposed on the oblivious, peaceful dining room, a charnel-house vision pulsated: shattered bodies on ruined ground, a scarlet blaze, a hell he'd seen on earth and never wanted to see again. Loïc, stationed at his desk ready to distribute the bags of house granola with which we sent guests on their way so they'd have something to remember us by next morning, noticed him first, and the sight of a chef on the floor without a dish in hand or scheduled task to complete was so alien to him that his expression became one of gorgeous bafflement, a supermodel asked to solve quadratic equations. Finn roved to the tree, grasping it for support, and listened. Conversation, our livelier late-in-the-meal music, the random percussion of cutlery on plate. And then, under it all, he and I both heard it: the loping bassline, the four falsetto gasps down from high C, the refrain that heard even once could get stuck in your head your whole lifetime – or maybe, it was starting to seem to me, even beyond that.

Finn's breath snagged. He turned his head like radar until he located the source of the music: the coat racks by the door. Now he was drawing attention from the diners too – bemusement turning to perplexity as he pulled out, patted down then let fall to the floor one coat after another. Finally, he located the ringing phone's faint tremble. He grabbed at the sensation, frisked the pockets of a midnight blue Crombie inside and out and, on finding the cheap Nokia bleating its dementing song, dropped the coat: it sank onto the damp-dog heap of the others, exposing a lining of peacock-blue silk. Murmuring behind him. The incoming call was cut off even as he tried to find the button to answer it, then the display flashed up its screed of missed calls: a handful each tagged with Midgard's name and Kima's, and more than twenty listed as Number Withheld.

Back to the kitchen: Joanna at the prow of the pass, flanked by the rest of the team. 'See?' he said, brandishing the phone. 'See? Hidden in the coats. They're mocking us. Someone here, now, knows what happened to her.' Behind Joanna, Gareth and Kelly exchanged looks: 'Her'? – Oh, he meant *me*. 'Lock the doors. Everyone has to be questioned.'

'It's just a phone, but,' Joanna's eye moving between his two, her tone so sedative, so cool. 'There are a million just like it, Finn, you know that. It could be anyone's.'

'Then call it. Come on, I know someone here has a phone on them.'

'All right. Let's do that.' Her tone so sedative. 'Hand it over, G. – No, don't start with me', and with a reproachful look he stooped to remove the phone from around his shin. Joanna had dialled my number often enough this evening to have got it by heart: she rang it again, turned the volume to full, held it out for Finn to listen. A distant peal as it connected, and then – in his astonishment he nearly dropped it – the Nokia phone in his hand lit up and the same song rang out again, the vocalist's breathy gasps now sounding fearful to me, snatched in panic amid something terrible unfolding. Finn cut the connection. Joanna lowered the phone. They looked at each other and Finn saw only a look of pleading.

'Tell them, Joanna. Tell them what we found in the alley.'

'Can't we—'

'*Tell* them.'

'Finn, man,' Kelly gently said, 'just cool it. Everyone's watching.' And they were, crowding in from the dining room, a series of faces exhibiting the prurient concern of the accident witness: the young man whose nose was leaking fresh blood, the boys looking to their critic friend for clues about how to react, the VIPs whose uncertain smiles suggested a dwindling hope that this was no more than a bit of theatre that would lead in to an unadvertised second dessert.

Joanna exhaled. 'All right. All right. As you're all here,' she began, and I recalled what she had told me about the importance of being able to improvise, 'there are one or two things I'm going to have to make clear. First of all—'

'Almost all.'

'I beg your pardon?'

'Sorry,' said the little boy with the signed menu. 'Sorry, Chef. You said everyone was here, but there's a man still sitting at his table. And he's eating.'

The screen over the pass showed only a blade of blue-white light. Joanna pounded its side with more force than necessary, and the line sprang outwards to show its overheard view of the dining room, the empty tables. A figure was making its way to

254

the heap of discarded coats. As we watched, he picked up the Crombie, dusted it down, replaced it on a hook and, leaving the other coats where they were, returned to Table Two. The Telefunken was malfunctioning: it showed interference patterns, ghost shapes that flared and flickered around the diner as he moved. Even after he took his seat, folded his hands in front of him and sat quite still, after-images continued to spit and thrash, other movements he hadn't made, or hadn't yet. My vision was filling up crimson but I still could make out the neat lines combed in his hair, the burnout discs of his spectacles: our latecomer party of one, Jadwin, patiently awaiting what we'd bring him next.

'He had the phone,' Finn whispering now. 'Table Two. It was in his pocket. How?'

He started to move towards the out-door to the dining room, but Gareth held him back, burly tattoo-dotted arms crossing round him quite tenderly. 'Mate, don't.'

My knees popped, loud as the ticking of the clock. My arm stung as if freshly hacked into. I felt an unplaceable ticklish sensation inside me, like frozen blood had started to thaw and sluggishly flow.

'He knows,' said the girl in the black velvet dress, tugging on her date's sleeve. 'Go on, Crispin, say what you saw.'

Crispin had an easy blush, and it rose up in his cheeks as the others all turned to him. 'I've been studying sleight of hand, you see. Misdirection. Making things appear and disappear at will.'

'What he's trying to say,' she interrupted, 'is that he saw who planted the phone.' She cleared her throat with a little showmanship herself. 'What he's trying to say is, who wants to know? And how much is it worth off our bill?'

For her last meal before her execution by lethal injection, Karla Faye Tucker requested a fruit plate – no pineapple – a salad and a glass of sparkling water. Charlie Morgan asked for barbecued pork ribs with all the fixings, and ate so slowly, with his one hand, that a skin formed on the beans. John Wayne Gacy, a former KFC manager, ordered KFC. Some refused the proffered meal, but they were the exception; most mass-murderers had a hearty appetite in their final hours. Filet mignon was a popular choice, but not as popular as cheese-burgers, commonest order of all.

Jadwin knew death row meals like other men could reel off football results. The information sank in with one reading, involuntarily memorised. In quiet moments he tormented himself with the thought experiment his reading naturally entailed: what would he choose for his one last meal or, if he really wanted to self-flagellate, what single dish? The answer – the answer was impossible. How could he be expected to choose between yellowtail sashimi in ponzu and a Friday night fish supper, chips doused in vinegar until they dissolved into tangy, starchy, salty sludge? Or between a proper murgh korma, with its subtle but unmistakable trace of saffron, and the chargrilled *bife do lomo* served in smoke-filled shacks on the dangerous backstreets of Buenos Aires? And what of your changing moods and tastes: some days he would probably settle for a simple bowl of handpicked brambles, black and juicy, the kind that slipped so easily from the thimble stalk as if being offered up in pride. Or, if the precise sense-memory could be recaptured, the slice of plain white toast, ten seconds overfired, that was the first thing he'd tasted on recovering from a seizure in childhood and which had been, in that moment, the finest, sweetest food of his life.

Sooner or later he had to stop. The experiment made him anxious. Nonetheless, he found the notion of the last meal poignant: the fact that these people had done wrong by society's lights, yet society wanted them to know at the end that they were people, after all, who should be treated civilly. Those who granted the request felt good about themselves, even as the electrodes were being greased, the toxic chemical cocktail prepped. They'd take pains to fulfil the condemned's request. When Corinne Huggett asked for a single scoop of boysenberry ice cream, her besotted jailers had searched the whole state of Arkansas to source it. The newspapers had called Huggett the Butcheress for what she'd done to her husbands, but that was long ago now. In these more enlightened times, Jadwin supposed, she'd just be called the Butcher.

Dessert at Midgard was marred, like every dish before it, by an aberrant undertaste Jadwin could not identify. Rotted gases in the crab, something foully metallic in the mackerel, and in the first couple of courses he'd assumed a deliberate continuity of ingredients, like those menus which found a way to put truffle in every dish and inflate their prices accordingly. It was not a distinctive flavour, more of a counterpoint to each dish he consumed, and it wasn't until it brought bile into the tallow-fat notes of the aged beef that Jadwin realised that what he could taste was not some contaminant that laced the food but a flavour his own body was producing, exuding, something that coated the interior of his mouth and tainted every mouthful he took. It was all he could do, when he realised, not to spit the gobbet of meat back onto his plate.

Jadwin often ate solo, by choice. His epicurean delight for food and its pleasures was, in his view, one of the things that made him a restaurant's ideal customer; among the others were his broad palate, open mind and disinclination to favour fussy etiquette over delicious food. And he found most things delicious: bring him fermented shark and he wouldn't bridle, Filipino fertilised duck egg and he'd slurp and crunch without hesitation, relishing these delicacies a second time when he described them later to his appalled co-workers. But tonight, his usual focus was lacking – impaired first by the polluting flavour, then by the intensifying line of ache in his face that meant the pills were losing effect.

The wound had woken him that morning. He'd come to life in a panicked instant, draped in bloody dreams, sheets clinging to his swinishly reeking body, with his eyes feeling deep-fried and the kick of his heartbeat in his face. A new symptom? No: in the bathroom mirror he confronted the long and jagged laceration that ran from beneath his eye socket to the side of his mouth, and from which pain pulsed outwards in seismic waves. He stroked his face around the cut, where the skin was swollen and shiny like cheap leather. He felt at its pulpy edges, first gently then more forcefully, until a pinkish ichor seeped from it and his vision flushed briefly white with agony. Then, as he showered, he discovered a second wound, clumps of blood matting the hair at the back of his skull. Water streamed red-brown over his shoulders as he massaged the clots away, cursing the creature who'd inflicted these injuries on him. That vicious, vile strumpet. Me.

It might not have been me, except that the first girl he'd been offered had mentioned over dinner that she was a social smoker. He phoned the agency first thing next morning to complain. 'She never said,' had come the rejoinder, in that Estuary croak. 'Not a mindreader, ducks.' The next girl they sent was unpleasantly pudgy; the third drank too much over dinner. He was genial in his remarks later to the woman who sent these girls, emphasised with an effort at humour that he was picky. Then there was me. Yes, I might do, he thought, but it was only when I mentioned that, since the gargantuan steak I'd endured a few weeks earlier, I'd sworn off red meat that I became perfect. Vegans, vegetarians, carnivores; topers and teetotallers, smokers and non-smokers – all attributes that must have an effect on texture. Flavour. He'd nodded earlier tonight when his server had described the indolent, stressless, fattening lifestyle of the heifer he'd eaten: quite so, quite so. Age, of course, that was a factor. Maybe even ethnicity, though he'd be castigated for saying so.

Even as he watched me faff with my chopsticks in the sushi restaurant, he hadn't been certain. Even as he brought me up to his flat, tipsy on the precise amount of sake he'd allowed me. But *Eat her* said the door that was slammed and bolted further along the landing, *Eat her* said the creaky floorboard I trod on as I followed him in. Yes, all right, it should be now, it has to be now. No more doubts – and then he heard me saying something so wretched that he nearly rounded on me and implored me to leave. Nearly told me to run. I'd ruined myself and made myself safe in eight words. But then we were in the kitchen and *Eat her* the ice was saying as it tumbled through the freezer compartment, and then all sympathy for me was washed away, replaced by malice, as if I'd set out to lead him on.

'My mother,' I'd said, and I'd been talking about getting in

259

cars with strangers, 'never taught me much of anything.' After that, it was my own fault I was doomed.

Still, Jadwin felt remorse. Not for his actions, not exactly. He'd waited so long, plotted and fantasised, knowing this was something he could only do once; and what he felt now was the bareness of fulfilment, the empty room of it, the under-standing that the anticipation of the act – the potential he'd drawn on for so long – was gone for ever, replaced by one small and rather sordid anecdote. But the fact was that he had had to do what he did now, now, now, and if I hadn't been perfect then I'd been good enough, and he wouldn't have to dwell on his regrets for long.

So it was poison in the coffee pods, poison in the bottled water. In the screw-top bottles of red and white wine and corner-store soda. He'd done his due diligence, calculating the precise dose of mistletoe extract that would first paralyse a person of my build, then put her in a coma from which she would slip quite peacefully from life. Ideally he'd have eschewed drugs, since any toxin would have a deleterious effect on flavour, but so too would any fear I were to feel, any tensing up or struggling releasing sour adrenaline into my system. Sweeter by far than slaughterhouse produce is the flavour of the animal reared domestically, a child's pet lamb, cossetted until the moment of death. Tenderness begets tenderness.

He'd been considerate. He'd tried to ensure I would feel no pain, and he had waited until I was on the brink of passing out before making the cut. Even then, he'd only taken the smallest scrap imaginable, a translucent sliver the shape and size of a rose petal, pink-white, ragged at one side where his hand had trembled as he cut. What percentage of me was that? Statistically zero. His hand, gripping the fragment of me in kitchen forceps, shook again as he watched the blood speckle into the round patch on my bicep. The red dots welled up and merged amoebically, gathering, drawn downwards by gravity, until they overflowed in two parallel tracks down my arm. From the kitchen, he could smell hot oil on metal.

All that, for just – a sliver? A taste? Adrenalised in the moment, next day he felt the slump of anticlimax. That's it, then, is it? That's all it was? And then the pain, the bad flavour, the sense that something had slid out of alignment: he should have been spared waking; merciful annihilation should have come in his sleep, blotting him out unawares. Instead, another dismal morning on earth, an eye swollen half-shut, the usual half-dozen pills before breakfast and three after, then yet more to dull the ache in his face, a fumbling search through the bathroom cabinet for alcohol and medical tape. Then, the inspection. He checked the living room first, hissed at the mess there, then closed the door over. From a cupboard in the hall he took out a suitcase, and was wheeling it towards the living room when its wheel turned on something I must have dropped there. A plush green pouch, a child's mascot, with a solid core. He unzipped it, and found inside a Stanley knife blade embedded in a cork, something I must have carried with me everywhere in this dangerous city, anticipating worse acts than Jadwin could ever be capable of. He held it in his hand like a diviner, waiting to feel a twitch of – empathy, pity, something, anything.

Jadwin knew enough to know that he should carry on with his normal routine. It was a Tuesday, and Tuesdays meant Nance. Years he'd been visiting her now, but recently he'd begun having to look up the address. He had to go out in the world, let himself be seen – tracked – surveilled. His route was being monitored and reconstructed from CCTV footage and card payments registered in centralised databases, and that wasn't the criminal's paranoia, that was the world everyone

261

lived in now, everyone carried around an invisible burden of data, lighter than the suitcase he was rolling along at his side and which, empty, kept hitting his heel and nearly overturning. At London Bridge he made spurious purchases to forge additional links in the chain of his traceability: first a scalding coffee, then an ice cream bar he selected partly for nostalgia, partly to soothe his mouth, and whose flavour he registered as a little off, a little acrid, which he attributed to either aftertaste from his Americano or to the wrapper's oxymoronic promise of a recipe both new and improved.

Whatever changes he had put himself through, biting into the sweet – shattering, then saccharine and chill – reconnected Jadwin immediately to the boy who had first tasted one of these. No externally compiled dossier could know that while eating and, as he'd been taught, folding the foil back bit by bit so as not to drip on his clothes, he was recalling one particular childhood trip to the beach, his mother's dress with the op-art pattern like sections of oranges, the blue car with the soft top rolled down. The ruckus when a petrol station attendant had expected Nance to handle the pump herself, and the choc ice she had bought her son as apology after the scene she'd made. Where had they been going that time? Margate, Hastings, Ramsgate, they did them all. Somewhere with a beach where he'd be deposited with a book on clammy packed sand through which sparse sharp blades of tough grass poked, while Nance waded into water too cold for bathing, the hem of her dress drinking the tide. A windbreak optimistically erected, soon flattened; gulls mocking; a sun that grew big and white behind clouds but never broke through. The drive home in silence, then maybe dinner, maybe not, because food and its withholding were the means by which Nance rewarded or punished her son for his conduct, good or otherwise, her judgment often impossible for him to predict.

What a cheeseburger – repast of choice for the condemned – meant to him was an annual stop-off at some motorway eatery while Nance sat prim on the far side of the table, trying not to let any skin come into contact with the moulded plastic chair, and smoked, and watched her son gorge himself. Long ago now, long enough that smoking in restaurants was unremarkable, even commonplace. He ate, torn between the instinct to bolt his food, maximising his pleasure and preventing her from taking it away before he was done, and the urge to savour it slowly, steep himself in it, make the memory of it last the year, which risked his mother claiming he was not appreciating it enough. At a certain point, she would reach over to select a single French fry from his plate. She would dip it in ketchup, suck it clean, drop it into the ashtray, and that meant the treat was over. On the way home, in a teasing tone, 'Getting a bit paunchy, aren't you?' A week of severe calorie counting would ensue: no such thing, one of her rules, as a free lunch. One day he'd realised that the words 'threat' and 'treat' were just one letter apart, and felt like he'd cracked one of the world's secret codes. When he lived under his own roof, she'd explained, he could cook and eat what he liked, but for now he had to abide by her rules. It was within these rigid parameters that the boy had grown – had been contorted and tugged and forced – into the shape, at least, of a man.

The train accelerated out of London Bridge. By now, Jadwin theorised, a neighbour might have made a call, his front door might be off its hinges, his home gone over by fingerprint-swiffers and specialists in blood spatter. He might be the cynosure of crosshairs, the subject of secret transmissions crackling between agents a constant few steps behind him at the station, on the train. Facts were being compiled, useless, unnuanced facts, from which equally drab conclusions would duly be drawn.

Sky-piercing glass cylinders and gaudy new tower blocks, cranes stately turning; then lumpen postmodernist experiments in suburban architecture, and Victorian terrace façades buttressed by I-beams, everything behind them excavated to blank sky. Sooner or later his pursuers would gain permission to access his medical records and examine the scans that depicted, slice by slice, the irregular oval of his skull, how in successive images its thick border bulged inwards, squashing – no, devouring – the matter within. He wasn't offended or upset at the thought of strangers scrutinising these private documents. The word 'inoperable' might even work to his advantage.

'Shall I store that for you?' asked the nurse as Jadwin signed the visitors' book. She reached for the handle of his suitcase, but Jadwin drew it towards him and told her he wanted to hang on to it. 'Valuables,' he said. She regarded him with some scepticism: he could sense her avoiding looking directly at his wound. He had dressed the cut, slathered yellow salve into it, but it was going to get worse before it got better: gelatinous black limning the gash, swelling and bruising as the blood collected there. 'Someone got the better of you,' she said at length, unsmiling. 'Nancy's looking forward to seeing you in the sunroom' – a sentence containing multiple falsehoods and fabrications. Jadwin, following her through the corridors of the home, the cheap carpets with the heavy plastic runners laid over to protect them, said suddenly: 'You should have seen the door I walked into.' She looked over her shoulder at him, baffled.

The day was bright but not warm and the heating in the sunroom – a large conservatory with a sea view and a discernible bodily tang – had been turned up high in compensation.

Games and magazines lay stacked on tables, but uptake was low; the residents had been arranged around the room in pairs and trios designed to encourage or simulate conversation, but this, too, was minimal. They were losing language along with everything else. Superannuated infants, they moved in ways they couldn't always control, kept odd sleep patterns, were prone to wails of frustration, ate a diet of pap administered by others.

'Nancy! Your visitor's here!' The nurse overenunciated, artificially bright and cheerful, the addressing-an-idiot tone he heard so often here, sometimes – shamefully – from his own mouth.

Nance was in green, and the resemblance to what I'd worn made him trip on an imaginary rumple in the carpet. Her wheelchair was set beside a window and faced a rattan chair in which Jadwin settled himself. 'Hello, Mum, how have you been?' Always self-conscious when he first spoke to her, almost a feeling of stage fright, as though the other men and women in the room might be paying close heed, judging this bad son. Her gaze dipped to inspect his hands' loose clasp around hers, then drifted away again, betraying neither recognition nor curiosity.

'Let's see, now. When did we last see each other? Just my little joke – last Tuesday, of course. Well, you'll remember that Friday was my final day at work. Right up until then I was wondering if I could stay on, but no, HR said I come with too much paperwork now, that if I were to – never mind, I shouldn't be morbid. So, no last-minute reprieve for me, though there was, as I'd feared, a presentation. You wouldn't call it a party, but out they all came from their cubicles, with their optimistically big card with signatures filling only about half the blank space and the gift for long service. So that was it, a card, a collection, a gift for which I'd rather have had the cash equivalent, two drinks, then out the door at six sharp to live the rest of my life.'

In the weak sunlight he could see spotted lilac scalp through her thin and freshly set hair. Nance was old now, terribly old, yet Jadwin felt indignant that she should be here among these other sad decrepits. Each time he visited he expected, still, an audience with his glamorous, spiky, assertive, vivacious, manic mother and was taken aback to be reintroduced, time after time, to this frail impostor.

'What struck me, Mum, is that all those plans people say they're saving for when they retire – they'll travel or learn a language or write that book they've always thought about – they all take time, don't they? That's the point of them, to fill your suddenly empty days. Only, I don't think I ought to be starting any big projects. Not many people knew, of course, at work. Otherwise someone might have mentioned that a ticking clock as a gift might be the tiniest bit insensitive.'

Afternoon tea was being passed around: drinks from catering urns, soft sandwiches and cake that wouldn't trouble the residents' teeth, maybe a jaw's worth among them. Seeing her slurp from a cup of barely tepid, brick-coloured tea, Jadwin again felt that some clerical error must have been made. He couldn't imagine his real mother ever tolerating this. Embarrassed for her, he reached out and again took her scraggy hand in his.

Against his will, he was thinking about me, and of what I'd said on the landing, or what I seemed to have said. 'Mum,' he said, 'someone was telling me something recently about . . . In a sense, I suppose, it doesn't matter now. You're you and I'm me. But this person thought that their mother didn't – want them.' He searched her face for some glimmer, some acknowledgment of what he was asking, who he even was. 'I know there's a thing called maternal instinct, but I don't think it's

266

always as simple as that. It's not something you can choose to do. To love someone.' There was a rule here that you shouldn't say anything that would upset the residents, but how could you know? Nance never seemed anything but placid these days, incapable of the ire which he and strangers used to continually spark in her. 'But did you, Mum? Do you remember?'

Nance's attention, such as it was, never lasted. Her gaze wandered now towards the conservatory window, then her head rolled to follow. Finding nothing to see out there, she turned slowly back to him. Her face bore the pleasant and incurious expression of a person before whom lay something bland and unremarkable, something that did not, could not, rouse a scintilla of her interest.

Jadwin felt a sensation like an ice cream scoop slipped in beneath the heart, rotated and withdrawn, a swift merciless extraction. 'Mum,' he said, 'was that an answer?'

Until he reached into his jacket pocket, Jadwin hadn't been certain he was going to hand over his gift. As he buffed it on his shirt, Nance's eyes brightened, drawn to the royal red shine, the little spiked coronet. 'Remember how you used to enjoy these?' She could make one last a whole evening, cracking open the pockets of waxy yellow pith, chasing out each tooth-sized seed with a pin. She had, hadn't she? Or was this the opposite of a memory lapse, some false impression based on an image he'd seen in a magazine, imputed to Nance? Her lips parted and closed on a silent plosive. Soft fissures in the fuzzy skin above and below her mouth recalled the furious way she'd once had with a cigarette, faced clenched like a fist. 'Poh,' he thought he heard her breathe. 'Poh . . .'

'That's right! Pommygranite!' He death-glared up at the nurse standing over them: that artificial brightness, that wretched condescension! 'Let me take that and cut it up so you can share.'

'Take some for yourself,' he called after her, vindictive. She studied the pomegranate as she walked away, and his breath caught a moment: but no, it was only the colours that she was admiring, the cherry red and peach paleness and the rich deep healthy crimson prickled with the dots of incipient decay – those little freckles, minute blemishes, quite indistinguishable from the other punctures in its dense skin, the ones Jadwin had made himself. 'And then a little walk,' he said to Nance, patting her hand. 'A little trip for you.'

Up and over the cliffs the wind blustered as Jadwin trudged back towards the railway station under the dying sun. The wind mussed his hair and clothes, drew back then rushed him again, cuffed and clobbered him, forced him to a standstill. His back and his arm ached from the weight of the suitcase, whose wheels seemed to catch on every uneven paving slab, threatening to capsize it. Should he go back? Maybe he ought to go back. But then he remembered how Nance's head had turned – how if she could almost produce a word, she surely knew enough to understand a question and find a way to respond – and then the wind would drop again and he could proceed, another few minutes before he had to rest or was interrupted.

The last train before rush hour. With each stop towards London the carriages grew busier and Jadwin, positioned by the baggage rack, more anxious. The air swam arid; foot-level vents pumped non-stop heat. Someone sat next to him and Jadwin was furious; then two minutes later they moved away, and he was irked by that too. He cupped a hand over his mouth, exhaled, sniffed, frowned: that same rancidity, surely not still from the coffee earlier – could others detect it too? Was it sleazing from his pores? At East Croydon he was surrounded, penned in, by teenagers passing back and forth grease-patched paper bags stamped with a ubiquitous logo, sharing the bounty; and as they ate and the stink of fast food filled the dry, hot carriage, and they yelled at one another, open-mouthed, displaying half-masticated chum – Jadwin could stand no more, stumbled through a cat's cradle of out-stretched legs, retreated to the vestibule between carriages where he retched in fresh air.

He'd been a teen himself once, yet as much as he struggled he could not recall the slightest evidence: no memories of a friendship, a uniform, a favourite subject. Any day now he'd be snuffed out, any hour or minute – maybe as he stepped off the train into the crush at the station, or afterwards, overstraining himself as he manhandled the case through London. He was sleeping more and more, as he'd been advised he would, a day at a time, unrefreshing hours, so on a purely statistical basis it was likelier to happen when he was already unconscious. But say he was awake. Just say. Would he feel it as an intensifying blaze that grew insupportable, making him beg for release, or would he simply be switched off, one moment present, the next – elsewhere?

He couldn't go home – sniffer dogs, incident tape – so instead he walked without any particular destination in mind, letting the city guide him first north-east against the tide of commuters leaving work for Tube stations and bus queues, then up Commercial Road in the direction of Spitalfields. Wet streets, rainless now, a mild evening with a festoon of mist around streetlights. Perspiration broke out on him, cooled to tackiness, broke again. He changed course whenever he felt himself approaching an invisible boundary, crossing which would have brought him too close to home or to his old work-place. He couldn't risk seeing his erstwhile colleagues. If he could have picked the moment, it amused him to think, he

269

should have chosen that sad drinks party at work. Quite the riposte to their measly party and the surpassing ugliness of the carriage clock they presented him with, that gaudy replica of Big Ben a fatal insult. But then he would never have had the chance to meet me, and he would have died never knowing.

Hunger occurred to him. Where could he go? Was he over- or underdressed? There was too much choice in Shoreditch, where every other business was a no-reservations restaurant already at capacity and with queues forming outside. How lively, how multitudinous, how diverse, and yet in all in these crowds – all this life – there could be no one person who knew what Jadwin knew, who had done what he'd done. Beneath the rail bridge by the church, the suitcase's trundling appallingly amplified by the archway, he saw a girl kneeling on the pavement, her forehead touching the dirty ground, and he stopped to place a handful of coins on her cardboard sign, because although this kindness might count for nothing, for her or for him, it seemed obscene to Jadwin that anyone living in a world of such gluttony and such waste should go wanting. It was here that he registered the trilling of his phone, realised he had been aware of but ignoring it for some time; the girl on the pavement started to raise her head from her kneel, and, fearful of whose face she might have, he hastened on. It was not Nance's care home calling, as he had expected, but a number he did not know. One authority or other, he supposed, and although it seemed bathetic that things should go this way – no squadron of cars, no loudhailered demand, no chase, just dodging the shower of black ditchwater from the tyres of a 243 bus careering to its stop – he swiped and answered. 'Yes?'

A snippet of muzak cut out, and a voice seeped from the phone like honey. 'Monsieur Jadwin?'

*

A little over quarter of an hour later, Jadwin had been surrendering his overcoat to his caller, a maître d' who had perfected the role's fusion of obsequious and aloof; and, as he scanned the dining room, rubbing the butter-coloured welts left in his hand from dragging the suitcase, his unease started to recede, his mood to lift. A restaurant was a refuge, a place where – so he had long ago come to believe – nothing truly bad ever happened.

'Lucky your name was on our waiting list,' the server had remarked as she was serving him his glass of Kentish champenoise, and he reflected again on how strange were the workings of his condition, for while he certainly remembered trying for a table at Midgard – a year ago, maybe, after the first star but before it received its second – his recollection was that, having been loftily informed, perhaps by this same maître d', that the next available table was in eight months' time, he had simply laughed and hung up. Eight months was an eternity: restaurants came and went in less time; people, too. But he must have been misremembering, must have left his number after all.

These long wait times did a restaurant as much harm as good, building a diner's anticipation to the point where dissatisfaction could only follow. Jadwin had been nonplussed all through the meal by its uneven pacing: some dishes were delivered within seconds of the last being taken away; at other times, long lapses stretched between courses, leaving him alone with his thoughts: of the slow meaningful turn of Nance's head, the tussle between them, the unwieldy ballet with a partner gone limp, so frail yet so unmanageable. Of bloodied me, recumbent on his couch last night.

I'd seemed so peaceful in repose. My hair wasn't disarrayed, my green-girl dress neither rumpled or torn; from certain angles at which the hole he'd made in my arm was invisible, I might have simply fallen asleep on his sofa, easily and completely. But I was motionless now, had been since the last tremor that had sent my head slumping over to one side. My mouth was a little ajar, exposing long front teeth, and my brows were drawn together in a slight frown, the look of someone realising she'd slipped up. What clue, it looked like I was pondering, had I overlooked? What had I missed?

The thing Jadwin clinched in his kitchen forceps was part of me and yet not. In a few seconds he would know something about me nobody else did or ever would. But that didn't mean he knew everything. I'd told him that I was an actor, but he didn't know that my classes had taught me how to tap into a formative emotional experience to inform a performance. That I'd spent my teenage years playing a game like a more dangerous hide and seek, where I lay doggo for hours while my mother marauded room to room trying to find me to give me hell. The stillness I'd learned then – trying not to let Martha hear me breathe, trying to force my heart to beat softer – had been what I'd drawn on to play Juliet while my fellow cast stuffed up their lines all around me and I had to stay perfectly still. It was a valuable life skill, knowing how to play dead, and he had no idea that I possessed it.

He'd planned this for so long – the auditions he'd conduct over dinner and then, once he'd made his selection, the humane method he'd devised to terminate his chosen girl by means of an all-natural, all-organic compound of mistletoe. A good and painless death, and then he'd do what he'd long fantasised about: place the wafer on his tongue and achieve transcendence.

Sometimes, though, toxicities were reassessed. On the train to the coast to see Nance, he had squinted and winced through search engine results and learned that the ingesting of mistletoe was no longer classified – as it had been when he'd placed his order – as lethal. The doses he had forced into me, diluted in milk and water, might have been enough to kill an elderly person, someone already compromised. For a young, relatively strong person, one who worked ten-hour shifts six days a week, drank late afterwards and could still bounce right back for the next day's work, it might mean a pulverising headache, crippling nausea, even a brief time unconscious. But it wouldn't kill.

Jadwin's first notion that his poison might not be as efficacious as he'd assumed had come as he was standing over the stove in the kitchen, rolling my elusive flavour around tongue and palate – I was pluma of pork, I was liver pâté. He saw movement blurred in the brushed steel of the extractor fan, turned, and I rose up behind him, my wild face and bloodied arm, holding a shining oval form in my hand. He opened his mouth to say something – even, in his astonishment and horror, to stammer out an apology – but what blurted from him was instead a fetid belch, and when I understood what his breath smelled of I less lunged at him than toppled into him, a violent swoon, bringing the object in my raised hand down on his face hard enough to crack the glass in the wooden frame and ruck its broken edge into his skin.

For a moment we both stood dazed. The wound in his face stung a little. He could see that I didn't know what to do next; the advantage would be his, only he couldn't think either. Then pain charged into the wound, and the blood I saw spring out on his face must have emboldened me, because I went to strike again. This time Jadwin was able to intercept me, gripping my arm and using my stilted momentum to spin me away. Nance's picture smashing smiling on the kitchen floor, and I grabbed at the sink, my knees buckling. Jadwin took a step towards me, hands raised in a gesture of harmlessness even he understood was futile. With a pained sound, a fox's bark, I hauled from the sink's scummed water the nonstick saucepan with the greasy blackened circle at its centre and swung it at him doublehanded like a racket. He recoiled, and I missed by a mile, carrying on the orbit of the blow to land against the kitchen wall. Nonetheless Jadwin felt a dreadful crunch of impact – not from the dripping pan, but where he'd struck the back of his head on the sharp corner of the cooker hood. His head lashed forward and back, flinging blood. The metal rang a deep sonorous note. He reached to the wound, felt a deep divot, brought his fingers back bright and wet.

He stared at me in disbelief as I rested the tip of the pan on the spattered tiles, supporting myself on my tool like a labourer on pause. My triceps were tensing and pulsing as I prepared to swing it up and at him again. There was locust buzz in his ears yet still through it he could hear the unrelenting tick of the carriage clock, counting him out. Was it now? Could it be? Was he gone? 'Please,' he said, and then I gathered the last strength I had, and I hit him one last time.

Of course he came back, and of course I was long gone by the time he did. No mercy, no annihilation. He was woken by pain and, with his face gummed to the kitchen tiles, his confused first thought was that I had staked him sidelong through the head. Then as he gasped and shook, the dry blood cracked and he was able to peel his face away, leaving a red imprint on the tiles. In cautious, protracted movements, Jadwin brought himself into a seated position against the wall, let his head loll backwards, felt then the other wound he'd sustained to his skull. Alone and in unbelievable torment: yes, maybe this was hell. The fatigue he felt, itself a kind of pain, was unlike any exhaustion he'd known before. How long it took he couldn't tell, though the clock ticked on remorseless, but in time he made it to his bedroom, tugged the sheets over himself, and passed out. And nothing happened; or everything did – the world reawoke and, eventually, so did Jadwin, to pills and more pills, his cack-handed clean-up job, the childish soft toy I'd left behind that was, apart from the mess on the sofa and the smashed picture in the kitchen, the only sign I had been there. That, and the sour brown flavour in his mouth.

It seemed, over time, to be growing more distinct. His dessert had tasted not of violet and lemon and all those wondrous ingredients his waitress had hymned, but of a distinctive feculence indescribable to any person who had not themselves tasted it. Inexpungible. Which, on reflection, Jadwin thought was only proper: the *ne plus ultra* of flavours should ruin everything that came after.

Some choices opened up new channels, some sealed them off. Still others did both. The decisions he'd taken over the last twenty-four hours had made Jadwin's fate inevitable. It wasn't surprising, then, when he detected movement in his peripheral vision and looked up in anticipation of more food, curious whether it would taste of anything but me, to realise that he sat alone beneath stark houselights in a room bereft now of music and conversation. It did surprise him, though, to think of them as houselights, to perceive the waitresses and chefs and other diners filing out from behind the frosted partition at the end of the room as emerging from backstage to find their marks.

He smiled in understanding and reassurance. He knew he'd been followed all the way. He'd even caught a glimpse of the spy lurking behind the tree in the middle of the room. He didn't mind it at all. They needn't fear him attempting to flee the scene. As the staff moved forward, converging on him, he was thinking of the old dilemma of the last meal and how, in a way, I had spared him an impossible decision. To force a person, as they'd forced Gacy and Tucker and Morgan and the Butcheress, to select just one dish, one final irrevocable option, was to Jadwin a cruelty beyond human endurance.

'Who's there?'

I flailed like a dreamer. My good arm struck metal, and above me I heard containers tumble and roll. Still here, still in my hiding place, but at last I could move. I could feel, and what I felt was cramp and ache, a body comprised entirely of injury, all sharp pains and new bruises overlapping old. Slowly, disbelieving, I unfurled and stepped forward onto the fat give of the rubber mats beneath my soles, reached to my side to stroke the fridge, feel its low constant vibration, how its doors were cold and its flank hot. When I looked at my arm I half-expected the wound to have been erased, but no: there it was, the blackened circle and the flaking parallel trails that had made it almost to my elbow, and my stomach flipflopped to see it. It had happened. And I – after I'd fought Jadwin I must have made my way here, on instinct, to the place I'd given so much, the place I'd been told there would always be a place for me.

In my rusted voice I managed to call: 'Joanna?'

But I knew Joanna was gone. She was assisting with enquiries in the police station at the top of Amhurst Road with Finn, her lieutenant and my last known witness, while Kima, on her way out the station having finally spilled what little she knew about my movements yesterday, had paused at the front desk to produce from her bag a brick-sized stack of postcards: 'Hey, while we're all here . . .' They were all gone, all my colleagues and all our diners, dispersed now to Putney and Greenwich, Ealing and Perivale. John surrounded by sympathetic friends in a Kilburn speakeasy: 'The place shut down on your first shift? Holy shit, Johnny, what did you do?' A quorum who, on autopilot in their shock, had gone to Pangaea, Tash and Sprudge and Nico, and Gareth, who felt his fatty knuckle of a heart bounce when a woman's hand fell on his shoulder and, in a tone she'd never heard from him before, swore: 'My god, girl, am I ever glad to see you.' Kelly's eyes sliding away from the needle as the tetanus shot went in, only to see on her other forearm the livid semicircle of the injury that had necessitated the jab. Addy shivering on the Thameslink, googling flights to Portugal. Loïc in a grey room explaining that all he had done personally was place a telephone call at the behest of a woman they would insist on calling his accomplice but about whom he knew next to nothing, not even her surname, and before that the simple clerical error of transposing two Post-it notes, which nobody could prove was anything but a genuine mistake – ah, all this was bullshit, and he waved his hands to try and wipe away what had happened and then, at his inter- viewer's insistence, told it all again from the start. Eleanor, her phone newly purged of evidence, grinning like a skull, totter- ing into the night on wasted limbs to another underworld . . .

The aches in my body coalesced and split, and one of them was the easiest to deal with: the gape of hunger. In the fridge I found a wedge of Danish Blue, ammoniac-ripe, and Tash's container of watercress leaves; in patisserie, quarter of a sour- dough loaf that Kima, affronted that it had gone uneaten, must have retained for herself. I made myself an ungainly sandwich, tangy, peppery, oozing, delicious. Careless, I depos- ited crumbs on the counters, splashed water as I lapped from one of the taps greedy as an animal. Disciplinary offences left and right.

Silent in the restaurant. And then, again, from the dining room: 'Who's there?'

Not Joanna's voice, but one that was also familiar, its vowels whiney and elongated. A voice I knew. A voice like mine.

I'd imagined it wrong. Even after hours, the restaurant didn't go entirely dark. In the kitchen, there were the cold digital displays of machinery, the orange on-lights of power sockets never to be switched off. And there was another glow, dimly perceptible, that came from front of house where, as in the theatre, a single bulb stayed burning all night, for ghosts.

It shone down from above Loïc's desk, illuminating overturned chairs, abandoned dishes on uncleared tables. In long shadows I glimpsed a wedge of banknotes shoved beneath a dessert plate by the conscientious regulars on Five. Cutlery on the floor, smears of food in the carpet, and a red shrapnel that crunched underfoot as I neared Table Two. How Jadwin had fought in those last moments, lashed with his teeth and his cutlery. The savage sounds he'd made as he uncoiled from his chair, about how he'd do the same in the next world and the next, how nothing mattered now. Which was when Kelly, unsure what had been discovered in the alleyway out back but realising that whatever it was had far exceeded anything she could have done to keep her position as the restaurant's perennial loser, used all her fury at being so definitively upstaged to drive her weapon of choice into Jadwin's maimed face, knocking him into bloody unconsciousness and shattering her block of cola cubes into smaller blocks that bounced across the carpet in every direction.

Even before service and after hours I'd never known the place so quiet. The ticking of a clock, the soft noise of my feet on the carpet as I shuffled about, setting this chair upright, stacking a couple of dishes then finding their clatter too disruptive to continue. What was the point? I didn't think a restaurant could come back from what had happened tonight. The brigade would splinter like Kelly's weapon. They'd find different occupations or else start again elsewhere, since in the end a cook – as Joanna had often claimed – was really just a restaurant's way of making more restaurants.

Above the windows' frosted panes glossy black night showed. I saw myself in their reflection, picking my way through the wreck of the room. And then I saw something else move behind me, in the vicinity of the ash tree.

I turned and said it right back. 'Who's there?'

From behind the tree, a plump and pallid hand spidered. It advanced, groping at the notches in the bark, sinking fingertips in deep, as if its owner hung away from the trunk at an oblique angle and was hauling herself bodily into the room from impossible space. Herself. From the dirty ragged fingernails alone I could tell.

All night I'd been hearing them and hearing about them: the would-be and the could-have-been, the wishful and the never-were. The absent, the overbearing, the willing and the dutiful. The whole night had been giving me clues, if only I had known what to listen for.

The figure heaving herself into the dining room was stocky and short. She emerged slowly from behind the tree, placing her feet on the ground with caution, as though she hadn't walked in some time, and the ghost light found the matted choppy haircut, the doughy face set in its eternally harrowed expression, the big black fearful eyes.

Of course, I thought. Who else?

'I was going to call,' I told her. 'I was. Honestly. Or write. But this job ...'

I fussed around Martha, guiding her into a chair at the least dishevelled table, playing maître d', server and cook all in one. 'Did you want something to eat? I think I took the last of the bread but I could fix you something else. There's definitely granola.' Martha didn't say anything, and the clock ticked. 'Have you been hanging around all evening waiting? Watching me? Ah,' I said, as I made the leap, 'Joanna tracked you down, didn't she? She wanted to reunite us, make us make peace. That is so her. Such a reconciliation junkie.'

Martha's eyes darted around the room. Her skin had the burnished ruddiness of a much older woman, or one who'd lived an even tougher life, and it gave me a sad insight into what she'd been doing since I walked out on her.

'I thought I could call from the airport in Singapore on my stopover, reverse the charges – do people still do that? Then I thought better wait until I landed in London. But each time there was a reason not to. I ought to have a place of my own first, a job that could impress you – I should be able to say I had left Melbourne in search of a certain life and now I was living it, a done deed. But I never quite was.'

Darkness pressed dense as flesh against Midgard's windows.

Pain was chasing itself back and forth between my elbow and shoulder, and I had to resist the urge to rub my hurt arm. If Martha had noticed my injury, even that didn't stir her to speech. I'd grown pretty skilled at interpreting her different silences – the furious ones, the ones where she was physically incapable of forming words, the brooding sulks that followed screaming rows – but this one was new on me. It was expectant. Maybe she was waiting for me to run out of excuses and tell the truth, because I wasn't, not yet.

'Look, I get it, you came all this way for something. Was it to hear me say sorry? All right then, I'm sorry. I should have talked more to you then. I shouldn't have run.'

Martha shifted in her seat, and I braced myself for her to come at me for a hug or a slap. Instead, she fumbled a pack of cigarettes from the depths of her shapeless black outfit, popped one in her mouth and canted her head to her lighter with a frown, the most animation she'd shown so far. 'You can't,' I started to say, then registered the bombsite the restaurant had become. 'Actually, fuck it.'

She was always dead set against smoking when I was a kid: she told me there were enough systems in the world poised to chew people up without us volunteering ourselves to the nicotine-industrial complex. She talked a lot about complexes and systems back then. I'd go to school in an unlaundered uniform but with a hundred stickers to distribute acknowledging we were occupying Wurundjeri land, and once I'd talked myself out of whatever fun situations that got me into, I'd come home to an empty house and a note to say she was up at parliament and didn't know when she'd be home, it usually depending on how swiftly the authorities detached her from the railings she and her fellow protestors would inevitably end up cuffing themselves to.

'When did you give up on yourself, Martha?' I tried

needling her. 'Was it a slow process of disillusionment or a snap decision, a fuck all this? Did the smoking come first, or the booze?'

The first I knew about the drinking was when I came back one evening from the after-school drama classes I'd started taking and found a note, not from Martha to explain why she wasn't home – new government, same protests, worse now because it was our guys in power and they were proving themselves just as shiftless and craven as the other lot – but from a neighbour asking us to stop filling up his recycling with our empty bottles. I went down to the walled bin-store outside our block and there they all were, replaced in our yellow lidded one: big clear glassware that gave the bins a sharp medical smell that I couldn't at first place, till I realised they smelled of her.

I blamed myself, later, for being nowhere near as worldly as I should've been by my middle teens. After that she stopped hiding the bottles and, as though that pretence had been the linchpin keeping everything together, everything else went to shit. She lost her job at the Chadstone Mall for, she claimed, encouraging the other workers to unionise, though I didn't buy this. The classes had made me better at perceiving when other people were putting on a performance. Instead of going out and getting another job, she took unemployment and started wearing sloppy jumpers, cry-for-help leggings. And I became the adult. I cleaned the house up a bit, I monitored Martha's bank statements, and I cooked, albeit kids' food: I toasted bread and tipped a tin of spaghetti hoops over it, or snipped up the local milk bar's cheese and mostly-water ham to make a sloppy omelette. On nights when I had drama class, I bought the good soured cream with bits of real herbs and put a potato on to bake for Martha before I went out. I sat my high school exams, came out with indifferent results. I got a job – first the milk bar at the end of our street, then the South Yarra coffee shop where a pastry and cup of single-origin cost almost as much as I earned in an hour. Then Martha got kicked off unemployment for not showing willingness to seek work, and I went full-time at Gumbys, not finding it very funny that I was now literally the household breadwinner. That put an end to my drama classes. And then it all came apart.

Smoke dribbled from the tip of Martha's cigarette, forming a vertical line that wavered, drifted, lost form. I hoped the restaurant's sprinklers weren't too sensitive. Her silence was riling me. 'Fuck. Look, I take it back. I'm not sorry I left. You were sinking and you were shitty to me about it. Stomping around the house yelling at me that I *should* be working, I *should* be paying you back for what you'd sacrificed on my behalf. It'd nearly killed you having me, you said. You said – well, what's the point in repeating what you said. But you made a point of telling me you were glad I'd had to stop going to drama, that the real world was the thing, not make-believe. And I'll give you this. As I was hiding from you, trying to be as small and quiet as I could, that dig of yours about the real world really put ideas in my head. You were right – the real world was more, so much more, than the rat run I'd got stuck in, the bakery, the tram home, those four walls. I needed to get out into it. I started to save, and, yeah, I started to sneak away a little of the cash you gave me for your drinks. A tax, for the further and further I was having to travel to different bottle shops so people wouldn't suss me.'

Even at that time, Martha could occasionally be charming, motivated – sober. Sometimes she'd talk about finding a job, though that impulse never really caught. On the last morning before our final falling out, I got up for work and found her already awake and on the sofa, watching the Olympics coverage from London. Everything looked so slick and ravishing in this city half a world away, a different planet. 'I'd love to go there someday,' I said as I watched, only half-aware I was speaking aloud, and Martha looked round and smiled a bit sadly and said, 'You would.' It wasn't a question. She was smiling. 'It's in your blood.'

I held my breath for more but she twisted her head back to the television where the teams were marching into the stadium, waving and beaming. I stood there in the corner feeling a dawning elation. She'd never said much about my father – when I was younger I'd told people either that he was an astronaut or that he was dead, which amounted to much the same thing – but something had loosened her up. Something on the screen? Through the volume turned low on the TV I heard a snatch of that daggy disco song by the Bee Gees, amplified by the drummers tattooing a live accompaniment, and knew I'd have it going round in my brain the rest of the day. 'Maybe we can talk later?' Her eyes were red with emotion or sleeplessness. 'We'll talk later,' I said, more confidently, and at least I kissed the top of her head before leaving.

It was June, lightless and foul, but I went to Gumbys feeling like it was the first day of spring. For eight hours I served up bad coffee and good croissants, I sliced loaves, I levered up pre-cut wedges of cakes and folded them into waxed boxes that absolutely would not stay sealed. I hummed as I worked, putting my own words to that earworm of a song. And then, half an hour before closing, the manager oozed in. In my effervescent mood I even smiled at him, which he took as licence to stand closer to me as I counted up the day's takings, to arrange himself around me when he wanted to retrieve the credit card receipts we kept impaled on a metal spike by the till.

'You got a nice smile,' he went, as I was bagging up the unsold cakes for the charity collection that would come by in a bit.

'Thanks.'

'Don't often see you smile.' There wasn't much to say to this, so I carried on working. 'Shame about the uniform,' he said. I was about to agree – synthetic fabric, fondant pink, like I was one of the cakes for sale. 'Bet you got nice tits under there. Gonna show me them, too?'

He was generically middle-aged, and his hair, waveleted with grease, was going not grey or white with age but yellow. He was neither fat nor skinny, not handsome, not ugly, not really anything, the kind of bloke no one ever gave a second look. He must have known it, understood that he'd have to do something to make himself memorable, and this was what he'd chosen.

The hands that came at me. The serrated tongs I happened to be holding. I left him poleaxed over the shelves of baked goods and ran out of there before I was tempted to have another go.

'And then I got home and found you sitting where you'd been that morning. You might not have moved, except that there was a tumbler in your hand, a bottle on the carpet. I told you what had happened, because you'd always used to warn me to not to take any crap from anybody, to always stick up for myself. I told you I was going outside to burn my uniform. Do you remember any of this, Martha?' – angry again now as I remembered. 'Do you remember how you perked up when I gave you those rolls I'd scooped up as I left? How you opened up the bag and then you looked up at me like it was full of dog shit. "Wholemeal? Fucken wholemeal?" And you threw them at me, one by one, chortling as they hit. Your awful catarrh-gargling laugh. I couldn't move, and you kept on pelting me. "If I let you off with your mistakes, how're you ever gunna learn?" They lay all round me on the carpet, and I was all flour, head to toe. And of course it wasn't sore. But god, Martha, did it ever hurt.'

Recounting this memory made my head fluoresce with pain, as if every blade in the kitchen had been whetted against my skull. But Martha listened without visible reaction: her chest rose and fell, she blinked every now and then. I felt like leaning forward to tweak her ear, pinch her cheek: 'Are you deaf? What's going on here?' She smoked, and the cigarette turned to ash that didn't flake or fall. Increasingly I felt that there was something wrong in the room with its solitary light, the smothering dark outside, the clock's inexorable ticking.

'That's when I stopped talking to you. That's when I bought the plane ticket. Everything between us was so snarled up and hurtful, and this felt like slicing through the knot of us. The weeks turned to days, and then it was the day of the flight, and still I hadn't told you what I was doing. I packed and said I was going out like any other day, and then I fanged it out of that house and that city and that life. I told myself you could make your own trips to the bottle-o. I told myself you could carry on raging at the TV and crashing round the house all you pleased without me there to interfere. I pretended it was tough love, but I knew it was revenge. I knew I was leaving you to ... to your own devices. And that's the truth, all right? That's why I never called. If I didn't call, I couldn't find out how bad things might have got. You were Schrödinger's mother. As long as I never learned any different, you'd go on being fine.'

Confession brought me no relief. I exhaled and pushed the chair back, gathered myself and made to stand. Gathered and readied myself. 'Talk or don't talk, it's fine. But we can't stay here all night, Martha. Maybe you hadn't noticed, but I'm going through something here, I'm maybe going to have to get this checked out.' The sensation in my arm was no longer pain but an organic discomfort, as if fibres were growing through – into – the exposed flesh.

'Ya tricked me.'

I hadn't heard her voice in so very long. Maybe no one had. That ocker accent, that smoker's rasp.

'"I'm going out for something to eat." That's the last thing you said before you walked out on me. Nearly a year and a half. Must've had some appetite.'

I sank back into the dining chair – or folded myself into it, because these chairs were not all that comfortable, but forced me into a weird, contorted posture. And the fabric seemed coarse, though when I looked again the arm of the chair was smooth as sealskin. 'I didn't mean to . . .'

'Yeah, you did.' Martha shifted, though she didn't seem agitated. She was stating a fact. 'And that's fine.' We faced each other across the table and in that voice so like mine she said, 'You've done first aid. Save a life, be a hero. I bet they didn't tell you this, though – there are some people who you try to rescue when they're going under, and all that happens is they drag you down with them. No big rescue, just two lives lost instead of one. You got it in the end. And in the end, you did right. You did what you had to.'

'Martha, I—'

'Ah,' she interrupted, turning her head and blowing the speech away with a lungful of smoke. 'Or it could be abandonment's in your blood and I didn't stand a chance either way. Who knows how like him you've turned out?'

'Who was he, Martha?'

Martha spread her hands, a raconteur. 'He was a trickster who spun me a shitty illusion. A student, meaning he was still a boy. He snarked and found fault with everything, and I was at that age where that's funny, mature-seeming, impressive even. He said he wanted kids, not just one, a ton of 'em. But above all he was a thief. He stole all the potential I had and replaced it with one word, mother, and then was gone.'

288

It was her voice and it wasn't. The words came from her like a devised piece.

'You tell me something, though,' she said. 'Since we're being honest. You weren't just running away from me, were you? You told yourself I was holding you back, which means that there was something you were running towards too. Right?' I stiffened. 'Right. So tell me, where does all this fit into the plan?' She gestured around the broken room, but the ash still didn't fall from her cigarette, and the smell coming off it, off her, wasn't nicotine at all but something metallic. 'Because I seem to remember you weren't in love with those café and restaurant jobs back home. And yet look where you are. Why aren't you doing the crappiest, most demeaning job imaginable at some shithouse theatre, getting a foot in the door? Why aren't you learning everyone's lines in case the impossible happens and they ask you to step in? Why aren't you fighting, girl, fighting?'

That little kick of pleasure I got here, bringing food out to strangers who gazed up at me with gratitude, who always wanted what I was giving them. I'd always be appreciated for the minor, vital part I played in whatever life story I made up for them. They'd never fling anything in my face.

'Something else I'm wondering. How was it you got all the way back here from that tower block, all covered in blood, without anyone seeing you or trying to help? Telling me this city's that cruel? And then you smuggled yourself in and hid out all night? Nuh-uh. Nah.'

Without warning, the water I'd guzzled in the kitchen surged up in my throat, black and scorching. It vented out of me and I thrashed in my seat, limbs too heavy to lift. Still Martha bore remorselessly on. 'And tell me, darl. What was it that your boss and your boyfriend found in that suitcase out in the alley?' I was choking, I was gagging on the hot-metal fumes of Teflon cookware overheating. Some bit of me was going under. 'Come on now. Clock's ticking.'

It was. It was, and it shouldn't have been. That was the wrongness I'd sensed. For all the time they were with us, Joanna had always insisted, nothing should remind the diners of the outside world. They shouldn't even be aware that time was passing, and that was why we didn't have – had never had – a clock in the dining room. So what was I hearing? A sign of time passing she never would have allowed. A time-bomb counting down, a carriage clock in the shape of Big Ben. A clock that snicked each second emphatically away, moments pared off and discarded, never to be seen again. Most likely.

Acknowledgments

Thank you to my parents, Alistair and Vida Stewart; to Becky Thomas and Saliann St-Clair at Lewinsohn Literary and their colleagues at Blake Friedmann; to Sarah Castleton, David Bamford, Katy Brigden, Katya Ellis, Marie Hrynczak, Nico Taylor and Alice Watkin at Corsair; to my friends Rebecca Fortey, Timothy J. Jarvis, Neel Mukherjee, Paul Murray and Elaine Ronson. Thank you, Marina O'Loughlin. For their advice and encouragement over the years, I would like to acknowledge and thank Walter Donohue, Natasha Fairweather, Willy Maley, the late Rosemary Goad and the late John W. Mercer.

In the course of researching and writing this novel I ate a lot of dinners, visited a lot of kitchens and asked a great many questions of patient chefs and restaurant staff. I am grateful to the following real restaurants for helping to shape my fictional one: Alinea, Chicago; Arzak, San Sebastián; Attica, Melbourne; Blue Hill at Stone Barns, New York; Boragó, Santiago; Dabbous, London; De Librije, Zwolle; D.O.M., São Paulo; Eleven Madison Park, New York; Le Grand Véfour, Paris; L'Enclume, Cartmel; Martín Berasetagui, San Sebastián; Mugaritz, San Sebastián; Timberyard, Edinburgh.

Thank you, now and always, Mark C. O'Flaherty.